The Mimbre Trail

By Duane Vadron Evans

(Sequel to Jacob's Hollow)

© Copyright 2010
Bluewater Publications
Protected

All rights reserved. No part of this publication may be reproduced or transmitted in any form or by any means, electronic or mechanical, including photocopying, recording, or by any information storage and retrieval system, without prior written permission from the Publisher.

Published by:
Bluewater Publications
1812 CR 111
Killen, Alabama 35645
www.BluewaterPublications.com

Dedicated to my Heart

Heidi, Alex, Kylie & Koedy
My Children

Table of Contents

FORWARD	III
NAH-KAH-YEN	1
DANIEL	15
WINTER TRAIL	25
FORT CUMMINGS	34
RACE TO THE BORDER	47
NEW COMPANIONS	52
THUNDER AND BREAD	62
THE CROSSING	71
TERAHUMARA	80
AT ODDS	93
COMING OF THE RIDERS	102
APACHE CUNNING	114
DUST CLOUDS	121
RIO GRANDE	128
ACROSS THE EXPANSE	141
EL RANCHERO	154
NIGHTFALL	163
THE UNINVITED GUEST	167
FRIENDSHIPS AND DARKNESS	179
CANDLELIGHT AND STARLIGHT	186
SADDLES	197
SHADOWS AND SHADOWED	204

THE STORM	212
BATTLE OF THE CLOUDS	221
TOGETHER	229
RETURN TO THE ABYSS	240
DARKNESS	252
RETURN OF THE MIMBRES	260

Forward
By the author

As I travel the back roads and forgotten trails of this great nation, I find in speaking with the people I meet along the way that there is so much history that is largely forgotten, or at least never makes it into the text books. Every small town and borough has its unsung heroes. There are tragic stories of loss and sacrifice that all tell of the human experience that we as individuals can relate to.

For me, I believe that these isolated glimpses into the past are the real story of America. These are not the epic moments like Washington crossing the Delaware, or the first shot fired at Fort Sumter, instead these are the quiet moments that reveal the love and the courage of the human heart.

When the name of an individual is more important than a date and a place, we start to see the strengths and frailties that are in all of us. The person in the story who stood tall or stumbled matters, and if they matter, then so do we.

To a large extent I write about fictional characters because it makes me uncomfortable to pen a story about a historical figure and put words into his mouth that he never said. That is merely my choice and I do not prescribe it to others. Each writer must tell the story in their way.

The Mimbre Trail is the continuing story of Jacob Keever, a former buffalo soldier. This book is the much requested and long awaited sequel to Jacob's Hollow. For the lengthy delay, this author humbly apologizes. I would also like to give a special thanks to my friends, Eric Honeycutt, and ol' Griz whose encouragement and support has meant so much to me. It is because of their constant needling that I kept my pen in hand.

The historical event behind The Mimbre Trail is the sad story of the Mimbres Indians, a courageous and fierce band of the Eastern Chiricahua Apaches. My story alludes to their tragic demises which will be covered in another book.

In The Mimbre Trail, Jacob Keever is forced to leave his mountain hollow and undertake a dangerous journey that carries him over the border into Mexico. He is accompanied by his beautiful Indian squaw Mea-a-ha, who is a force of her own. Their small band is hounded by death from all sides. Cowards and heroes are shown for what they are. Adventure and history are replete but in the end it is a story of deep love.

Chapter -1-
Nah-kah-yen

With a mournful howl, the biting wind drove a heavy snow up the face of the slumbering mountain. Half-frozen, the Indian pony stumbled but caught himself and struggled on through the deep drifts.

Nah-kah-yen woke from his stupor. Blinking ice from his vision, he took in his bleak surroundings. Reaching a brittle hand from beneath his tattered blanket, he patted the poor beast.

"Take heart, my friend; soon we will be in the sacred pines. Ussen forbids the wind spirits to walk among the ancient ones. There we shall die in peace."

Wolves had trailed the lone warrior since first light and though Nah-kah-yen had three shells for his rifle, he made no attempt to drive the menace away. Better to fill the belly of brother wolf than the bowels of maggots.

The Apache was tired, cold, and heartsick. His was a trail of consuming despair. Three full moons had passed since the Massacre at Tres Castillos. Weapons had volleyed and thundered. The Mimbres were gone. His squaw, Mary Lost Pony, lay beyond his reach. He had failed them all. Nah-kah-yen had watched his people die. Soon he would join them.

****

Cheery red, yellow, and blue flames chased each other over the pine pitch logs in the cozy fireplace. Wrapped in a bright, warm quilt, Mea-a-ha took in the comforting scent while lost in blissful thoughts. It had been less than two months by the white man's reckoning since she had married the buffalo soldier and moved into his house of stone. Their snug little ranch was secreted in the hollow of a lonely mountain—lost in the vast southwest desert.

An Apache and a soldier, well… ex-soldier, Jacob had left the army to boldly follow his dream. Mea-a-ha giggled to herself. An Indian girl was not what he had planned, but the future is an unwritten page. Gods and mortal men often scribble in our books, keeping life a mystery. So it had been for them.

The howling storm that blew through the night had finally died down, yet distant howls more sinister echoed through the tall dark pines that bordered the Hollow.

Wolves! Pulling her quilt tightly around her, Mea-a-ha timidly came to her feet and tiptoed to the window. Drifting fog curled over the snow, shrouding the barn in a gossamer haze that opened and closed like a tattered veil. All was safe. The chickens were locked away in their coop, and the wolves knew better than to challenge the horses. Even so, the mournful cries sent a chill down her spine. Casting a fretful eye over her shoulder at the bedroom door, the small girl reassured herself that Jacob was nearby... still sleeping. Just knowing he was there made her feel protected. He was a good man.

Had this brave soldier not found her, Mea-a-ha knew she would have died without knowing how wonderful life could be. After enduring a brutal existence, the Indian girl marveled that so many treasures had waited just beyond her vision.

Lost in languid reflection, Mea-a-ha closed her eyes and melted against the wall. The soft crackle of the warm fire lulled her into blissful dreams. All was well.

Like a sudden rush of cold wind, loud vicious snarls jolted her back to the window. Filled with urgent dread, she anxiously rubbed the frost from the small glass pane. "Jacob!"

Not waiting for his answer, the girl dashed to the door and threw it open. "Shoo! Get away!"

Mea-a-ha only made it a few yards from the cabin before stumbling in the knee-deep snow. "Get away! Shoo!" Her voice was shrill. Struggling up on one hand, she waved her blanket in the frigid morning air. Startled wolves darted about a body lying at the feet of a haggard pony. Hunger gave them courage.

A hulking silver male, seeing a tender meal in the diminutive girl, bared his yellowed fangs and bounded across the snow with startling speed. Shrieking in terror, Mea-a-ha jerked the quilt over her head and collapsed into the deep drift just as the wild beast pounced upon her.

Intent on his kill, the Lobo sank his jagged teeth into the thick blanket, tearing at it wildly. In the same instant, a powerful ebony hand thrust itself into the fray, grabbing the scruff of the creature's neck and lifting it from the ground. The giant man flung his arm wide, sending the wolf hurdling high through the air. It rolled once and came up snarling.

With the beast clear of the girl, Jacob's pistol exploded in his hand. The vicious animal dropped in mid-leap. As if by magic, the entire pack faded into the gray mist. Their disembodied yellow eyes seemed to linger a heartbeat longer, then all was quiet.

Pulling back the blanket, Jacob gave the foolish girl a disapproving glare. Her startled face let him know she was unharmed.

With a snarl of his own, the naked man trudged through the snow to the frozen body. Kneeling, he turned the prostrate figure over.

"Apache. Still breathing. He's chewed up a bit, but his blanket saved him, too."

Handing Mea-a-ha the heavy pistol, Jacob shivered. "Best get him inside, before I get frostbite on places that might ruin our honeymoon."

Their humble stone house was rather rustic in its mountain setting, but Jacob had built two snug bedrooms just off the main room. In the smaller of the two, Mea-a-ha bathed and bandaged the dazed warrior's bite wounds. His glazed eyes opened and closed. He had neither the strength nor wit to speak.

"How is he?" Jacob ducked through the door fully clothed. Mea-a-ha lifted her eyes to her husband.

"Not much bleeding. Frostbite much worse."

"Do you know him?"

The Indian girl tucked her patient's bandaged arm under the wool blanket. "He is my people." Her face colored with emotion. "His name is Nah-kah-yen. Mary Lost Pony is his squaw." A bitter tear rolled down her cheek. "...was his squaw."

Stunned, a low whistle escaped the big man's lips. "Wonder how he escaped the massacre?"

In one terrifying night, the entire Mimbre tribe had been slaughtered by Mexican troops on a desolate mountain. It was butchery at its worst. Warriors, boys, and old women were brutally scalped. The children and pretty girls who survived were sold into slavery south of the border. Though Mary Lost Pony's fate was unknown, Jacob only knew that she had been Mea-a-ha's friend.

Holding a tin cup of steaming coffee, Jacob tossed another pine log on the fire and then settled into his comfortable leather chair. The snow was falling softly now, blanketing the Hollow in a quiet tranquility that he loved. A door opened and closed. Mea-a-ha stepped near and timidly rested the tips of her fingers on the back of his chair. She waited a moment before speaking. Her ol' bear could be grumpy when troubled. The Indian girl studied her husband. He seemed deep in thought but he did not look like he would bite her head off.

Lovingly, she draped her soft arms around his neck and kissed his stubbled cheek. "Nah-kah-yen will sleep long time, I think. His body and heart are tired."

The old sergeant continued staring into the blue flames but made no response. Mea-a-ha slid over the arm of the chair and folded into his lap. Wrinkling her brow to mock her husband's frown, she lowered her voice as deep as she could. "You have that hatchet crease in your forehead. Are you angry he is here?"

Taking a final sip, Jacob set his cup on the stone hearth and hugged the girl to him. "Not angry; just worried."

The big man's thoughts drifted to something else, and he quickly ducked his head, hiding a sheepish grin. Mea-a-ha caught it and raised his square jaw in her small brown hands. "What?"

Shrugging his shoulders, Jacob pulled away, a little embarrassed. "It's just seeing someone sleeping in Daniel's room…I guess I miss the boy."

Mea-a-ha smiled and kissed her husband. "Nchaa Shash, my big ol' bear, not so tough as he pretends."

Snuggling deeper into his lap, Mea-a-ha rested her head on his chest and thought of her little brother. Jacob had taken the young Apache in and been a father to him. A deep bond was forged between them in the fiery days after Jacob found the Hollow. The two were inseparable, but the youth was fifteen and needed to be with boys his own age. Luis Rincon, a close friend, had offered Daniel work on his big ranch. Her brother accepted, mostly to be with his friends, and perhaps because of a pretty little senorita, though he was too shy to admit it.

Nuzzling softly, Mea-a-ha kissed Jacob's neck. "Daniel promised he would visit in the spring," she teased. "Big tough soldier."

Jacob gave the Indian girl's bottom a firm swat, but he knew enough to keep his mouth shut. The last word was something he seldom got when dealing with this little savage. It was best to change the subject. "We were talking about Nah-kah-yen. Kind of puts a crimp in our honeymoon."

If she could have snuggled closer, Mea-a-ha would have. "It is sad. Our people are gone. Mary is, too. Nah-kah-yen should have been killed in battle with the warriors. Much shame. I think he came to the sacred hills to die."

Lost in thought, Jacob stroked the girl's cheek with a curved finger. Taking a squaw was one thing, but the Army would shoot a warrior on sight. No matter how he cut it, the Indian was trouble.

Weighted with concern, Jacob hugged the girl, knowing she would be right in the middle of it. His little Mea-a-ha had a big heart. This buck would be one more stray for her to save. Jacob reached for his cup. Yes, there was going to be trouble.

****

Stomping in through the front door, Jacob leaned his Winchester against the wall. Playful laughter coming from their bedroom drew him across the stone floor. "Mea-a-ha!" His voice was deep and gruff.

The Indian girl bounced up from a pile of blankets where she had been wrestling with her brown-and-white puppy. The dog quickly jumped to the floor, knowing the big man did not allow him on the bed.

Jacob raised a reproachful brow, scolding the girl without words. Mea-a-ha's large dark eyes opened wide, feigning fright at being caught, but a mischievous grin was already working its magic on the surly giant.

A low growl rumbled in Jacob's throat. "You know the rules."

Mea-a-ha rose to her knees amid the tangled sheets and innocently tilted her head to one side. "I was practicing with my puppy for when I have to fight my ol' bear." She raised her hands like claws and mimicked a cute little growl of her own. Jacob retreated from the room, knowing well when to leave the battlefield.

Jumping out of bed, the girl wiggled, straightening the large blue shirt that she slept in. It was Jacob's old Army shirt, and it fell to her knees. Mea-a-ha scurried into the big room and buried her cheek against her husband's red flannel shirt. "Hold me."

"Holding you usually gets me in trouble."

She smiled up at the big man. "No different this time."

Jacob scooped up his bride and twirled her around, then held her close. With a quick kiss to the top of her head, he tucked her under his chin and pensively stared out the window.

The burly soldier loved this savage beauty, but he found words difficult. Mea-a-ha snuggled closer, understanding what was in his heart. She could hear it beating now. It matched her own.

If only he could...the girl smiled. When he held her like this, words were not so important. Mea-a-ha pressed her warm lips to his cheek, telling of her own love, then softly laid her head back on his shoulder and absently toyed with a loose thread. "Jacob, did you miss me?"

The soldier pulled his gaze from the window. His adoring eyes were the only answer she needed. Life was tenuous on the desert, and her quiet hero had proven his love many times.

Mea-a-ha lifted her hand to his face, but he turned and stared back out across the snow-covered meadow. Curling her fingers on her ol' bear's chest, the Indian girl accepted his change in mood. A part of him would always be a soldier; it was his lot to protect. While others found time for love and jest, Jacob silently stood his watch.

"Has Nah-kah-yen spoken yet?"

Mea-a-ha took a deep breath, and her voice rose in a long, wondrous whisper. "Mary Lost Pony is alive."

She wrapped her arms around her husband's thick neck and pulled herself higher. "Oh, Jacob. It's terrible. The Mexicans have her." The girl softened as she nuzzled her cheek against his, seeking comfort. "I told Nah-kah-yen we would help him."

"No, Mea-a-ha!" Placing his bride firmly on her feet, Jacob towered over her. "Little Apache, I can't save everyone. I have you now, and I am not going to risk what we've got after the price we paid."

Lifting onto her toes, Mea-a-ha tried to climb back into his arms. "But Jacob, the Mexicans have made Mary a slave. She is my best friend."

"No, Mea-a-ha! Mexico is too far and too dangerous. I couldn't leave you that long."

"I would go with you," Mea-a-ha's large brown eyes pleaded as much as her words.

Jacob pulled her arms from his neck and turned away. "I have spoken." Grabbing his hat and coat, he headed out the door.

Mea-a-ha stamped a bare foot on the hard stone floor and puckered her lower lip into an injured pout. She hadn't really expected him to agree. Not yet. It would take a lot of little-girl tears and sugary kisses, but she would bring him to her way of thinking.

Scowling at the window, Mea-a-ha folded her arms and watched Jacob disappear into the barn. He always went to the barn when he didn't want to talk. She stamped her foot again and then knelt to hug her puppy. "I hope its bitter cold out there," she murmured into the soft fur.

****

In the western sky, the clouds were finally breaking. Heavy storms had battered the lonely mountain for most of January locking the newlyweds indoors, which they hadn't minded at all. Still, food was needed, so taking advantage of the temporary respite; Jacob saddled up the Buckskin and went hunting at first light.

Stirring a thick pot of pinto beans, Mea-a-ha guessed his departure was probably hastened by a desire to avoid her nagging. She shrugged. It didn't matter. They could use some fresh meat. An impish light twinkled in her eyes. He would not escape her tongue for long.

While Jacob was gone, Mea-a-ha tended to chores and kept watch over her sleeping patient. Above the Hollow, the clouds continued to give way. As the day grew brighter, the Apache girl eventually calmed down. At least she wasn't angry with her husband any more. In her heart, Mea-ah-a knew she really had no right to be. They had survived against overwhelming odds while defending their little home in the Hollow. She understood why he would be unwilling to risk it all for an Indian he had never met.

Mea-a-ha knew the ol' bear loved her dearly, but she knew that her being an Apache had caused problems for the black soldier. To expect him to rescue every Indian in trouble would be foolish. Nowadays, every Indian was in trouble.

Mea-a-ha added several wild onions to the bubbling pot. Still, Mary Lost Pony was her friend, and it broke her heart to see the grief in Nah-kah-yen's eyes. Something had to be done. With her people all but wiped out, rescuing even one Mimbre would give hope that in some small way her tribe might live on. She would talk with Jacob again.

The sound of shuffling footsteps pulled the girl from her thoughts. Nah-kah-yen stood behind her, steadying himself with a bandaged hand on the back of a wooden chair. He nodded, but his eyes darkened as he searched his new surroundings. A house was a strange and frightening place for the Apache warrior. It held the white man's medicine. Wrinkling his brow, the warrior's stern gaze finally returned to the girl. "I came to the sacred hills to die. Now I stand in the lodge of a soldier and I see an old friend, only she is dressed as a white squaw. How is this so?"

Quickly pulling a chair from the table, Mea-a-ha invited the Indian to sit before he fell. She had only talked briefly with Nah-kah-yen when he had first regained consciousness, and then only to doctor his wounds. Most of the time, he had been half-delirious. A full night's sleep had renewed his strength. The time had come to get reacquainted.

Mea-a-ha placed a warm plate of food in front of the brave. He was famished, and started wolfing down the first meal he had tasted in days. Taking a place beside him, Mea-a-ha touched his arm. "Old way is gone. Apaches can choose the path of the white man, or choose death. No other."

Nah-kah-yen frowned, and spoke through a full mouth. "Better to die."

Mea-a-ha gave a sympathetic smile. "And yet you eat."

Shifting his eyes, the warrior swallowed his food and then cleared his throat. "Even in youth, it was never consider wise to trade words lightly with little Mea-a-ha. I see you have not changed." His face pained. "... but had you seen our people butchered like the white man's beef, our women herded like cattle, maybe you would not be so eager to forgive."

"Brave Nah-kah-yen, I don't forgive because it is easy. I forgive because hatred is a poison that sickens the one who holds it."

The heavy stomping of boots on the porch drew their attention to the door. Nah-kah-yen rose from his chair as the huge black man entered the room in a gust of cold air. Leaning his rifle against the wall, Jacob's eyes darted from his wife to the newcomer. He offered a guarded nod.

Visible anger shuddered through the warrior's body. His muscles tightened like iron sinew. Before him stood his mortal foe. Had they met by chance on a trail, Nah-kah-yen would have killed him without the slightest hesitation. Years of war and the slaughter of his people had seared his heart. All that was left was charred with hate. "Soldier, your woman tells me you saved my life. I did not ask you to do this thing."

The eyes of the big man narrowed. He owned the other half of the coin. "My name is Jacob Keever. The Hollow is my home. If you wish to die, do it someplace else."

"Jacob!" Mea-a-ha rose from the table and gripped the back of a chair.

In a burst of rage, Nah-kah-yen balled his fist. "I know this name! It hangs bitter on the lips of every warrior. You killed Sholo. You are the enemy of my people."

Apache curses were nothing new to the soldier, but be they just, he would not endure insult under his own roof. "You have no people. If you call me enemy, you do it for yourself."

Nah-kah-yen snarled. "All buffalo soldiers are my enemy."

The big man frowned. Pulling his knife from its sheath, Jacob stabbed the blade in the table. "If you would rather die than accept my hospitality, then there's your chance, Apache."

Mea-a-ha screamed. Dashing between the men, she snatched up the knife. "You two stop it!" The girl turned to her husband and stamped her foot. "Jacob! Would you kill a man in his grief?" Without waiting for an answer, she whirled around and glared at Nah-kah-yen. "...and you. This is my home too, arrogant warrior. Mary would be ashamed of you."

The Apache girl shoved the knife back into the sheath on her husband's belt. "Jacob, I too am much ashamed. Now tell Nah-kah-yen he is welcome in our home." She wrinkled her nose, letting him know she meant it.

The big man stared down into the girl's smoldering eyes. It was hopeless. Jacob reluctantly surrendered his anger. In a low growl, he forced a half-hearted peace offering. "The girl is one Indian I don't want to fight. If you come in peace, you are welcome in my home."

He turned away, letting the warrior digest his words in cold silence. Mea-a-ha folded her arms and raised a threatening brow to her old friend.

With little else he could do, Nah-kah-yen relented and unclenched his fist. "Mea-a-ha is right. Mary would be ashamed. She would thank you for saving my worthless life. I come in peace."

Both men glanced at the fiery girl, hoping she was satisfied.

Answering their question with a sweet smile, Mea-a-ha's demeanor instantly changed. "Now let's sit down and have this nice meal together. It has been long since we had company in the Hollow."

Mea-a-ha dished up a plate of beans for Jacob as he sat down at the head of the table, then gave a second helping to Nah-kah-yen. She didn't expect them to be cordial, but she would tolerate no rudeness.

"Jacob, would you pass the biscuits to Nah-kah-yen?"

The big man shoved the plate towards the Apache with the back of his hand. A simple nod was the Indian's only response.

Sliding a chair between the two men, Mea-a-ha enticed them to eat plenty. No one fights on a full belly. She took a dainty bite and then turned to the warrior with an encouraging smile that was clearly meant to erase the altercation. "Do you like my beans, Nah-kah-yen?"

The Indian mopped his plate with a biscuit. "Beans good."

"I make them with molasses and salt pork. Jacob taught me."

He gave another nod and said nothing more.

Doing her best to change the churlish mood of her companions, Mea-a-ha kept up a lively monologue. The discourse changed from beans to the lifting of the storm, and then to reminiscing about their childhood at Warm Springs. It seemed a safe topic. "It is good to see an old friend. Not many Indians nowadays." Mea-a-ha smiled sadly, letting her eyes drift to the window. "Once our campfires burned brightly..."

For a long moment the girl was silent as beloved faces, now gone, hung vividly before her. Each faded in turn, leaving an emptiness that time would never fill. The Mimbres were gone.

Shaking off her gloom, Mea-a-ha returned her gaze to her stoic companions and tried to be cheerful. "Yes, and there were noble chiefs, too." She recalled great men and their brave deeds: Mangus Colorado, Old Nana, and seeing Cochise when she was a little girl. The conversation came at last to Chief Victorio. His name brought sadness and pain.

Mea-a-ha's eyes darted to her husband and then settled on the warrior. He alone knew the truth about the death of their people, a truth she feared yet desperately needed to hear.

Slowly, she stretched her fingertips across the wood table towards Nah-kah-yen's hand, but did not touch him. "My dear friend, there is much we should hear. Tell us what you can of Mary, the death of Victorio, and of the final battle of the Mimbres."

Swallowing his last bite as though it were a dry lump, Nah-kah-yen pushed away from his plate and hid his grief in the shadows of a lone kerosene lamp hanging dimly over the table. Gruesome visions of the hellish night burned in his brain like hot coals that could never be extinguished. The once-proud warrior slumped like an aged man, burying his head in his hands and silently cursed that he alone still lived.

Slowly, Nah-kah-yen's dark eyes lifted to his hosts, and then fell. To speak meant to open the wound, but the story had to be told. Surrendering to what he knew he must do, the warrior took a tortured breath.

"Soldiers. Accursed soldiers. Our hearts sick, we wanted only one thing, to stay at Warm Springs, the land of our fathers, as we were promised. There we would live in peace, but the soldiers came again and said we must go to the camp of death at San Carlos.

"After all our people had been through, we cried, 'Enough!' Our young and old would surely die. 'Enough!' But the soldiers would not listen. They said that on the next day they would come for us, so in the black of night, Victorio, the bravest of the brave, told us to rise, and he led us into the desert." He stopped to take a long, ragged breath and continued.

"The Long Knives would be rid of us, but even that was not good enough for them. To be free was all we asked. Was it too much? Finding us gone, the buffalo soldiers gave chase, biting at our heels like hungry dogs straining at their master's leash."

Nah-kah-yen lifted a scornful eye towards Jacob, and then once more was swallowed by his grief. "Victorio said he would take us across the border to a secret place. There we would be beyond the reach of Long Knives. Our families could forever live free as Apaches.

"The trail was hard, much hunger. It was difficult on Mary, with the baby. The soldiers hounded us, many battles, but Victorio outsmarted them. Even hindered by our women and children, he made fools of the black horse soldiers. They were a thousand strong and yet they could not catch us. We escaped into the land called Mexico."

Pride flickered in the warrior's weary eyes. He embraced the rare moment of victory before continuing. "When we were sure the soldiers had turned away, there was rejoicing. The mighty army of the blue coats could not cross an imaginary line.

"Ahead, the spires of Tres Castillos lifted towards the heavens. This night we would sleep without fear. Our hearts glad, we built fires, but it was not for me. Victorio had me fall back to watch for Blanco, who had gone to find ammunition. After fighting the buffalo soldiers, we had few bullets. Mary came to my side. She wanted to stay with me. I told her not to worry. Our people were safe now, and I rode away. She stood there in the middle of the trail, holding our baby. After what we had survived, it was hard to be parted."

Nah-kah-yen buried his head in his fists and whispered. "I see her still. She cried, 'Yadalanh shi shikaa.' 'Farewell my husband.'"

In the shadowed light, he bit a quivering lip. "I should have let her come. I...I...Mary...my gentle Mary."

Mea-a-ha wanted to reach out to him, but remained silent, knowing there was nothing she could say. He was a warrior; comfort from a woman would be an insult.

Taking a deep breath, Nah-kah-yen shook off his guilt. "Late in the night, I reached a high mountain pass. The air was clear and cold. Sound carries a great distance on such nights. Looking behind me I could see Tres Castillos in the moonlight. It was beautiful. Then my ears heard a faint sound, like the breaking of dry twigs. The sharp cracks did not stop. Suddenly I realized it was gunfire. Our people were being attacked! Mary!

"Whipping my pony, I flew through the night as fast as I could. My heart ached as if a lance had been driven through my chest. Could I have flown like an eagle, it would not have been fast enough. My pony raced long beneath the cold stars. In the vast darkness the trail seem as though it would never end.

"Haste was needed, but I would stop and listen...fearing. Rifles still spoke, growing louder. With each cruel report I felt a Mimbre fall.

"Finally, my horse spent, I came upon the shore of the lake where our people had camped. I was too late. There were only bodies. Shots still rang through the dark, but they were scattered far and wide, mixed with the trampling of hooves and the shouting of a cursed tongue. Rising above the gunfire, I could hear the screams of women and children as they were hunted down. 'Mary!' It was pointless, but I cried her name. 'Mary, Mary.'

"Then out of the darkness, horses raced towards me. In the moonlight I could see Mexicans. Drunk on the blood of my people, they started shooting. My grief was so great that I stood my ground and emptied my rifle into the vile murderers. Some fell. More came. I went to reload, but my pouch was empty. Mexicans were all around me. There was nothing to do but flee. Bullets and shouts rang from everywhere. Muzzle flashes burst in the dark. I knocked a rider from his horse with the butt my gun. Another one took his place. Tall rocks stuck from the earth like saguaro cactus, offering some protection against the gunfire. I drove my poor pony higher up the mountain. They followed for a time, but eventually the Mexicans either gave up the chase seeking easier prey, or hungering for a share of the women, they turned aside.

"My pony was lathered and coughing. I let him walk for some time, moving away from my enemy, higher, always higher. When the sun joined the moon, I was in a saddle between the stone spires of Tres Castillos. Far below I could see black shadows as evil soldiers searched the hills and shore, some with torches. I looked for warriors, but there were none. My heart wept. Victorio was no more."

In anguish, Nah-kah-yen opened his tortured mouth, but could find no words to release his despair. His trembling hands clutched helplessly on the table before him. The warrior's eyes closed tightly against the pain as he struggled for control. It seemed as though he would never breathe nor speak again. The death of the Mimbres was a weight too great.

Wiping her tears, Mea-a-ha whispered. "What of Mary?"

"Mary." The very mention of her name gave him courage. Nah-kah-yen lifted his tired head once more. "Yes. Mary. My Mary. I searched. Keeping to the rocks, I made my way down the mountain. By the time I reached the shore, they were gone, at least the living. The dead were everywhere—warriors, women, and boys. All of them scalped. I knew them, my brother, my sister's son, their white skulls stained with blood. Our people, wiped from the earth. I retched as I turned over the bodies of the squaws, searching for Mary. Every face, I knew. All of them butchered, some naked. What kind of people makes war on women?

"With each body I found, my soul tormented, fearing it would be Mary. Then, standing among the dead, it suddenly came to me. There were no girls or young squaws. Mary is young and pretty. Surrounded by the carnage of my kin, though it shames me, my heart soared. Mary was alive. I stole bullets from the dead, then jumped on my pony and raced after the killers of my people.

Midday, I spotted movement on the horizon. There were hundreds of Mexican soldiers on horseback with whips, herding our women like animals. When evening came I was able to get closer. Finding a ravine, I hid until morning.

At first light, I could see the women and children. My eyes searched each one. Finally I spotted Mary. She held our baby. They were alive."

Nah-kah-yen stopped. His face brightened once more. He looked to Mea-a-ha, wanting her to read in his heart the emotions he could not speak. Her eyes misting, she nodded.

A fragile smile flickered then quickly faded as the warrior returned to his tale. "All the next day I kept to the arroyos. When I could, I would crawl to the rims and steal glimpses. Each time was like the first. So close, yet so far. Seeing her tormented me. If only there was a way to steal her back, but how?

"Then, towards evening, I spied a party of riders coming from the east, vaqueros. The soldiers welcomed them.

"The squaws were made to walk in front of a very fat man. He turned them around, looking at them, touching them." Nah-kah-yen clenched his fist. "Touching them...A few squaws he pushed to the side. He chose three women. One was Mary. Our baby was pulled from her arms. Mary screamed and pleaded. I could hear her cries. I put the fat man in my sights. He would die with my son. But as I tightened my finger on the trigger, our baby was given back. Perhaps only to silence Mary's screaming. There is no caring in such men.

"I recognized the other two women: little Son-gee, and Lori White Feather, a white child captured long ago. They were the fairest."

At this disclosure, Mea-a-ha wept. She knew the other girls.

Nah-kah-yen paused for her tears, then his face clouded with anger. "The fat one gave a bag to an important soldier, a little man, with big hat, big coat. For this small bag, the three women were bought and tossed on horses behind vaqueros.

"Their trading done, the fat man rode back the way he came. I waited for the Mexican army to leave with the rest of the women, and then I followed after Mary.

"We did not go many hours before we came to a great rancho. There were lots of buildings and high walls. Plenty guns. I could not get close enough to see where they put the women. So I waited. For three days I watched, living on lizards that came out to sun themselves. Only once when I dared reach the wall, did I see a woman, but not Mary. There were so many guards, I could not get close.

"Even if I found her, without more bullets, I could not have gotten her out. I would only put her in greater danger. I failed my people, and I could not even save my own squaw. It was a stone too heavy to bear. In despair I left, telling myself I would find help, but there was no help, and in the end, after wandering for many moons in the cold desert, I came here to die. I failed at that, too."

Nah-kah-yen looked weary of life. He raised his sad eyes to his hosts. Death was the only relief for his suffering. Mea-a-ha sniffed and fought back her tears. "Do not give up hope. In the Hollow there is magic. I believe it can reach beyond this lonely mountain. Mary is alive. Somehow we will find her."

Jacob remained silent. The girl's words were meant to comfort, yet he felt they held a promise she could not keep. He loved Mea-a-ha and understood her anguish, but their life together in the hollow of this mountain had come at a great price. In a land where Indians were being slaughtered merely for being Indians, he fought to keep this Apache girl safe. He could do no more.

Slowly Jacob rose from the table; Mea-a-ha's eyes followed him. He looked down at the grieving warrior. "I am sorry for your loss, Nah-kah-yen."

Putting on his coat, he glanced at his wife. "I'm going to the barn."

Chapter -2-
Daniel

Steam curled from the nostrils of the large gray shire standing patiently in a patch of trampled straw while Jacob ran a curry comb down her flank. The log barn opened to the corral on the east side, allowing the low winter sun inside. Mea-a-ha quietly stepped through the door and patted the horse's nose.

"Hi Peaches," she whispered. Without a word to her husband, she hurried to the grain room. Moments later she reappeared with a burlap sack of cracked corn and headed out to feed the chickens.

Brushing harder, Jacob watched her with a raised brow. He knew a battle was brewing inside his little savage, and he wasn't looking forward to it.

Uttering a curse, he thrust the comb onto a wooden barrel with more force than necessary and followed her out the back door. It was best to be done with it.

Jacob slowed as he approached his sullen bride and rested a hand on the low, shingled roof of the chicken coop while measuring her anger. At times like this he saw more of the Indian in her. She was full-blooded Apache with long shiny black hair that hung to her slender waist. Today she chose her buckskins over a store-bought dress. When she was in one of her defiant moods, it was hard not to see the savage in her. It caused him pain, or perhaps it was guilt. Tonight when they lay together she would be his little Mea-a-ha again, but right now she was full-blooded Apache, and it put a distance between them.

When the silence began to take on a voice of its own, he forced a smile. "You're cute when you're angry."

Mea-a-ha ignored him and kept talking to the five hens and one strutting rooster. Each bird had a name, and would get a personal greeting while she doled out the grain. As always, her little brown-and-white puppy was by her side.

Apparently Jacob would not be accorded the same kindness as the barnyard fowl. Reaching down, he scratched the playful ball of fur behind the ear. "Hello, Friendly."

The pup wagged his tail, but returned his attention to the chickens, causing the big man to vent a sigh. "Looks like everyone is going to ignore me."

The Apache girl did not respond. His patience waning, Jacob tipped his hat back and tried the direct approach. "Are you going to give me the silent treatment?"

Mea-a-ha tossed another handful of corn. "Maybe so."

"Have it your way." Jacob shoved his icy hands into his pockets and turned to walk away. Mea-a-ha scrunched her nose. "Dumb soldier, you are supposed to hold me and ask, 'What's the matter?'"

Rolling his eyes, Jacob accepted his part in the game, and took her in his arms. "I know what's the matter."

The Indian girl squirmed away. "Don't hold me. I'm mad at you. Husband, you are the only one who can get Mary back."

Jacob let his hands fall. "It is a very long way to Mexico. Might as well go to the Moon. The trip would take a month."

A quick sideways sneer told him that his cold male logic was summarily rejected. Mea-a-ha went back to feeding her hens.

Taking her by the shoulders, Jacob turned her firmly around. "Wife, in these times there is no safe place for the Apache, even here in the Hollow. You would be alone and unprotected. I can't leave you."

Mea-a-ha suddenly rushed back into his arms, clutching at his coat. "I could go with you. I am not so small. Mary and the baby will need me."

"No! There is death on this trail. With no money to buy Mary Lost Pony back, we would have to take her by force, and the Mexicans will outnumber us. No, you can't go, and I won't leave you. It is impossible."

He raised her chin on a bent knuckle. "No more talk of this. I have said my piece. It is for you to obey me, not nag me to death."

Releasing her, Jacob gave the girl a loving swat. "Feed your chickens, woman. Let them do the pecking, not you."

Mea-a-ha's lower lip curled into a familiar pout, but a fire burned in her eyes. "I will obey you, my husband, but I am not a little child to be ignored."

Jacob grinned. "I don't think anyone has ever succeeded in ignoring you."

The young girl ducked her head, hiding her guilt in the strands of her dark hair, knowing it would be no different this time.

She pulled away and let the last kernels of yellow corn slide through her dusty fingers. For now she would silence her tongue, but a pert little twitch of her nose let Jacob know that the very same silence made his victory a hollow one.

He shook his head and tucked his insolent bride under his arm. "Come, little warrior. If you are to treat me coldly, let's do it by the fire."

Ending the battle, Jacob led her back towards the house. Mea-a-ha accepted her husband's commanding embrace. She knew she could only push so far before his temper would burst like thunder, and then he would be impossible to convince.

The Apache girl risked a cunning smile. Her husband didn't know it, but she had won their little exchange. He was already thinking about the dangers of the trip, and what to do with her. Mea-a-ha had also made up her mind that if they had to go to the Moon to find Mary, they'd do it together.

As the newlyweds crossed the narrow footbridge over the icy spring, they were brought to a sudden halt by the dull thud of hoofs on the snow-covered trail that laced its way through the tall pines bordering the Hollow. A lone rider appeared on a beautiful Paint Stallion. Jacob's voice broke with uncommon surprise. "Daniel!"

Unconsciously, the veteran soldier truncated his outburst, but couldn't help whispering again. "Daniel."

A lean boy bundled in a frost-covered coat and a heavily wrapped scarf, his face taut from the rigors of the wintry trail, lumbered up to them and stopped. In spite of his haggard appearance, he broke into broad grin.

"My brother! Are you crazy? It is a two-day trip in the dead of winter." Gushing with alarm, Mea-a-ha reached up to him and scolded, "Foolish boy!"

Stiff and cold, Daniel stumbled from the saddle. He pulled his sister to him and held her tight. Women were a rarity in the harsh land, making her emotional embrace all the more cherished by the young lad. "It is good to see you, too."

Mea-a-ha buried her head in his neck and softened her voice. "Foolish boy."

With a final squeeze, Daniel exhaled an icy breath then easing his grip, smiled over her head at the big man who stood stunned with disbelief.

The Indian girl laughed. "Men! Jacob, hug Daniel so we can all go inside and sit by the fire."

The buffalo soldier eagerly pulled the boy into his arms. "You could have froze to death. What were you thinking?"

The boy pressed an icy ear against the big man's warm chest and closed his eyes for a long moment, accepting a long-awaited embrace. "It's your birthday."

Daniel's announcement caught Jacob by surprise; Mea-a-ha, too. She stared at her brother, wondering how he would know this. The boy lifted his head in a sly grin. "Jubaliah told me."

Jacob held the boy tight. Jube would know. He was Jacob's best friend. They had soldiered together since boyhood. Daniel now lived with Jube on the huge Rincon Ranch, where Jube was the foreman.

The big man hid his emotion in a final hug before pushing Daniel and Mea-a-ha ahead of him. Their family was together again. It was a birthday gift he'd treasure forever.

17

Reaching the stone porch, Mea-a-ha suddenly turned with wide eyes. "Brother, you will be sleeping by the hearth. A guest has taken your room."

Daniel stared in surprise. "A guest?"

"Yes! Nah-kah-yen has come to the Hollow."

The boy's jaw dropped in astonishment. "Nah-kah-yen is alive?"

His sister quickly nodded and pushed open the door as Daniel hurried into the room. Before him stood the startled brave. Nah-kah-yen stared at the lean boy, questioning, then a light of recognition flickered in his eyes. "Young warrior, you have grown."

Eyeing the boy's clothes, a cavalry hat, and a holstered pistol hanging low on his hip, the Indian frowned. "And you have become a white man."

Daniel squirmed uncomfortably. "I have two people now." He looked to the big man by his side. "Jacob has taken me as his son." Pride sparkled in his youthful eyes.

With a sigh, the warrior relented. "It is good to see you. Any Apache is welcome in these times."

The rest of the morning was spent in noisy conversation that seemed to flow in one direction. Daniel endured his sister's mothering. Though he was much taller, Mea-a-ha was still his big sister, and always would be.

"Have you been eating well, my brother? Too thin. We have fresh venison. Boys should eat plenty meat." Mea-a-ha started rattling pans. "Two have come home. Who would have thought three Mimbres would ever stand together again, and on Jacob's birthday. Good reasons to celebrate. Jacob…"

"I know. Get some water…Daniel, there's a bucket by the back door."

"Jacob!" she admonished.

"Well, it's my birthday."

Mea-a-ha pushed her brother back down into his chair and held his head to her breast. "He is cold as snow."

"I am okay." Daniel tried to rise, but Mea-a-ha held him firm and glared. "Jacob..."

"Alright, alright, I'll get the water. Do you want me to kill a chicken too?"

"Jacob!"

Closing the door behind him, the big man tried to sneak in the last word. "They're chickens, not pets, for hell's sake..."

The Indian girl stamped her foot. "Next he will want to eat my puppy."

Jacob returned a short time later with a dripping bucket, making a point to shiver effusively as he stamped the snow from his feet. Mea-a-ha took the pail from his hand and paid him with a kiss.

"No hunting in the Hollow. You know the rules."

Out of politeness, Jacob and the boy accepted Mea-a-ha's feminine fuss as she calmed her emotions. In truth, her emotions were *their* emotions. This beautiful girl, with her bright eyes, laughter and tears, nurtured a part of their hearts that masculinity hungered for but could never show.

When Mea-a-ha's attentions eventually turned to the meal at hand, the two conspirators exchanged a quick glance and ducked outside.

Daniel quietly followed the tall man to the barn as he had many times before. He loved his sister dearly, but women were like sugar; too much made him sick.

Jacob tossed the boy a curry comb, then leaned against the wooden railing and watched the young lad brush his pony.

"So, are you working hard?"

Glancing over his shoulder, Daniel nodded. "Si, I mean yes." The boy laughed. "I am learning Spanish, too. Well, a blend of English and Spanish. Maria tries to teach me English. She says it's the new way. Roberto and Juan speak English too, until they get excited, or angry, then it's Spanish." The boy kept grooming. "I am working very hard...father."

Jacob glowed from an inner warmth. The words "father" and "son" carried the affection that men seldom spoke of. He continued his questioning.

"Is old Luis happy with you?"

There was a light in the boy's eyes. He quit brushing. "Senor Rincon says I am doing good. He offered to pay me, but I have no use for money, so I asked him if I could work for a mare."

"A mare?"

Daniel beamed with pride. "You have a fine breeding pair. When I come home, I want to help you build a herd of great horses...our herd." The boy's eyes darted, searching for his father's approval.

A broad grin spread across Jacob's face. Lifting a big hand, he mussed the boy's hair. "It will be our herd...son."

Returning to his brushing, the boy hid his delight, and continued dreaming. "Pa, Senor Luis, let me pick out the mare." Daniel nodded to his horse. "I've already put Snow Raven with her. Senor Luis said when she drops, the foal is mine. If Mea-a-ha's mare drops in the spring, well, that will give us six of the best horses in the whole territory. In a few years, well..."

****

Jacob's Hollow was hidden high upon a lonely mountain at the base of a towering cliff that ran for miles in both directions. Behind the cabin spread the ancient forest. Its tall cedars and firs grew so close together that their branches were interwoven. Neither light nor snow fell on the woodland floor. The upper boughs were buried in several feet of white powder, creating a vast cavern amongst the trunks of the mighty giants.

A soft pale light filtered through the perimeter of the forest, bathing the inner woods in a twilight that belied the noonday sun. Nah-kah-yen's breath steamed in the cold, clear air beneath the canopy of trees. His keen eyes searched the deep shadows. Somewhere ahead was the buffalo soldier. The Indian's moccasins fell silently on the thick bed of damp pine needles. The big man was brave; he would give him that. Nah-kah-yen had seen him enter the woods without a weapon. Wolves and lions hunted these trails. Even the spotted jaguar still roamed this isolated domain.

Raising his long-bladed knife before him, the warrior hurried on. At the edge of his sight, the path dipped into a deep bowl. Water bubbled beneath a silver ribbon of ice that laced its way around the roots of the trees. Stepping past a massive cedar, Nah-kah-yen searched for solid footing to cross the frozen stream.

"Looking for me?"

The Indian whirled around. He could see nothing. Then, from the shadows, the enormous black man loomed before him. "In here, the advantage is mine."

Lowering his weapon, Nah-kah-yen frowned. The soldier was mocking him. "Your advantage is lost with foolish words."

Jacob eyed the heavy blade in the Indian's hand. "Are you hunting me?"

A sneer replaced Nah-kah-yen's frown. "Not hunting you, but hunting for you. I have given you my pledge of peace unless you would desire it otherwise."

The soldier cocked his head in thought. "I would have honesty. In war or peace, it's a good place to start. You don't like me, do you?"

Turning away, Nah-kah-yen stood in a narrow shaft of light. The shadowed lines of his face deepened with grief. "It is one thing to do battle; in that my guilt is no less than yours. But victory was not enough; you of the black skin had to wipe my people from the earth. Now the Mimbres number less than twenty and still you hunt us. There will be no more children of the Chihene. Can you ask me to feel any different?"

Stuffing his hands in his coat pockets, the soldier shrugged his broad shoulders and moved to the Indian's side. "No, I suppose not."

Both men stared quietly into the distance. Evil had been done that could not be undone.

Slowly, Jacob turned to the warrior. "Ever since I was a little boy, all I have known is killing. And I regret that the blood of your people is on my hands. I came to this hollow in the mountain vowing that I would never kill again." A gentle smile softened the big man's face. "Mea-a-ha will tell you I saved her life. The truth is, she saved mine."

His eyes rose once more to the warrior. "You want to kill me, but wish for my help in rescuing your woman: a difficult choice. I tell you now, Nah-kah-yen, I will not help you. To rescue your squaw would endanger mine."

Jacob hardened. "As much as I yearn to live in peace, I would break my vow and slaughter every living thing to protect that girl. So make your choice."

The Indian turned grim. A desperate hope had vanished. He knew of the black man's valor, but he would find no help from his enemy.

For a long moment the brave remained silent, weighing what the soldier had said. Finally he turned to face him. "Mea-a-ha says you are no longer a soldier. That is hard to understand. For an Indian, a warrior is. There can be nothing else. If a lion chooses to sleep, do we forget he swallowed our children?"

Deep in thought, Nah-kah-yen rested his hand on the rough bark of a tree. A narrow shaft of light played cold on his skin. "You will not help me. So be it."

The Apache warrior took a breath and forced a smile. "I did not come here to kill you. I came to thank you. I had given up when you saved my life. In doing so, you have given me a chance to restore honor to my name. My love for my woman is no less than yours for little Mea-a-ha. And know that I too will do whatever it takes to protect her."

Jacob extended his hand to the Indian. "Mea-a-ha says the Hollow is a healing place filled with magic. Rest a few days. I will give you food and ammunition for your journey. That, at least, I can do."

Nah-kah-yen accepted his hand.

Somewhere deep from the shadowed trail trilled the shrill voice of a woman. "Jacob!"

The dark form of the Indian girl suddenly appeared on a mossy rise by the massive trunk of a giant tree. She quickly hurried to the silhouettes of the two men. Coming to a stop, she gasped for a breath. Her moist eyes darted around wildly. Seeing there was no danger, Mea-a-ha tried to hide a huge pistol in the folds of her skirt. Both men smiled, knowing what fear had carried her into the sleeping forest. Jacob leaned forward. Kissing her, he took the gun from her hand.

"Foolish me. Can't very well kill him without this, now can I?" Both men broke the snow-padded silence with laughter.

The girl fell against her husband and slapped his shoulder. "You're both terrible. What was I supposed to think? You can eat cold beans tonight."

****

The rest of the day passed in a quiet truce, and Jacob rose the next morning at first light, as he had always done. Their simple home in the Hollow was managed with the same discipline Jacob had learned in the Army. By the time Mea-a-ha called him to breakfast, he'd have an hour's work done.

Tossing a pitchfork heavy with grama grass to the horses, Jacob turned in time to see Daniel storm into the barn. The boy was usually shy and waited for the big man to speak, but this time his face was flushed with anger. "Why won't you help Nah-kah-yen?"

Stabbing the pitchfork into the hay, Jacob turned from his labor. "He told you?"

The boy shook. "I heard him talking with my sister, so I ask. Why won't you help?"

Jacob reached for Daniel, but the boy pulled away. "Father, you are the only one who could get Mary Lost Pony back. I will go with you."

"No!" Jacob snapped. "That is exactly why I am not going. I will not put this family in danger."

Daniel's eyes pleaded, hoping desperately his father would understand. "But you've always told me to do the right thing, no matter the cost."

"The right thing is to protect my family."

Whirling in anger, the young boy shook his fist. "You can't turn your back on them, Pa. They are the last of our people."

"Son, I cannot fight every battle…"

"This one you must fight, Father. You're not like other men; you are a hero. You just have to. Pa, you have to."

"Son, it is not easy…"

The boy raged. "You always say it is not easy. It is your way of not doing what is right."

"Daniel!" Jacob flared.

Refusing to relent, Daniel stood his ground. "I'm sorry, Father, but you are wrong."

Backing away from emotions that were about to overwhelm him, Daniel ran from the barn. Reaching the door, the boy turned one last time. "You are wrong."

****

    Four days had passed since Daniel had left, and Nah-kah-yen had departed shortly after. Mea-a-ha cast quick glances at her husband as he sat staring remorsefully into the fire. He had not made amends with his son. Jacob loved the boy, and the rift stabbed at his heart. Mea-a-ha wanted to comfort him, but the decision was his. Mary was lost and so was her child. He would have to live with his decision.

    Returning to her work, Mea-a-ha busied herself, cutting venison into chunks for a stew. When she turned around, Jacob was gone. The Indian girl hurried to the door and flung it open. Her stoic husband was standing alone on the front porch, leaning against the log railing.

    Folding her arms, Mea-a-ha stepped quietly beside him. It was beautiful in the Hollow, even in winter. Dark green pines bordered the snow-covered meadow. The humble stone-and-log barn, adorned with icicles, added its own enchantment to the pastoral scene. In the corral, the Buckskin stallion trotted proudly to the edge of the frozen pond while the Pinto mare and the Gray Shire looked on. As always, a soothing tune carried from the bubbling spring. In its icy water flowed the magic that protected the Hollow from the outside world.

    Softening just a little, Mea-a-ha slid under the big man's arm. "We are safe. Is it enough?"

    Jacob pulled away. "You and the boy can hate me if you want, but safe is enough."

    Her face straining with sudden alarm, Mea-a-ha threw her arms around the soldier in a tight embrace. "Jacob, do not say that. We love you, but we grieve for the loss of our friend. You are a hero to the people in this land, yet your own family cannot turn to you."

    Jacob pushed her away. "And when I refuse to do your bidding, will those who say they love me turn on me? I am not going to Mexico. If your love comes with strings…"

    Clenching his jaw, Jacob headed off the porch. The girl chased after him. "Jacob!" She folded against his chest, crying. "I'm sorry. Hold me. I am mad at you, but I love you more than the air I breathe. Above all, there is love." She wept. "Hold me. I'm sorry."

    Clenching his teeth, Jacob took the Apache in his arms. "Damn it, Mea-a-ha. I'm not going to Mexico. You have to accept that."

    Old Buck plodded over the familiar snow-covered trail that he had traveled many times before. Jube patted his frosty neck. "We's almost there ol' friend." After a long cold ride, they finally came into the border trees that surrounded the Hollow. A sturdy packhorse trailed behind, and a whiskered old gent rode by Jubaliah's side. Jacob's Hollow would be a welcome, if temporary, respite.

The last time he had seen his friend was the night Jacob married that little Indian girl. She was a good woman, barely twenty, but she was an Apache, as violent a race that had ever lived. It would take time for old prejudices to die. Jube had wished Jacob had married one of his own kind, but black women in this forgotten wasteland were scarce—even more so than Apaches. A pang of guilt rose in the old soldier's chest; little Mea-a-ha did not deserve his disdain.

At last, the trail came out of the shadowed pines. Halfway between the stone cabin and the barn, stood his old friend, holding the Indian girl in a tight embrace.

"Hi-ho!"

Looking up, the couple's eyes grew wide with surprise. Jube rode up and pulled his weary bay to a stop. With a twinkle in his eye, he broke into a broad grin. "Don't cha two ever stop pawin' each other?"

The girl hid her face against her husband, wiping the last tears from her eyes. Jacob held her close, shocked to see his friend.

"Jube, what in thunder are you doing here?"

The jovial soldier tipped back his hat. "Sarge, we's goin' ta' Mexico."

Chapter -3-
Winter Trail

Jacob paced the floor while his new guests warmed themselves by the fire. He turned several times, and then suddenly pounded his iron fist on the heavy table. "Damn it! Damn it to hell. Tell me what you know, Jube."

Sipping a warm cup of coffee held tightly in both hands, his old friend mugged a face. "That's it. The note said Roberto n' Juan was going with Daniel ta' meet up with some Apache warrior feller, and go ta' Mexico ta' rescue Injuns."

Jacob cursed. "Damn that boy. I'll tan his hide. It's just crazy."

Jube chuckled. "Yea, not like when we done run off at fourteen n' joined the Union army in that bloody war. We was much smarter." He brayed once more and nudged his shabby companion with an elbow.

Turning to the bewhiskered old man who had remained silent, Jacob cast a glance at his bandaged foot. "Hamp, what happened to you?"

The old man grimaced. "Gone from bad to worse, I'm afraid. A horse stepped on it. Messed up the circulation I guess, 'cuz frostbite set in on the way up. Figured I'd go with you, but now I don't know. Maybe I'm too old for such adventures."

Things were going from bad to worse, all right. Jacob continued to pace. "Hamp, you best not risk it. If you think you will be okay, you can stay here while I'm gone and protect Mea-a-ha."

Hamp stretched his foot out in front of him, relishing the warmth of the hearth. "Suits me jes' fine. Liked not to make it here, as it was."

From the corner of the room where she had sat quietly listening to the men, Mea-a-ha stood and folded her arms resolutely. "I'm going."

Jacob scowled. "I don't have time for this childish nonsense. Things are bad enough without dragging a woman along. You'll stay here with Hamp."

The girl took one step forward and stretched to her full height. Her large brown eyes burned with a fire that would melt steel. "Damn you, Jacob Keever! You will hear me this time." Her fragile voice shook with emotion. She had never sworn, and it gave the big man a start.

"Daniel is my brother. That is reason for me to go. Mary Lost Pony will need me, too. And because you rage like a storm, I must come to stop you from killing Nah-kah-yen. I may be just a woman, but I know something you don't, and that's the Apache route across the border." Mea-a-ha bristled with defiance. "If you leave me, I will follow. Then I will be alone and in more danger. I am your woman; my place is with you. It is the Apache way. There will be no more talk. I have spoken."

His chest swelling in anger at the girl's audacity, Jacob towered over her. "You ain't going!" he bellowed.

"Am too!"

A menacing growl like that of an angry bear rumbled deep in the big man's throat. He'd have no more of this.

Undeterred, Mea-a-ha shoved her nose into his face, bristling with a sneer meant to peel his hide from his bones. "Am too!"

Her belligerence was too much. It was all Jacob could do to control his temper. He had to save his son, and she didn't know it, but he was trying to save her, too. His husky voice hissed low and threatening. "You ain't too big to spank, little missy."

Her eyes flashing, Mea-a-ha grabbed a thin stick of kindling from the firebox and thrust it into his hand. "Then do it, nchaa ndeen'…'big man.' You are wasting time. Too much talk. Do it."

The battle-hardened soldier glared down at the diminutive Indian girl. He expected to be obeyed, and her insubordination made his blood boil. At a loss for words, his temper exploded. Jerking her arm, he turned her sideways and raised the switch high. Mea-a-ha bit her lip, refusing to cry.

Frustrated beyond all measure, he lifted his hand higher and held it for a moment. "Damn it, girl!" He couldn't do it. "Damn it to hell." No matter how dangerous the trail, he wasn't that kind of man.

Releasing her, Jacob threw the stick hard against the wall and turned away. A whipping would not cower her and he knew it.

Mea-a-ha exhaled a breath. She had won. Jacob could never hurt her. Her voice softened. "I go with you."

His mighty fist clenching and unclenching, he faced her. "Very well, little girl, you can go," he spat. "But don't think you've won. You can come because you know the trail Daniel will take, but you won't have it all your way. When we find the boys, we are turning around without Mary Lost Pony. And one more thing—you can't stop me from killing Nah-kah-yen."

Jacob grabbed his hat and stormed out. "Jube, I'll be saddling our horses."

As the door slammed, shaking the very stones of their home, the girl stood, staring at the two stunned guests. Her eyes filled with tears. Suddenly she tore after her husband, screaming, "Jacob…Jacob!"

He refused to turn around. Hurrying across the yard, Mea-a-ha caught his arm as he stomped into the barn. She was crying freely now. "When you disagree with me, will you turn on me? Are there strings to *your* love?"

Jacob stood shaking. "You don't get it."

The girl clenched his coat. "I get it. The big, tough soldier who's afraid of nothing is scared for the first time in his life...for me."

She curled against him. "Better get used to it; you will be watching over me for a long, long time."

A frustrated groan escaped his clenched teeth as he took the girl into his arms. "Damn you, woman."

She kissed him passionately. "You swear too much."

Daylight was burning. Jube climbed onto ol' Buck and bid goodbye to poor Hamp, who was balancing in the doorway on one foot. "Don't cha' be dancin' all night. Ya hear."

The old man faked a little jig and smiled broadly.

Backing away from the hitching rail, Jubaliah turned and grinned at Jacob, who was leading his Buckskin from the barn. "Took yo' time ta' saddle them horses."

The Indian girl quietly rode up beside him on her spotted pony. Jube stretched out a hand. "Ya' gots' some straw in yo' hair." He brayed like a donkey. "If you two don't control yo' selves, we'll never reach Mexico." Mea-a-ha blushed and hid her eyes.

Arching a brow, Jacob mounted to the saddle and rode past his friend. "You'll have plenty of time to laugh, Jube...while you're freezing your ass off sleeping alone. She may be a handful, but she is soft n' warm."

Following her husband, the Indian girl smiled bashfully at the soldier. "Very warm."

The two men, dressed for winter, wore heavy leather coats with thick sheepskin linings. Their tall boots and tan hats told that they were once Cavalry. Most black men in this part of the territory usually were Army of one kind or another.

Mea-a-ha wore a dark gray dress with several slips for warmth. She had made the dress herself during a long stay on the Rincon ranch. Carmelita Rincon had taught her how to sew. The Mexican girl was a new friend in the Apache girl's rapidly changing world. Just a few short months ago, she wore only hides. The fringed doeskin dress was tucked away in her saddle bag just in case. Mea-a-ha was not sure how civilized women's clothing would hold up on the trail. They were beautiful, but delicate.

The only thing detracting from Mea-a-ha's feminine attire was the cowboy hat she chose instead of a bonnet. Her shiny black hair clearly showed she wasn't a white woman. Dressed as she was, maybe she could pass at a distance for Mexican. It would help on both sides of the border.

Jacob's high mountain retreat was buried in deep drifts, but as they descended into the desert, stiff gray brush and cactus of all sorts slowly replaced winter's snowy mantle. The horses were fresh, and now was a time for haste. The plan was to reach Robber's Knoll by nightfall, so he pushed hard.

In their lush, hidden Hollow, vision was often limited to the next tree. Here the land fell away under the cold, cloud-filled sky. The Apache girl gazed forlornly at the endless horizon that never seemed to get closer. Somewhere beyond the vast expanse rode Daniel. Finding him before he reached Mexico seemed an impossible task. It was daunting, but Mea-a-ha knew if anyone could do it, it was Jacob.

Winding down a steep ridge, they came out onto the flatlands. The young girl had spent little time in a saddle. Horses were for warriors, and she found the pace both grueling and painful. Mea-a-ha pouted, growing more miserable with each mile; sure that Jacob was riding hell-bent to punish her for insisting on coming. It was certainly a paddling of sorts. Her husband was far out ahead and seemed not to care that she was having a hard time keeping up. He was being a brute.

Leading the packhorse, Jube brought up the rear. As the trail widened, he came alongside the Indian girl. She was fighting back tears. When he caught her eye, he tipped his hat. "There might be a few things ya' still gots' ta' learn 'bout ol' Jacob."

Mea-a-ha rebelliously sniffed away her tears, but said nothing.

Pulling off his gloves, Jube blew into his hands for warmth. "Jacob sets a mean pace. I know what ya's thinking. But even his own men complained about wearing out their britches before lunch. He was mighty harsh on them boys, but we knowed if we survived Sergeant Jacob Keever, there weren't nothin' we couldn't face. He's tough as nails, n' pity the man who gets in his way. Before this is over, you's gunna' thank 'em for puttin' blisters on yo' pretty little backside."

The girl looked ahead to her husband. She winced with each bounce of the saddle, but her heart hurt a little less.

Jube started to fall back, then decided to speak his mind. "Jes' so it's said, Jacob was right in not wantin' ta' bring ya.' So don't go bein' angry at him. He shoulda' spanked ya' like he was thinking.' This ain't no place for you."

Having said his piece, Jube tipped his hat once more and dropped back in line. Mea-a-ha's pout returned, but she knew it was partly because the buffalo soldier was right.

For a while she rode on, wrestling with what Jube had said. His cold, hard logic did not sit well with her feminine emotions. She wiped her cheeks, but continued fuming over his parting words. "...shoulda' spanked me. Dumb soldier."

A flame in her eyes bursting anew, Mea-a-ha leaned forward and patted her pony. "Come little Ch'ikii. Maybe he is right, but he should not be so arrogant."

Digging in her heels, the Indian girl whirled her pony around and raced back to confront the haughty soldier.

It infuriated her that, because she was smaller and much younger than the men, they often treated her like a child. In some ways, she still was. The white man's world was new to her, so there was much to learn, but she was trying, and she would not be scolded. She had earned her right to ride with the men, and it was time to let Jube know.

Pulling beside him, Mea-a-ha spun around once more and glared. She let it burn, then spoke. "Is it because I am small, or a girl, or Apache that I should not go?"

The burly man looked down at her reproachfully. "All three."

"Do I love less because I am these things?"

Jube frowned. "No, ya' probably love more."

"Then I go because of a greater love. There is no better reason."

Mea-a-ha kicked her pony to ride away, then abruptly pulled her reins and waited for Jube to catch up. She wrinkled her nose. "Let's talk about spanking my pretty little backside. Which of these things that I am, should I be spanked for?"

Jube narrowed his eyes. "Don't be tryin' ta' rile me, child. I know your wicked tongue. Ya' should be spanked 'cuz you is a little girl that sasses yo' husband, n' he knows a lot better n' you what dangers this trail will bring."

Mea-a-ha shrugged her shoulders. "Maybe so. But if I am to be spanked for following my heart, then maybe your hand falls as unjustly as your words."

Her voice started breaking with emotion. "Jube, I'm not a child. If I harm my husband because I am these things that I am, then you should spank me hard, but maybe, brave soldier, my love is something he needs as much as the strength in your arm. Maybe."

The Indian girl slapped her reins and rode away.

By afternoon, the horses had run themselves out, and three travelers slowed to a gentle lope. The deep snow of the Hollow was now far behind as though it never existed, and a land bereft of moisture dared them to go on.

The Indian girl knew no other place. This was her world. It was harsh, like life itself, and she accepted it simply for what it was. She had never been to a town, nor known any luxuries until Jacob took her to his cabin. For her, their humble feather bed was a treasure beyond her greatest dreams. How she longed for it now.

Mea-a-ha's limbs ached, and she was thankful for the slower pace. Her mind drifted to other thoughts. They were traveling the Mimbre trail. She was following the death march of Chief Victorio. Her people—everyone she knew—had tragically perished in one bloody night. How the women must have wailed watching their braves cut down before their eyes. How helpless they must have felt huddled together, knowing that they were now the chattel of these brutal men, to be gutted or raped at their whims.

The Apache girl was riding towards a death that should have been hers. Why had she survived when everyone she loved lay murdered on a lonely mountain? It caused her guilt, but the answer was simple—Jacob. He had taken her in when she had nowhere to go. This quiet man had given her a home and loved her with all his heart. The night her people were slaughtered, she was lying safely in his arms. Yet now she was defying him. It troubled her more and more as every hour brought them closer to that fateful place.

The day of the Mimbre Apache was over. There would be no more villages with laughing children or barking dogs, no noble chief, no joyous dances. Her people had played their sad part, then passed out of time.

A lump came to her throat. She now lived in the white man's world, an invading race that cheered the passing of her tribe. *Apache* was a word they spit with hatred, just nameless savages who would not be mourned. She knew the meaning of the word *savages*; it embarrassed her. Her people were primitive. Faced with so much she didn't understand; it was hard to hold her head high.

Unable to bear her grief, Mea-a-ha wept. Nameless savages. She knew each of the dead by name. She remembered their voices and saw their beautiful faces in her dreams. For the Apache there was no written language to tell their story, no poetry to sing their praise. The Mimbre may have been poor and ignorant, but they were her people, and she would never forget. This she vowed.

Mea-a-ha lifted her eyes, scanning the horizon. She and a handful of hunted warriors were the last of the free Mimbres. Would anyone remember them when they were gone?

Saving Mary Lost Pony and her baby would not change the fate of her people; yet now on the brink of extinction, every life, no matter how small, was more precious than the rising sun. Mea-a-ha looked to her husband. He alone had the strength to make a difference. She must make him understand. Protecting his family was not enough.

The hard ride had paid off. As the fading sun cooled on the horizon, the weathered pinnacles of Robbers' Knoll came into view. Mea-a-ha had come this way before. She shivered, wishing they could have made camp elsewhere. It was a dreadful place, but it was the only shelter for miles around.

Jacob lifted Mea-a-ha from the saddle and realized her alarm. "It will be okay my love. I'll build a white man's fire so big it will scare away old ghosts."

Mea-a-ha did her best to hide her fear. Robbers' Knoll held painful memories of a battle that still haunted her. Jacob's reassurance did little to calm her.

With the day's last rays of amber burnishing his ruddy face, Jube rode into the circle of stone. "Everything okay?"

Holding Mea-a-ha close, Jacob raised his chin. "Will be as soon as you build a fire." He kissed the girl. "And the little lady wants it big n' cozy."

Jube shook his head. "Sending me off fo' kindlin' so ya' can be alone. Ya' been kissin' on that little filly so much, amazed her lips ain't falled' off."

Mea-a-ha dipped a wooden spoon into the pot of beans and breathed easier. She couldn't change the world, but she could soothe a hungry belly, and for now that was enough. Dried meat was plucked from a sack and added for flavor. Next, she warmed some tortillas to the delight of the men. It was not bad fare for the first night on the trail.

Rubbing his stomach, Jube broke into his familiar broad grin. "Iffin' I knowed' havin' a woman along woulda' meant we coulda' had vittles this tasty, I'da' been capturing squaws long ago."

The Apache girl sneered. "And long ago, I would have poisoned you."

Jube grinned. "Wouldn't of been any worse than my own cookin.'"

Mea-a-ha ignored the crude soldier and looked to her husband. He hadn't been listening. His cold eyes stared off into the darkness towards the south. Mea-a-ha rubbed a comforting hand on his shoulder. "Don't worry, ol' Bear. You will get a chance to wring the boy's neck."

Jacob turned back towards the fire and lowered his eyes. "They have a two-day lead, and the border could be made in four."

The big man shook his head and sighed.

Pulling the blackened coffee pot from the fire, Jube offered a cup to Jacob. "True, but the boys didn't take a packhorse or any provisions. Them younguns' will have ta' live off the land, an' that'll slow em' down."

Turning the tin cup in his hands, Jacob mulled it over. "Let's hope it's enough. Mexican soldiers got no love for Americans or Apaches."

Rising to his feet, Jacob turned to other thoughts. The stone pinnacles surrounding them held echoes of sadness and pain. He wandered alone into the evening shadows. As he walked, his hand clutched at his chest. Around his neck hung a small medicine bag given to him by the Indian girl. Braided to it was a length of silky horsehair. It carried memories of an old friend.

Mea-a-ha watch until the dark took her husband. She knew that somewhere beneath the stars he would stop by a pile of stones. A tear rolled down her cheek. There were too many stones, stones in the Hollow, stones at this lonely place, and on a distant mountain far ahead. Much sadness, yet beneath the stones, there were good memories that would endure beyond the pain. A tender smile softened her face. Jacob would be okay.

By the time he returned, the strain of the day was telling on their faces. Knocking down the fire, Jacob joined Mea-a-ha. She was already wrapped in several blankets and had slipped into his comfy blue shirt that she always slept in. Jacob climbed in and pulled her close. Turning in his arms, Mea-a-ha pressed her back to his chest. She found the energy for one last healing smile, then snuggled deeper beneath his muscular limbs. Her sleepy eyes looked past the dying flames. Poor Jube, he would be freezing by morning. "Good night, Jube," her voice rang, honey-sweet. "Keep your ass warm."

It seemed like she had just fallen asleep when Jacob's firm hand shook her shoulder. Mea-a-ha rubbed her eyes with a tiny fist. "What's the matter?"

"Time to go."

The girl slumped. "It's night."

Jube's dark shape blotted out the stars. "While the boys sleep, we'll be ridin.'"

Groaning, Mea-a-ha stumbled to her feet. "I'll wring Daniel's neck myself."

Feeling grumpy, she shoved Jube with her tiny hands. "Turn your back while I change."

Through the cold, moonless night, they plodded on in silence. Tucked beneath her hat, the Indian girl's head bobbed. Her mare followed Jacob's tall stallion, and if she slowed, Jube was there to move her along. The smell of sagebrush and the sounds of the trail faded from her mind. She dozed once more.

After several long hours of riding, details began to appear on the silent desert landscape as a sleepy winter sun struggled to rise behind her beloved distant mountains.

Taking in their surroundings, Mea-a-ha spoke through a yawn. "We should be farther east to join the Mimbre Trail."

Jacob sighed and slowed to let her catch up. He knew she wouldn't like what he had to say. "We're going to Fort Cummings first."

"No!" Mea-a-ha leaned forward and gripped Jacob's arm. "It's a bad place..." She pleaded. "No, Jacob."

To the Indian girl, forts were dark, evil abodes where soldiers poured out like deadly wasps through a gaping hole to hunt her people.

"Do we have to?"

Jacob placed a gloved hand over hers. "We need supplies. You heard Jube. We don't have time to live off the land. And I fear we are going to need a lot of ammunition."

The girl's shoulders slumped. "You won't let them take me from you?"

Lifting her chin, he tried to reassure her. "You know Colonel McCrae. He'll be happy to see you."

She gazed up at her husband with doubting eyes. "But there are many soldiers there. You don't let them take me."

Jube rode alongside. "They only wants the bucks, they ain't huntin' squaws."

"Stop calling me a squaw. I'm a girl. You, you, Dar-kee."

She whipped her pony and bolted away, leaving the men staring at each other.

Jube broke into a surprised grin. "Darkie! Where'd she learn that word?"

Watching her disappear, Jacob chuckled, "Don't know, but next time you talk to her, I think you better lose the word squaw, or plan on losing your scalp."

Jube kicked his horse and defended himself. "Ya' knowed' I don't mean nothin' by it."

Jacob pulled past his friend. "I'll write that on your tombstone. *'Here lies a dar-kee, tried to be fair. He didn't mean nothin' but he's still missin' his hair.'*"

Tugging on the packhorse, Jube hurried to catch up.

"Ain't funny, Jacob. With that girl, it's the soldiers who need protectin.'"

Chapter -4-
Fort Cummings

Cresting a low hill of crumbling earth, the trio pulled to a quiet stop. Below them, the foreboding adobe walls of Fort Cummings rose from the cold earth. A dreary winter sky added to Mea-a-ha's dismay. Kicking her painted mare close to her husband, the girl's heart beat like a fist pounding inside her breast. She had never been to a fort, a town, or a settlement of any kind. While the two men were eager to greet old friends, the Apache girl was filled with memories of thundering hooves on a dark night. Screams of women and children mixed with the sharp crack of rifles as her mother lay atop her in a ditch. Fort Cummings was her childhood nightmares come true.

Seeing her distress, Jacob reached out a reassuring hand. "You belong to me; they won't hurt you."

She understood what her husband meant. To the soldiers, she was a possession, like a horse or a saddle, an item of little concern. It was a sad thing, but with the fort looming before her, being so regarded gave her comfort. She would play her part as worthless baggage.

Jacob headed down the knoll with Mea-a-ha hanging close to his side. A sharp glance over her shoulder let Jube know she wanted him near, too.

The gate of the old fort was what was known as a sally port—a large guard tower that rose above the wall over the entrance like a gaping mouth ready to swallow her. Entering the fearsome jaws, they went through a short tunnel to a second gate. It was dark. The clip-clop of the horses echoed an unsettling tone on the flat stones. Mea-a-ha nervously looked left and right, peering into every shadow.

At the end of the tunnel, a disheveled black soldier with the butt of his carbine resting on the ground snapped to attention. Upon recognizing the approaching men, his face broke into a cheery grin. "Well, lordie, lordie. Sergeant Jacob, it's good to see ya'. Good times n' bad times. Ya ain't gonna start shootin' up the place again is ya?"

Jacob's last trip to the fort had ended in the untimely demise of a dishonest rancher. "Not today, Luther. Just needin' supplies."

Mea-a-ha had met the scrawny soldier before. He gave her a polite nod, then greeted Jube with the same exuberance he showed Jacob. "See you is all healed up. Sure you don't want your old job back? It ain't been the same without ya."

Inside the fort, they rode down a broad street lined with many doorways and passed into a large courtyard surrounded by long buildings, constructed against the outer rampart. Other structures cordoned off a corral for livestock. It looked like a walled city. Though Mea-a-ha was amazed by how big it was, this den of soldiers had none of the beauty of the Rincon ranch. There were no graceful arches or covered walkways. It lacked heart. Everything was square, unadorned, and covered in dust.

Riding to the west side of the parade grounds, they pulled up in front of an adobe building with a small wooden porch. Jacob tied his horse to the hitching rail. Dismounting, he lifted Mea-a-ha to the ground. "We need to pay our respects to Colonel McCrae."

This, the girl was relieved to do. McCrae was the chief. If he welcomed her, she would be safe.

A white trooper stepped onto the porch. He nodded to Jacob, then opened the door for them.

Once inside, Mea-a-ha looked through another entryway and saw the colonel sitting at his desk. Lifting his head from his work, he instantly broke into a big smile and stood up. "Jacob Keever, come in. What a surprise."

Hesitation in his voice made Mea-a-ha think somehow it wasn't such a surprise.

McCrae shook Jacob's hand, and then Jube's, who remained uncommonly quiet. The rank of the man demanded respect from his two ex-sergeants. After a few pleasantries, the colonel turned to the Indian girl. Taking her hand, he gave it a kiss. It was a white man's custom she approved of.

"Little Mea-a-ha, so you accompanied your husband to the fort." He continued holding her hand while searching her eyes. "I can tell you are a bit nervous, but you needn't worry. You are perfectly safe here." He slowly pulled away, still studying her. "Our job is keeping the braves on the reservation, not scaring pretty girls."

The smile faded from the colonel's face as he turned back to Jacob. "So Jacob, what brings you to the fort?"

Jacob paused, returning the colonel's scrutiny. The officer was an honest man. He had always treated the buffalo soldiers fairly. At this greeting, his politeness seemed somehow thin. When the long silence grew awkward, Jacob finally spoke.

"Hoping to get supplies from the sutler with your permission, Sir."

Staring up at the tall men, Mea-a-ha could feel the tension growing between them. Their words were guarded as each sought to read the other's mind. She realized with a start that a silent battle was being waged. The colonel finally smiled at the big man. "Going on a trip, are you?"

Setting his jaw, Jacob glanced at the girl. McCrae quickly looked down at Mea-a-ha.

"I'm sorry, it must have been a long journey, and I am sure you are tired." He turned to Jube. "Jubaliah, the guest quarters are empty; why don't you take Mrs. Keever next door so she can rest."

Mea-a-ha looked anxiously to her husband. She was being dismissed so the men could talk freely. She felt like a child. To the colonel, maybe she was, or even less, merely an Indian.

Jacob gave her hand a reassuring squeeze. It was useless to protest. Mea-a-ha smiled politely to McCrae. "Thank you, Colonel."

Shrinking back, she slipped her hand into Jube's. The burly soldier nodded to the colonel and cast Jacob a wary eye.

"Jacob, be outside if ya need me." His voice was cold as ice.

The two men watched as Jube led the girl away. McCrae glanced at Jacob, then turned and stared out the window.

"Jube's words sounded almost like a threat, Sergeant."

Jacob smiled. He knew the colonel calling him by his old rank was meant to place him in a position of subordination. "Call it a friendly warning. Colonel, I don't have much time. Maybe it would be better if you just say what's on your mind."

McCrae laughed. "Damn if you aren't the boldest darkie I've ever met."

The thinnest trace of a grin eased the hard lines of Jacob's face. "It's tough being timid when it seems like somebody's life is always hangin' in the balance."

Leaving the window, Aaron McCrae stepped to the center of the room and squared with the big man. "Is there a life hanging in the balance this time?"

Jacob's eyes glinted like cold steel. He didn't like being questioned, and he let a silent stare be his answer.

Easing his stance, McCrae turned back to the window. "You've become a famous man out here in the New Mexico Territory. It's hard to know how much is truth, and how much is myth." The colonel's shoulders shrugged as he smirked. "My friend Judge Hein left me the dime novel written about you. Guess it's how legends are born." He whirled around. "Jacob, I got a job to do, and I don't need the Hero of Apache Springs stirring up trouble."

A fierce, penetrating glare added a warning to McCrae's words. "There are a dozen braves led by a crafty old warrior from Mea-a-ha's tribe. They are wreaking bloody vengeance for the slaughter at Tres Castillos, and they are embarrassing the whole damn U.S. Army. Having a local legend side with them would give the papers a field day."

Again the colonel waited for some kind of response, but the sergeant stood as silent and unyielding as the adobe walls surrounding them.

McCrae shook his head, frustration furrowing his face. "Jacob. For some reason you turned away from the Army and took in an Apache family. You're a soldier, damn it, and you know that the last of Mea-a-ha's people are going to die. You also know I'm the one ordered to hunt them down. What I want to know is, do I have to fight you, too?"

The giant finally moved. Stepping past the colonel, Jacob glanced out the window at the guest quarters. "Colonel, without women and children, the Mimbre Apache are already dead. The few braves that are left wouldn't want my help. They expect to die, but they're going to kill as many soldiers as they can. Rubbing your nose in the dirt just shows they ain't lost their sense of humor."

McCrae hung his head. This he understood. "Sergeant, there are still those who think you should hang for the killings you've done. I want to know where you stand."

Turning, Jacob drew himself up to his full height. His square jaw locked in grim defiance. "I'll stay out of it, but know this: I will protect my family. If you send soldiers to the Hollow, don't expect them to return."

For a tense moment the colonel held Jacob's icy stare, bristling at the bold threat. Slowly he broke into a calculating smile. "Yes, your secret Hollow. You own the whole damn mountain, so I hear."

"Enough of it."

"Fair enough, Jacob. I have no interest in your Indian squaw or sending troops to your Hollow, but you are not in the Hollow now. That brings us back to why you are here. You want to tell me the real reason?"

Once again the big man turned to stone, refusing to answer. The colonel angered. "Very well. Then *I'll* tell you. Private Zeke Potter, one of your own men, is stretched out over in the infirmary right now. He's answered his last bugle call." McCrae's eyes narrowed. "Private Potter was scouting with Sergeant Bolley and a small detachment of troopers yesterday morning when they spotted an Apache warrior riding with three young men who looked like Mexicans, but they could have been Apaches in stolen outfits. They were too far away to tell. Sergeant Bolley gave chase and took fire."

Aaron McCrae paced to the center of the room. "One of them was riding a tall painted stallion, fast as the wind. There's talk that Mea-a-ha's brother is known for such a horse." McCrae's voice rang sharp. "Where is Daniel, Jacob?"

The big man turned away, balling his fist. Zeke Potter had been more than one of his men; he was a friend, and now one more of his soldiers lay dead. Would it ever end?

Shaken, Jacob put his hand to his head. "Did they see who did the shooting?"

McCrae pounded his fist on the desk. "Damn it, Jacob, I've been honest with you. If you are the man I think you are, then it's time to be honest with me, or it's only going to get worse for your boy."

Jacob slowly turned. His face was heavy with grief. He knew the colonel was trying to be fair. He could do no less. "Nah-kah-yen. An Apache warrior, Nah-kah-yen, came to the Hollow. His squaw is a captive in Mexico. He wanted me to help him, but I sent him away. Daniel was furious, so he took off."

Jacob raised his dark eyes. "I'm going to get my son back. That's all. As for Zeke, I don't believe Daniel did any shooting, but if someone was chasing me, lookin' to kill, I wouldn't hesitate, and neither would you. The boy's only crime is being Apache."

"Out here it's crime enough." The colonel folded his hands behind his back, much relieved to hear the famed hero didn't want trouble. "What of this Indian, Nah-kah-yen?"

Jacob shrugged. "He means nothing to me. I just want my son."

McCrae rubbed his face. "You know I can't guarantee your son's safety. Any buck off the reservation is to be shot. Not all the warriors of Mea-a-ha's tribe are dead. With that old scoundrel, Nana out there murdering ranchers, and a soldier laid cold from an Apache bullet, I got generals breathing down my neck."

McCrae paced the distance of the room and then turned to Jacob. "Get your boy and go home if you can. Keep him there until the last Apache is dead."

Mindful of his duties, the colonel adjusted his collar and came to attention. "But you know I have to send troops after him. My hands are tied."

The big man didn't try to hide his distress. Daniel was in a grave danger. The colonel had orders, and Jacob couldn't blame him, but Daniel was his son. "Maybe you will have to fight me after all, Colonel."

McCrae clenched his fist but then calmed. "Let's hope it doesn't come to that."

Changing his mood, the Colonel stepped forward and put his hand on Jacob's shoulder. "I remember your wedding to that little girl. I'm not without heart. Maybe we can find a way."

Reaching into his pocket, McCrae pulled out an ornately engraved gold watch and flipped it open. "You know, I have a son, too."

Jacob looked surprised. "No sir, I didn't."

Staring into his watch, the colonel smiled proudly and showed the picture to Jacob. "Guess fatherhood isn't something you expected from a starchy old fort commander."

Taking the watch in his big hands, the sergeant studied the picture. "He's a soldier too." Jacob raised his eyes to meet McCrae's.

The colonel closed the watch and returned it to his vest. "Yes, a young brash lieutenant. He's been back east attending school, but Mason is here now at the fort. Came in a few days ago."

Walking back to the window, McCrae looked off into the distance. "Jacob, beneath the legend, I know you to be a good soldier. You never lost a man under your command. I'm going to ask you to do something you are not going to like."

Taking his time, McCrae moved to his desk and settled into his chair. "You want to protect your son. I want to protect mine. Mason, on the other hand, wants to join General Crook in pursuing Geronimo. He is young and hopes to see action before this damn Indian war is over." The colonel cursed under his breath. "Crook is pushing too hard. Good men are going to die. I don't want my son to be one of them." The colonel pounded his fist. "The boy won't listen to me."

With hardly a breath, McCrae's eyes narrowed. "Jacob, my son has heard about you. That little dime novel got around. When he found out that you were under his daddy's command. . .well, he wants to meet you. I intend to use his enthusiasm to change the young pup's mind about going with Crook. Here's my proposal. Instead of me sending a detachment after Nah-kah-yen and your son, I'll send Mason with you. You'll be my detachment. When you find your boy, you turn Nah-kah-yen over to my son as a prisoner. The generals get an Injun to hang. Mason gets to meet a real, live hero, track Apaches across the desert, and play a part in the great damn Indian war."

Jacob leaned on the desk. "Colonel, I can't."

McCrae came to his feet. His voice boomed with authority. "You can, you will, and you will bring my boy back safely."

"But Colonel, I'm in enough trouble with Mea-a-ha as it is. If I turn the last of her people over to the Army..."

"You take my son, or when you leave here, a detachment of white troops go with you."

Jacob stood speechless. The colonel was giving him no choice. "Sir, it ain't fair."

"War's hell, or haven't you heard?"

McCrae eyes danced. He knew he'd won. Taking a bottle of whiskey from a shelf, he filled two glasses and handed one to Jacob. "To our sons."

"I tell ya' Jacob, you'd think that out here in the most desolate dung hole in the po' side of hell, where ya' gots' ta' ride for day jes' ta' hear a body sneeze, that people could live their life in peace, no matter their color."

Jube fumed as he followed Jacob to the sutler's store. "Whatcha' gunna' tell Mea-a-ha?"

Jacob pulled up short. "The truth—always the truth."

"Jacob, she'll go wild."

"I don't like it, either, Jube, but we don't have any choice."

"So we is suppose to babysit this officer's brat and hand over a Mimbre warrior to him in front of Mea-a-ha and expect her not to lift our scalps. Jacob..."

Gripping the door, Jacob whirled around. "I know, Jube, but saving Daniel comes first."

With a flap of his arms, Jube relented. "Well, I don't know how things could get any worse."

The sutler's store was a large square building, just outside the fort. It was well-stocked with dry goods and anything else soldiers or weary travelers might be willing to buy.

As the two men ducked through the low door, Jacob noticed a tall, lean man talking with the sutler across the dusty plank counter. The stranger was young, yet had an air of dignity about him, along with a scholarly face. He had a long straight nose and dark, piercing eyes. Their conversation appeared to be small talk. Whoever he was, he wasn't buying anything, unless it was information.

As Jacob stepped up to the counter, the man smiled and moved aside. Paying customers came first, especially one as big as Jacob. Returning his smile, Jacob nodded and then looked to the bearded gent behind the counter. The portly sutler recognized him immediately.

"Well, by golly, ain't seen you in a long time, Sergeant. What brings you down from your mountain?"

Wanting to get his provisions and be on his way, Jacob hoped to keep conversation to a minimum. "Just some supplies for a little trip, Mr. Broyles. I'll need som-..."

Jube interrupted the pleasantries by dropping a heaping handful of potatoes on the counter. Then, reaching behind him, he grabbed a blanket and added it to the pile. "Don't need no spicy girl to curl up with, jes' a little sheep's wool." He mugged a face at his friend. Jacob turned back to the red-haired proprietor. "I will need ammunition, Winchester, Springfield .45-70, Colt .44, and lots of it."

Mr. Broyles grinned. "You ain't planning on massacring the Apaches again, are you Sergeant Keever?"

The stranger came to attention. "Sergeant Jacob Keever?"

Jacob tipped his hat, but paid the man no more notice. Jube returned with a sack of flour and another of beans. The pile was growing. A wrinkled brow showed Jacob's concern. "Do you have an extra packhorse in the corral that you can let go cheap?"

The sutler feigned sympathy. "Sergeant, you know ain't nothin' cheap out here. Least ways horse flesh." He scratched his head. "Got one I could let you have for twenty dollars."

Drumming his fingers on the counter, Jacob looked at the necessary supplies before him. His old friend returned with a box of matches and a pair of socks. Jacob clenched his fist. "Jube, how much money you got on you?"

Screwing his face in thought, Jube tried adding in his head—"Ten-dollar gold piece, one sawbuck, three nickels, n' two pennies."

Trying on a ten-gallon hat that made him look absurd, he quipped, "Squirrelly Martin is back at the fort. He's got a gold tooth, n' I don't mind bustin' him in the chops if it will help the cause."

Jacob rubbed the back of his neck, "Mr. Broyles, do you give credit?"

The sutler frowned. "Sorry, Jacob, but a man buying this much ammunition might not be coming back. Even you. Truly sorry."

A sense of hopelessness strained the big man's face. There wasn't time to hunt. Every minute put Daniel closer to the border and lessened their chances of finding him.

Stepping to the counter, the thin man who had remained silent until now, pushed his billfold towards the proprietor. "Give Sergeant Keever whatever he wants...and throw in enough for one more person. I'll be traveling with him."

Not believing his ears, Jacob turned and stared at the stranger. Behind him, Jube quickly added a brick of chocolate to the pile. Jacob shook his head. "Mister, you don't even know where I'm going, and the sutler's right. I might not be coming back."

The young man managed a nervous smile. "Sounds perfect; when do we start?"

Fearing Jacob might refuse the stranger's generous offer, Jube stepped forward. "Jacob, time's a-wastin.' We need the supplies, and an extra gun could come in handy."

Jacob grimaced. Jube was right. Time was running out, but this was too much.

"Mister, a green soldier and an Apache girl are already coming along against my will, and I'm not keen on adding a total stranger, no matter how badly I need his money. So maybe you just better tell me who you are and why you are so eager to ride the Devil's trail."

The man nodded politely and then picked up a paperback from a pile of dusty books on the end of the counter and pushed it towards the big man. Jacob read the cover: *Hero of Apache Springs.*

"So that's it."

Though this little book had plagued him, Jacob had never seen it before. He turned it over in his hands, studying a dramatic picture of a fearless buffalo soldier surrounded by screaming Indians. Slowly Jacob lifted his eyes.

"You are willing to throw your money and your life away because you read a dime novel about a man you don't even know?"

For a moment, the tall stranger stared at the reluctant hero, his face almost glowing. Reaching out his hand to Jacob, he took the book back. "I didn't read it, Sergeant Keever; I wrote it."

Jacob gave a start. "You! You're Barnabus Kane."

The author humbly bowed his head. Lunging forward, Jacob grabbed the young man by his lapel and lifted him off the floor. Jube, knowing what was coming, reached for his friend's arm.

"Jacob, man ain't done nothin' wrong, n' we ain't gots' time ta' bury 'em."

Jerking free, Jacob cursed, "Nothing wrong? Turned my life into to a damn three-ring circus!"

Jube forced his way between them, trying to be cordial while struggling to keep his friend off the young man. "Pleasure to meet you, Mr. Kane. Jubaliah Jackson's the name. Read your articles in the *Gazette*. Pretty writin'…"

"Pretty writing, my ass. It's a pack of lies." The veins on Jacob's neck bulged.

"Calm down, Jacob, he only wrote what the boys told him. Give the generous man a chance."

The writer shrank back in fear, completely stunned by the soldier's rage. "That's true, Sir. Everything I wrote about you came directly from your soldiers."

"My soldiers don't talk like that. You colored it with your fancy tongue, when you ain't got no idea…"

"I...I'm sorry, Sergeant; I hoped you would like my book." The author looked genuinely hurt. "I tried to find you, but you were already gone. If I exaggerated, it's only because I truly admire a brave man such as you. This country needs heroes, and your men praised you as one of the finest. I'm truly sorry. I…I…"

Jube smiled over his shoulder while pushing his friend back. "Ah, Jacob don't mean nothin'. Heroes' is like that…but he pets dogs n' children. Grows on ya'…well kinda' slow-like. Some days slower n' others."

Getting the situation under control, Jube offered a sympathetic smile to the shaken lad before turning to his friend. "Jacob, he seems like a nice kid, n' here you go bein' yo' self again. Maybe they's a reason why people is always tryin' ta' kill ya'. Give 'em a chance."

Jacob stared over his friend's shoulder into the writer's injured face. The poor boy was truly saddened.

Taken aback, the author straightened his collar and tried to defend himself. "Sergeant, I'm not like you. I have never met a hero until this very moment. I've written about courageous deeds, even dreamed about them, but I never had the nerve to do anything daring. Hearing about you from your soldiers…well, it fired my heart, Sir. It changed me. I came here looking for you. This fort made me feel almost a part of your brave adventures. And to suddenly see you in this shop and realize you are planning something bold. . .and I am here. Well, Sergeant Keever, I don't care where you are going, but I must go. It's providence. If I don't do this now, I may never have the courage again. Please accept my money."

Jacob cooled as he listened to the boy's heartfelt sincerity. "Mr. Kane, it's not what you think. Every day out here is a coin toss between drudgery and death. If you come with us, saddle sores might be the most exciting thing that happens to you, or you may not come back at all."

The author offered a weak smile. "Sergeant, drudgery to you is a bold adventure to me. I sit behind a pencil. Please let me come. This time everything I write will be absolutely true."

Trying to regain his composure, the proud youth did his best to stand tall. "I am a good writer. Really, I am."

There was something about the young man's spirit that touched a tender spot in the soldier's heart. Despite his gruff exterior, Jacob had always been a sucker for strays, and Jube was right, time was wasting.

Blowing his anger through his teeth, the big man relented. There was no way to rescue Daniel without the writer's help. Jacob grudgingly turned to his friend. "Jube, show Mr. Kane how to pack a horse, and throw in some more shells. I'll decide afterwards who I'm going to use them on."

Storming past the pile on the counter as he made his way out the door, Jacob grabbed the chocolate. "I'm gonna need this."

Mea-a-ha refused to let her husband get close. Her scolding nearly shook the adobe bricks from the room. "I told you we should not have come here. It is always a bad place, but you would not listen. You, the big boss!"

The Apache girl turned to the wall and pounded her fist. "And now instead of helping Nah-kah-yen save Mary, you give him to the soldiers. It is death for him and for Mary." She whirled around, eyes burning. "You always say, 'Do the right thing.' How is this the right thing?"

Jacob reached for the Indian girl, but she pulled away. He let his hand drop to his side. "Darling, it's a bad thing, but if I don't go along with it, they will kill Daniel. I am choosing the lesser of two evils."

"No, Jacob. You find another way."

"Mea-a-ha, there is no other way."

"You find one. If you do this thing in front of Daniel, he will spend the rest of his life hating you."

The big man hung his head. "But at least he will have the rest of his life to hate me."

The thought was too much to bear. Jacob turned to the door. Before he could open it, the Apache girl rushed to him, burying herself against his chest. "...and I will never forgive you...but I will always love you."

Jacob wrapped her in his arms. He wanted to roar against the injustice, but there was nothing he could say. It was a terrible thing.

Pulling up on the cinch, Jacob adjusted the saddle of the tall Buckskin. It was his third time to do so. He stood waiting outside Colonel McCrae's office. Fussing with his horse gave him an excuse not to face Mea-a-ha. She was right about coming to the fort, and she was right about Daniel hating him. Jacob sickened with anger, most of it at himself.

The door in front of him creaked open. An eager young officer with sandy-blond hair stepped onto the porch. "Sergeant Keever."

"I ain't no sergeant, son; just call me Jacob."

A smile faded from the boy's face upon hearing the surly retort. "I am Lieutenant Mason McCrae. My father said you will help me track down a notorious Apache who kidnapped your son."

The eager soldier offered another smile. "I assure you, Sir, we will bring the savage to justice."

Jacob ignored his comment. "Get your horse, boy. We're burning daylight."

Taken aback by the cold abruptness of the hero he had read so much about, Mason stepped several paces back, dismay telling in his eyes. "Ah...right away, Sir. I'll get my mount." The young lieutenant did a crisp about-face and quickly disappeared.

When Jacob looked up again, the sad-eyed colonel was standing in the open door, watching his son hurry away.

"Sergeant, I understand your resentment of me, but he's a good boy, and he shouldn't have to bear the sins of his father."

Jacob did nothing to hide his bitterness. "Did you consider how *my* son is going to feel?"

Across the narrow lane, a door clicked shut and the Indian girl stepped onto the porch. Her dark eyes held the colonel's attention as she slowly crossed the courtyard. Colonel McCrae tipped his hat. Without a glance at her husband, Mea-a-ha walked straight up to the officer. She stared long and hard, not hiding her scorn.

Unnerved by the girl's scrutiny, McCrae felt compelled to speak. "I'm sorry, Mea-a-ha, I know what you must think of me, but I have a job to do."

The diminutive Apache girl looked so small next to the tall soldier, as though she were a child being scolded by an adult. Aaron

McCrae was a powerful officer of a civilized nation; she, a lowly squaw of a savage race.

Unwavering, her voice came soft and slow. "Why say you are sorry for doing a bad thing, when you could choose not to do a bad thing?"

Surprised by her question, McCrae sputtered. "I, I have my orders."

With a quizzical tilt of her head, the girl weighed his answer, and then politely persisted. "If someone tells you to do a bad thing, does that make it right to do it?"

McCrae swallowed and gave Jacob a sideways glance. He was a gentleman, and debating with a female was unmanly. His face reddened. "I guess it doesn't, but we are at war."

Mea-a-ha's tiny doeskin moccasins edged closer. "War—yes. Tell me please, great Colonel, how many soldiers do the mighty bluecoats have?"

The towering officer seemed to shrink. "Thousands, ma'am."

For a moment the girl was quiet, letting his answer be its own absurdity. Her eyes lifted once more. "Nah-kah-yen is but one man. Are the Long Knives so threatened that you must kill him?"

"Ma'am, the Apaches must remain on the reservation."

"Yes, the reservation. Many deaths. Great hunger." The girl saddened. "I am just an ignorant savage, but I wonder how many officers would remain in such a place, watching their children die?"

She shrugged. "...but if it were orders, I suppose they would understand. Orders are very important…lives are not."

The girl waited, her penetrating gaze stripping the officer bare. McCrae had no answer, so she continued. "Tell me, please, if your wife and son were held as slaves, would you not find them?"

McCrae's words fell weakly. "Yes…Yes, I would rescue them."

"So you will kill Nah-kah-yen for doing a good thing, while you do a bad thing. And now you force my husband to do a bad thing to save his son. Tell me, mighty Colonel of the bluecoats, what kind of man would do such a thing?"

McCrae bowed his head. "I'm sorry, ma'am."

Mea-a-ha stepped away. "I know, you told me."

Jubaliah, Mason and Kane returned, leading the horses from the corral. Without a word, Jacob lifted Mea-a-ha onto her Paint. Aaron McCrae leaned against the hitching rail, his face drawn tight. "Jacob, you're a soldier; you understand."

Taking the reins of the Buckskin, Jacob climbed into the saddle. "Thought I did once. But no, Colonel, I guess I don't. Do what you have to do, then live with yourself if you can. I'll try to do the same."

The other men mounted up. Mason rode forward and saluted his father. The colonel slowly came to attention and stiffly returned the salute.

As the party headed out, Jacob lingered.

"We are both fathers, Sir. Don't worry; I'll take good care of your son. One last thing, Sir—Nah-kah-yen is a father, too."

Chapter -5-
Race to the Border

The sharp crack of a rifle echoed across the barren knolls. It rumbled over the horizon and seemed to continue on forever, like a noisy bird taking wing to herald the presence of an intruder. Hopefully they were alone on this endless sea.

For a moment it was quiet again, as though sound did not exist in such a place. Then muffled hoofbeats in the loose sand rose from the distance, once more disturbing the slumbering desert. A young boy appeared riding over a small berm on a silky Piebald Paint. Daniel's beloved Snow Raven was the fastest of the horses, and he often rode farther afield. In his hand he held a freshly killed rabbit, bringing their tally to two rabbits and one desert tortoise. Along with a few tortillas Roberto had the good sense to bring, they would have an evening meal.

In the distance the boy could see his friends building a campfire at the base of a crumbling rock. Sage and greasewood pulled from the loose earth ignited easily. A watchful raven perched atop a tall yucca was the only notable sign of life.

Daniel urged his horse forward. Inside, he felt a growing uneasiness. The boy wanted the rescue to be over and done with; then he wouldn't have to worry about having run away. He would return a hero and show his father. But now he felt like a naughty child. Jacob would be mad, Mea-a-ha too, though she would hug him and kiss him when he returned with Mary Lost Pony and the other Mimbre women. Jacob would still be angry. He would say, "If you are going to do something, do it in the light of day. A man doesn't sneak off like a kicked dog."

He knew his father wouldn't understand, but he hadn't planned on running away. When Nah-Kah-yen had caught up with him on the trail and told how he was going alone to rescue Mary and their little baby, well, Daniel just knew he had to go. Turning his back on a warrior of his tribe was wrong. Jacob would be able to see it, too, if he weren't so damned stubborn.

Daniel hadn't meant to bring his friends, either. He planned on sneaking in and leaving a message while Nah-kah-yen waited in an arroyo near the ranch. It would have worked too, but when he tried, he couldn't spell enough words to write a note. While he was struggling with quill and paper, Juan walked in on him. When he told his best friend what he was doing, well Juan wanted to go. It sounded exciting. Then Roberto came looking for Juan, and when he couldn't talk them out of it, he decided it was best to come along to keep them out of trouble.

Daniel knew he was lucky Maria hadn't found them. She would never have let them do such a foolish thing. A smile replaced the frown on the boy's face. Juan's sister sure was pretty.

A lot of worries were spinning in the young boy's head. Yesterday was the worst. The buffalo soldiers had surprised them. They were far away, but Daniel thought he recognized one or two of them. He hoped they hadn't recognized him. With a horse like Snow Raven, that was unlikely. They gave pursuit, but he knew buffalo soldiers had the worse horse flesh in the Army. Escaping the bluecoats would have been easy. There didn't have to be any fighting. Daniel frowned. Nah-kah-yen wanted to fight. He turned and fired several rounds, knocking one of the soldiers off his horse. He would have kept on shooting, but Roberto rode in front of him. Nah-kah-yen was furious. The warrior had every right to hate the soldiers, but Roberto stood up to him and said, "We came to rescue women, not fight our new country."

Things were tense. The two hadn't spoken much. Nah-kah-yen was a noble warrior, but he didn't like being challenged by a mere boy, and Roberto called it like it was, so there was likely to be more head-butting. Not a good thing.

Daniel's thoughts returned to the scraggly rabbit. It wasn't a lot of meat to share four ways. Juan had brought a sack of beans. They sure would be tasty, but he forgot to bring a pot. That was like Juan. Daniel's smile returned. The Mexican boy usually did the unexpected. Juan had befriended him once when they were enemies, Apache against Mexican. Juan even gave him Snow Raven. What kind of person does that for an enemy? It was a wondrous gift for a poor Indian boy. Snow Raven had saved his life, and changed it. Daniel patted the Paint's glossy neck. Juan would always be his best friend.

Roberto was different. He was more like Jacob; kind of bossy. It wasn't just that he was bigger, he was just bossy, always thinking about what was most responsible instead of just having fun.

The taller boy was usually right, but when he got to giving too many orders, Juan would salute him and say, "Yes, sir, Sergeant Bossy." Everybody would laugh. Still, Roberto always made sure the work got done, and Senor Rincon never had reason to be angry with them. Daniel was glad that Roberto was here now.

As the Apache youth jumped from his horse, Nah-kah-yen took the rabbit from him. "Good shot, through the head. The meat is not ruined. You shoot like your father. He was a great warrior before the buffalo soldiers killed him."

Daniel lowered his eyes. He knew what Nah-kah-yen meant. The boy wanted to tell him that Jacob was his father. Mea-a-ha had memories of their parents, but he was too young. Daniel busied himself with his pony, knowing Nah-kah-yen would not want to hear about Jacob.

Not far away, ever-watchful, Roberto stood erect on the crumbling rock, his Winchester folded in his arms. He scanned the horizon one last time before looking down at his Indian friend. "Did you see any tracks?"

Daniel shook his head. "No. The land is empty. It is like man never existed out here."

Pulling the pelt from the rabbit, Nah-kah-yen shoved the meat onto a sharp stick.

"They are out here. Always they are out here."

Juan's eyes grew large. "Who?"

The warrior propped the stick over the fire. "All of them. Soldiers, Gringos...and Scalpers."

The Apache made a face. "They are the worst. Very bad Mexicans. Scalpers do not fight for honor. They are coyotes that trade Apache scalps for yellow stones."

Nah-kah-yen thrust a finger at Roberto, then Juan. "They will not care that you are Mexican. Your hair is black like the Apache. Your scalp sells just as good."

Shrinking back, Juan swallowed hard at the thought of losing his hair in such a grisly manner. Roberto nervously scanned the horizon once more.

Until yesterday, their race across the desert had been an adventure. Juan looked about and anxiously rested his palm on the butt of his revolver. It gave him comfort. They were just boys, and few in number. Jacob wasn't here to protect them. What had seemed like fun, became frightening with the killing of the soldier.

Once not so very long ago, the Mexican boys had stood beside Jacob with guns ready against the Indians, but they had never really fought. Daniel was the smallest of the boys, a full-blooded Apache. He alone knew what it was like to kill.

Turning the meat, the warrior sat on his haunches and draped his arms over his knees. The boys eagerly gathered around. Half a rabbit each and a little bit of tortoise was okay for a meal, but there would be no breakfast, and their bellies would be grumbling before they ate again. It made the meat that much sweeter.

Wiping his greasy hands on his bare chest, Nah-kah-yen talked with a full mouth. "When we find Mary, she will cook for us. She good cook. So is Lori White Feather." He made a sour face. "Son-gee, pretty, but bad cook. Her tortillas taste like cow pies."

The boys laughed.

Nah-kah-yen leaned back and chewed a large mouthful in quiet thought. "Maybe other squaws escape. Maybe they find Old Nana. The soldiers forget. Maybe they move on, and the Mimbres could return to Warm Springs. Our people might start over. My son would grow up Apache. Maybe..."

Daniel forced a smile. He knew the brave's heart. He wished it, too. If all the Mimbres could be found, maybe their tribe would live again. Daniel lowered his eyes. It was a beautiful dream; a sad, beautiful dream.

Tossing a bone onto the coals, the proud warrior rose and turned from the fire, hiding his grief in the shadows. The squaws were gone, the braves were dead, but Nah-kah-yen's pain was great, and for awhile longer he would seek comfort in delusions that would never be.

Daniel cleared his throat and tried to sound cheery. "When we rescue the women, they will sure be surprised."

Gnawing a bone, Juan stopped to agree. "Si. The fat rancher, he will be surprised, too. We will show him."

Nah-kah-yen turned with a grunt. "We go quiet. If they see us, much killing."

He looked to each of the boys. Their eyes held both excitement and fear. The warrior grunted again. "Bad men kill my people and steal our women. Deserve to die. Much killing once we have the squaws."

Daniel swallowed. The words were said. 'Much killing.' It was something he had given no thought to until now. 'Much killing.' Nah-kah-yen was full of hate. Tres Castillos haunted his mind, poisoning him.

Uneasy, Roberto stood and walked towards the setting sun. The warrior watched him go. "The tall one is weak. He has no stomach for fighting."

Juan cast his eyes to the ground. "Roberto will fight if he believes it is right."

The warrior turned his back. "Is right."

While the boys were pondering what lay ahead, Nah-kah-yen looked north, worrying about who might be trailing behind. There was a chance Jacob didn't know, but if he did, he would be riding fire. In Nah-kah-yen's brief stay in the Hollow, the warrior learned that Jacob was not a man you wanted for an enemy. By taking Daniel, he had crossed the line with the giant. The soldier named Jacob would follow the boy to hell and take any man with him who got in his way.

Nah-kah-yen wandered one direction, Roberto another. The Mexican boy had heard the warrior's insult about no stomach for fighting. He was young, and it hurt. Only a few days ago they were happy friends on a beautiful ranch. Now they were swallowed by the cold, uncaring desert, following a bloodthirsty Apache, and hunted by soldiers. How had things gone so wrong?

He felt like the world was on his shoulders, and the Mimbre warrior had told his friends he was weak. Roberto trembled with anger.

Behind him he could hear light steps. It wasn't necessary for him to turn around to know it was Daniel. The Indian boy had learned much in his savage youth. While others stomped, his feet fell soft as a whisper.

For a while, Daniel stood quietly beside him, staring south—staring into tomorrow. The last rays of the sun bathed the boys in a fading amber light. Its warmth offered comfort. When the moment seemed right, the young Apache took a breath. "Nah-kah-yen is a great warrior."

"He is stupid."

"You are mad at him for shooting the buffalo soldier."

Roberto shook, trying to control his anger. "We are Mexicans and Indians living in the world of the gringo. Killing soldiers gets you dead."

Daniel shifted uneasily. "It was a bad thing, but you must know how the Apache have lived."

"I know how they die. I know Nah-kah-yen's life is measured in days, not years."

The Indian boy stiffened. "The Apache understands this, too. It is why we fight so hard."

Roberto turned to his friend. "The soldiers do not forget when one of theirs is shot. They are coming." He swallowed a lump in his throat. "I am not weak because I don't want to kill."

Daniel nodded. "I know. We will be in Mexico soon. We will rescue the women, then you will see. It will be okay."

The Mexican youth sneered. "A crazy warrior and three boys against an army of vaqueros—it is insane."

Daniel defended. "We are almost seventeen, and you are as tall as a man ...well, nearly."

"We're barely sixteen. Well, Juan and me. You don't know how old you are."

"I do, too. I'm as old as you, even if I'm not as big."

Roberto turned away. "It don't matter; we will never reach Mexico."

Daniel looked shocked. "What do you mean?"

"Ah, never mind." The lanky Mexican boy hurried away, ending the conversation.

Chapter -6-
New Companions

By noon, they had left the fort and were making good time across the unbroken terrain. Fueled by anger, Jacob spurred his uninvited companions on at a cruel pace. There had been little time to speak. Mea-a-ha tried to console herself that maybe it was just as well. When Jacob was in his dark moods, distance was a good thing.

The Indian girl stayed back with Jubaliah. Despite their differences, she trusted the black soldier. He kept it simple.

Ahead of them rode the man called Kane. Farther up the trail, the young lieutenant was pushing his mount, trying to keep up with Jacob. Neither of the new men looked too accustomed to the saddle. Mea-a-ha didn't feel so bad about her own bruises anymore.

The officer, she didn't trust. He was a soldier, which was reason enough. Being his father's son did not help. He even looked like his father, muscular with chiseled features. Mason was green; she could see it, but there was strength in him. Still, he was a soldier.

The man called Kane intrigued her. From out of nowhere he came to their aid. He was a writer, and she loved books even though she struggled with most words not found in children's stories. Kane was quiet and mysterious as she thought writers should be. He was lean and tall. His shiny black hair and handsome dark complexion made him seem closer to her own kind than the blond soldier.

Both men were only a little older than she. Jacob had a few more years, and sometimes he seemed more like a parent, but she knew she was safe in his arms. She loved him for his courage, not just in the face of danger, but his courage to make his dream come true. Even now he was fighting for that dream.

Mea-a-ha hoped someday he would find the peace he yearned for. She felt sad for him and angry at him for what he was going to do. Jacob was a man born to face the storms that other men feared. It was not in him to shrink away or make excuses when danger lay ahead. He would do what he believed was right, no matter the price.

This giant of a man had saved her life. It caused her pain that now she added to his sorrow, but she could not back away or forgive him, even though what he was doing was for her brother. For the love of Daniel, this man would risk his life and everything he cherished.

A hand reached out and patted her arm. Mea-a-ha looked into the caring eyes of Jube, who realized she had been crying. She ducked her head. Jube was a hard one for her. They had nothing in common. He had no love for Apaches, but he was honest about it.

Circumstance had thrown them together. She hoped time would make them friends.

Mea-a-ha raised her eyes and tried to smile. "Sorry. You must think me a silly girl. It's just...just everything."

Jube returned her smile. "I don't think you is silly. Maybe we should all be cryin'."

He looked to the front of the line. "Ya' must find it in yo' heart ta' forgive him."

Mea-a-ha shook her head. "I can't."

The soldier's face showed sadness and understanding. "No matter how important something is, it ain't no good what kills love. Try, little missy. He's just a man doin' what he hast ta'."

Jube tipped his hat then slowed his horse and fell in behind, leaving the girl alone with her thoughts.

Dark clouds boiled menacingly overhead. March was coming on, and gusty winds out of the west meant warmer temperatures in the days to come. For that they could be thankful. The trail was wearing enough without fighting the cold.

The young officer raised his gloved hand and droned out a long "Hoooooo." Everyone pulled to a stop. Looking annoyed, Jacob returned to the circle of horses. "What is it, Lieutenant?"

"It's time for a rest, Sergeant."

Jacob's eyes narrowed. "I'll say when we stop." The big man turned his horse around, resuming the lead.

Astounded, McCrae burst into an angry protest. "Now look here, Sergeant, you may be a big hero and all, but my father put me in charge of this patrol, and you'll follow my orders. Is that clea..." Mason stopped in mid-sentence as the huge black man pulled up short. By the way the muscles in his back tensed, the young lieutenant knew he was in trouble.

Jacob deliberately turned his horse once more. His big hand clenched into a fist that made a sickening squeak as it hardened.

Mason swallowed. "M-maybe y-you don't need a rest...Sir." He licked his lips, looking nervously to his side. "But perhaps your squaw does."

The pretty face of the Apache girl scrunched into an angry sneer. Putting her heels to her pony, she charged right into Mason's horse. The startled animal reared in panic, dumping the young man rudely to the ground. As the stunned officer rose to a sitting position, Mea-a-ha rode in close. "Don't call me squaw!"

Scrambling to his feet, Mason rubbed his butt. "I didn't mean any offense...Mrs. Keever."

"No one ever does." The girl pulled her reins hard and raced down the trail.

Bursting into a grin, the big sergeant turned and headed after his bride. Kane prodded his horse past the hapless lieutenant and stifled a smirk of his own while scribbling in his journal.

Flustered and feeling unjustly treated, Mason lifted his face to Jube, who waited patiently. "She had no call to do that."

Jube leaned down. "She's a little savage, that one, but smart like a fox. She jes' saved you a busted jaw, n' don't think she didn't know it."

The young officer looked after her. "I just wanted to rest for a bit."

Rubbing his backside one last time, Mason climbed back into the saddle. "What does Sergeant Keever have against me?"

"Son, you will find that everything ya' read about ol' Jacob is true. You'll find it out a lot sooner if you lighten up on the military, and stop calling him sergeant."

The boy rode in silence, nursing his bruised ego. He had gotten some schooling the hard way, and it took the wind out of his sails. "Mr. Jube."

"Jube is good enough."

"Jube...Sir. Have I done something to make Mr. Keever hate me?"

The old soldier laughed. "It ain't what you done, it's what you is gunna' do."

The young man looked confused. "I don't understand. What is it I'm I going to do?"

"Break his heart, boy. Break his heart."

The next several hours seemed the hardest, as the endless trail pounded their bodies into numbness. Every stomp of the horses' hooves was like an iron hammer to the riders' spines. Closing their weary eyes to the pain, no one complained.

Mason resumed his place behind Jacob. Kane dropped back with Jube, both men trailing a packhorse.

As time went on, the Apache girl nodded off. She would jerk awake each time she started to slide from the saddle, and then do it all over again. It was a fitful sleep, but her aching body took what rest she could find. With no energy to spare for words, everyone settled in for the long, weary ride.

A pale moon shone through the broken clouds, allowing Jacob to push on late into the night. Finally Mea-a-ha had enough and rode up to his side. "Jacob...Jacob! Maybe you can go on forever, but you're killing the rest of us."

"Then you shouldn't have come. Should have been just me and Jube. If I don't catch Daniel, it's your..."

The big man cursed and looked away. Lost in her bitterness, Mea-a-ha had not realized that Jacob was festering anger of his own. "Jacob, I..."

He cut her off. "Don't."

Pulling his horse to a stop, the sullen giant raised his hand. "Ho." Resentment telling in the taut lines of his face, he turned to the others. "We'll stop here. Four hours. Then we ride."

Dropping to the ground, Jacob pulled the saddle from his horse and then stormed off into the dark, leaving Mea-a-ha to fend for herself.

Fighting tears, she climbed down and struggled with her heavy cinch. It was too tight, and she was too upset. A kind hand reached past her. "Here, I'll do it."

Kane pulled the strap and set the saddle on the ground. Mea-a-ha kept her face in the shadows. "Thank you, Mr. Kane."

"A pleasure, Mrs. Keever."

No one felt like building a fire, so the tired companions made due with dried meat. Mason spread his bedroll out in front of his saddle. "Is he always like this?"

Jube chewed on a bit of gristle then spit. "Like what?"

The boy fussed. "Well, you know."

"Guessin' I don't."

"Always pushin'. Mean-like. He's supposed to be a hero, not a slave driver."

Jube took a swig from his canteen and wiped his mouth with the back of his hand. "Maybe that's what makes a man a hero, always pushing when others won't...or can't."

Kane looked at the poor exhausted Indian girl bathed in the cold, silver light of the sinking moon. She was sitting on her blanket with her head slumped on her knees, looking more dead than alive. The writer lifted his voice in agreement with the officer. "At this pace, he won't have anyone to be a hero for."

Jube tugged off a boot. "You is a bunch of sissies."

Not expecting the older man's rebuke, the young men fidgeted uncomfortably, not knowing what to say.

The burly soldier tossed his boot aside and struggled with the other one. "Jacob didn't ask any of ya' ta' come, and you is all whining like a bunch of prissy schoolgirls."

Turning, Jube scowled at Mea-a-ha, who had raised her head. "You, too, little missy. Jacob ain't doing this to be mean. He's trying ta' save his son for God sake, and now he's got ta' baby-sit your candy asses."

Kicking his boot away, Jube made no attempt to sugarcoat his disgust. "This ain't nothin'. I've seen ol' Jacob ride for three days straight. And now he might not reach his son in time, because he's kind-hearted enough to mollycoddle the sorry likes of you. We come ta' save a boy, n' not one of ya' could do it on yo' own, so ya' tag along with the only man that can, n' bicker behind his back cuz' he kept ya' up past yo' bedtime."

Plopping his head on his saddle, Jube rolled onto his side and pulled a blanket over him. "Don't matter anyway. Daniel will end up hating Jacob in the end. The good colonel done seen to that."

Mason jumped to his feet. "What do you mean?"

The black man had said his piece and ignored the officer. Mason turned to the girl. "What did he mean? What'd my father do?"

Kane voice rose from the shadows. "Did you know Jacob's son is a full-blood Apache?"

Jube muttered beneath his hat. "Kane, that's enough. It don't matter now."

"Sorry, Jube, but Mason is one of us, and he has a right to know."

Mason turned to the writer. "No. I didn't know. I figured he was black."

The Indian girl finally spoke. "He is my brother. Your father traded Daniel's life for the Apache warrior you are going to take back to be hung."

Jacob stared south even though night was upon them. It didn't matter; he was searching with his heart and not his eyes. "Damn that boy. Damn them all." He spoke his thoughts out loud. The long ride had not quelled his anger, anger at the colonel, anger at the little Apache girl, and even his own son. Even those who loved him had turned against him.

Bending, Jacob picked up a stone and hurled into the dark. "Keep them safe, and everything else be damned." Keep them safe. Yes, that was his mission. What happened afterwards, if there was an afterwards, was beyond his control.

Seeing his duty, Jacob fell back on what he was, and had always been—a soldier. His curse was his strength, but no matter what happened, he had to stay focused, or Daniel was lost.

All he had ever known was killing. Since his youth, men had died before his gun and by his side. Growing up that way, he learned that when battle roared, you put feeling aside like so much useless baggage. Those who didn't fell face-down in the dust. It was survival.

When Jacob staked his home in the Hollow, he swore he'd never take another life. Now he was standing on the brink of the abyss. If he didn't catch Daniel in time, death once more would be upon them. Why couldn't they understand?

When Jacob had walked off some of his anger, he headed back to the camp site. He would keep the others safe and trust that luck would play in his favor; otherwise, they would arrive too late.

For now he would try to make amends with Mea-a-ha, or it would be a cold night. He couldn't blame her, but there was no way he could have known about the colonel's treachery. She had told him to find another way. Short of killing Mason McCrae, he couldn't see any answers.

The moon came out from behind a cloud as Jacob reached the camp. He gave a start. Everyone was mounted and ready to ride. Lieutenant McCrae led Jacob's horse to him and handed him the reins. "Didn't feel much like sleeping. We've got your son to save."

Jacob stood speechless as the riders filed past him. Mea-a-ha reached down from her saddle and let a delicate finger trail across his cheek, then rode on.

****

Somehow the weary companions made it through the night without falling from their saddles, and morning brought new hope. As a pale sun began to warm her back, Mea-a-ha edged up beside her husband. He had asked no questions about what had changed their mood. It wasn't his way. They were heading towards the border, and that was all that mattered.

The Indian girl flashed him a teasing grin, temporarily drawing the big man's attention from the distant horizon. His voice rose pleasantly for the first time since they left the Hollow. "We are making good time."

Mea-a-ha looked out of the corner of her eyes. "There is hope?"

Jacob breathed. "There is hope."

Throughout the early morning hours, Mea-a-ha rode by her husband's side, accepting an unspoken truce. The Indian girl remembered Jube's words. "Ain't no good what kills love." In her heart she knew it to be true.

What lay ahead was unwritten, but if they were to survive, they would need to pull together. Now was a time for healing, for new injuries were sure to come.

Looking over her shoulder, Mea-a-ha noticed the young officer was not far behind. He looked miserable. There was more healing to be done. With a nod to her husband, she dropped back and let Mason come alongside. Somehow he seemed less like a soldier and more like a timid boy. This morning he was not so much like his father.

Mea-a-ha offered a forgiving smile. "Good morning, Lieutenant."

Mason exhaled a tense breath and tried to calm his troubled mind. "Good morning, Mrs. Keever."

A warm smile blossomed on the Apache's face, exposing perfect white teeth. "Mrs. Keever does not seem to fit the trail. It is such a big name for one so small as me. I am just Mea-a-ha."

The lieutenant repeated her name. "Mea-a-ha."

It was the first time the Indian girl had talked with him, and for the young man it was his chance to clear the air. "Mea-a-ha, I'm sorry for calling you a squaw."

The girl's eyes sparkled, but she said nothing. Mason accepted her silence as forgiveness, and continued. "It might seem strange, but I'm from back East, and you are the first Indian I've ever met."

Mea-a-ha looked surprised. The lieutenant quickly added. "Please don't be offended, but I thought that all Apaches ran around naked, screaming and killing. To see you in a dress and speaking English...well, I thought 'squaw' was correct."

The Indian girl did not change her expression. "We do run around naked sometimes, but usually when we have nothing to wear. It makes us scream and kill."

For a moment the lieutenant looked unsure, then he broke into a grin. "You're teasing me."

They both laughed. With a fading chuckle, Mea-a-ha grew quiet. "If you saw naked Indians, you would call them savages. No?"

Mason nodded his head. "Yes. I guess I would."

"This word, 'Savage,' it means like a wild animal. No?"

The lieutenant nodded. "Yes."

"I wear a white woman's dress so you treat me kindly, but if I was one of the naked savages, you would think less of me, too. No?"

"It is hard to see you that way."

"I was once too poor to own the dust on my own skin, but I was the same person I am now. No difference, only a dress."

Considering her words, the lieutenant shrugged. "I understand what you are saying. Still, it is hard. Seeing naked savages, whooping and screaming, well you know..."

The young girl's eyes stared off into the distance. "Another man's tongue may sound like the howls of wild beasts." She saddened. "A day will come when you will be ordered to herd my people like animals, as it has happened many times before. When it does, and you see naked savages stained in dirt, their eyes wild with fear, unable to speak your language, I hope you will see me among them and show them the kindness you show this dress."

Mason was visibly moved. "Mea-a-ha, thank you for telling me this. I will try to be kind. I don't think I could look upon any naked Indian now without seeing you...I mean, ah..." The lieutenant bit his lip and turned red.

Mea-a-ha giggled. "If you were kind, then maybe I would not mind you seeing me naked or calling me squaw."

The young man grinned shyly. "Maybe we should talk about your husband, and not about naked squaws."

Mea-a-ha cocked her head in thought. "Squaw is not a bad word. It's just the way people say it. Sometimes it is bad. Sometimes I use it."

Mason rubbed his rump. "I don't think I'll be using it." They laughed again.

Letting a blissful silence signal their newfound peace, the Indian girl looked ahead. "My husband is a good man, but he is an old bear, and old bears growl. Little squirrels do not growl, but they are not very good protection. We need bears."

The lieutenant smiled. "Thanks, Mea-a-ha. I guess I misjudged him too, and I need to try to make things right with your husband."

Mea-a-ha pulled back on her reins. "You tell him I have decided not to scalp you...not today, anyway."

Mason gave the girl a nervous glance and spurred his horse forward.

The young lieutenant joined the stoic sergeant at the front of the line. Traveling through the night had gained them a day, which left Jacob in a better mood. Overhead the air was clear, but black clouds rumbled in the southwest.

For several miles, the two men rode together with little more than a nod. Yet the buffalo soldier didn't seem to mind the officer's presence, so the trail became tolerable considering the circumstances.

As they dipped down into a dry wash and came up a steep bank on the other side, the horses faltered and struggled for footing in the crumbling earth. Reaching out his hand, Jacob patted the big Buckskin's thick neck. "Steady, Mister. Get up there, boy."

His comment was directed to the horse, but it was the first words the tight-lipped soldier had spoken. Mason screwed up his courage and decided to risk a little conversation. "You call your horse Mister?"

At the top of the gully the trail leveled off, and the two men once more were riding side by side. "He's a civilian."

The big man's words carried a taint of bitterness that hid nothing of his disdain for the military. Mason decided to let it be and changed subjects. "You have a beautiful wife, Mr. Keever."

Jacob rode on, expressionless. His voice rolled soft and slow. "That she is, and a whole lot more. Call me Jacob."

"Jacob it is. Call me Mason if you like."

For some time the men rode on in silence, accepting a truce. There was a lot to set right. The young lieutenant took a deep breath and summoned a little more courage. "Jacob, I'm sorry about the position my father put you in. It wasn't right." Mason frowned. "But that's my father. It's his way, or no way."

Jacob mulled it over. "My son said the same thing about me."

The lieutenant smiled thinly, but then reclaimed his frown. "It puts me in a bad position. I am a soldier, and like it or not, I follow orders. There doesn't seem to be any way around it."

Keeping his eyes on the horizon, the big man's reply rumbled deep in his throat. "I could kill you."

Lieutenant McCrae tensed, then caught a faint twinkle in the sergeant's eye. Mason grinned. "I'll have to get used to your family's dry sense of humor. Your wife said she wasn't going to scalp me today, but I hope you will consider she might take offense if you beat her to it."

Jacob nodded. "You ain't the only one she's thinking of scalpin', so let's hope we can find another way."

Finding another way wasn't going to be easy. Mason was bound by orders, Jacob by a promise. It was a chasm that seemed too far to cross, and in the middle lay the life of a warrior and the love of a boy.

Beneath the descending clouds, the sterile land bathed in a blue-gray light. Weathered rock jutting from the parched earth slowly grew to ever-deepening arroyos. Eventually the broad expanse became a choice of narrow trails, and the riders were forced to follow in single file. There was no rain, but the threatening air was cold and damp.

Ahead, a wall of dark, reddish rock rose to the west of the trail, sheltering a broad, sandy grotto that made a natural fortress against the elements. In the middle, an abandoned fire pit heavily strewn with charcoal told of nameless riders who had passed this way countless times before. Indians and soldiers, Mexicans and miners, perhaps even Spaniards had stopped by this circle of stones, leaving their stories buried in the ashes. To this the weary rescuers would add their own.

Jacob raised his hand, halting the beleaguered riders. Stiff of joint and weary of limb, they climbed from their horses. It was time for rest. Mea-a-ha untied a canvas sack from the packhorse that Kane had led. The men were already breaking up dry brush to build a fire.

Dropping his tinder into the circle of stones, Mason followed Jacob's eyes to the horizon. "Looks like we're in for a little rain."

The big man nodded. "With any luck, a lot of it."

Jacob saw the confusion on the young officer's face and added, "The boys will take shelter. We'll push on through it."

Jube set fire to the wood. Stepping back to dodge the smoke, he added; "Then now's the perfect time to eat some of Mea-a-ha's delicious cookin'.'" Returning to the subject at hand, the cheery buffalo soldier nodded to the young lieutenant. "Their horses will also leave tracks aplenty in the mud. Blisters n' storms, things is looking up."

Accepting the sardonic wisdom of the veteran soldiers, Mason returned his attention to the fire. The Indian girl was attempting to balance a pot on the burning brush. He knelt beside her.

"Can I help you, Mea-a-ha?"

Jacob smiled at his wife. "So, little Apache, miracles happen even out here. You have made peace with a white soldier. Mason said you are going to let him keep his hair."

The girl busied herself, stirring pinto beans into the pot of bubbling water. "Yes. Good talk. He wants to see me naked."

Coloring with fright, the young officer jumped to his feet. "So help me, Sir, that's not what I meant..."

The big man was already grinning. Mason looked to the Indian girl, then to Jacob. He caught his breath. Mea-a-ha smiled up at the officer's bright face.

"And you call us the red man."

Carrying a steaming plate of beans, Jube joined his old friend at a craggy overlook. He took a few bites, then cleared his throat. "When ya gunna' tell 'em?"

A raised eyebrow was Jacob's only response as he turned back to the horizon.

Jube chewed a moment longer, then swallowed. "They's thinkin' we is jes gunna' get the boy n' go home. That dealing with the Apache is our only problem."

Jacob tugged down his hat. "If we catch him this side of the border, it is."

"An' iffin' we don't catch them this side of the border, this is likely a one-way trip."

The big man rose to his feet. "Eat your beans, Jube, it's time to ride."

Chapter -7-
Thunder and Bread

In the thin space between the black sea of clouds and the broken mesa, a tiny line of riders hurried on in the gathering darkness. An unspoken sense of urgency outweighed their growing fatigue. No one had uttered so much as a word for some time.

Without warning, a thunderous bolt of lightning tore a jagged path across the turbulent sky. At last, the rain, feared and hoped for, finally came. With each thunderclap the downpour increased in intensity and amplitude until it beat down in torrents.

Peering over his shoulder, Jacob could see the frightened young riders lying against their ponies' necks. With hats and coats drawn tight, each tried to disappear inside their clothes. Only Jube seemed to be unchanged. He sat his mount as usual, surveying the hostile terrain. Desert storms, no matter how intense, did not excuse a soldier from his duty.

Lightning hit the ground in front of and behind them. Riding tall horses was asking to be smote by the hand of God.

In the dim light, Jacob picked a rocky trail that led down the face of the ragged mesa. From this narrow ledge, the arroyo fell thirty feet or more. The wet trail was treacherous, but the cliff offered safety from the lightning and hammering rain.

Squinting against the tempest, Jacob studied the sky. The storm was blowing in from the southwest. Nah-kah-yen and the boys had to be in the thick of it. Pulling his collar about him, Jacob pushed on.

The trail dipped lower, but the floor of the canyon fell away much faster, leaving the companions winding along a dangerous face in near-darkness. The once-deadly lightning was now welcome as it momentarily lit their perilous path.

An hour was endured with slow progress on the slippery rocks. Somewhere beneath the rain soaked clouds, a forgotten sun had set unnoticed. The darkness became impenetrable. Jacob wisely let the big Buckskin find his own way. Turning in his saddle, he waited for the next bolt of lightning and quickly counted six horses, four riders and two pack animals.

He knew they had to keep moving if they were going to catch Daniel, but the elements were taking a toll on both man and beast. With a nagging fear, Jacob worried for Mea-a-ha's safety. A fall from this cliff was certain death.

The Buckskin suddenly turned sharply to the right. The trail followed a narrow cut into the cliff. Another flash of lightning revealed the opposite wall, which was maybe fifty feet away. Jacob guessed the cut would go in a short distance, then double back out and continue down the steep face.

The rocky crag gave shelter, and the rain finally dropped off, giving then their first break from the storm.

Pulling to a halt beneath the massive walls, the companions could finally hear their voices, and everyone started talking at once. Good-natured grumbling released their tensions about the darkness and the rain.

Mason hollered back to Kane. "Are you writing this all down?"

The writer's voice shook with fright. "Words are swimming in my waterlogged brain."

Through it all, the young man had managed to keep his humor.

A little further into the cut, the trail widened. Stiff and cold, everyone climbed from their saddles and stretched their legs. Mea-a-ha inched past Mason's horse and snuggled against her husband. By the way she was trembling, Jacob knew she had been crying. He kissed her. "You shouldn't have come. Next time, you will do as you are told."

Mea-a-ha buried her head against his chest, accepting his admonishment. He was correct; a trail like this took the strength of hard men. She was too small, and sheltered beneath his muscled arms, she felt the fragility of her sex. Still, she came for a reason, and no matter how terrifying the storm, the reason remained.

A heavy finger wiped the rain and the tears from her face. He was not without some compassion. Suddenly the Indian girl looked up. "Fresh-baked bread!"

Jacob gaped at her, surprised. She repeated herself. "Smell. Fresh-baked bread."

The big man lifted his nose to the air. Mea-a-ha was right. Drifting through the downpour was the definite aroma of freshly baked bread. Everyone started sniffing the damp breeze, relishing the delicious smell. Jacob hollered to the lieutenant. "Take Mea-a-ha's reins. She will be riding with me."

Lifting her into the saddle before him, he tucked her inside his slicker and nudged the Buckskin into the darkness. Echoes fading against the walls and flashes of lightning overhead showed the cut was gradually opening up. The downpour continued its noisy patter, but the riders realized none of it was falling on them.

Mason stuck his hand straight up. "Ouch!" He hit a large overhang of rock above their heads. "Well, that's handy."

Mea-a-ha poked her button nose out from Jacob's coat. "The smell is stronger."

Her eyes suddenly grew wide with alarm. "What if it is a gang of dangerous desperados?"

Jacob flipped the reins, encouraging the horse forward. "Never known outlaws to take time in a storm to practice their cooking skills."

The winding trail continued to widen as they made their way beneath the overhang. Safe from the downpour, the fury of the trail was all but forgotten as the mysterious aroma brought pangs of hunger to the starving companions. Mea-a-ha thrust a tiny hand into the darkness.

"Look!"

Jacob strained his eyes. Several hundred yards ahead, a faint red glow shimmered in the blue-black mist. It faded in and out then finally took form. Another flash of lightning revealed an uneven manmade wall stretching beneath the low overhang where it curved around the back of the canyon. Dark broken stones reached all the way to the roof of the low cavern.

Next to a dilapidated wooden door, a shuttered window leaked an inviting light that defined the rustic stonework as a dwelling of sorts. Cords of wood, yucca and sage, were piled helter-skelter in the shelter of the black cliff. A series of rickety sheds linked together with haphazard fences were tucked deep beneath the winding ledge.

At the far end of the shanty, a stone chimney puffed blue smoke into the cold night air. The amazed troop pulled to a stop outside the little door. From within, an old man's voice rose in song. He was painfully off key, and seemed to be making up the words as he went.

"It don't matter that its rainin',
I ain't complainin'.
Cuz its better n' bein' dead
As long as I can holler,
I'll earn meself' a dollar,
Singin' n' makin' cactus bread..."

Jube edged up next to Jacob. "Let's hope the old codger cooks better n' he sings."

Jacob filled his lungs. "Hello inside?"

The merry tune came to an abrupt end. After a moment, the flimsy door slowly creaked open. A lantern was thrust out at arm's length, followed by a pair of startled eyes blinking beneath a silvery head. The stooped man had shoulder-length hair, a groomed mustache, and a tapered goatee. He was clad in faded long johns and thick wool socks with holes in both toes.

Once he might have looked quite normal, but now he resembled a man who had spent too much time in his own company. His face was wild and full of surprise. "Well drop my drawers' n' take a gander. Did-ja' come for my singin' or my bread?" He burst into a broad smile. "Bread will cost ya. Singin's free."

The hermit held the lantern while the men stripped the horses. He politely escorted everyone inside. Setting the lantern on the table, the old man craned his neck and looked his guests up and down. Seeming perplexed, he scratched his rump, leaving a floury handprint. "Seen Injuns, seen greasers n' gringos, and even a few darkies, but I ain't never seen em' all together. This is truly a wonderment."

Kane, unable to contain his writer's curiosity, pulled his journal from his coat.

"Begging your pardon, Sir, but who are you?"

The old man grinned widely, almost doing a little jig. He waved a wrinkled hand toward his kitchen piled with bread, biscuits, cakes and tortillas. "Why, I'm the Baker." He smiled. "Ain't no butcher or candlestick maker."

His amazed guest looked in need of a better explanation. The animated gent quickly slid an uneven stool made from yucca wood to the Indian girl. "Everyone sit, and I'll get ya some hot bread, just baked. Do it from sunup ta' sundown. Always better in the rain, when it comes."

The hermit started cutting a loaf into thick slices, *"It don't matter that its rainin' . I ain't complainin' better n' being wed..."*

Scooping up the bread in his hands, the funny man passed the thick warm slices about. "Nasty night out." He waited until everyone had taken a bite. "Cost ya a penny a loaf, unless ya got somtin' else to trade."

The old man looked to the girl and gave a wink. "Pretty. Mimbre, ain't cha'? Know my Injuns. Is she for sale?"

Without waiting for an answer, he started in. "Come this way in forty-nine. Wagon full of chicken, head full of dreams. Was gunna' get rich in the gold fields of Californ-ee-ay sellin' eggs. Heard they was fetchin' a dollar each. Can ya' imagine! Well, ran out of water, n' my gall dang horse Evangeline up n' died. Got a wife back in Missouri. Her name is Evangeline, too. Wandered for three weeks in the desert followed by a flock of Rhode Island Reds till I stumbled on this place half-dead. Them hens was loyal; women, they ain't. There's water year-round, so me n' the chickens took a vote n' decided to stay. One ol' rooster, Ike was his name, voted to go on; he wound up in the pot. But couldn't eat em' all. No sir, most of em' is my friends, so we eat lizards, 'ceptin' when a chicken dies of old age or rattlesnake bite, then its pot heaven.

"Started making cactus n' mesquite bread. Made bread out of everything that grows in the desert. Some like ta' kill ya, others right tasty. I figured iffn' I made enough food for whoever came my way, well, ain't nobody gunna' kill a body that feeds 'em. Even if he charges a penny. Been feedin' civilized n' savages alike."

He lifted Mea-a-ha's chin with the tip of his powdered fingers. "Right pretty. Gots' some twilt-kah-yee, iffin' you is thirsty."

Kane looked confused and looked up from his writing. The old baker reached for an earthen jug. "Twilt-kah-yee. Apache booze. Them Injuns was getting drunk long before the white man came along ta' blame."

He poured the writer a drink and watched him take a sip. "Cost ya' another penny."

Before setting the jug down, the baker hauled it to his lips and gulped his fill. "Yes, sir, even make a Twilt-kah-yee bread. That's two cents. Though I eat most of it myself when I get to feeling melancholy." He looked back to Mea-a-ha. "Miss my Evangeline. Mean the Missus, not the mare. Every now n' then, a buck will bring a squaw with him. Ain't seen a white woman in thirty years. Guess they still look the same. Evangeline's hair was raven, like yours. I didn't run out on her; I meant to go back."

The baker looked longingly at the girl. "She was small like you." He rubbed his weathered hand across his moist eyes and turned his thoughts to other matters. "Yes, sir, it's a nasty night. Best you stay 'til mornin'. That ol' gully is piled with bones of travelers that ignore my warnin'. Too old ta' bury 'em."

Everyone turned eagerly to Jacob. The big man looked at his wife nibbling a piece of bread she held in both hands. Her large, hopeful eyes peered above the crust. Jacob's heart melted. He couldn't force her back into the storm. Removing his rained-soaked hat, he sighed. "We will stay until first light."

A cheerful murmur rolled across the room. The old man clapped his hands. "Well, get your bedrolls n' stake your claim to the floor. It ain't no fancy hotel, but its dry n' the mice are too polite ta' bite."

The old man danced aside as everyone rolled out their bedding in the many corners of the cluttered room. "Got me a fiddle, would play ya' a tune, but only have one string. Still, the hens don't mind."

When everyone was settled, the baker passed around another helping of warm bread. He gave the thickest slice to the girl and stroked her cheek with a soft, leathered hand. She gave him a sweet smile, letting him know she appreciated his kindness.

With a forlorn sigh, the hermit turned and shuffled to the stone fireplace. "Yes, sir, now let's see." Craning his neck, the old man reached up and plucked a folded piece of paper from the dusty mantel. He held it at arm's length, turned it over, and squinted his wrinkled eyes. "Which one of you darkies is Senor Keever?"

Jacob jumped to his feet. His gaping mouth answered the hermit's question. The baker thrust the letter to the big man. "A tall Mex' boy said ta' give ya' this. Said ya'd' pay a nickel."

Suddenly everyone was on their feet, all talking at once. Fumbling with the paper, Jacob looked to the old man. "When?"

"About mid-afternoon. They bought twenty-five cents' worth of tortillas. Been a banker's day."

Jube could see the question on Kane's face. "Roberto's a good boy, a Mexican; he left his first note fo' me ta' give ta' Jacob. That's how we knowed' where they was goin'. Looks like we ain't far behind."

The gentle patter of rain beat a soothing rhythm on the stony perch outside the door while distant thunder echoed down the canyon walls. The terrible storm that had driven them to this strange shelter now seemed soothing, almost musical.

In the darkened room, the Indian girl snuggled closer to her husband in their blanket on the floor. Mea-a-ha filled her nostrils once more with the delicious aroma that lingered in the cavernous house. A contented smile softened her delicate face. For the first time since they had left the Hollow, she was warm.

Through the thick stone walls, she could hear the snoring of the funny old hermit in a back room. Mea-a-ha kissed her husband on the cheek. "He is a nice man."

Jacob let the back of his fingers stroke the girl's soft belly. "Real nice." Mea-a-ha pushed him away.

"Shhh. The others will hear." She wiggled closer. "Will we catch up with Daniel tomorrow?"

Nibbling at her velvet shoulder, Jacob mumbled, "Maybe."

He toyed with the girl, but his thoughts drifted back to the letter. Roberto feared that Nah-Kah-yen intended on more than just rescuing his family. His vengeful heart hungered for blood. The boys would be caught in the middle. Speed was now even more urgent. At first light they would be off, riding hard. Jacob had paid the baker his due and bartered for an early breakfast, ten cents each, except for the girl, who could eat for a nickel.

Taking a deep breath, he cleared his head and turned his attentions back to his bride. He tickled her and muffled her squeals with a kiss. "Shhh. The others will hear."

A warm crackling glow from the large stone oven slowly awakened the sleepy room. As his guest began to stir, the baker drifted into singing another made-up song:

*"Morning is comin' n' slumber is done.
There's biscuits n' gravy for everyone.
Pull on your boots n' take a chair.
The Injun girl will get her share
Eat before the rooster crows.
There's biscuits n' gravy ta' warm your toes..."*

Maybe singing wasn't as crazy as talking to oneself. The old man had put on some clothes. One pant leg was tucked into his boot while the other dragged beneath his heel. His odd manner of dress seemed to repeat itself. Only his front shirttail was tucked in, and he had one suspender up with the other one dangling to his knee.

Opening her eyes, Mea-a-ha glanced shyly around the room. The old hermit was stoking his fire. Mason was sitting against the wall, pulling on his tall black boots. Her sleepy gaze drifted over to Jube. The crude soldier blew her a kiss and gave a sly wink, letting her know that he knew of their amorous night. Blushing, the Indian girl pulled the blanket over her head and hid. The last laugh would be hers, she would see to that.

Jacob's big hand came down firmly on her bottom. "Get dressed, little one, we will be leaving soon."

Clutching the blanket around her while gathering her rumpled dress, Mea-a-ha scurried into a shadowed corner, where she blended in with clutter. A blast of cold air chilled her bare shoulders as Kane hurried out the door to relieve himself. The door stayed ajar, letting a little more light into the room.

The baker's old eyes sparkled as the Indian girl dropped her blanket and quickly pulled her dress down over her head. Mea-a-ha smiled sweetly not seeming to mind, and then she sharply eyed Mason, who colored and quickly turned away. Jacob sat at the table reading the note again and paid no notice. Last night's storm was now a gray drizzle. Wherever the boys were, they no doubt were soaked.

Irregular-shaped wooden plates filled with scrambled eggs, biscuits and gravy were passed about the table as Mea-a-ha took a chair next to Jacob. Holding her shoes in her hands, she turned her bare back to her husband. "Button me."

Jacob grumbled. "My big fingers always have a hard time with these little things."

Mea-a-ha scolded. "They didn't have any trouble unbuttoning them." The half-dressed girl flashed her eyes at Jubaliah. "Jube, you are good with buttons. Do you remember?"

Jube hung his head over his plate and busied himself in his meal. Jacob tugged his bride's hair, reminding her to behave.

The hot meal was consumed by the men with a minimal amount of chatter. The chase was about to resume, and with Daniel close, there was little doubt that very soon Jacob would set a painful pace.

Mea-a-ha cautiously poked at the unfamiliar food before taking a timid bite. She licked the gravy from her lips and grinned with delight. It was delicious. The Mimbre girl smiled at the hermit and dove back into her plate.

After his own meal was done, Kane slid back from the table and watched with amusement as the Indian girl finished her breakfast. Taking his pencil from his pocket, he added an entry to his journal.

Mea-a-ha finished her last bite and lifted her eyes. "If your book tells about an Apache girl eating biscuits, I think no one will buy it."

The quiet author smiled. "I believe you might be more interesting than you think."

Mea-a-ha wiggled in her chair. "Read what you just wrote."

The young author closed his journal. "Oh, it's nothing."

Seeing Kane's reluctance, Mason prodded him good-naturedly. "Come on, Kane, we would like to hear of our exciting adventures on the Mimbre trail."

Kane resisted. "It's really nothing."

Turning his mind from Roberto's note, Jacob raised his voice. "Read it to her, Kane, or she will give you no peace."

Reluctantly, the young writer gave in and nervously opened his book. "Well...it's just a rough paragraph. It needs polishing."

The girl bounced. "Read now, polish later."

With an awkward glance around the table, Kane cleared his throat and began.

"The beautiful dark-eyed Apache sat in the secret stone cavern of the mysterious baker, her tiny bare feet swinging in contented delight as she tasted her first plate of biscuits and gravy. In a deep crevasse beneath a storm-drenched mesa, the small savage girl, on a perilous quest to rescue her brother, found reason to be happy. Perhaps we could learn from her that in the midst of our trials, there is joy to be taken in the simplest pleasures."

Kane sheepishly closed his book. "Like I said, it needs polish."

Mea-a-ha blushed at the flowery sentiment. "You got all that from biscuits and gravy?"

"From your happiness."

Cocking her head, the girl wrinkled her brow. "Do you think I am a savage?"

The author quickly avoided her eyes. "Savage and Indian mean the same thing. It is how people see Indians. I'm sorry."

Mea-a-ha frowned. "Maybe you could tell them Indian and people mean the same thing."

She turned to the young officer. "Maybe Nah-kah-yen would not have to die if he were people instead of savage."

Jacob led the horses out from the shelter of the rocky overhang. The curious baker held a sack of biscuits and watched from the side as the men mounted up. "Ya sure she ain't for sale?"

Mea-a-ha turned to the old man and gave him a kiss. "She ain't."

Clapping a wrinkled hand to his cheek, the old hermit chuckled. "First kiss since Evangeline told me goodbye."

Jacob lifted his bride into her saddle and took the sack from the old man. "If I ever decide to sell her, we'll trade for biscuits."

As the rescuers rode away from the stone shanty, the hermit danced sideways, trying to keep pace. "I'd give a mountain of biscuits fo' this little Mimbre. N' I'd take good care of her, too."

Giving up the chase, he stopped and let them pass by. "I dint' abandon my Evangeline. I know what ya' is thinkin'. It weren't my fault. Couldn't stand ta' see her cry…"

Chapter -8-
The Crossing

    Barnabus Kane tugged on the reins of the packhorse. The apprehensive procession was strung out along the rocky face of the mesa. He made a note in his journal that as usual, Sergeant Jacob Keever, formerly of the Ninth Calvary, was in the lead, followed by Lieutenant Mason McCrae. Behind them, on her painted pony, rode the dark-eyed Mimbre girl, Mea-a-ha. He would try and talk with her when they reached the desert floor. She certainly wasn't what he expected from an Apache Indian. Despite her size, there was a strength in her that seemed to charge the very air around her. Maybe all savages were that way. The unspoken word caused him a pang of guilt, but he couldn't help thinking it. She was a beautiful savage, but a savage nonetheless. Old prejudices die hard.

    Kane glanced behind him at the stalwart Jubaliah Jackson, who had resumed his place as rear guard. He alone remained unchanged by their great adventure. Jube was a jovial man, yet solid as stone. He didn't have Jacob's air of authority, but Kane had no doubt that this humble buffalo soldier could be depended on to the very end. It was something you sensed about him. The young writer envied the soldier's courage.

    Kane's thoughts turned back to their leader. This was the man he had written a book about, making him famous. In turn, the writer had garnered some fame of his own, but not the kind he had dreamed of. Jacob was a real hero who rode into battle outnumbered and outgunned, never wavering. The valiant fighter had passed through hell only to come out on the other side. All Kane had done was put words on paper about other men's deeds. That was why he had to come on this dangerous journey, desperately hoping to find courage in himself. The other men were soldiers. He alone had never faced death. Kane fidgeted uncomfortably, fearing they could tell he was riding scared. His eyes fell on the Apache girl. Mea-a-ha turned and looked back at him. She knew.

    His own story, Kane kept to himself. It wasn't exciting like Jacob's. His father was a schoolteacher in Denver, where life was civilized. Coming from a respected family, Kane had spent much of his time attending parties and social events. Yet there was a part of him that dreamed of a good, old-fashioned barroom brawl. He sighed. It just wasn't in him. The most dangerous thing he had ever done was write a scathing article about a corrupt politician, and it got him in trouble. But instead of weathering the storm, Kane had headed to

Silver City, where he bought a struggling newspaper and turned it around. There he passed the boring seasons reading and writing about the heroic deeds of others. With each word he penned, Kane's regret grew over how timid his life had been. It was his book and articles about "The Hero of Apache Springs" that made him realize his constant fear had become his own quiet hell. It plagued him until he could no longer face what he'd become.

The morning when Kane met Jacob in the sutler's store, he knew it was his one chance to be like the men he wrote about. He would quell his trembling heart or die trying. This he vowed.

Kane lifted his eyes to the Apache girl once more. She knew, but something told him she would not judge.

****

Eventually the steep trail reached the desert floor. It had started in shadow and ended in light. The writer hoped it was an omen of good tidings to come. Kicking his horse, Kane took a deep breath and settled in by the Apache girl's side. She had tied her coat behind her saddle and was enjoying the early morning sun. Despite the cool air, she was still barefoot, her small feet dangling in the stirrups, something a civilized lady would never do.

Still, Kane couldn't help but admire her. She was slender. Her Spanish dress accentuated a tiny waist and perfect breasts partially hidden beneath her long silky hair. The girl's brown skin was smooth, and the delicate features of her petite face might have easily been sculpted by an artist's skilled hand. She was truly beautiful; art come to life. He was amazed how young she looked, like a child ushered into womanhood before her time. Only her eyes betrayed her age.

Though a mere savage, she seemed lost in deep thought. This contradiction puzzled the writer. Her dark eyes held secrets he hungered to hear.

Kane rode quietly for a long while, trying to find something to say. Words were his living, and now they abandoned him in the presence of this enchanting Indian maiden. He awkwardly cleared his throat. "Looks to be a nice morning."

The girl smiled. "Do you want to talk?"

Kane was surprised by her honesty. Savage also meant innocence. She had not learned how to play subtle games. He smiled. "Yes, I guess I do. Tell me about your tribe."

Staring ahead, the girl's sweet face wrinkled in thought. "When we were many, the white man did not want to know us. Now that we are gone, they want to learn who we were. It is hard to understand."

The writer sighed. "I suppose that is true. It's sad that we got it so backwards and your people had to suffer, but I do want to know about you."

Appreciating his sentiment, Mea-a-ha felt a desire to speak. "I am Chihene, the Red Paint people—what you call the Mimbres." Her voice lowered in a comical fierceness. "Last of the savages."

She looked forward again, but cast the writer a mischievous sideways glance. "We unjustly killed gringos who only came in peace to take our land. Write your story. Say that you rode with one of these wild savages and lived to tell about it. You will sell many books. It is what they want to hear."

Kane lowered his head. "I am sorry for my choice of words. Believe me, I want to write the truth. Please tell me."

For awhile the girl rode on in silence. She appeared to be struggling with some deep emotion. It took her some time, but at finally she spoke in a soft melodic tone. "Once I stayed at a great ranch when Jacob was wounded. A friend read me your book about him." Her eyes flashed. "You said great things about Jacob. I love him, and know what you say about his courage is true. You also told of the Apache chief Sholo, who Jacob fought. You call him a godless bloodthirsty heathen."

The Indian girl tossed her hair away from her face and captured the author's eyes. "Mr. Kane, did you know Sholo?"

Kane stirred uncomfortably. "No ...no, I did not."

The girl repeated his words. "A godless bloodthirsty heathen. You said this thing of a man you never met...I'm sorry—a savage you never met."

The young writer turned away, unable to meet her gaze. Mea-a-ha patted her pony's neck. "If you write about me, please say, 'This small Apache girl was proud to be the friend of a bloodthirsty heathen who loved his people and died for them. That is the truth."

The girl smiled. "That, and she likes biscuits and gravy."

A quiet breeze lifting off the cool morning desert swirled whiffs of dust around the horses' plodding hooves. The parched earth had already consumed last night's rain. What moisture remained quickly drained into shallow water courses making its journey to a distant sea, and leaving not so much as a tiny sip for any living creature who might be foolish enough to pass this way.

It was early, and the urgency of their journey seemed far away, at least to Kane. A myriad of thoughts tormented his mind. He had fallen back, shaken by his exchange with the Mimbre. As a writer, words were his to command, yet from this girl's simple tongue flowed a courage and honesty that failed him. He didn't know how to speak to her.

From behind, the buffalo soldier watched the young man for awhile, then nudged his mount close. "Saw ya' talkin' with the little Apache. By the look on yo' face, guess ya' got scalped from the inside out."

The author looked up with an embarrassed grin, still at a loss for words. Jube gave him a sympathetic smile. "She can cut deep as a lance, n' make ya' look inside where it ain't always pretty."

Kane nodded. "Never met anyone like her."

"That's a fact." Jube chuckled. "My advice is, don't try to figure her out. Injun or not, she's still a woman. Jes' be honest with her, n' she will treat ya' fair."

"Have you known her long, Mr. Jube?"

Turning his thoughts inward, Jube pushed back his hat. "Not long. But this world is new to her. Guess I knowed' her a little longer n' that."

"What do you mean?"

The buffalo soldier cast his eyes ahead at the young girl. "She was a savage once, I guess. Captured her myself. Wearin' little more n' the desert. Cute little thing." A brief smile brightened the soldier's ruddy face, and then faded slowly. "But everyone she knowed' or ever loved died in a single night on a mountain up ahead. Her world ended. That's the sadness ya' see in her eyes. This here world is all new ta' her. Started with Jacob, it did. Probably more frightened than she cares ta' let on. Livin' with the enemy, so ta' speak. Only knowin' her savage ways, not sure what's right. Takes courage, it does. So I tries ta' go easier on her."

"Mr. Jube, what about her husband? He seems to almost ignore her."

"Oh, don't get ol' Jacob wrong. He might surprise ya'." Jube grew silent for a moment as he studied his curious young companion. "Mr. Kane, ya' ever kilt' a man?"

The author looked surprised. "No! No, I haven't. Thank God."

"For some men it's hard ta' love n' hate at the same time. You ain't seen Jacob, jes' the wall."

Jube smiled. "Don't be afraid of either one of 'em. What you is searching fer can be found in both of 'em."

"Thank you, Mr. Jube. I think I understand."

With that, the buffalo soldier faded back to his place at the end of the trail. Kane thought about their exchange for a moment, then slapped his reins. He would try to make amends with Mea-a-ha. If nothing else, he'd show some courage in at least facing her after the things he had written.

As he neared, the Indian girl appeared to be conversing with a dusty raven balancing on a thin juniper branch hanging over the trail. It squawked, then hopped to the next limb, staying up with her pony.

If the writer hadn't known better, he would have sworn the raven was trying to talk. When Mea-a-ha noticed Kane, she quickly shooed the bird away.

Kane grinned. "A friend?"

She blushed, then turned serious. "Never sure with ravens. They are tricksters."

Mea-a-ha studied her companion for a moment, wondering if he was making fun of her. An eagerness in his caring face seemed to beg for a story. Obliging, she cocked her head in serious thought. "Ravens are born old and live long. They are clever like coyote and owl. Gringos pass over this land, but ravens are a part of it as were my people. We came from the earth." Mea-a-ha paused to search the sky. "The raven's keen eyes see all that is done and all that is to be. They listen to the wind. Every word that is spoken they keep. Sometimes if they feel kind, they will share what they know."

The small girl's eyes grew wide as she continued her tale. "But mostly they just wait and let evil come. Tricksters."

The Indian girl seemed almost comical in her seriousness as she leaned close to the writer, warning him. "Watch for the ravens. When danger is near they will gather so they can rob from the dead. It is not the meat from the bones they seek, but the truth from the dying man's soul." She thrust out her chin, adding importance to her words. "Watch for the ravens. They know."

Kane held his breath, almost believing her story. His eyes darted to the rocks, fearing the ravens were gathering now. To his relief, he spied only one lone bird. It was sitting far away, sharpening it beak on a lofty stone. A shudder went down his spine. Though this trail would be long, some instinct told him he would see that raven again.

The Indian girl smiled. "Teach me how to write."

Surprised by the sudden change in her innocent face, Kane chuckled out loud. He had not expected this. Mea-a-ha persisted. "I can spell..." She blushed. "Well, little words, but I am learning. My friend Carmelita gave me a book about animals that talk." She blushed again. "It is a children's book. I think I would like to write a children's book about a puppy that can talk. Could you teach me?"

The writer smiled. "I'd be delighted."

Sitting tall, Kane took on a serious air. "If the puppy is going to talk, the first thing you need to do is decide is if he will talk in the first person or the third person."

The Indian girl wrinkled her brow. "He's a puppy."

A laugh broke from the author's lips. "I am talking about how you will tell your story. If you tell the story in the first person, the puppy might say, 'I'm happy,' but if you tell it from the third person, then you would say, 'The puppy is happy.' Do you understand?"

The girl looked confused. "I'm the third person?"

Kane nodded his head. Mea-a-ha gave it some more thought. "Who's the second person?"

"There is no second person, unless, I guess it's the dog."

The Indian girl frowned. "He's not a person. He's a puppy." They were back to that.

Kane chuckled again. "It seems illogical, doesn't it?"

Shaking her head, the girl tried to understand. "It makes no sense. A puppy can be a person, but Apaches can't. What if the puppy writes a story about a little Indian girl?"

The writer shrugged. "Maybe we should write in the first puppy."

Mea-a-ha smiled. "Okay, but there may be many puppies."

Kane could see it was going to be a long morning.

Coming to a muddy wash, Jacob pulled the band of rescuers to an abrupt halt and jumped from his saddle. Motioning everyone to stay back, he knelt on the shallow bank.

A trail of hoof prints crossed the damp ground. Following the tracks into the brush, Jacob read them like a man turning pages in a book. After a moment, he hurried back and spoke to Jube. "Four horses, three shod, one not. Maybe three hours old."

Jubaliah held his hand to the sun. It was not yet noon. "The rain slowed 'em down."

Kane was surprised how easily Jacob had read the tracks, but guessed the soldier saw even more than he had told. His writer's curiosity got the best of him. "Sir, what else can you tell?"

The big man shrugged. "Nah-kah-yen is leading. The other tracks are over his. Daniel is riding wide, flanking to the right. They seem to be in no hurry, which is good for us."

Jacob could see the amazement in the writer's face, so he obligingly continued. "If it matters, a boy named Juan is in the middle and Roberto is bringing up the rear. I'll let you figure that one out."

Jacob turned to Mea-a-ha and lowered his voice, adding a tinge of reproach. "There are horse droppings. Daniel is still sneaking tortillas to his pony. He learned that from you, little one."

Mea-a-ha ducked her head and grinned.

Jumping back on the Buckskin, Jacob slapped his reins and broke into a gallop. For his greenhorn companions trying to keep up, it was a bone-jarring ride. Everyone understood the urgency of the big man out front. He carried the greater weight, but they all were racing to the same end.

When the horses were winded, Jacob would slow to a walk, and then start again. He kept this up for several hours. Lunch came and went without rest. No one dared complain.

The terrain became hilly once more then fell into arroyos. Scrub trees began to replace the cactus and sage. Finally, in mid-afternoon, the relentless sergeant called a halt. Mea-a-ha rode to his side.

Too stiff to climb down, she stretched out her arms. Jacob lifted her to the ground and held her until she found her feet.

There was no time for a fire. Biscuits, dried meat, and a canteen of water would be their meal. Fatigue weighed on the girl and even the young men. Only the two veteran soldiers remained unchanged.

Jacob paced back and forth. Taking a bite of meat, Jube watched his friend struggle with his thoughts. Several times Jacob glanced at Mason, then continued pacing. Jube finished his meal and washed it down with a swallow of stale water. "Silence don't change the truth, Jacob. Tell 'em."

Mason realized by their glances that they were talking about him. Nervously, he rose to his feet. His eyes darted to both men. "Tell me what?"

Jacob turned his back in frustration and stared south. Pulling his hat from his head, he let it slap against his side. "We failed."

The young officer swallowed. "What do you mean?"

"We didn't catch them in time. We're in Mexico."

Lieutenant McCrae gave a start, knowing what this meant. He was an American soldier on foreign soil. If caught, he'd be shot.

Here the awesome power of the United States Army vanished like smoke on a high wind, and with it any authority he had. His starched blue coat with gold bars, a uniform he wore with pride, now mocked his presence.

With a piercing stare, Jacob measured the young officer. It was time to see what the lad was made of. "With all the problems of late, the Mexican army patrols the border regularly. Do you have any civilian clothes in your saddlebags?"

McCrae tugged at his coat. "Well, yes..."

"You can change and come along as a civilian, or you turn around and hightail it home where it's safe."

Mason unconsciously backed away, as thought the illegal crossing could be erased with a few steps in the opposite direction. "I...I have my orders to apprehend the Apache."

Jacob growled. "Your daddy's orders ended somewhere in that last valley. You have no authority here."

Lifting up from his rocky perch, Jube broke into a grin. "Fact is, down here, you is an outlaw...jes' like Nah-kah-yen."

The young officer was stunned. He came from a regimented world where men followed orders handed down through a chain of command. Mason had grown up as part of a powerful military force of thousands, yet now, barely in his twenties, in a foreign land, he stood alone. For the first time in his life, Mason didn't have someone telling him what to do. He swallowed nervously. "What about you?"

Jacob's dark face stared back with unwavering resolve. "Nothing's changed. I'll follow my boy to hell. Time's wastin'."

Mea-a-ha grabbed Mason's arm. "Come with us. My heart tells me there will be trouble. Jacob needs your gun." She looked to her husband. "Forget your pride. Tell him you need him. I can see it in your eyes."

The big man stepped towards the girl. "You told me to find another way. If Mason comes, he will arrest Nah-kah-yen. If he leaves now, the problem is solved. It's what you wanted."

The girl filled with distress. "But you said he has no authority here."

Mason bristled with a sense of duty. "Nah-kah-yen is in as great a danger as me on this side of the border. If we find him, I will stay with him until he crosses onto American soil, with or without his family. Then he will be my prisoner, as Jacob has promised."

Mason shot a glance at Jacob, letting him know he expected him to stand by his word.

Jube climbed into his saddle and looked down at the girl. "Iffin' he says so or not, yo' husband needs Mason's gun. You now have ta' make the same decision, ya' been condemning him for. Trade a life for a life—Nah-kah-yen for yo' brother. What's the right thing now, Missy?"

Jacob barked. "Jube! Leave her alone."

The black soldier whirled his horse around. "It ain't jes' you, Jacob. We all gots' a say…an there's Daniel."

The Indian girl's heart pounded. She was trapped between her own anger and love. A painful gasp escaped her throat. There had to be another way.

Mason pulled his arm free. "It's my decision. I'm coming."

Taking a deep breath, Mea-a-ha looked to her husband then lowered her eyes. With guilt on her face, she turned to white soldier, grateful the decision was taken from her.

The young officer stripped off his coat and opened his saddlebags. From here on out, he would be measured as simply a man. "Like I said, I expect you to keep your promise, Jacob."

Jacob cast a glance at his bride. "I will or die. Best lose them fancy striped pants, Lieutenant, and throw away your saber. too."

Mason spun around. "My saber? It was presented to me by General Schofield himself at West Point."

Jube hunched forward, layering his arms over the pummel of his saddle. "The love of a boy n' a shiny tin sword. We all gots somethin' precious ta' loose. Throw it away, Mr. McCrae. There's a price ta' be paid by all."

The lieutenant's face burned as he held the engraved scabbard before him. It was a symbol of his solemn duty. When it was presented to him, he swore an oath that he'd never surrender it or let it fall in battle. His hands trembled at his impending loss, yet now there was a greater oath to duty.

Mason gritted his teeth and let the sword drop in the sand at his feet. Seething with anger, he snarled up at Jube. "So be it. It's just a sword."

Fuming, he kicked out of his boots and stripped off his pants. "It's not the uniform that makes a soldier, Mr. Jackson. It's the man who wears it."

Mason pulled a pair of denim jeans from his saddlebag. His eyes flashed at the Apache girl. "Ma'am, you asked me to look past the dress. Yet there you sit scorning this uniform while wanting the gun that goes with it. Look at me now. Look at me, damn it, and remember that soldiers are people, too."

Mea-a-ha stared forward in guilty silence. He was right about how she felt, yet as she watched him cast his gold braid and shiny buttons aside, she knew that there stood a man of honor.

Buckling on his holster, Mason mounted up and glared at the others. "The trappings are gone if it amuses you, but my mission remains, and I'll see it through or die."

Slapping his reins, the young cavalry officer bolted away.

Mea-a-ha lowered her head to avoid Jacob's eyes as he took her by the waist and lifted her into the saddle. The white officer had let her off the hook, but his rebuke shamed her. Would she have made the same decision that she condemned Jacob for?

As the procession moved out, Jube kicked his horse past the writer. "Sharpen yo' pencil, Mr. Kane. Heroes come in all colors 'n sizes. Looks like you is going ta' get yo' story after all."

Chapter -9-
Terahumara

A stand of scrawny pinions grew up the side of a distant ridge. The trees were too sparse to offer any cover for an enemy. Yet something was wrong. Nah-kah-yen sat patiently on the back of his pony, searching the rolling hills. He kept coming back to the stand of trees. In nature, there is an unseen harmony. When it's right, you don't notice it, but when something is wrong, it scratches at your nerves. The Apache had been taught since birth that one must listen to the songs of the earth. Fail to do so, and life is cut short.

In the arroyo behind him, he could hear the boys whispering anxiously. Daniel pushed his beautiful horse forward, hoping to join the brave warrior on the crest of the hill, but Nah-kah-yen dropped his hand to his side and turned his palm to the young Indian, stopping him in his tracks.

The Mimbre remained unchanged. Calmly, he looked in the other direction, towards the blinding sun resting on a distant hill. Night was coming, and dark cloaks evil. If anyone was shadowing their trial, now was the time to find out. "Daniel. Bring your rifle and crawl through the grass to me."

The Apache youth risked a nervous glance at his friends, then obeyed. Among the boys, he alone knew how to move without being seen. Not a blade of the tall, dry grass shook as he made his way to the feet of the warrior's pony.

Without turning his head, Nah-kah-yen's voice rose softly from deep in his chest. "Look to the far ridge to the east."

"I see trees."

The warrior patted his horse, showing no concern. "Look hard, young brave."

For a long time, Daniel studied the stunted trees. They were short and too thin to hide behind. Much too thin. He gave a start. "The shadow. They cast too big a shadow on the side of the hill."

Nah-kah-yen smiled. "Good boy. There are those who know how to hide like the Apache. It is a long shot. Take your time."

His palms sweating in the cool evening air, Daniel laid his cheek against the smooth wooden stock of his Winchester. He aimed at the shadow, judged the sun and moved his sight slightly lower and to the left. Taking a final breath, he released it and squeezed the trigger. The shot shattered the peaceful silence. As his bullet tore its path across the vale, Nah-kah-yen jerked his own rifle to his shoulder.

In the distance, a horse reared and screamed, throwing its rider to the ground. The frightened animal turned and raced away. It was an Indian pony. With incredible speed, Nah-kah-yen levered three shots into the base of the trees. Coming to his senses, Daniel rose on one knee, spending two more rounds of his own. An Indian jumped from the tall grass and raced after his horse. He stumbled, and fell, then regained his feet and kept going.

The distance was too great to hit a moving target. It was better to save their ammunition. Nah-kah-yen shouted to the boys. "Ride!" He kicked his pony and headed down into the next arroyo. Daniel mounted Snow Raven on the run. Roberto and Juan whipped their mounts and followed. They had to get off the exposed ridge.

Their small band charged down the hill at a full run. Puffs of smoke rose from trees deep in a shaded glen to their right. The Apache boy laid his head against his pony's neck as the deadly zing of bullets screamed like hornets overhead. His mighty Paint quickly caught Nah-kah-yen's Mustang and moved into the lead. For a moment they were beyond the vision of the trees, and the shots silenced. Then, from behind the knoll, screaming horsemen poured into the bottom of the arroyo, cutting them off.

Instinctively, Daniel pulled his rifle to his shoulder and fired. Far below, a rider fell from his horse. Nah-kah-yen, shouting, turned the boys and headed up the steep hill to their left. It was their only route of escape.

Heavy bullets tore up tufts of earth around them and ricocheted off the rocks. There was no time to think; they must ride, and ride hard. Daniel had been farther down the mountain, but Snow Raven quickly overtook the other horses. The boy could hear their raspy breathing as he raced by. From below, a score of riders gave chase.

Snow Raven was as fast as the wind, but bullets were faster. They had to make it to the ridge. The courageous youth passed several pinnacles of fractured stones rising from the grassy hill. The steep climb tapered off. Daniel led the way between the rocks and made for the top. Once down the other side, he knew their horses could outrun Mexican or Indian ponies. The Rincon stallions were bred for speed.

The Apache youth pulled his horse to a stop and waited for his friends. Juan's eyes were wild with fright as he flew past the line of jagged stone, followed closely by Roberto. Nah-kah-yen was the last to reach him. For a moment, they were safe, but it was only a temporary reprieve.

On top of the hill the strata of rocks had tipped up on end. Two broken outcroppings, maybe a few hundred yards apart, ran parallel along the length of the ridge for five hundred yards or more. A field of dry yellow grass lay in between the crumbling walls. Any second the enemy would be upon them.

The warrior gave a yell and whipped his horse towards the second line of rock. Daniel pulled ahead and raced through a narrow gap. They were almost free. He began to breathe. Suddenly, the boy jerked hard on the reins. Snow Raven reared. At his feet, the mountain fell away. They had come to the edge of a steep mesa. Stones dislodged by the pony's hoofs fell through fifty feet of air.

As Daniel brought his horse under control, his friends came barreling to the ledge. Nah-kah-yen whirled around. It was too late. Already their pursuers had passed the first wall and were spreading out into a deadly line. This was their land, and they knew the terrain. The Apache warrior and the boys were driven to this place to be slaughtered like frightened deer.

Not giving up, Daniel drove his pony between his friends and raced farther up the grassy ridge. A few hundred yards ahead rose a high rocky point. He prayed they could squeeze past the swarming riders before they had a chance to cut off their escape. Shots rang out to his side. Daniel leaned against his pony. "Fly, Snow Raven, fly."

The beautiful Paint raced up the incline at a blinding speed. His hooves pounded the earth like rolling thunder. "Fly, my pony, go, boy, go."

Before the enemy could bring their sights to bear, the boy and his horse made the shelter of the rock.

Daniel pulled up short and looked over his shoulder. The others were following far behind. He was free, but his friends would never make it. Already, mounted riders were moving to cut them off.

Daniel cursed and threw his Winchester to his shoulder. His shots hammered in rapid succession. The enemy scrambled to get out of his deadly barrage. He emptied his rifle and loaded again. Out of the corner of his eye he could see Nah-kah-yen and the boys turn their ponies, trying to retreat to the safety of the stony spires at the edge of the cliff.

The Apache youth knew he had to flee now if he were to make it to safety. Already riders were closing in on his side. Daniel ignored them and fired instead at those chasing his friends. With a hail of bullets he dropped the lead pony, sending the rider plowing head-first onto the ground. The others turned and raced for the safety of the first ridge, allowing his friends to make it to the sheltered cliff. Nah-kah-yen and the boys were safe, but trapped.

Shots ricocheted off the rocks by Daniel's head. He had waited too long. Pulling back behind a stone wall, the boy returned fire. He was surrounded, and alone. Soon the enemy would be upon him.

Feverishly, Daniel reloaded his rifle. It held seventeen shots, enough for every one of his killers. His fingers fumbled with each bullet he shoved into the breech. "Damn them all." They would pay dearly for this young Apache's life.

Daniel finished loading and looked around. He realized there were tears streaming down his cheeks. Battle had come to him; he had seen riders fall. Men now lay dead, killed by his hand. The boy cried openly.

A shot cracked, and a rock broke near his face. Daniel wiped his tears and returned fire. There was a distant scream, and then all fell silent. The Apache listened. Not a sound could be heard. Why weren't they attacking?

Suddenly he realized the shadows were stretching out from the rocks. Soon the blood-red sun would leave the craggy knoll, and the deadly hunters would come for him in the dark. He trembled as a chill ran down his spine.

Daniel had seen both Indians and Mexicans. Whoever they were, they held the first ridge. His friends held the second, against the cliff. He could see darting shadows move along the jagged walls.

Suddenly shots rang out far below. The bad men were attacking his friends. Daniel shook with anger. There was nothing he could do. Then from the narrow ledge, flames licked the evening air. Nah-kah-yen and the boys were defending their tiny plot of earth. If they were to die this night, they would not be alone.

Just as quickly, the shots died down and all grew silent once more. The enemy was only testing their resolve. The boy wiped his nose and tried to calm his breathing. With death closing in, he thought of his father and how angry he would be. Daniel wished he could tell him he was sorry.

On the outer side of his rocky shelter, he heard the scraping of boots. The boy moved his pony deeper into the shadows and held his rifle against his chest. His eyes darted left and right. A stone fell, but now from behind. Someone was climbing the rocks to get above him. When it was completely dark, they would shoot down into his rabbit hole, killing him with ease. It was only a matter of time. The light was almost gone.

Daniel remembered his father's words, "Never give up." In his savage heart, a smoldering ember burst into flame. "Not this night," he swore.

There was one chance. Snow Raven had brought him to safety. The brave horse had to carry him back. In the last flicker of light, he must charge out at full speed and try to reach his friends. The enemy would not expect him to return to the jaws of death. Foolish as it may be, it was his only hope. His breath came in pants as the young boy thought about what he was planning to do.

Daniel slid his rifle into his scabbard and drew his pistol. It felt powerful in his hand, as if it always belonged there. Death was no longer a feared stranger. This night it would be his companion.

Listening carefully, he fixed the position of each scrape on the rocks and judged the distance as his would-be killer inched closer to him. Every sound, each loose pebble that fell, was carefully calculated.

'Quiet as a warrior's heart.' It was something his grandfather used to say. Daniel repeated it to himself. If there was the slightest noise, it would not be his. The boy nudged his pony forward. He paused and listened. A faint trickle of dust falling from the rocks above his head caught the last pale ray of light. Daniel fired his pistol upward, then bolted forward. Behind him, a heavy black shadow came crashing down. As he cleared the shelter of the stone, a dark form jumped from the rocks by his side. Daniel felt icy fingers clawing his leg as his attacker sought to drag him from his saddle. The boy fired point-blank as his pony flew by. In the brief flash that leapt from his muzzle, he saw the vacant eyes of the dying man.

Snow Raven tore into the open at a dead run. Leaning close, Daniel shouted him onward. The men crawling up the rocks behind him were unaware the boy had fled their trap. For a second there was silence, then flashes of light appeared to his left. Daniel veered towards the gunfire. It would have been human nature to stay to the right of the vale, closer to his friends, but there he would be exposed for a longer period of time, allowing the killers to draw a bead. By moving to the outcroppings held by his enemy, only those directly beside him, would be able to fire, and only for a brief instant, like someone bolting past a open door.

As Snow Raven devoured the distance, Daniel fired his last four shots into the dark shapes that appeared between the rocks, forcing the shadowed figures to retreat. He saw a flash and felt a tug on the fleece collar of his coat. Snow Raven raced on. So fast was the incredible speed of the painted stallion, that every shot misjudged its mark.

In a surprising feat, the boy had made the length of the gauntlet and somehow survived. Now he had to turn his back on his enemy and cross the open field to his friends.

On Snow Raven, it took less than a few seconds, yet plenty of time for the hunters to find their target. Daniel heard the rifles. Bullets rang past his ears, each one closer than the last. A bullet caught the flap of his coat. Another burned the back of his hand.

Suddenly flames leaped in rapid succession before him, lighting up the night. His friends had seen his valiant charge. Screaming defiance, they emptied their rifles into the shadowed spaces between the rocks, silencing every gun. Daniel raced into the fortress of stone and pulled up amid the cheers of his friends.

Before he could dismount, Juan was hugging him and crying. Nah-kah-yen patted him on the back. Roberto cheered as he stood guard from above. Embarrassed, Juan wiped his face. "You did it! You did it." The warrior rubbed the boy's head. "You came back for your friends, young brave."

Daniel slumped against the rocks. They were together. It sank in; they were trapped together. He took a breath. "Who are they?"

The warrior spit. "Scalpers. Very bad."

He had feared as much. Scalpers. Nah-kah-yen had warned them that they were the worst.

Juan looked to his friend, still amazed. "How many did you kill?"

Daniel shrugged and quickly turned away. Nah-kah-yen climbed back up on the rocks. "How many? We need to know."

It was something Daniel wanted to forget. He hid his eyes. "Three or four."

The warrior growled. "How many?"

The boy took a deep breath. "Five."

Juan stared in disbelief. "That is more than all of us. Nah-kah-yen got two, and Roberto winged one. I didn't get any."

The warrior turned to the Mexican boy. "You did good. Come morning, you will have your share."

The Indian stared into the darkness. "They number no more than a dozen now. Still, it is enough. They have us surrounded. We cannot escape."

The night settled in with an unnerving silence. Every second became its own eternity. Nah-kah-yen had Daniel and Juan rest while he and Roberto took first watch. The warrior had changed his mind about the tall Mexican. The youth had kept his head under fire. He lacked experience, but made up for it in cool courage. He would have made a good Apache.

Juan could not sleep. Unable to calm his mind, the silence worked against him. After tossing and turning, he sat up and looked at Nah-kah-yen. "How do you think it will happen?"

The warrior showed no emotion. "They will send some men behind us. When it is light, they will attack and pick us off from both sides." He nodded towards Daniel. "Kill as many as this young warrior, and you will die well."

"Apache!" Somewhere in the darkness a voice rang out. "Apacheee!"

A high, sick laugh carried from the distant rocks. "I saw you, Apache. What kind of warrior rides with young Vaqueros? Have they tamed you?"

Nah-kah-yen raised above the wall. "I know what kind of Indian rides with Mexican scalpers. I am Nah-kah-yen of the Chihene, and who is the Terahumara dog, that yaps in the night to impress his Mexican masters?"

The sick laugh rose again. "I am Rutaio. But you lie, Apache. There are no more Chihene. No more Mimbrinos. I was there at the spires of Tres Castillos when we cut them down like old women."

Daniel could hear the air hiss through Nah-kah-yen's teeth as the warrior rekindled with rage. His eyes blazed in the dark.

Rutaio laughed again. "Apache, I was with Mauricio Corredor when your chief Victorio rode into the valley. The fool let his guard down when he saw we were Indians. Mauricio shot him from his saddle with no more effort than swatting a mosquito. Killing the rest was easy. Many scalps that day."

A wound unhealed was reopened. Nah-kah-yen seethed with madness. He was beyond words, not so for Rutaio. "Apache. The scalps lift easy from your women...and...little children. Some I scalped before I killed them just for fun. How they cried. Come see. I kept one scalp for me."

Leaping to the top the stones, Nah-kah-yen screamed insanely while emptying his rifle into the darkness. It was not enough to quell his fury. Tortured by the horrors of that distant night, he continued to lever his empty gun. Roberto pulled him from the rocks as bullets tore about him.

Coming to his senses, the warrior jerked away. The gunfire faded as it echoed down the vale. Silence returned. Then once more the haunting laughter fouled the air. "Many scalps, Apache. This night we add yours. Will you beg like your women?"

Nah-kah-yen feverishly shoved more cartridges into his gun. Daniel scrambled up the rocks and grabbed the warrior's arm. "Save your ammunition. Do not let him win. Tomorrow we will kill the coward before we die."

The Apache warrior slumped to the ground. His feet would no longer hold him. He whispered to himself. "Victorio, I will avenge you."

Daniel settled by his side. For a long time the two Indians did not speak. The words of Rutaio played in the boy's mind. It troubled his heart. "Nah-kah-yen. It ain't true about Victorio. They didn't shoot him, did they? He fell on his own knife, like our people say?"

Nah-kah-yen calmed his breathing and rested his rifle across his knees. Once more he was his old self. "Perhaps both are true, my son. Victorio was the greatest warrior. He made fools of the skilled white soldiers. If he were uninjured, no Mexican dogs could have beaten him. They always ran like cowards. I think he was wounded by treachery as the Terahumarian traitor said. And with no ammunition, unable to fight, he took his life, like our people said."

Daniel leaned his head back against the rocks. "I knew they couldn't beat him."

As the night wore on, Juan sat his post on the high rocks. Daniel had taken a position farther down. A half-moon provided enough light to discourage any sneak attack. The boys slowly moved closer until they could whisper to each other.

"Daniel? You okay?"
"Sure. You see anything?"
"No. It's quiet."
"Daniel?"
"Yes?"
"...Nothing."
The boy understood. "I know."

Resting his chin on the rock, Juan exhaled a long slow breath. It was a time for reflection in his very short life, even though there was little to reflect on. Juan had been the smallest kid until Daniel came along. Maybe that was why he took to him. Maybe he was protecting himself. It was funny how things change. After Daniel's wild charge, he would never be looked on as the little kid again. Juan suddenly trembled. That would all end with the morning sun. No one would know of Daniel's heroism. Juan slid a little closer to his friend. "You could have gotten away."

Daniel shook himself from his own thoughts. "What?"

"You could have gotten away. No sense in you dying with us."

The Apache boy had thought many times about the folly of his decision to return. He feared death, but he knew he had done the right thing. "Don't matter. Maria would have killed me anyway if I came back without her stupid brother."

It was a joke, and it brought a much-needed smile to the young boys.

Daniel thought of Jube and how he was always cracking jokes when things were bleak. The boy's smile grew wider. Maybe he was growing up.

The cool air braced Juan's young cheeks as he peered into the darkness. The rifle clutched in his small hands seemed awkward. It was for killing. In his heart he was still a boy, and guns were for men. "Apache, what's it like...Killin'?"

For a long time Daniel was silent. It was a difficult thing to answer. "Guess it's different for everyone."

The Indian boy rolled over on his back and leaned against the cool rocks. "There's how you think about it before...and after, but when it's happening...well, ya' just do. You don't have time to think. You just do."

Daniel knew what his friend feared. "Don't worry. When the time comes, you'll be ready. And you won't even know it's done until it's over. That's the way it is."

Juan fidgeted. "Guess I was scared about getting in trouble for killin' so I didn't really aim. You know. What if I killed someone, and then the adults say I done wrong..."

Reflecting on the battle, Daniel chuckled nervously. "Heck, if that happened, I'd get the whipping from hell...but Jacob told me not to worry about what others thought, just do my best to do the right thing. It's all anyone can ask of you."

Juan slumped back against the rough stone, feeling miserable. "I shoulda' aimed."

"You will come mornin'. It wasn't that you were frightened, it was that you were scared of doing the wrong thing."

The young Mexican released the air in his lungs. "Thanks for understanding." Juan swelled with new determination. In his young hands, the Winchester rested a little more easily. Maybe he could fight like his Apache friend.

He looked down at the Indian. Daniel still looked like a boy, but he was different now. "Apache?...What changed you?" Juan's eyes shined like the stars. "I mean, it's more than you having fought soldiers before, or the first killin' you done. This is different, like a hawk takes wing for the first time, n' soars higher than the clouds. One day you are a dumb kid, then all of a sudden you are a...well...what us Mexicans call a pistolero. What changed you?"

The question caused Daniel to shake deep inside. It was a question he'd tried to ignore, but now it hung in the cold night air, waiting for an answer.

He turned away from his friend, wishing the dark would hide him. Was being a killer of men just something he was meant to be, his savage Apache blood answering the inevitable call of battle, or...was it guilt?

He'd disobeyed his father, and everything had turned horribly wrong. A soldier had been shot, his friends were facing death, and it was his fault. Daniel closed his eyes tightly. The men who now lay dead beneath the cold night sky—had he murdered them for his own sins?

Daniel swallowed a trembling breath. "What we are doing would change anybody." His whisper rose more defensively than he'd meant. "But I'm still me. Honest! Nothin's' different. We're still best friends...right?"

The plea in his young voice startled his companion. Juan awkwardly smiled. "Well, sure. Yeah! I was just wondering. That's all."

Juan cursed himself. It was a question he shouldn't have asked. He tried to make light of it. "Just wanted to know what kind of guy was going to marry my sister."

Daniel's heart leaped at the mention of Maria. "Juan, do you think your sister would have married me... I mean, when we got older?"

Juan scooted a little closer, happy to talk about something else. "Heck, you dumb Injun, she's wondering why you haven't already asked her."

"Uh-uh!" For a second, Daniel's thoughts were over the hill and far away. "You're making that up...aren't you?"

Juan took one last peek above the wall, then turned back to his friend. "She's almost fifteen. Why do you think my mother is always inviting you over for dinner? It ain't your table manners."

Daniel scanned the moonlit landscape. Suddenly his desire to see Maria one more time became overwhelming. "She sure is pretty. Why ain't she said something?"

The Mexican boy shook his head. "No wonder there are so few Indians, if they are all as brainless as you. That's the way it works with girls. The boys have to say mushy stuff."

"Why?"

"Haven't figured that out."

"If you make it back, well you tell her I would have married her...maybe say some mushy stuff for me."

Juan's voice rose with hope. "Do you think there's a chance? I mean...one of us could make it back."

The Apache youth's heart suddenly beat with a new fire. "If there is a dozen of em' left like Nah-kah-yen says, then we only have to kill three each. Heck! I can do that for Maria."

From down below, Roberto's voice carried from the shadows. "What's going on?"

Sliding back to his post, Juan whispered excitedly to his tall friend. "We've decided we ain't going to die. Daniel's going to marry my sister."

Rolling from his blanket, Roberto joined his friends. "I like that plan." He eagerly embraced their resolve. "Jacob always says, 'Never give up.'"

The boys looked to the east. A thin, red glow outlined the distant mountains. Morning was near. Nah-kah-yen picked up his rifle and climbed up the rocks to the boys. "Maybe it's a good day to live." The brave did not believe so, but it was better to die with a glad heart.

Time was running out. Already, the land was taking form. Beyond their rocky perch, the enemy hungered for the break of day. Behind them the world dropped away, and more guns waited for the cloak of darkness to be lifted from the ledge.

Soon they would be exposed. They could hold the rim no longer. The warrior had the boys climb down from their posts, hoping the scalpers would delay their attack a few minutes longer.

Nah-kah-yen's eyes narrowed. "It is no good here. We must ride out and meet them."

Roberto frowned. "They will cut us down."

Defiant to the end, the Apache warrior leaped onto his pony. "They will cut some of us down." His eyes grew cold. "Do not stop to help your fallen friends. One of us must live to sing our tale. Now ride, young warriors."

A narrow cut led back to the grassy plane. Still shrouded in the receding shadows, the boys quietly mounted their ponies. Nah-kah-yen and Daniel knew how to shoot from a running mount. They would go first. Moving away from the rocks, they made their way forward.

"It is time." The warrior kicked his heels, but barely pushed forward when he suddenly stopped. His eyes scanned the inky dawn. "No good. The enemy are mounted and ready. Too late."

Daniel peered into the pale light. Ten riders were fanned out and slowly moving across the grassy expanse. Through the morning haze, he could discern the cold, deadly glint on the steel barrels of their rifles. The boy looked nervously over his shoulder. At least two more must have been sent to lie in wait behind them.

Nah-kah-Yen thumbed back the hammer on his Winchester and took aim. "We go anyway."

In less than a heartbeat, Daniel thrust out his hand and grabbed the warrior's arm. His keen eyes caught motion to the east. "Wait! The sun."

Over the ridge, came horsemen galloping four abreast as though they had burst from the brilliant orange sun rising from their backs. A deep, familiar voice rang out. "Charge!" The silhouetted riders broke into a dead run. Caught by surprise, the scalpers turned their eyes and were blinded. Flames from horsemen's rifles flashed in the morning air. They were four against ten. Their bullets sang of death. Now it was eight. On the riders came, sending a hail of lead before them. Some of the scalpers whirled to fight the new foe, but others, unsure of what they were facing, raced away. The Mexican rabble quailed against the trained U.S. Cavalry. Rifles volleyed. Three more scalpers traded their saddles for a patch of earth.

Nah-kah-yen unleashed a blood-curdling scream and kicked his pony forward. The wolves became rabbits. Seeing the rout, the boys raised their voices and joined the fray, their young hands now firing at will. Outnumbered, the scalpers fled with the Apache warrior, screaming vengeance at their heels.

Jacob broke off the attack and turned his line to protect his son. The boy, seeing his father, pulled up, but Nah-kah-yen, insane with rage, flew on. Mason veered to follow the Apache, and whipped his horse to a greater speed.

Breathing hard, Daniel rode up to the giant man and stopped. His smoking rifle hung in his hand. "Father!"

The buffalo soldier's eyes burned cold. "Check the bodies." His voice growled with a ragged hiss as he searched the ground. Not the slightest glance did he make to his son.

Daniel stared, crestfallen, his young heart ready to burst. He had gone through a night of hell, and the boy needed the man. His father's scorn left him shaking.

Daniel started after him when a frantic voice called from the top of the hill. "Daniel!"

Mea-a-ha came riding down the ridge, with two packhorses in tow. "Daniel!"

Jacob looked up and swore. Spurring his Buckskin forward, he charged through the tall, dry grass and blocked her path. Her pony reared. On the ground in front of her lay a wounded Mexican struggling to lift his head. He turned his eyes to the girl, pleading in a pain-ridden voice. "Senorita. Please...please..."

Thumbing his pistol, Jacob fired a round into the man's back. The Mexican jerked with the impact of the slug and crumpled back into the weeds. The big man turned his fury at the girl. "Damn it, woman, I told you to wait until I came and got you."

Mea-a-ha steadied the pony, her mouth agape, horrified by the deed he'd done. "You killed him."

Jacob twisted with rage. She had never seen him like this. Unable to comprehend, Mea-a-ha turned her eyes away. Suddenly Daniel was by her side. She reached out and wrapped her arms around the boy. "Brother."

Daniel ducked his head, hiding his tears. His sister did her best to comfort him. "It's okay, little brother." Lifting her eyes, she looked over him into the angry face of her husband. Mea-a-ha had not seen Jacob kill before. What he had done was murder. She sickened.

Having checked the dead, the other men came riding back to the circle. It had been a hell of a thing. No one had time to sort it all out. A moment later, Nah-kah-yen returned at full gallop. He pulled his winded pony to a stop by Jacob's side. The brave was furious. "You let the Terahumara dog get away."

Without warning, Jacob's huge fist flew fast and straight, knocking the Indian out of the saddle.

"Jacob, no!" Mea-a-ha screamed, and drove her pony between her husband and the prostrate warrior. "Will you murder him too? ...in front of Daniel?"

The big man looked to his son. Jerking his reins, he spurred his horse away.

Chapter -10-
At Odds

The yellow sun rose into the morning sky, warming the quiet hilltop. Ravens soaring low over the ragged cliffs broke the stillness with their mournful cries. This carrion perch was a lonely place, seldom visited by man. No water flowed, no trees grew on this untillable ground, yet this barren plot of earth served one purpose: beneath freshly turned stones lay the unmarked graves of the forgotten dead.

The small Indian girl moved gracefully through the tall, dry grass. Her long shiny black hair, catching a silent breeze, floated gently around her. Mea-a-ha brushed the errant strands from her face and stared into the distance, her dark eyes searching for an answer she could not find.

"Mea-a-ha."

The girl turned. Kane stepped cautiously towards her, not wishing to intrude. "Are you okay?"

A grateful smile slowly erased the troubled lines from her sad face, making her look young again. "Many thoughts."

She continued walking. The author hung his coat over his arm and settled by her side. He broke the silence with a nervous chuckle. "I guess I got my story."

The young man held his hand before him. It was shaking. "My God, I was never so scared. Jacob and the others sat their horses like stone. "I was terrified…"

Ashamed, Kane lowered his voice to a husky whisper. "Mea-a-ha, I couldn't kill those men. I, I fired my gun into the air. When Jacob needed me, I let him down."

The girl looked up with understanding and took the writer's trembling hand in hers. "They are trained soldiers. For Jacob, many battles. You did not run. He will respect you."

"No Mea-a-ha, your brother and the boys, they never fought before. Look at them, and I'm still shaking like a leaf."

Mea-a-ha's gaze instinctively went to a distant rock by the cliffs. Daniel and the boys were quietly talking. She held Kane's hand close to her breast as though comforting a small child. "Daniel has fought." She returned her eyes to the troubled man. "It is fear, you fear, but you did not run. If the opinions of women matters, I think you are brave. Do not judge yourself by a trembling heart. Mine trembles too."

She placed a kiss on his hand and let it go. Her eyes returned to the horizon.

The young man took a deep breath and exhaled. "Thank you, Mea-a-ha. When I write my book, I will tell of the kindness of the Apache."

Mea-a-ha smiled. "Tell also of your courage. You rode to protect my family. I will remember."

The Indian girl turned and walked away. Kane stared after her. She carried a great weight on her small shoulders, yet she willingly took time to give comfort. There was much to learn about this beautiful savage.

****

Mea-a-ha twisted the long grass into tight bundles so it would burn slower. The boys would return soon with what wood they might find, but for now her grass logs would keep the fire burning. She tasted the beans and added a pinch of salt, then a tiny handful of sugar. It was her secret.

Jubaliah walked up and tossed a small weathered branch that he had kicked loose from the dirt onto the flames. The girl scowled at his measly contribution. "You get an extra bean."

Unruffled, the soldier knelt on his haunches. "Is the coffee hot?"

"No coffee."

Jube frowned. "Why not?"

"No water."

She tossed another straw log onto the fire. "No coffee, no water, no wood. If the boys do not return soon, no beans."

Going to his horse, Jube returned, shaking his canteen. "Well you sure is a cheery sort."

Mea-a-ha abruptly threw down her spoon and burst into tears. Startled, Jube awkwardly slid to the girl's side and put a clumsy arm around her. "Hey, now, little Apache. I'll do without the coffee."

She sniffed. "Oh Jube, why did he murder that man?"

"Is that what this is all about?"

"Part."

Jube pulled her too him. "You might call it murder, but that man had come ta' kill, maybe Daniel. If we'd a patched 'em up, spent weeks tendin' 'em, he'd only kill again. Probably us. He lived by the gun, he died by the gun. He'd a done the same ta' Jacob, n' no apologizes. Way it is. Done it myself."

Mea-a-ha leaned against him. "Men are terrible. Jube, why is he so angry? I have not seen him this way."

"Well, little Apache, you is jes' a woman. You want what ya' want. Yo' brother, them Mimbre squaws, get 'em n' go home. Jacob sees all the things in between. He knowed' this was a comin'. Knowed' it since the Hollow. Been fretin' on it ever since. He sees more, n' he's frightened he will lose you n' the boy. Everything he's fought for. It's his dream, n' he's havin' ta' fight you n' Daniel ta' boot. Everyone he loves. He's heartsick, n' it ain't over. Hell, it ain't barely begun."

Stunned, Mea-a-ha searched the soldier's eyes, then collapsed in tears. She threw her arms around his neck. "Oh, Jube. I've been so terrible. I've treated him very bad."

"Ya' ain't bad, jes' a woman."

Jubaliah lifted his head to the sound of hoofbeats. Jacob rode up and dismounted. "Any coffee?"

His old friend scowled. "You ain't mad I is holdin' yo' woman?"

Jacob fished a tin cup from his saddlebag. "She's got clothes on this time. Didn't kill ya' then, no sense in killin' ya' now."

"Well if you ain't the most romantic…"

Mea-a-ha jumped up and threw herself against her husband. "I'm sorry. I…"

Jacob frowned. "Don't want to talk about it. What's done is done. We're here. We'll deal with it."

The girl stood on her toes and buried her head in her husband's neck. "Much to talk about."

"No! I want to get the boy and go home, and I know you ain't going to let that be. There's been enough fighting this morning. So right now I just want to eat some grub."

Jube dropped the wooden spoon into the pot. "Fire's out."

The boys rode in carrying several cords of yucca wood. Jubaliah reached up and untied the bundle on the back of Daniel's saddle. "Hey, Injun."

Breaking into a timid grin, the boy climbed from his horse. "Hey, old man." Daniel knew that at some point, Jube would give him hell, but not until the wound had closed a bit. Right now everything was raw.

Seeing Jacob's horse, Daniel voice came in a timid whisper. "Where's my sister?"

The black man rolled his eyes. "Behind them rocks by the cliff, an iffin' you don't wants ta' go blind, I'd stay away. You'd think they was rabbits."

Snickers erupted from the boys.

Daniel wiped the smile from his face and stood quietly by the soldier's side, watching him light the fire. A thick plume of smoke and ashes settled over the open pot of beans. Taking the spoon, Jube stirred the gray coating of cinders into the meal. Satisfied, he looked up at the troubled boy and read his mind. "Yo' Pa's okay, son."

Jube stuck his dirty finger into the pot and licked it. "When he gets his pants on, he'll talk to ya." The hulking soldier gave the young boy a wink. "Then he'll kick your scrawny ass plum back ta' the Hollow."

Daniel stared at the opening near the cliff where, only a while ago, they had ridden out to meet the scalpers. A lifetime had happened in one night. Nothing would ever be the same, but he had to make things right. He must square with his father.

Mea-a-ha came walking through the opening, carrying her boots. Her thoughts seemed to be far away, but her dark eyes slowly lifted to her brother. She knew what he had to do.

Daniel rubbed his hands nervously on his trousers. As his sister strolled by him, she looked sideways with a shy grin. "I put him in a better mood for you."

The boy tried to smile, but failed. Mea-a-ha glanced over her shoulder. "Don't worry, brother. He won't throw you over the cliff...I think."

When Daniel stepped on to the ledge, Jacob was pulling on his boots. A raised eyebrow told the boy not to expect open arms. The big man stomped his foot into the boot, then stood waiting. A dozen feet separated them, but for Daniel, it was a mile on hot sand. "Hi, Father."

Jacob folded his arms, letting the boy sweat for an interminable moment. When the boy stood before him, the big man hung his hands from his hips, looking every bit the disapproving parent. "I could tell you I'm not very proud of you, Son."

Daniel lowered his eyes, accepting his father's scorn. "I could tell you you've worried your sister sick. I could ask you if you realize how much danger you put us in. But you know all that."

Jacob hid none of his disappointment. Releasing his anger, he threw his arms in the air and shouted. "I ought to beat your ass for what you've done...toss you over my saddle and drag you back home."

The boy's eyes filled with fright. He started to speak, but Jacob silenced him with a raised hand. "I want you to figure out how to make it right."

Jacob thrust an accusing finger towards the cut in the rock. "A host of men lay dead out there."

The big man abruptly stopped and swallowed his pain. "I killed today, Son. Something I swore I'd never do again." He set his jaw, then thundered, "Could have just as easily been us...our family. Boy, I want you to think it through, and come home because maybe family should matter."

Daniel stood silently, trying to find the courage to meet his father's eyes. There was nothing more the boy wanted to do than fall into the big man's arms, but he had to make him understand. "Father, I do love my family, but I can't go back if someone else's family must die."

Jacob frowned. "And what am I supposed to do, Son? Do you think I can just ride out and leave you?"

The boy shook his head. "No, Father, I can't do it alone. I know that now. Mexico is too big."

Turning away, Jacob walked to the edge of the cliff. "And you would still go on even if it means your family may die?"

The boy took a deep breath and slowly came to Jacob's side. "Yes, Father. It's the right thing. You can't look at the price when deciding if something is right. You taught me that."

Daniel edged a little closer. "So I will fight for what I know is right...even if I must fight you my father."

Jacob whirled around and gathered his son in his arms, hugging him so tight he could hardly breathe. "Damn it, boy. You put me in a fix. You want me to stand by you, but will you stand by me?"

Daniel buried his head into the man's shoulder, accepting his love. "Yes, Father. I will always stand by you."

"Don't make a promise you can't keep."

Sniffing, the boy hurriedly wiped his eyes. "Father, if you were to jump off this cliff, I would follow."

A sarcastic chuckle escaped Jacob's lips. "You won't get off that easy."

Stepping apart, Jacob grasped Daniel by his shoulders. "Son, you need to hear me. I made a deal with the soldiers. Nah-kah-yen's life for yours."

Daniel screamed. "NO! You can't do that."

Jacob took the boy's face in his hand. "It's done...We've both done something we shouldn't have done, and now can't be undone." He pulled his son back into his arms. "But we must find a way."

When Jacob and the boy returned, everyone was waiting, even Nah-kah-yen. Mea-a-ha saw her husband's eyes narrow at the sight of the warrior. She hurried between them. Jacob reached down, and picking her up by the waist, he set her aside. "Woman, you are developing a bad habit of getting in my way."

He turned to the warrior. "I ought to kill you where you stand."

Nah-kah-yen rubbed his jaw. "I do not blame you, Black Gringo. But you would have done the same thing for little Mea-a-ha that I have tried to do for my woman."

Jacob stepped towards him, his fist clenched. "That's one of the reasons you are still alive." The big man looked ready to kill. "...but if you ever come back to the Hollow, I'll bury you under my doorstep."

Jacob turned and faced the small group of misfits. He shook his head. There were Indians, Mexicans, coloreds, and gringos. Before him stood warriors, soldiers, and fools without a clue, but somehow they had become kindred souls, hell-bent on disaster. He knew he must find a way to protect them against their own hearts.

Filling his lungs, Jacob decided he would try one last time to change their minds. "Going to keep this short. We ain't got time to cry it out." He thumbed over his shoulder at the warrior. "Me and the Indian are going after Mary Lost Pony."

Nah-kah-yen gave a start. There was a sudden clamor of voices, but Jacob raised his hand. "This goes for all of you." He looked to his old friend. "You too, Jube. Turn around and go home...It's a fool's errand; we won't be coming back."

Jacob turned to his boy, his face heavy with pain. "Daniel...Son. Will you go home? Take your sister?"

The boy shook his head and whispered. "No, Father, I go with you."

Jacob grimaced, but pushed his emotions down into his chest. "So be it."

He had tried and failed. Slowly he turned to the others. "Short of killing the boy, I can't stop him. But the rest of you got no business here. Go home."

The big man lowered his sad eyes to his young bride. "My wife, there is no time for tenderness. You can only get in the way. From here on out you'd be safer traveling back alone than continuing on. I tell you this, knowing you are going to ignore me, but know that hell has a place for women who disobey their husbands. Soon, you are going to regret your insolence."

The Indian girl took her husband's hand and held it to her breast. "I do not know this word 'in-so-lence,' but I will disobey you, because my heart rides with you. I am sorry for being a woman, and I will try not to get in the way. But I am not a gringo, and Apache women follow their men."

Jacob took the delicate girl in his arms. "I hope the Hollow will make some decent family a good home."

Leaving the couple to their embrace, Jube stepped towards the Mexican boys. He was their foreman on the Rincon ranch. Though he had never spoken of it, he had come because he felt it was his duty to protect them, even from themselves. Still, the old soldier knew that for boys to become men, their hearts must be tempered by fire, and they must be free to choose the flames. He would leave it up to them. "Is you turnin' back or is you as foolish as the Apache kid?"

Roberto gripped his rifle. "Maybe foolish, but we've come together, and we'll stay together. That's what friends do."

Juan rose to his full height. "We stand."

Nah-kah-yen watched, deeply moved by the boys' bravery. After the violent night they'd endured, they were still willing to die for his family. Unsure what to say, he came silently to their side. Without warning, Jube doubled his fist and threw a right hook that knocked the warrior to the ground. Mea-a-ha screamed in disbelief. "Jube!"

The buffalo soldier stood spread-legged over the stunned Indian and thrust an angry finger. "That's for Ol' Zeke. You killed a good friend of mine. He didn't deserve ta' die. N' neither do these boys, so ya' thank 'em for what they's about to do."

Having said his piece, Jube stretched out his hand to the Apache. "If you still want my help, say so, else wise' I'm a headin' home. Gots' a woman of my own."

Nah-kah-yen wiped the blood from his lip and accepted Jube's hand. As the soldier lifted him to his feet, the warrior suddenly drove his head hard into Jube's chin, knocking the big man back several feet. He squared with him. "My people didn't deserve to die. Some by your hand, Black man." Nah-kah-yen's voice shook with pain. "...but if you offer it now to save my Mary, then the blood that stains us both may find some forgiveness. I thank the boys...and I ask for your help."

Mea-a-ha pushed forward and slapped Jube's arm. "Is there so little death on this trail that we must fight each other?"

Jube backed away from the little Apache. "We ain't fighten'; jes' clearin' the air."

Jacob pulled the Indian girl back into his arms and turned to the two young men who had yet to make their decision. Time was short. "Mason, Kane, this isn't your fight; if you ride out, no one will think the less of you."

Hesitantly, the young lieutenant stepped forward and ran his fingers through his sandy blond hair. "Until this morning, I've never seen battle or killed another man." Mason fell silent, trying to come to grips with what had happened and what it all meant. "My father sent me on this errand because he has no faith in me."

His voice breaking, he took a needed breath, but it didn't help. "No matter how pointless, this is my first command. If I turn back now, I prove the pompous son-of-a-bitch right."

Swelling with resolve, Mason faced Jacob. "I know it's a fool's errand, Sir, but that doesn't make it wrong. I'm going on."

His decision made, the courageous young officer came to attention and turned to the warrior. "Nah-kah-yen. Despite my lack of a uniform, I am a soldier. My name is Lieutenant Mason Aaron McCrae, U.S. Cavalry. I've been ordered to arrest you and take you back to Fort Cummings to be hung for the murder of Private Ezekiel Potter." He let his words sink in. "I have no authority on this side of the border, but if we survive and make our way back to the United States, Jacob is charged with turning you over to me. Once on American soil, I will do my duty."

Mason softened his stand. "Until then, I will make what amends I can by offering you my help in rescuing your wife and son. Hopefully you will die knowing they are free."

The warrior stared at the officer in disbelief, then turned to Jacob. "You will hand me over to this soldier?"

Jacob made no apologies. "I traded you for my son."

Nah-kah-yen shook his head. The irony was not lost on him. "My life buys two sons." He raised his weary eyes to the big man. "Tell me, Black Gringo, what price will you pay?"

Jacob pulled on his glove and turned away. "Your son will remember you kindly." He glanced at Mea-a-ha. "And so will your squaw."

The men saddled the horses and packed the supplies. Mea-a-ha stared off the edge of the cliff, looking across the strange land. There had to be a right in all that was wrong, but she couldn't see it.

The Indian girl wished she was a bird. She would take wing and leave this horrible place. Her husband had yielded to her berating. He would go on, but his heart had grown cold.

A faint rustling rose in the dry grass. Mea-a-ha kept her eyes fixed on the distance. "My brother, you have come to talk?"

Daniel stepped beside his sister and took her hand. "Father said what is done, can't be undone, but we must find a way."

A deep sadness labored the girl's fragile voice. "Do you think there is a way, little brother?"

The boy shrugged his shoulders. "He wouldn't lead us to our deaths. Would he?"

Mea-a-ha stepped closer to the edge. "No; it is we who have led him."

A breeze whispered up the cliff, chilling the boy's moist cheek. "Father is going on, to stand by me. And when he turns Nah-kah-yen over to the soldier to be killed, I am supposed to stand by him." The boy hid his eyes. "Only it will never happen because we will all be dead. It is my fault."

Mea-a-ha leaned her head on Daniel's arm. "It is both our faults. Our hearts are the same. Maybe we have traded our small family for one that cannot be saved."

It was time to ride. In the little time they had, and in their own way, the nine companions each did what they could to accept their inevitable fate. One by one they walked their horses into a circle. If Jacob was right, from here on, it would be as much about survival as a rescue.

Lost in her own worries, Mea-a-ha had forgotten about the man who wrote books. He stood alone, looking sick. Going to his side, she smiled softly and rubbed his arm.

Kane lifted his troubled eyes to the Indian girl and gratefully accepted her comfort. With an angel's touch, she had lifted a great weight from his heart. The writer breathed for what felt like the first time.

Rescued from his fears, Kane laid the back of his finger against her cheek. Maybe there was magic in this mysterious race of people, or maybe it was just in this Indian girl alone. Still she calmed his mind, allowing him see things clearly.

Jacob led his horse in close. "Well, Kane, everyone has had their say but you."

The slender man adjusted his coat, and throwing his shoulders back, did his best to stand tall. His show of courage was more for the girl than for himself. She believed in him even though she knew his heart. Kane's eyes scanned his companions then fell on the man he deemed a hero. "Mr. Keever, I came on this adventure to find something in me that I fear isn't there. I haven't found it yet."

Facing the group, his voice shook. "I do not know Nah-kah-yen's family, and I will not pretend to care. I am not as noble as the rest of you. What I do, I do for myself, but I must follow the damned or die."

The forlorn writer took one last glance at the Indian girl, then climbed into his saddle. "I've penned in my book, *The Mimbre Riders*, and listed my name among the brave few. Jacob, I promised you that this time I'd write the truth. No matter what happens, I am going to see it through."

Turning his horse, Kane headed down the trail. Mea-a-ha stepped away from her husband and watched the sad man ride away.

Jube shrugged and mounted up. "Well, that makes it unanimous. We is all stupid."

Chapter -11-
Coming of the Riders

Nah-kah-yen galloped his pony alongside Jacob and the officer McCrae. "We would not be in such great danger, Black Gringo, if you would have helped me hunt down the Terahumara vermin this morning, instead of throwing your big fist."

The Indian rubbed his bruised jaw while brandishing a reproachful smile.

"Perhaps you're right." Jacob raised a sardonic eye to the warrior. "But this morning, I was planning on getting my boy and going home. Knocking you on your sorry ass was just an added pleasure."

The Indian let the insult pass, and taunted the young lieutenant instead. "The scalp hunters will bring the Mexican soldiers. When they find you are a Gringo, officer, they will peel your skin and burn you alive."

McCrae smiled. "I'm sure that will give you comfort, while they are cutting the flesh from your skull so they can sell your scalp."

Erupting into a hearty laugh, Nah-kah-yen rode away.

Mason turned to Jacob. "Is it the Mexican army you are worried about?"

The big man headed his horse into a stony wash between a stand of tall cactus. "The Mexican army, the vaqueros, the Terahumara, scalpers. There are plenty of ways to die. Whoever comes, knows the land, and we don't. All told, we have eight guns. No matter how it plays out, we're on the losing end of the bullet. Still, Nah-kah-yen is right. The Mexican army is vast, and they are looking for vengeance over losing to the Americans. If it were just the scalpers or the Terahumaria, they might let us pass, but the army won't."

The trail dropped over a small crumbling bank, then leveled out. The big man continued. "If history records this moment, it will say that in a despicable act, Lieutenant Mason Aaron McCrae, of the U.S. Army, led a detachment of buffalo soldiers deep into Mexico, attacking an innocent rancher without provocation." Jacob raised his brow. "Remember, history is written by the victors."

Mason swallowed. "I hadn't considered that. So I am facing not only death, but dishonor."

"Hell, you will probably be court-marshaled posthumously."

Reaching into his cartridge belt, Jacob pulled out a bullet and stuffed it into the officer's vest pocket. "Keep that one for yourself. It won't do much for your honor, but it might save you from seeing your intestines tied to a fast horse."

Mason patted his vest. "And what of you, Sergeant Jacob Keever? They will have less trouble mistaking you as a buffalo soldier."

Glancing over his shoulder, Jacob looked remorsefully at the Indian girl riding beside her brother. "I have three bullets set aside. After the first two, the third will be welcomed."

As the sun moved across the sky, the trail wore on with little change, matching the riders' disposition. It's hard to be at ease when a day starts with killing. No matter how far they rode from that rocky hillock, the smell of death was never far from their thoughts. Mea-a-ha prodded forward to be with Kane, and Daniel dropped back to ride with his friends.

Juan was glad he did. "I think I winged one." The boy looked to his friend. "I mean this morning, when we rode after the scalpers. I saw a hole appear in a scalper's sleeve. Maybe some blood."

It was important to the boy. Juan looked ahead at the stranger riding next to Mea-a-ha. He didn't want to be like the nervous man, running scared, riding with women.

Juan had not met the measure of his Apache friend, but this day brought him closer. He had fought in battle, and he had fired his first real shot.

His nerves still unsettled, the Mexican boy needed to talk. "Wasn't it amazing how your pa figured out what we done, then rode all the way from the Hollow and found us in the nick of time?"

The Indian boy nodded. "It was like he knew right where we would be."

"He did." Daniel and Juan looked to Roberto in surprise. The tall boy repeated himself. "He did. When I couldn't talk you donkey brains out of going, I left a note for Jube, and another with the hermit. When Nah-kah-yen thought I was lagging back because I had no heart, I was marking the trail. Your pa is a good tracker, and when he found the scalper's hoofprints, he just waited until sunrise to mount his attack. Pretty smart."

Juan nearly burst. "You betrayed us."

"I saved your scrawny necks. Maybe the next word out of your stupid mouth should be thank you."

The smaller boy turned to Daniel, but the Indian shrugged. He was just happy to have his father. Juan sneered at Roberto. "You saved our necks, but you put one over on us, so you can't expect us to be all giddy. If we make it back home, then you saved our lives, but until then you are a low-down, side-winding snake."

****

Three horses pulled to a breathless stop atop the low ridge. Snow Raven eagerly pawed the earth and shook his shiny mane in the afternoon sun. Beside the boy warrior, Nah-kah-yen and Mea-a-ha sat their painted ponies. Three Apaches, last of the Mimbres. In their own tongue, they were the Chíhéne. With solemn reverence, their hearts beat as one.

Ahead, rose the towering spires of Tres Castillos. At the base of these desolate stones, the Mimbres had met their doom. The great Chief Victorio, yearning for his people to be free had fled with hundreds of warriors, squaws and children to this desolate land. Only seventeen managed to flee the carnage of that dreadful night only months ago, and even now the American and Mexican armies hunted them to extinction.

Mea-a-ha's breath caught in her throat. Had it not been for the chance meeting with the buffalo soldier, she too would lay among the dead. Reaching out her hands to the warriors beside her, she bowed her head, letting her long black hair hide her tears.

Behind them, Jacob brought the riders to a stop in respect for their grief. The brave girl was full-blooded Apache. They were the warrior race who had defied the U.S. Army longer than any other band of Indians. Their courage had cost them dearly. Here beneath the spires, Jacob Keever, former soldier, finally understood how much they had lost.

Lifting her mournful eyes, Mea-a-ha turned her pony and rode back to her husband. There was too much sadness to speak. She reached out, and he took her into his saddle. The little Apache would come into the valley of the dead in the safety of his arms. Mason snatched up her reins, and the silent rescuers moved on.

A small fire was built in the shelter of the rocks, not far from the lake. It was set back so that an enemy would have to be right on them before being seen. The Mexican boys stood guard, knowing their Indian friends needed time to mourn.

Mea-a-ha and Daniel walked the lonely shores with Nah-kah-yen.

Gesturing without words, the warrior pointed to the charred earth where the Mexican soldiers had piled their people like so many cords of wood and burned them. Mea-a-ha leaned her head on her brother's shoulder and slipped her arm into his.

Here the Mimbres had their last stand as a free people. Tears of great loss rolled down the Indian girl's soft cheeks, comforting the two warriors beside her. It brought them closer.

Mea-a-ha looked down. The dark ashes of her tribe clung to her moccasins. Were her people reaching to her even in death? Closing her eyes, time faded. A sudden gust of wind cooled the air. Mea-a-ha could hear the deadly reports of the rifles and the helpless screams of those about to die as though she were among them. Though it was daylight, she was standing in darkness; the dreadful moon telling overhead. Silhouettes of darting figures crashed and crumpled to the ground, trampled by horses. Babies lay in the dust like shattered dolls. She could bear no more.

Dropping to her knees, the Indian girl took the ashes in her hands and clenched them to her breast. In a trembling breath she whispered. "Be at peace. I will hold you in my heart forever."

The warriors knelt by the girl's side and in turn reverently took up the ashes. Nah-kah-yen lifted his hands above his head and chanted. It was a song of life and death. All that was left of the Chíhéne slipped through his fingers, vanishing like smoke. Slowly he stood and danced in a circle, chanting ever softly until his hands were empty. "Our people are of the earth and now they have returned. They are beyond pain. We who live envy them."

Many sad stories had ended here. Some were lost, yet some were known. As they walked, Nah-kah-yen occasionally paused, remembering someone he'd found lying in a certain spot. Braving his sorrow, he would whisper their name.

To the Gringos, they were wild savages, deserving no more consideration than a gutted deer, but to Mea-a-ha, the dead were family and dear friends who would be grieved.

Coming to the clearing where Nah-kah-yen had entered the valley on that fateful night, he turned aside and followed his trail up the side of the mountain. Mea-a-ha patted Daniel on the shoulder. "Go with him. It is not a time to be alone."

She watched her brother disappear into the high rocks. Left with her thoughts, Mea-a-ha continued on down the stony shore in quiet reflection. It was quiet; not the caw of a bird or the whisper of the wind. For a brief moment, the world had paused in remembrance of its lost children. The Apache girl lifted her head to the dying sun in gratitude.

In the distance Mea-a-ha could see Kane coming towards her. She stopped and waited.

When the writer drew near, he slowed. "I don't mean to intrude, but if it is okay, there is so much I wish to know."

He had expected to see grief in the girl's dark eyes. Instead he saw peace. Kane sighed, wishing he could face life with such courage. "I worried you would be in tears."

Mea-a-ha moved closer, and they slowly walked side by side. "My people came here with hope. They perished. It is sad. Now it is for the few of us who remain to carry them in our hearts so that they live on in some way. It is a great honor they have given us."

Kane sidestepped a stone, and his hand brushed Mea-a-ha's. She innocently slipped her hand into his. The Apache girl's skin was soft and warm. Her touch calmed his nerves, but his pulse raced. "Mea-a-ha, I don't know how you do it."

She wrinkled her nose. "Do what?"

"Survive all this tragedy. I couldn't."

Mea-a-ha leaned her head to the side and pulled her long, dark hair away from her enchanting eyes. "We face death as we face life. It is one and the same. Hopefully, we faced life well."

She watched Kane quietly repeat her words to himself, then asked, "Are you going to write that in your book?"

Kane smiled and squeezed her hand. "Probably, but I was remembering it for myself." He stopped and turned towards her. "I came on this adventure in desperation, hoping to fight wild Indians, instead I meet you. The littlest savage." He grinned. "You have opened my eyes. Thank you, Mea-a-ha. I no longer wish to fight Apaches. In fact, there is one I think I would die for."

Mea-a-ha gave a nervous smile and slipped her hand from his. "Let's not talk of death." She turned and headed back the way they had come. "…You came on this adventure, as you call it, to find courage. You would find it without me. The courage is in you. It only needs to be awakened."

The writer ambled on, quietly thinking. "Perhaps, but is it not better to have it awakened by a beautiful maiden instead of a warrior's lance?"

Mea-a-ha stopped and stared up at the handsome young man. "Kane. Both have dangers. Be careful with your words."

Lowering his head, Kane continued on. "Forgive my boldness. I mean no disrespect. But please try to understand; you have changed my life. It is not easy to pretend you don't matter."

The girl smiled, accepting his compliment. As they strolled down the shore, their hands once more found each other. Mea-a-ha didn't mind. This man called Kane was kind and gentle. His words were thoughtful; so unlike the coarse soldiers that had been her only experience in the civilized world. Amid the carnage, she found comfort in his presence.

"Mea-a-ha." Kane gave a shy whimsical grin. "Are all Apache women as gentle as you?"

The Indian girl laughed. "Are all Gringos so bold?"

"Well, you are my first Indian." He chuckled. "You know what I mean."

"Maybe so. It is sad that people can share the same land and never know each other."

The little savage and the writer of books bumped shoulders as they meandered in thought. Each touch brought them closer. The girl tossed back her hair. "I do not know if I am different from other Apaches. I am simply Mea-a-ha."

As dusk fell, Jube did his best to make a meal of beans and salted meat. When he finally got it going, Mea-a-ha walked into the circle of stones with the writer not far behind. "I will do that." She knelt and took the wooden spoon from Jube's hand. After stirring the pot, she frowned. "Are you cooking beans and twigs?"

Jube grinned. "They just sort of fall in. Calls it a taste of the land."

As the evening sky turned to lavender, the men finished brushing down the horses and gathered around. Nah-kah-yen was the last to return. In his hands he tenderly held a broken necklace he'd found among the stones. He knew the young Apache girl who had worn it. She had a name, too—Chenleh.

When Mea-a-ha handed him his plate, he ate for some time in quiet thought, but the warrior was full of memories, and finally he began to tell the stories of his people. Kane pulled his journal from his pocket and wrote. His interest made the Apache happy. With his eyes shining, Nah-kah-yen told of great battles and their harrowing escapes. His arms flung wide, soon he was moving about, acting out the stories in the fashion he'd learned around the campfires of his youth. He'd often look to the writer, making sure the white man was still scribbling in his book that remembers.

As Nah-kah-yen danced, Mea-a-ha would interject with the names of Indians who had played their small part, and her memories of them. He spoke with pride of great warriors. She told of women—Gouyen, Lozen—and the children. In the midst of death, there was healing.

Lieutenant McCrae listened to Nah-kah-yen as he told of great deeds and families lost. Here was a man full of life, yet condemned to die. The young officer's duty seemed so clear a day ago, but now... He tried not to think about it, wanting instead to lose himself in the wonderful tales and forget the part he was doomed to play.

At last the Indian's stories finally brought them back to Tres Castillos. Reliving good memories had improved their moods, though this mountain held a wound that would never heal.

Nah-kah-yen pressed his hands to his knees and sat up. He gestured to Daniel. "If this little warrior had been here, it might have been different that night. He fights like the brothers of Goyaałé. Kill many scalp hunters."

Jacob tensed and looked at the boy hiding in the shadows. "I heard nothing of this."

Jube set his plate aside and cleared his throat. "When Mason n' me drug the bodies off the field, we found nine more, some stiff from the night before." The officer nodded in agreement.

"Nine!" Nah-kah-yen looked surprised. "Nine, I only kill two. Little warrior, maybe you shoot better than you count."

A gasp of fright escaped Mea-a-ha's lips. "Daniel! Seven men?"

Every eye turned to the young Apache. Daniel slid farther into the darkness. "Maybe."

Mea-a-ha clutched her heart. "Oh, Daniel."

The boy defended himself, sputtering his words. "Well, Father says you never give up. I did what had to be done."

Rising to his feet, Jacob went to his son. "That I did, little Buck, but each bullet kills twice. We die a little, too. Are you okay?"

Daniel leaned towards the big man. In his father's arms he could be a child again, yet a cold was growing inside his chest. Death was upon him. He had not grieved for the slain as he had done the first time, and he felt shame. "I'm fine." The boy pulled away.

By the light of the fire, Jacob cleaned and oiled his prized Winchester carbine, his deadly Springfield, and his Army Colt. As the flames burned low, the other men saw his wisdom and did the same. The looming spires of Tres Castillos were a reminder that death was near. Life was a fleeting moment, not a promise of endless years. Every breath had to be earned. The Mimbres had learned this the hard way.

Leaning against a shaggy tree, the young Apache girl watched the men readying for battle. They were in it now. When Nah-kah-yen had come to the Hollow, she never considered what rescuing her friend really meant. Jacob tried to warn her, but she didn't listen, and everything he said about killing had come true. The next time it might be one of these brave men who would die. They were her friends and her world. It terrified her. Jacob's words echoed in her mind: 'You will be in the way.' She was a woman, and if fighting started, she would endanger those she loved. Her stomach knotted. Mea-a-ha edged closer to her husband. Reaching out a timid hand, she touched his arm. "Is there something I can do?"

Jacob shoved another cartridge into the Colt and spun the cylinder. Without looking up, his voice rang cold. "Nothing you can do. If battle comes…I want you to stay close to Kane. Do you hear?"

"Kane?" Mea-a-ha was shocked.

"Can't have you underfoot."

Mea-a-ha's breath caught in her throat. His words hurt. "But…"

"You will be safer if I'm free to fight...and Kane..." His words trailed away, lost in a sadness of his own.

Tugging tighter on his arm, she protested. "But I want to be with you."

Jacob holstered his gun and finally met her injured stare. "I want you to obey me this time, little one. You stay with Kane. Do you understand?"

Swallowing a lump in her throat, the girl nodded. "But..."

Jacob strained face looked as hard as old wood. "Do as you're told. Didn't want it to come to this, but killing's been done and more to come. I haven't got time for your tears."

Ending his scolding, Jacob turned away from the stricken girl and walked from the light. There were more urgent matters to tend to.

Left standing alone and shaken, Mea-a-ha fled into the seclusion of the tall rocks, leaving the light of the campfire behind. There she sobbed. Jacob had made her feel even more worthless. Why must he be so cold? Did she not ride beside the men, and cook their meals while they rested? Was that not enough? Did he expect her to fight like a man, too?

A hand softly touched her shoulder. "Are you okay?"

From out of the shadows, Kane came to the girl's side. "I saw you run away."

Mea-a-ha wiped her cheek, thankful for the dark. "Little bit not okay. It's just..." She gave an embarrassed glance, knowing she was hiding nothing. "Just sometimes I feel very small."

"Me, too."

Stifling a sudden giggle, Mea-a-ha turned towards the writer. "But you're a man."

Kane offered a sympathetic smile and caught both her hands. "Just saying I know how you feel."

The Indian girl's moist eyes lifted towards the writer's caring face. Before her stood a rare man who truly did understand the emotions of a woman. "Thank you...Jacob does not always have time for me...for my feelings. It hurts."

"One so pretty should not weep."

Mea-a-ha looked down, but she did not pull away. Right now she was grateful for his comfort. If nothing else, this tall stranger was honest and kind. She could trust him to speak the truth, yet temper it with compassion. Jacob spoke the truth, only his words laid her bare. He was used to barking orders at coarse soldiers, and he gave her no consideration for her being a woman.

When their closeness became awkward, Kane squeezed her hands, then released her and turned away. "The stars are so beautiful out here on the desert. I never get tired of gazing up at them. The evil we do will never tarnish their brilliance."

He stepped a little further into the night. "I think the stars make everyone feel small…but they also fill us with wonder. Beneath them there is no shame in being insignificant."

Mea-a-ha moved closer. "I do not know this word. 'In-sig-nif-i-cant."

Kane chuckled and once more took the girl's warm hand. "It is a big word that means small. I guess writers say silly things."

"I don't think you say silly things. Your words are beautiful. Most men do not talk of stars. Is there not courage in that?"

The writer's chest swelled. "Hey, I came to you cheer you up, little warrior."

Mea-a-ha's eyes glistened. "You did."

"Well, I hope you will consider me a friend, and if you ever feel small, know I am here. We will share a star together."

The Indian girl trembled and didn't know why. "My first white friend." She giggled again. "It is no in-sig-nif-i-cant thing. No?"

Pulling her closer, Kane laughed. "Yes. And you are my first Indian friend. Maybe there is hope for mankind yet."

When everyone had gathered around the campfire, Jacob stepped forward. His eyes caught the flickering light. "Five days in. Five days out." He let his words sink in. "It ain't going to be easy. If you believe we can ride through hell and come out the other side, well, then maybe there's hope."

He shifted his attention to Roberto and Juan. "Boys, your childhood has ended. You'll never get it back. You have come to war. If you think you need permission to kill, you've got it. In the days that follow, there will be blood on your hands, or your blood will surely be on someone else's. You decide."

The two boys swallowed and looked at each other with wide eyes, realizing the full meaning of what Jacob was telling them. He had given them the right to be judge and executioner—to take a human life. They were just sixteen, and his words held no compassion for their young age, only the cold promise of death.

Lastly, Jacob looked to his son. "Follow your instincts. They have served you well." In deliberation, the big man let his eyes trail across the worried faces. "Fear will kill you, so let it go. We've got a job to do; now let's get some sleep."

As Jacob walked from the circle, he once more leaned close to his son and lowered his voice. "Don't fret. There will be time for grieving when the butchery is done."

Daniel's throat tightened. His father understood what was tearing him apart. They had both lived by the gun. Perhaps he understood his father a little better now, too.

Jube doused the fire, and the nine companions buried themselves deep into the rocks. Jacob warned then that from here on out, they were to sleep in their clothes.

Making one last round, he was the last to crawl into his bedroll. Mea-a-ha snuggled against him. Jacob stroked his thumb across her cheek. She was crying.

For a moment the trail was forgotten. The bitter soldier pressed his lips to her ear. "Little One...I... I'm doing what I must. Just know I need you. Never doubt that."

Mea-a-ha wrapped her arms around his thick neck and warmed his lips with a kiss.   Something she had almost forgotten broke forth with new meaning. 'When darkness besets all, true love is a bond that cannot be broken.' On this trail, death might find them, but nothing would destroy their love.

She was not worthless. The Indian girl had her part to play. Her love for the buffalo soldier was more powerful than any gun. He needed her. Mea-a-ha closed her eyes. Surrounding her were eight brave men. They had courage. With Jacob to lead them, it would take an army to bring them down. She slept.

In the distance an owl hooted. Jacob opened his eyes.

Mason and Kane awoke with a start. A heavy hand pressed over their mouths. Jacob's deep voice whispered from the darkness. "They're here."

Both men slid silently from their bedding, eyes wide, searching the night.

The boys were roused, and the horses were quickly saddled. With hardly a sound, they hurried to make their escape.

Moving past each man, Jacob warned, "Follow in single file."

When he got to Kane, The soldier leaned close. "Writer, take care of her." He moved on.

The band of rescuers led their ponies beneath the starlight. Jacob knew war; whoever was out there was waiting for the moonlight. Already a dim glow outlined the stone towers. They had to move quickly. Seconds mattered.

On cat's feet, they silently wove through the labyrinth of rocks with a sixth sense. Pausing, Jacob looked back. He guessed they had come maybe a hundred yards. For the moment they had slipped the trap, but here the shelter of the rocks ended. If he pushed forward without knowing what lay ahead, he might deliver his trusting companions into the hands of the enemy. If he waited, the moon would betray them. He passed the word back. "Mount up."

They would have to make a run for it and pay the devil's due. If the guns lay ahead, it would be a short ride.

The veteran soldier had battled his way out of many tight spots, but this was different. It was one thing to charge against enemy guns, cursing and laughing at death as bold men do, but now his delicate bride was by his side. His heart quickened. Fear is an unwelcome companion that causes a man to hesitate when a mere second is all that hangs between life and death.

The moment had come to challenge the unknown. If he were wrong, the Apache girl he loved more than life itself would fall in a hail of lead. Jacob hesitated. He couldn't bring himself to give the call. His mind tormented, "Fool! Do something!"

Uncertain, his eyes, and ears strained against the night a moment longer.

"Father." Jacob gave a start. Daniel was by his side. "You told me to trust my instincts. Be ready to ride."

The big man's heart knotted in his chest. "Daniel. No!"

He heard the boy's pistol slip from his holster and the quiet slap of his reins. The great horse shot through the darkness like a phantom light. A faint shimmer on his spotted coat marked his passing, and then he vanished. Beyond the clearing were rocks unseen, known only by memory. In a heartbeat, Daniel was upon them, drawing the enemy out. Without warning, the boy's deadly pistol flashed to the left and the right. Jacob heard Mea-a-ha swallow a cry. Hell opened its gates.

Flames burst in the night, illuminating thick, black curls of smoke. Whoever was out there had answered the boy's challenge. A thundering wall of fire rose from straight ahead and to the left, but to the right there was darkness, and with it a path to freedom.

Jacob kicked the Buckskin hard. "RIDE!" The band of rescuers charged forward as a multitude of guns belched like angry cannons. Lost in the maelstrom, the Mimbre Riders made their escape.

With keener sight than man, the horses found their way through a low outcropping of rocks while behind them the deadly roar filled every inch of breathable air.

As yet, no bullets had cut their path. The attackers were thrown into chaos by a demon horseman racing down their line spending every bullet. Daniel broke through their ranks, drawing fire in the opposite direction. The enemy now thought they were being attacked from the rear. They turned their guns on themselves.

As the moon burst over the spires of Tres Castillos, Jacob led his small band down the shore of the black lake. Their hearts prayed they had slipped the trap, but the night has eyes. A watchful scout at the edge of the battle caught their flight. Shouting and screaming, swarms of riders took up the chase.

Duty-bound to hold the rear, Jube turned and laid down a volley to slow the enemy. He sent his bullets and curses into the thundering hoard. As he fired his last round, the young cavalry officer appeared by his side, valiantly adding his gun to the fray. The bold lieutenant held his pistol steady at arm's length and coolly hammered every round. If Mason had fear, he didn't show it. The rest of the companions rushed on, hoping to extend their lead. Off the steps of the mountain and into the empty desert they charged.

Daniel had bought them precious moments that would not be squandered. Jacob cursed the boy for his foolish courage and whipped his horse to a greater speed.

In the distant rocks, shots still rang, only fewer now. The enemy had realized they had been tricked. Scrambling to their horses, the attackers hurried to take up the chase, but an army that size needed time to regroup.

Jacob thought about this. It was a large, organized assault. Their ranks fired in unison from a straight line. He had no doubt it was the Mexican army. To Tres Castillos, the soldiers had returned. Once more they faced the Mimbre, only this time it was a lone boy.

The big man gritted his teeth and swore to himself. If Daniel fell, he would never leave Mexico. His last breath and bullet would be spent settling the score.

At a thousand yards from the skirmish, Jacob pulled to a halt and abruptly turned. From his second scabbard, he dispatched his Army Springfield 45/70 and fired several rounds into the distance. Jube did the same. No Mexican rifle could carry so far, and Jacob wanted to remind them of it. They would not have it all their way.

"Ride."

Mea-a-ha pleaded. "Where's Daniel?"

Jacob ignored her. "Ride! Damn it."

The girl screamed. "No! You can't leave him." The big man grabbed the reins from her hands, and the band tore into the night.

Chapter -12-
Apache Cunning

The half-moon filtering through the cold haze made its solemn journey across the desert sky. Casting furtive glances over their shoulders, the rescuers pushed on. A mile behind them a great host rolled like dark water over the barren earth.

Their solitary trek to rescue the Mimbre women had become a desperate escape. Jacob pulled to a stop and waited for his companions to gather around. His hard, chiseled face in the silver light glinted like black steel. "Nah-kah-yen, stay here and buy us some time. Everyone one else, dismount. We will walk for awhile to save our horses. It's going to be a long night."

Climbing from the Buckskin, Jacob turned and lifted Mea-a-ha to the ground. She fell into his arms and sobbed. "Daniel."

The big man did not comfort her; they had to move quickly. Taking the girl's hand, he turned and marched forward. Her weary legs did their best to keep pace.

The ground beneath their feet was hard with a thin layer of dust that swirled and caught the pale light. Kane noticed it. Funny, how in the midst of a nightmare, something so trivial as dirt would register in the human mind. If he survived, he would always remember it as Mexico.

Ahead of him, the Indian girl lifted her dress in her small brown hand and took quick steps, trying to stay with her husband. Somewhere on the trail, she had traded her store-bought shoes for the soft doeskin moccasins of her people. Her tiny feet scurrying next to Jacob's long strides in his heavy leather boots made her look childlike. All these things passed through the writer's mind.

As they walked, Kane made note of his companions and what he might write about them. There was Jacob, cold and hard; Jube, strong as a bull; and McCrae, trying to do what was right while knowing it was wrong. Each had his own story.

The writer noted them all, yet his eyes kept drifting back to the beautiful Apache. There was a magic in her that seemed to come from the land. She was a part of it, and could not be separated from it. This captivating girl was the color of the earth, and warm as the desert breeze. Small and unarmed, she had a strength that endured. If death were to take them this night, he somehow knew that she would be the last to fall.

As eloquent as he was, her force wasn't something he could put in words, and he struggled with it. Water flows while rock crumbles. Maybe that was it. She was soft and yielding. That was her magic.

The Indian maiden lifted her head and looked back, aware that he was watching her. Kane quickly lowered his eyes, but he knew his gaze would soon return to the beautiful savage.

The rescuers had walked in silence for several minutes when Nah-kah-yen's rifle suddenly awoke the night. Levering as fast as he could, the Apache set every round in flight. It was a great distance, but he knew that with so many of the enemy bunched together, his bullets would find their targets. In answer, a faint din rose and fell. Waiting a few minutes longer, the warrior raised his rifle and fired again before fleeing on his pony. Fearful of the Apache's sting, the soldiers would follow more slowly.

Another hour passed beneath the hated moon. Mea-a-ha was exhausted, but she had stayed up with her man. At the top of a ridge, Jacob called a halt. Mea-a-ha collapsed against him, breathing heavily. Mason pushed forward, gasping for air himself. "Sir, who's back there?"

Jacob smoothed the girl's hair. "Like I said before, you name it. The Mexican army, Terahumara scouts, and the last of the scalp hunters thrown in, just to keep things nasty." Jacob called to the Indian. "You got the closest look. How many do you think?"

"Sixty. Maybe more."

Dropping to one knee, Jacob motioned for everyone to gather around. "Don't need to tell any of you that if it comes to a fight, we ain't going to win. Thanks to Nah-kah-yen, we've increased our lead by a couple miles. But if we continue on to the fat Mexican's ranch to rescue the Mimbre women, we will be up to our asses in vaqueros and soldiers."

The big man took off his hat and let it dangle on the tips of his fingers. In the moonlight he could see the worry carved on the warrior's face. "Don't fret. We made our decision and we ain't giving up."

Jacob turned to the others. "...So we will learn from the Apache. 'If you can't beat em', make 'em look stupid.'"

Jacob filled his lungs with a deep breath. "We have some advantages. They don't know who we are, and they don't know our plans. So what we are going to do is lead them away from the ranch, heading east to the Rio Grande. Then we will turn north along the river. They will think we are heading home like any sensible people would do, but being the fools we are, we will double back and make a mad dash to the Mexican's ranch and rescue the women. The soldier will be to the east, and we should have a clear shot home."

Jacob rose from the dirt and faced his companions. "If you think that's a good plan, its cuz' you don't know any better. I told you before; we ain't getting out of this. All I'm trying to do is keep my promises and live one more day. Anybody got a better idea, say it now."

Eyes heavy with exhaustion darted uncomfortably, but no one spoke. Jacob had proclaimed their doom. All they could do was see it to the end.

Nah-kah-yen finally stepped forward. "It is a good way to die." He slapped Jacob on the shoulder and grinned. "Sad. There will be no one to remember what a brave ride we made."

Jacob forced his hat down over his eyes. "Any ideas, Injun?"

The warrior nodded. "As you say. Keep learning from the Apache. You soldiers wonder how Indians disappear. Tonight we show the Mexicans. They are looking for many, so they will be blind to a few." Nah-kah-yen pointed to the east. "From this ridge, many arroyos. We break up. I take the boys as before. The black soldier with the big fist, he knows how to fight. Let him take the young Gringos. You Jacob, take your woman, we go many directions, meet later."

Jacob turned to his friend. "Jube. What do you think?"

The buffalo soldier grinned. "Hate breaking up our cozy bunch-o-friends, but it makes sense. We will be harder ta' follow. Fewer tracks, it divides the enemy n' disrupts their communication. Yes, sir. It should slow 'em down a might. All we's' gots' ta' do is not get lost."

Jacob nodded. "We'll keep the distance short, head due east once we leave the arroyos, and meet up noon tomorrow out on the desert. So let's get to it."

As Jube mounted up, he chuckled to Kane. "Well, writer, ya' got yo' story n' then some, so it ain't been a total waste. Maybe one of them Mexicans will publish it for ya'. The Mimbre Riders, by Pedro Sanchez." Jube laughed again and slapped his reins.

Nah-kah-yen took the arroyo to the north, Jube to the south, and Jacob headed up the middle. Each arroyo was like a furrow in the earth, twisting and meandering out of the low foothills. Eventually they would peter out on the hard-baked desert floor.

The Indian girl watched uncomfortably as the night swallowed her companions. There was no time for goodbyes.

Jube and Jacob had both taken one of the packhorses. Kane's generosity had given them ample supplies and ammunition. When it came to it, there would be one hell of a last defense.

A few hours were left before sunrise. They would make good time while the army tried to figure out what happened. Jacob kept high on the east ridge, knowing their tracks would stay in shadow longer there. Then, when it came, the blinding morning sun would in turn hide their trail as well. It wasn't much, but every trick would add to their lead.

For several hours they rode at a fast gait. The soft thud of the pony's hooves on the dusty, clay earth was the only sound save for a distant coyote.

Mea-a-ha turned her thoughts to her husband. She knew he could head out alone and escape, but he was not that kind of man. It saddened her. This was not his fight. She and Daniel had forced it on him. 'Daniel.' She nearly wept.

When the hill widened, Mea-a-ha rode to her husband's side. "Jacob..."

"Mea-a-ha I don't know any more than you. He could be alive, injured or..." The big man's thoughts echoed her own.

"Jacob, if he is okay, will he be able to follow us?" Her voice was small and fearful.

The big man sighed. "Yes, but I wish he couldn't, then maybe he'd go home."

It was a nice thought. 'Home.'

"Jacob?"

"What?"

"I'm sorry."

Pulling to a stop, Jacob leaned in his saddle and touched a finger to the Apache girl's cheek. "It's not important anymore." He let his hand fall away, but Mea-a-ha caught it and held on as they rode in silence. She remembered an old saying; 'When death is near, love outshines gold.' Mea-a-ha felt this way now.

"Jacob."

Slowing the horses, the soldier looked back over the trail they had traversed. No one was following. There was time to listen. "What, little Apache?"

"Kane is a good man."

Jacob searched his wife's face, then prodded his pony forward. "I know."

Mea-a-ha let her eyes drift to the moon. "He likes me...much."

"I know." Jacob's answer lingered. "...and you like him."

Lowering her head, Mea-a-ha spoke softly. "Yes."

Bursting in sudden emotion, she gripped Jacob's arm. "Much, but a thousand Kanes could not steal me away from you. I am your woman, always and only. You must believe me."

"I was never worried."

"You are not mad that I enjoy this man's company?" She sounded like a child expecting to be scolded.

Cupping her worried face, Jacob leaned close. "Little Apache, we are banging on the gates of hell. I won't deny you a little comfort when life is so uncertain. You are new to the white man's world. There is so much for you to learn. Kane is a good man, and he can teach you things I can't. Take what you can from your friendship with him. I trust you. If I didn't, I wouldn't be here."

Faintly in the distance, a rifle shot echoed over the hills. Their conversation ended. A moment later a second shot followed by several more reports. They held their breath as each sharp crack slowly rumbled over the arroyos.

For a while there was silence, and then it started again. Jacob spoke quietly. "It's to the north. Sounds like Nah-kah-yen and the boys are in for it."

Climbing from his horse, Jacob stood on the ridge, listening intently. Mea-a-ha hurried to his side. She looked up at her husband, realizing that her soldier had understanding she didn't. "Jacob, tell what you hear."

He rested his hand on her shoulder and stared into the darkness. "Winchesters and Mexican muskets sound different. There are rapid bursts from the Winchesters, but the Mexicans are laying down more fire. It's my guess that a party of scouts, most likely Terahumara Indians, have caught up with Nah-kah-yen and the boys. Coming from behind, they will have high ground. I'd put their number at eight. If they were soldiers, there would be more shooting and the shots would be evenly spaced."

Nah-kah-yen cursed himself. He had stayed too low in the arroyo and now the enemy was upon him from both sides. For the moment he held the south rim, and the boys held the north.

The Terahumara were too close for them to bolt and run. It was the mountain Indians; he knew that. They often scouted for the Mexican army. He could see them in the moonlight. Rutaio was not among them, or there would be taunting. These warriors killed for profit, not for hate.

Nah-kah-yen fired again, then stuffed his hand into his leather pouch. He had spent precious ammunition keeping the army at bay earlier in the night. He hoped the boys had filled their saddlebags. Even if they had, it would do him little good now. Slipping past a jagged wall of rock protruding from the thorny cactus, he found shelter and slumped to the ground.

In the moonlight he could see Roberto fire three rapid shots. An Indian fell and rolled down the ridge. The tall Mexican boy did what he had to do and never flinched. Nah-kah-yen was sure this brown-skinned youth must have some Apache blood.

Suddenly, Juan firing his pistol wildly, charged across the arroyo on his pony like he had gone plum loco. For a moment he disappeared in the underbrush as bullets shattered branches and ricocheted off stones. Then just as suddenly, his Paint came charging up the steep slope at a full run. The boy fired twice more and jumped from his saddle. He was actually smiling. In his hand was a cartridge belt. "Roberto said you might need some ammunition."

The Indian shook his head. "You are foolish, little Mexican." Nah-kah-yen took the belt. "Foolish, but brave."

The warrior loaded his rifle and then quickly emptied it. The Terahumara would learn that one Apache was too many. Across the arroyo, Roberto fired again and slipped lower down the hill. He was pinned down. Nah-kah-yen turned to Juan. "I think we will end it here. It is no good running."

The warrior looked to the east. "Sun come soon. If we die, our souls will not get lost."

Juan stared anxiously up the hill. "Maybe we can beat them."

The Indian nodded. "Yes, we beat them. But the gunfire draws the soldiers. It is why the cowards have not rushed us. They wait."

Juan lowered his eyes. The long trail to this lonely arroyo in the wastelands of Mexico had started out as an exciting adventure. But it had changed, and so had he. The boy lifted his chin with new determination. The enemy would not take him easily.

Juan jumped to his feet and throwing the Winchester to his shoulder, sent several rounds screaming through the vanishing night. A rifle cracked from above. The boy went flying backwards to the ground. "I'm hit. I'm hit."

Nah-kah-yen fired in answer, then reached for the boy. Juan held his hand near his neck. He was bleeding above his collarbone. The warrior ripped a strip from the boy's shirt and pressed it to the wound. "You will live long enough to die, foolish one. Reload your gun."

The boy swore in Spanish, then broke into English. He fought back tears of frustration. "Damn it! I ain't killed no one yet, and I'm the first one shot. Ain't fair."

The Indian scouts saw the boy fall. They had driven Roberto into the bottom of the arroyo where he could no longer see. Emboldened, they rushed down the ridge, firing on Nah-kah-yen, going for position. With them came the first rays of the morning sun. There would be no more hiding.

The Apache warrior fired rapidly in multiple directions, trying to hold them back alone. Bullets started crashing all around them. It was no use. Nah-kah-yen stopped to reload.

A daring scout taking advantage of the moment, ran towards them, shooting and screaming. Before Nah-kah-yen could chamber a round, his attacker jumped onto a rock and threw his sights down on him. Nah-kah-yen franticly grabbed a stone, ready to throw, when suddenly the Terahumara's brains blew out through the front of his head. The scout crumpled forward, falling on top of him.

Juan pointed. "Look!" On a far ridge catching the first light, a dark figure knelt on one knee. The big man fired again. Another Indian tumbled into the gulch.

Juan jumped to his feet, cheering. He emptied his pistol at a brave closing in on Roberto. The Indian ducked the shots and scrambled away. Nah-kah-yen's hand pulled the young boy to the ground. "Fool. Do you have to be shot twice to learn?"

Jacob's heavy Springfield roared again. The Indians gave up, quickly retreating over the ridge. Nah-kah-yen slammed a bullet into the chamber and fired a parting shot. Another scout stumbled and fell.

Lying on the ground, Juan continued cheering. "Come back and fight, you cowards."

Hearing his friend's elation, Roberto poked his head from the brush in stunned surprise. Somehow they had won.

Minutes later, Jacob rode down the ridge. Mea-a-ha followed, towing the packhorse. The girl jumped from her pony and quickly dropped to her knees by Juan's side. "You are hurt, little Mexican." She immediately started mothering his wound. "Poor boy."

Juan nuzzled his head in her soft lap.

Looking up the hill, Nah-kah-yen frowned. "Three got away. Bring the rest."

Jacob shrugged. "I think the others already know."

Tearing a bandage into strips, Mea-a-ha scowled at the brave. "Too much noise. Not how Apaches disappear."

The warrior laughed. "It is this land. No good for Apaches."

Mea-a-ha turned her attention to the boy. "Are you in pain?"

Juan, looking close to death, moaned and nuzzled closer.

Gripping the pummel of his saddle, Jacob prodded. "We need to get moving now."

Mea-a-ha, lifting her eyes in distress, cradled the boy's head to her breast and protested. "The poor child is shot. He is too weak to move."

Nah-kah-yen shook his head and climbed onto his pony. "If you hold him to your breast, he will never move."

The girl looked to her husband for support. Jacob rolled his eyes. "I ain't no doctor, but the boy is grinnin' from ear to ear." He looked down at the Mexican. "Mount up, you little rascal. And find your own damn woman...or stand in line for mine."

Chapter -13-
Dust Clouds

Stunted mesquite trees dotted the flat, barren expanse as far as a man could see. Jube shaded his eyes and studied the sun, then turned to the writer. "About seven minutes after the hour, as close as I can figure." As the surprised writer checked his watch, Jube secretly slid his own back into his pocket. Kane looked up in amazement. "You are only off by a minute." The black soldier checked the sun again. "Nope, yo' watch is off by a minute."

Jube kicked his pony. "Bes' get ridin' n' keep n' eye to the north."

Far in the distance, a rounded knoll raised from the desert floor. A spire of crumbling rock beckoned like a flag. It was the only landmark. Jube headed towards it. The night had been uneventful. He hoped the day would be the same. Still, it concerned him. If they hadn't been followed, then the others had. Jacob was alone except for the girl. Nah-kah-yen had the two boys.

Jube knew that with Mason and Kane by his side, he stood the best chance of survival in a running battle with the Mexicans. McCrae could fight and hopefully the writer would find his courage when the time came; if not, then good riddance to him. At least they were three grown men, and people cry less over the death of a man.

Kane broke the long silence. "How are we going to find the others out here?"

The buffalo soldier shrugged. "Jacob said it weren't a good plan. Findin' each other is one of the kinks we gots ta' work out."

Jube let the young man chew on it for awhile. The writer was visibly upset by the obvious flaw.

Turning to other thoughts, the soldier cocked his head. "Saw ya writin' in that journal of yo's', most of the night. Gonna be some book?"

For a moment Kane was uncomfortable, and then suddenly he blurted out, "Yes. It is going to be some book. Everything I write this time will be honest and true …"

The writer realized he had become excited and took a breath to calm himself. "When I wrote 'The Hero of Apache Springs' about Jacob, I sat at a desk and tried to piece together things that others had told me. I tried hard, but it was only pieces, so I made up the parts I didn't know without having any idea how it really was. This time I am a part of it."

Jube shrugged. "Least ya' have the courage ta' make things right. Most men wouldn't. It speaks well of ya'."

Kane slowed his voice. "Thank you, Mr. Jackson. That's mighty kind. I'll tell it right this time. My own part is small, but there are plenty of heroes. And I will say that heroes are just everyday people who do the right thing even when it's the hardest thing to do. It will be a good book."

Studying the young man, Jube saw something he hadn't expected. Buried beneath the writer's fear was honor. There are different reasons why a man will shoulder a gun. If it came to it, Kane would fight.

The buffalo soldier broke into a grin. "Hope you write somthin' flowery about me. I gots' a little senorita back home, and seein' my name in print, well it can't do no harm. Plannin' on askin' her to marry me if we gets back."

Kane returned his smile. The writer had pages for all his brave companions, Jube among them, but there were more pages for the beautiful Apache girl. He dared not print everything he'd written about this gentle savage. He still called her 'savage' when he put pencil to paper. It was an endearing word, just for her. A word full of life that spoke of love and tragedy and something so rare that no other words he knew came close to describing her. She was Mea-a-ha the Savage.

The writer touched his hand to the journal in his vest pocket. Yes, he had written things about her that no one would ever know.

"Look!" McCrae pointed to a flash of light. It burst three times from the distant knoll and then stopped. Jube pulled a polished metal shaving mirror from his saddlebag. After rubbing it on his shirt, he flashed three times and waited. His signal was quickly answered. "Well, we is going to find out real quick if it's friend or foe." He kicked his horse forward and loosened his pistol in its holster.

Kane swallowed. "Isn't there any way of knowing?"

The soldier looked unconcerned. "Sure, there is. Ride behind me. An iffin' you see my brains explodin' all over the front of yo' horse, then it weren't Jacob, an' you might consider vacating this here desert."

Mason laughed. "Maybe I should ride behind Kane."

Jube gave an approving nod and continued his sage advice to the writer. "Kane, iffin' the lieutenant's brains get splattered all over yo' horses ass, consider it a sneak attack, and after informing me, we can both vacate this here desert."

The writer did not appear consoled by the buffalo soldier's humor. "Well, who do you think it is?"

Continuing in his droll manner, Jube urged his horse faster. "It's Jacob, all right."

Kane hurried to keep up. "How do you know?"

"Cuz' that giant dust cloud comin' over the rise to the west is the Mexican army."

Jube burst into a full gallop. The young men frantically matched his speed. Holding his hat to his head, Jube hollered to the writer. "This is the part where we vacate this here desert iffin' ya' wants ta' write it down."

As they reached the knoll, a line of familiar horses galloped from behind the rocks and matched their speed. Coming alongside, Jacob slowed just long enough to let his old friend catch up. "See you brought some friends."

Jube nodded. "Didn't want ta' make a liar out of ya' 'bout us gettin' out of this here shindig alive."

The reunited companions continued east with only mesquite trees to hide their trail. They had increased their lead by several miles, so the night had not been without profit.

Coming over a small rise, they headed down into a shallow, dry wash that dropped them below the horizon. Jacob slowed the horses to a walk and then turned the party sharp north, up the sandy depression. Settling into a slower pace, the men finally had time to talk.

"What now?" Mason pushed his mount close to the older men.

"They can't see us in here, so we head north and keep the dust down." Jacob took a moment to catch his breath. "Mesquites don't look like anything you could hide behind, but with enough of 'em between us and soldiers, they will give us coverage."

Nah-kah-yen butted in. "Scouts will follow our tracks, but without sight of us, they will move slower."

When the dry wash played out, they headed east again for several hours. The dust cloud was still behind them, but farther south.

Eventually the mesquites dwindled away. Spanish bayonet, yucca, and prickly pear broke up the monotony of the bleak plane. Without concealment, Jacob hoped they could remain undetected until nightfall. It was still more than an hour away.

Once again, Jacob had the rescuers dismount to breathe the horses. Mea-a-ha was already exhausted from a night without sleep. Walking was another trial to endure. She looked to the yellow sun in the western sky and started moving. The girl tried to stay out in front of the men, knowing eventually she would be struggling to keep up. Their conversations ceased to register in her weary mind.

Mea-a-ha sobbed, and realized she was crying. The girl cursed the dust cloud, feeling she needed a reason to weep. The warm tears on her cheeks comforted her. Hurrying her steps, she decided to have a good cry. She was overdue. "Darn dust cloud." She felt better.

A large hand grasped her delicate shoulder. It was Jacob. Mea-a-ha wiped her cheek and turned away, embarrassed. The big man caught her up and lifted her in his arms, then kept walking. Mea-a-ha allowed herself several good sobs, then balled a tiny fist and slapped his chest. "I did not want you to see me cry."

Jacob kissed her forehead and kept walking. "I won't look."

"It's too late." She folded her arm and snuggled against him. "You can't carry me forever."

The big man gave her another kiss. "I'd like to." Stepping back, he tossed her in his saddle and snatched up the reins of both ponies. "My horse is a lot bigger than yours. After carrying my heavy carcass all day, I don't think he will mind a little squirrel on his back."

The girl smiled down at her husband, appreciating the special treatment. She sat up straight and looked behind her, wondering if the men knew she had been crying. No one seemed to notice except Kane. She quickly turned her beautiful eyes away, hiding in the distance.

"Jacob!" Mea-a-ha screamed and pointed. The men were instantly alert. About a mile towards the northwest, half-dozen riders or more were making their way towards them.

Nah-kah-yen growled under his breath. "Terahumara scouts."

The men climbed back onto their saddles. Jacob let Mea-a-ha remain with him. Everyone strained to see the new intruders, trying to determine their intent. Kane looked confused. "We outnumber them."

Reaching into his saddlebag, Mason pulled out his binoculars and lifted them to his eyes. "Daniel!"

Mea-a-ha screamed. The young lieutenant adjusted the focus. "He's being chased."

The girl clutched Jacob's shoulder. "They won't catch him. He's on Snow Raven."

Mason shook his head. "Something is wrong. The Indians are gaining." Tossing the binoculars to Jacob, Mason shot out at a dead run. In an instant, Nah-kah-yen, Kane and the boys tore after him.

"Jacob!" Mea-a-ha was near panic. She stared towards her brother. The distance was too great. They would never reach him in time.

Jacob thrust the binoculars into her hands and jumped from the saddle. Pulling the heavy Springfield from its scabbard, he ran several yards to a small rise. Jube followed. "It looks to be more n' a mile, Jacob."

The big man did not respond. Dropping to one knee, Jacob flipped up the windage sight and turned a small brass knob. He pressed the large bore rifle to his shoulder, took a deep breath and released it slowly.

Mea-a-ha held the glasses to her eyes. One Indian was out in front and riding hard. He was almost upon Daniel. The brave raised his rifle above the thundering pony and took aim at the boy. "Jacob!"

The big Springfield leaped. Without waiting, Jacob chambered another round and shouldered the rife again.

Shaken by the roar of the gun, Mea-a-ha steadied the binoculars. She was sure the Indian would fire when suddenly his horse rolled out from under him, throwing the warrior to the ground.

Jube calmly lifted his rifle to his shoulder. "Ya missed the Indian."

He drew a bead and fired. A moment later another horse reared and collapsed, hurling its rider through the air. Jacob aimed down his barrel. "Bad day for horses."

The girl watched the remaining Indians gain on her brother and wailed. "How can you joke?"

Jube reloaded. "Calms the nerves."

Once more Jacob's rifle spoke. An Indian jerked in the saddle and turned away. Jube lowered his weapon. "Mason is too close. It's up to the boys now."

Through the glasses, Mea-a-ha saw smoke from the lieutenant's revolver. A third Indian fell. Nah-kah-yen fired his rifle and raced past Mason. The boys were shooting as well. It was over.

Mea-a-ha was crying and shaking badly. Jacob lifted her from the saddle before she fell. "He's okay, little Apache. He's okay."

Sometime later the men slowly came riding back, Mea-a-ha, unable to wait, broke into a run. The diminutive girl, screaming her brother's name, all but disappeared in the shimmering dust. Jacob could see Daniel stop and jump from his saddle. He hugged his sister in the orange light as the other men rode on by.

Mason dropped to his feet and came storming to Jacob. He looked sick. "Crazy Indian bastard." The young officer turned full around and swore. "Damn it, Jacob. He scalped them. Two were still alive." McCrae grabbed Jacob by his vest, his eyes were wild. "Jacob, a wounded scout was lying there screaming, holding onto his bloody skull, and Nah-kah-yen castrated him. He...he castrated him." It was more than Mason could bear. "Crazy Indian bastard. What makes a man so sick?"

Jacob stepped away and shoved the Springfield back into the scabbard. "Seeing his people, women and children, butchered the same way." He came back to the lieutenant. "Nah-kah-yen's actions were just."

Jube stepped forward, taking a swig from his canteen. "Son, it weren't all vengeance. When the Mexican army comes across that grisly scene, it'll slow 'em down. They'll fear us just a little more.

The Injun knows this. He's doing what Jacob told him ta' do; buy us some time."

Mason swallowed his sickness, trying to comprehend.

Gathering up his reins, Jacob slowly walked away. "Some things they don't teach at West Point, but ya' learn 'em if you want to stay alive out here."

The lieutenant trembled. "My God, I nearly shot him."

Jube grinned. "N' spoil yo' daddy's hangin'."

Leading Snow Raven, Daniel walked up with his sister, still clinging to his side. When he saw Jacob, he ran and threw his arms around him. "They shot Snow Raven."

The boy was in tears. "They shot 'em, Pa."

Jacob hugged Daniel close, comforting him, and stealing some comfort himself. After a moment, he stepped back and mussed the boy's hair. "Come on, Son. Let's take a look at him while there's still light."

With Daniel steadying the great horse, Jube examined the wound on his flank. "Ain't too bad. The bullet traveled 'bout a foot underneath the hide. Din't tear up too much muscle. Once we dig it out, he should heal jes' fine."

Pulling a flask of whiskey from his saddlebag, Jube sighed and poured it on the horse. "Was savin' this to celebrate somethin'. Guess you returning from the dead is cause enough, though I kinda' thought I'd be drinking it." He took a swig and poured the last of it on his knife.

With the bullet just beneath the hide, Jube didn't have to dig too deep. He wiped the blood on his britches and tossed the slug to Daniel. "There ya' go. Any bullet that don't kill ya' is a good-luck charm."

Jacob patted the boy's back. "We will distribute the load from one of the packhorses. You can put your saddle on it and let Snow Raven rest for a day. Imagine you've been pushin' him pretty hard."

Daniel only nodded. He was too emotional to speak. Jacob studied his son. "We'll talk later. Go be with your friends." After a lifetime of soldiering, he had a pretty good guess what the boy had been through. It would have to come out, but now was not the time.

With the last rays of the sun, Nah-kah-yen finally came riding back. He seemed unaffected by the fight, or his grizzly deeds. Mason took a step forward. "Wondered where you went." He looked to the warrior's pony. "Where are the scalps you lifted?"

The Indian's eyes flashed. "Made a trail to the dust cloud. Dropped them one by one. Soldiers pick them up on the way. Give them much to think."

Mea-a-ha's attentions had been on her brother. But now the boy had wandered into the evening shadows with his friends. She knew they'd talk as boys do, retelling their stories, and come to grips with horrors they survived. It was a rite of passage to manhood. What Jacob had told the boys was true. Their childhood was over.

Mea-a-ha drifted away as the men talked of killing. Kane was not with them. He had stayed at a distance ever since returning. The writer was standing near his horse, looking distraught. Folding her arms, Mea-a-ha walked slowly to him. He was shaking. She rubbed his back. "You okay?"

Kane took a quivering breath and rested his chin on his saddle, staring into the distance. "You hear what Nah-kah-yen did?"

The girl nodded. The writer balled his fist. "He castrated him, scalped and castrated him, and he wasn't even dead."

Mea-a-ha leaned her head against his shoulder. "It's hard to understand."

"Damn him. He left that poor bastard writhing on the ground. His skull all... Mea-a-ha, I couldn't stand it. His screaming."

Kane turned and reached for the girl, needing her comfort. "I wanted him to stop screaming. I..I took out my pistol, and, and...I killed him, Mea-a-ha. I killed him. I took a man's life."

Wild-eyed, he pulled away and wiped his nose. "The worst thing is, I didn't do it for the Indian. I did it for myself." Kane buried his head in his hands. "I couldn't stand his screams."

Putting her arm around him, Mea-a-ha spoke softly. "Today is to cry. Tomorrow is to understand."

Chapter -14-
Rio Grande

They prayed for darkness, and it finally came. The foreboding dust cloud pursing them vanished with the last flicker of a blood-red sun. Until morning's first light, they were hidden from the Mexican army.

Another hour's ride brought them to a low, sandy berm. From here the land sloped gently away. In the distance, moonlight sparkled on a tiny ribbon of water. Soon they would drink from the Rio Grande.

Everyone was dog-tired. They had gone two days without sleep. Behind them spread a violent trail of death, and though the river beckoned, even it could not wash away the evil that had been done.

The Mimbre Riders were alive, but not much more. They had taken a beating down to their very bones. Continuous battles since crossing the border left them numb. Jacob looked into the vacant faces. Something had to break or his little troop surely would.

As they drew near the thin dark line of brush, the sound of the river drifted through the night, bringing with it a breath of cool air. The inviting water made little more than a soft gurgling as it flowed over mossy stones. Night birds and insects living along the banks sang a different tune than the desert creatures, so by moonlight and sound, the company knew they had finally arrived.

One by one, weary horses dragging hooves, loped forward and lined up on a grassy slope. The tired riders longingly stared into the shimmering stream. The river and the moon seemed bound together. It was a beautiful sight, made even more so by their perilous desert flight.

Without encouragement from their masters, the horses lumbered to the river's edge and drank from the cool water.

"Build a fire."

Everyone blinked away their stupor and stared at Jacob, wondering if he had gone crazy. He repeated his command. "Build a fire. Build it low, keep it dry. If it is below the bank, it probably won't be seen at a distance."

Lieutenant McCrae looked around nervously, then spoke what everyone else was thinking. "Isn't that taking an unnecessary risk?"

Pushing the Buckskin up the bank, Jacob turned the horse around and faced the others. "Listen up." Beneath the shadowed brim of his hat, his voice rang, cutting through the fear of his companions like a sharp knife. "We've been running for our lives, and we're scared. Too scared."

The big man took a moment to measure the faces of his friends. "A man can only run so far before he starts thinking of himself as a helpless rabbit waiting for wolves to decide his fate. That's what we're all feeling now."

Jacob pushed both his hands against the pummel of his saddle and rose tall. "Boys, you build the fire. Mea-a-ha, cook a meal fit for men. Keep some food warm for Jube, Nah-kah-yen, and me. We got some business to attend to."

He turned to the lieutenant. "Mason, you're in command. Keep up your guard, but have some fun, real fun. You've earned it. If we are not back by dawn, follow the river north. It will take you home."

Jacob could see the fear welling in Mea-a-ha's large eyes. He held her gaze with unshakable confidence. "Don't worry, little one. You will see me again, so you party tonight. Dance with the men if you like. Have fun."

Mea-a-ha gave a trusting smile. "Your meal will be waiting for you, my husband."

When the three men had ridden well away from the river, Jube brought his mount alongside the Buckskin. "Well jes' what is it we rabbits is gunna' do?"

The big man kept riding and stared straight ahead, lock-jawed. "I'm getting pissed. Nobody is going to put a bullet over my head and have a good night's sleep. We're going to attack the whole damn Mexican army."

An evil laugh crackled from the Indian.

Knowing it must be a good meal, Mea-a-ha fixed her special beans with an extra handful of sugar and twice the dried meat. There were plenty of biscuits thanks to the old hermit, and along the bank of the river she found some stonecrop. It was a simple meal, but after what they had been through, it seemed like a feast.

The food and the fire had the effect Jacob intended. In a short while, the small band was doing their best to have fun. What Jacob had said about being rabbits struck home.

After dishing up a second helping for the men, Mea-a-ha stared into the darkness, thinking of her husband. It seemed silly. Had Jacob not given the order to have fun, they surely would have gone on being miserable. She smiled, understanding what he meant. With a full belly, a warm fire, and a sparkling river, the change was miraculous. Danger seemed far away.

There was talk and even some laughter. The three boys, celebrating Daniel's return, slipped off into the shadows, giggling like schoolgirls. Apparently they had found a bottle of whiskey among the supplies that Jube had forgotten to mention.

Enjoying the tranquility of the campfire, Mea-a-ha sat on a low, flat stone next to Kane. It was a time for cheery talk to distract them from their plight. The Indian girl excitedly told him about her home in the secret hollow and its magical spring. Kane wrote while she rambled on quite merrily. Content, Mason sipped his coffee and listened.

For the writer, Jacob's Hollow sounded most enchanting. The little Apache girl's eyes grew wide. "...and behind our small house there is an ancient forest older than time. It has magic, too. If you follow it far enough, and long enough, and high enough, you will find a lost city of stone that hides in the clouds. Spirits still dwell deep in the mountain, but I think you will not find it because you have to swim dead water, and the passage is blocked by a giant tree that fell from the sky."

The young girl paused and looked up from her fantastic tale to see the men's amused grins. She blushed. "You don't believe me."

Kane put his book away. "Well, let's say I would have a hard time selling it."

Mea-a-ha puckered her lip and shoved his shoulder. "Then I will not tell you the story of the small naked girl who slew a ferocious wolf for stealing her rabbit."

Both men laughed. "Now that's a story that would sell."

They were teasing her, but the men were happier, and that was what mattered.

Ignoring their jest, Mea-a-ha tugged off her moccasins and turned her back to the writer. "Unbutton me, please."

Kane froze, shocked by her request. She looked over her shoulder. "It's okay. I'm taking a swim."

Not sure what to do, the young writer glanced at the lieutenant. Mason rolled his eyes while shaking his head in bewilderment. All he could offer his friend was a bemused grin.

With little else he could do, Kane took a deep breath and awkwardly started unfastening the Indian girl's dress. She giggled. "Maybe this is where you could write about the naked savage."

His fingers trembling, the writer struggled with the tiny buttons while she chattered on. "Gringos are strange. Their dresses fasten in the back. It takes two people to dress...or undress...a girl. Hard to understand, but the clothes are soft and pretty." She shrugged her petite shoulders and giggled again. "Fair trade."

When the last button was undone, Kane parted the delicate fabric. He released his breath in an all-too-quick exhale of air that tickled the girl's bare skin and unwittingly revealed his rattled composure.

Holding her dress loosely to her breasts, Mea-a-ha stood, eyeing the young men. "Both of you smell like bad end of horse. Do you want to swim with me?"

Mason sputtered a gulp of coffee. He knew what he wanted, but had better sense, and grinned. "No, ma'am, we want to go on living. I think if Jacob rode back and found us skinny-dipping with his pretty little Indian princess, he might not give us a chance to explain."

Mea-a-ha smiled innocently, and on tiny bare feet danced a step backwards. "I forget that Gringos are embarrassed by their own skin." Accepting the young men's decision, she turned away from the fire. Cloaked in shadows, the petite girl let her dress slip to the ground.

With a few more steps, she was knee-deep in the Rio Grande. The languid river was deliciously cool. A week in a filthy dress was too much for any girl to bear.

Allowing the current to take her, she drifted, relishing the feeling of being naked and clean.

The flickering glow of the campfire and the cool caress of the moon etched the girl's delicate form onto the surface of the black water. Her slender legs kicked as she dove in a sudden splash of silver light that quickly disappeared, leaving not so much as a ripple.

All was quiet, as if she'd never been. A precious jewel had been stolen away. The meandering river flowed on, saddened by its loss. Crickets along the bank returned to their song, while the baritone croak of frogs added their lament.

Hearts that had quickened only a moment before suddenly feared for the maiden's safe return. Growing concerned, the men came to their feet and moved closer to the river's edge.

As they strained to see beneath the dark water, the Indian girl suddenly burst above the surface near the shore, giggling like the bubbling spring. She splashed at the men, teasing them for their startled expressions. "Jacob said, 'Make fun.'" She laughed and drifted backwards, returning to her play.

On the bank, Mason and Kane both took a deep breath. The heaven-sent moonlight kissed the girl's wet skin. In the midst of a horrible dream, a shimmering angel appeared, chasing their darkness away.

Lieutenant McCrae shook his head. "Crazy little Indian, I wonder what she is thinking."

Kane moved closer to the shore, unable to pull his eyes from the enchanting vision. "Something tells me she understood exactly what Jacob was saying. Right now, my friend, we feel less like rabbits and more like men than we have in a long time."

Mason came to Kane's side and watched the girl dive once more. "Bless her heart. Guess it's her strength as much as Jacob's that holds this desperate band together."

The writer sighed. "She's got courage."

Sitting in a sheltered spot, hidden in the tall reeds, Daniel shoved Juan, knocking him over. It didn't take much effort. For the first time, the boys were drunk. "Quit staring at my sister."

The Mexican sat up, his glossy eyes fixed on the dancing water. "You stare at my sister."

Daniel jerked the stout whiskey away from his friend's hand. "That's different. Maria's got clothes on."

The enchanting girl eased out of the river on the opposite shore and walked into the moon shaking sparkles of water from her long, dark hair. Daniel took a swig and passed the bottle to Roberto. She sure was pretty.

****

"Fools!" Nah-kah-yen stared at the dying campfires scattered among the sea of bedrolls. "They make it easy. Only two guards."

Kneeling by the Indian, Jacob surveyed the sprawling camp and mused. "Even jackals sleep."

He wanted the Mexicans to know that their pursuit of the gringos was a battle of worthy adversaries and not a hunt for frightened prey. If there was fear, let it be theirs. No matter what the days ahead would bring, this night he would teach them respect for Americans.

The three men watched the sentries. One was charged with the horses, the other with guarding the sleeping camp. Each soldier walked his assigned post, and when they met, they quietly traded a flask of mescal. Then they would turn and march away, only to do it all over again. By their unsteady gait, it looked like they had been doing it a long time. Obviously, no one expected an attack.

"How's we gunna play it?" Jube gripped his rifle, eager to settle the score.

Leaning close, Jacob whispered. "Killing what few we could ain't going to change the odds. There's too many. We just want to take the wind out of their sails."

The big man quietly nodded as he thought it through. "With Nah-kah-yen's grizzly trail-markers last night, and us leaving them with a few soiled bedrolls, it should give them second thoughts."

Jacob let his eyes trail across the sleeping figures. "We need to take care of the guards. Then we will kick this slumbering giant where it hurts and get the hell out of here."

Jube nodded. "So how is we going to conk them guards without wakin' the whole dang camp?"

Nah-kah-yen put his finger to his lip. Dropping to his belly, the Indian simply disappeared where no one would have thought it possible. It was a talent that never ceased to amaze the soldiers.

Several long minutes swelled to eternity while the two buffalo soldiers held their breath. Once more the guards came together and shared their drink. The drunker one clowned a salute, and then they walked apart. No sooner than their backs were turned, the Apache raised to his full height right where they had been standing. Lunging at the nearest sentry, he covered the man's mouth and slid his knife across his neck. The other Mexican turned in response to the muffled sound. Whirling, Nah-kah-yen's blade, thrust at arm's length, plunged deep into the soldier's throat. A quick second thrust stopped the beating of the Mexican's heart. No one in the camp stirred.

Jacob nodded to his friend. "Guess that's how we do it."

The two soldiers joined the Apache. Moving quickly and silently, they made their way around the sleeping forms to the north end where the Mexican horses were tied to rope lines. Most of the trail-worn animals were of little note, but a few were great steeds, obviously the well-groomed mounts of officers. One in particular, a tall white stallion, was picketed apart from the others. The general who led this army certainly had an eye for horse flesh.

Cutting the first rope, Jacob motioned to his companions. "Each of you pick a horse you can use to spell your own when we hightail it out of here. The rest of them we will stampede right through the camp. A hundred hooves will cause more injuries than a few bullets."

Eager for vengeance, Nah-kah-yen took the white stallion. Stealing it would be a humiliating insult to the Mexican commander. The two buffalo soldiers chose darker horses, less conspicuous in the night. Moving with great care to not frighten the animals, the men hurriedly cut all the lines. Their task done, they quietly slipped behind the herd and mounted up.

Grinning to his companions, Jacob thrust his colt .44 high above his head and let loose with a blood-curdling scream. In unison, the three men emptied their weapons into the air. The rapid shots blended into one explosive roar more deadly than all the lead cutting through the midnight sky.

The startled horses bolted as planned, charging straight through the slumbering camp. Startled screams of men scrambling from their bedrolls joined the thundering of hooves. Jacob holstered his pistol. "Ride!"

With a braying laugh, Jube eagerly followed, knowing they stood no chance against nearly a hundred men. The two soldiers had barely made their escape when Jacob looked over his shoulder. "Damn!"

The Indian had ignored his command. As angry Mexicans crawled from the clamor, Nah-kah-yen fired his Winchester, making every shot count. The trampling herd passed out of sight, and from the lingering cloud of dust, the dark shapes of soldiers took form. Muzzles flashed, swearing revenge on their arrogant foes. The army had been stung but not vanquished, and now this formidable force reached out its deadly hand.

"Crazy Injun." Jube triggered his rifle in defense of the Mimbre. Whipping his horse, Jacob raced back. "Nah-kah-yen!" The big man leaned from his saddle and kicked the Indian, knocking him out of his hate-filled trance. "Ride, you damn fool."

It was still dark when the men lumbered back into camp, leading their new horses. The boys were asleep, lulled by the whiskey. Jacob glanced toward his son, curled peacefully in a blanket. They had not yet talked about the boy's battle at Tres Castillos. It would have to wait until morning.

Mea-a-ha left the company of the two men and hurried to her husband's side. She rose on her toes and kissed him. "Your dinner is warm, buried beneath the coals."

Jacob lifted her chin and searched her eyes. The girl held her head high. "You will find no tears. I knew you would return. Besides, I was busy chasing away rabbits."

Mason nodded his head towards the white stallion. "Been horse tradin'?"

Giving a chuckle, Jube dropped his saddle on the ground. "Had no gold, so we bought 'em with lead."

Kneeling by the smoldering fire, the Indian girl brushed away the ashes and scooped up the meat and beans for the men. Jacob took the plate from her hand. "You are wearing your Indian dress."

"Other dress dirty." She flipped her long, shiny hair. "I took a swim. Had fun." With an impish sparkle, her eyes darted to Mason and Kane. "Everyone do as you say. Watched over me real good."

Caught by surprise, the lieutenant nearly choked on his coffee. The buffalo soldier eyed the young men with an arched brow. Mea-a-ha modestly straightened her dress over her knees. "Do you want to kill them now?"

Jacob dug into his plate. "Can't blame them for lookin'. It's touchin' that will get em' dead."

****

Jacob rolled out of his blanket and rubbed his stubbled face. The cover of darkness was necessary for his plan to work. An hour of sleep and a cold cup of leftover coffee was all he was going to get.

When the Mexican army reached the river, they would have to wait until morning light to take up the chase. By then he hoped to have laid down a false trail for them to follow. With luck, the rescuers would be long gone.

He swallowed his last bitter gulp and struggled to his feet. Another hour's sleep would sure be nice.

The Mimbre warrior was already up and staring south. His family was so close, yet so far. Each mile became longer than the last. Jacob knew how he felt. This journey was about family, only for Jacob each mile became shorter as they rushed towards a deadly end that he couldn't see how anyone would survive.

"Jacob, the men is up, n' I rousted the boys. Best wake yo' little bed-warmer n' gets ta' goin.'" Jube spit out his last sip of coffee and watched the young men saddle their ponies without complaint. "Ya know, they's a good bunch. Green, but a good bunch jes' the same. Looks like yo' little raid chased away the rabbits n' turned 'em back to men."

Jacob gently rubbed the sleeping girl. "Not sure who had the bigger hand in that." He brushed her hair from her cheek. Mea-a-ha wet her lips and slowly woke. He gave her a second longer. "Hey, little Apache. Time for another swim."

Rubbing her fist to her eyes, Mea-a-ha sat up and yawned. "Too cold to swim."

Before they broke camp, Jacob made sure they left plenty of tracks on the muddy banks heading in every possible direction. With a final glance behind, he turned his small band of riders north along the western shore towards the American border. They would turn back south long before then. He had made his choice, and with grim determination he'd see it through.

In the still night air, a lapping of water among the reeds was the only sound. Even the frogs had gone to bed. It was too early to be awake, and no one had the energy to speak. Dreading the long day ahead, they did their best to steal a little more sleep, nodding in their saddles.

The Indian girl slowed her pony and fell back, allowing her husband to turn his thoughts to surviving another day. She could see by the way he sat his horse that the stone soldier had returned. His heart would have no time for her.

In the faint light of the setting moon, Kane silently rode to her side. She wasn't sure how, but this tall, mysterious man, tormented by fear, had become her protector and companion. He was an unlikely choice. The others didn't respect him, yet in a strange way Mea-a-ha found courage in his honesty. Gruffer men might boast to hide their fear, but not Kane. He admitted what he was. The Indian girl wondered if that was not the greatest courage of all.

After several miles, Jacob turned his Buckskin down the steep bank and led the rescuers into the slow-moving river at a shallow crossing. On the other side, they continued north again for about a mile until he found hard rock.

He knew they were cutting things close, but the subterfuge had to be convincing. Being careful to not leave signs, they headed back into the black river. Only this time they waded out several yards from the shore, and then turned south for the last time. Here, their tracks came to an end.

As her pony stepped from the shore, a cool current tugged at the Indian girl's feet. She hiked up her doeskin dress as the water quickly rose above her knees. How different the river seemed from last night. The chase had resumed and with it the realization of their desperate plight. It sent a shiver down her spine.

A hand reached out of the darkness and touched her bare leg. Kane whispered. "It's okay, little warrior."

His gentle stroke warmed her. Like their night beneath the stars, this quiet man understood how she felt. The writer's hand lingered. Mea-a-ha thought that perhaps he should not have touched her so boldly, but when his caress slipped away, she missed it just the same.

Under the cover of darkness, Jacob planned to travel south in the river for several miles before turning west again and making a dash for the Mexicans' ranch. It would be a cold ride.

The Mexican army would have to search north to see if the Americans were heading to the border. Hopefully the subterfuge would buy them the necessary time.

Nearing the shore where they had spent the night, Jacob sent Nah-kah-yen forward. The moon had dropped beneath the black horizon, but there was still enough starlight to spy their horses if anyone was watching.

Holding his rifle at ready, Jacob kept his band of would-be rescuers in mid-stream. Moments passed; then all of a sudden, faint sounds drifted from the bank. Something was happening, but what? The air grew silent once more save for the metallic click of Jacob sliding back the hammer of his Winchester. Another moment of hushed silence held before a loud rush of hoof beats broke the still of the night. Nah-kah-yen came fearlessly charging across the river unconcerned about noise.

Reaching Jacob, he stopped and spoke out loud. "Only one scout." He drew a finger across his throat. "We kill many scouts last day. Maybe they are running out of Indians. It is a good thing, no? Much harder to track us."

The warrior lifted his hand above his head and flung a bloody scalp to the shore. His eyes burned with hatred. "Not Rutaio. I get him soon."

The Apache was obsessed with killing the Terahumara Indian. Jacob worried it might make him reckless. Last night it nearly got them killed.

After another few miles in the river, the shivering companions returned to the shore and headed west. They had to make the most of the vanishing darkness.

Unless he had miscalculated, they'd have a clear ride to the ranch, and the Mexican army should be a full day behind. Still, to Jacob, it seemed like precious little time to deal with the fat rancher and his score of vaqueros. For now he would forget about the army and bend all his attention to what lay ahead. They would need a daring plan if they were going to pull this one off. Somehow he must find a way.

Before dawn, they came upon a grassy marsh. Stagnant water pooled among the stiff weeds, leaving a foul odor hanging in the air. It was brackish, and tiny worms oozed in the mud, but it was drinkable if one was thirsty.

Jacob called a halt. Man and horse desperately needed rest. He had pushed them hard. The exhausted riders dropped into the dry grass as though they'd been knocked from their saddles.

Mea-a-ha snuggled close to her husband and fell asleep the instant her head touched the ground. No guard was posted. At this point, dying from fatigue was a greater threat than the Mexican army.

Not far from the girl, her brother was already in deep slumber. A hungry grass snake chasing a field mouse slithered over his exposed hand. The boy did not wake.

In what seemed like only a moment, Mea-a-ha's heavy eyes blinked open to a graying sky. The Indian girl frowned and lay still, fearing that she might wake the men. All too soon they would be riding again, but for now she would steal every last second she could.

A few more minutes passed and her eyes slowly opened again. The day had come, like it or not. Her sleepy gaze drifted to her brother, his brown hands tucked peacefully beneath his cheek. Mea-a-ha smiled, softly remembering holding him when he was a baby. If there was nothing else to cheer, at least Daniel had returned safely.

So much had happened in such a short time. Weary from so many battles, and numb from lack of sleep, there had been little chance to talk. Many questions remained about the boy's flight. With the commotion over Nah-kah-yen's grisly scalping, Daniel's own story had gone untold.

Putting it from her thoughts, Mea-a-ha snuggled deeper into Jacob's arms. For a taunting moment she savored another deep breath as her mind sought sleep, but almost instantly the camp began to stir. Labored coughs and blankets being tossed aside heralded the unwelcome day.

Daniel slowly lifted his head, greeting his sister with vacant eyes. The innocent child was gone. She ached with a motherly concern.

Uttering a heavy groan, Jacob rose on one elbow and followed his wife's gaze to the boy. "Good morning, Son."

Daniel rubbed a hand across his sleepy face and took in the new surroundings. "Guess we are all together again."

Jacob threw back his blanket. "That we are, but don't think that just because you returned safely, you are forgiven. If you ever pull a stunt like that again, grown up or not, I'll lay you across my knee. You worried your sister something fierce."

Mea-a-ha elbowed her husband. "We know who worried fierce."

Sitting up, Daniel yawned a protest. "It's Juan who needs a whipping. I didn't get shot."

Jube lifted his head from his saddle and tipped his hat from his eyes with a stiff finger. "Iffin' it hadn't been for a couple o' Springfields', ya' would of. So don't be thinkin' yo' is invincible."

Juan kicked out of his own bedroll, taking offense at being drawn into the scolding. "We all saved your Apache butt, so don't go saying I should be whipped."

Daniel dropped his head. "You did. I was out of ammunition and those scouts would have had me if you hadn't come." His voice dropped to a whisper. "Thank you."

Mason came to the boy's defense. "And you saved our lives too by what you did back there at the towers. Either you got nine lives or you had a pretty rough go of it." The lieutenant sat up and stretched his arms. "I know you had at least a hundred rounds on you, so if you ran out, there had to be some shooting."

The boy hid his eyes, but Juan thrust out an arm and shoved him. "I told you how I got shot. It's your turn."

"Yeah. You told us a dozen times."

Daniel looked to his father, hoping he could remain silent, but the big man seemed ready to listen. Unconsciously, the boy rubbed a tear in his shirt and winced. "Not much to tell. By the time I had raced down their line, you were gone. The Mexicans were mounted by then. They chased me, and I fled up the mountain. Much shooting. Snow Raven was fast, but no matter where we turned, they were there like bats swarming out of the night. I finally charged through their ranks. It surprised them."

Daniel lifted his eyes to Nah-kah-yen. "Rutaio was with them." He rubbed his side again. "I know because he taunted me, said bad things. Fortunately his horse pulled up lame. The boy grinned sheepishly. "With a bullet in his hoof...My last bullet. That's all, until I found you."

Everyone sat quietly, mulling over Daniel's tale. Juan spoke up. "How many did you kill?"

Getting to his feet, Jacob's deep voice rumbled. "Don't tally the dead, Son. Remember every one of them, but don't count your kills. If a man becomes known by a number, he is branded a gunman and shunned by decent folk. Kill when you must, but don't tally the dead."

The early light was already bringing color back into the drab landscape. The men were packing and recounting the late-night raid on the Mexican camp. Nah-kah-yen boasted of vengeance, and Jube joked about nothing being prettier than stampeding horses by moonlight.

With the dangers behind them and the beckoning of a new day, a little bragging was healing after their harrowing escape.

Roberto and Juan gathered around Nah-kah-yen to listen to his tale, but Daniel kept his distance. He wanted to hear nothing more of killing.

Leading Snow Raven away, he busied himself tending to his pony's wound. It looked much better. "Soon you will be racing eagles, my friend."

The bond between the boy and the horse was as close as his own skin. On Snow Raven's back, the Mimbre youth was transformed. The beautiful stallion's unmatched speed made him fearless. Perhaps more importantly, the horse accepted him completely, asking no questions about the number of dead that lay in his wake.

Watching from a distance, Mea-a-ha dipped a rag into the spring, and then went to him. "Take off your shirt, little brother."

"I'm okay."

His sister pulled out his shirttail. "I decide."

Daniel stood quietly and let her undo his buttons. "Shidizheé, I raised you after mother died. You were always sweet and gentle. Now you kill like ten warriors."

The boy tried to look away, but she turned his face with a stern finger. "Why?"

His throat tightened. "Because."

She slid his shirt off his shoulder. "Why?"

The only answer he could muster was a dejected shrug. Mea-a-ha traced a deep, ugly gash on his side. "Do you fight so hard because you think it is your fault?"

The boy's eyes grew red. "It is my fault. Father and you are here because of me. He said our family is going to die. It's my fault."

The boy turned, not wanting his friends to see him cry. "Please leave me alone."

Mea-a-ha combed her fingers through his glossy black hair. "First I wash your wound. It is bruised like your heart...Come."

She led him away from the camp so they could speak freely. "It was my choice, too, little brother. It is sad that Jacob has to protect us, but it is also who he is."

Mea-a-ha cupped the boy's face in her hands. "If you die, it will kill him. If you die inside, it will kill his heart. What is done, is done. Dying is no way to repay his love. Talk to your father. Mend hearts."

After a hasty breakfast of boiled pemmican wrapped in tortillas, everyone was ready to ride. Daniel lingered by Snow Raven, sharing a biscuit with him. He nuzzled his face against the horse's neck. The boy was tired in body and soul, but his sister's words helped.

Behind him, he heard heavy boots. "It's time to ride, Son."

Daniel made no response as he quickly dried his cheeks. His father's caring hand reached out and mussed his hair. "How's your pony?"

Daniel slowly turned, but kept his head down. "He's fine. Maybe I ride him tomorrow...Father..." Daniel looked up, then hid his eyes again. "Father, I will be careful from now on."

A deep breath rattled in the big man's chest. "Your sister will be glad."

Chapter -15-
Across the Expanse

There were nine riders. The number of horses had swollen to fourteen. The Mexican general was sure to be livid over the loss of his magnificent stallion. If the two guards had not met their untimely demise at the end of Nah-kah-yen's blade, the general would have no doubt shot them over the loss. A filthy Apache riding his horse was the ultimate humiliation.

If they rescued the Mimbre women, extra mounts would be needed. Besides, their own horses were about done in.

Lieutenant McCrae took his usual place by Jacob's side. Jacob welcomed his company. It had taken time, but the shadow of the father had given way under the harsh desert sun. Mason had proven himself a worthy companion.

The three boys rode next in line, talking about what perils lay ahead. At a tender age, they were testing their mettle. A few short weeks ago the young friends seemed so much alike that they were often referred to collectively. Now, tempered by blood, they were beginning to stand on their own. For good or ill, Daniel was known for his gun while Juan still seemed like a boy trying to figure it out. Their youth had been stolen, but Juan somehow managed to hold on to a part of his. His tender heart still resisted the cruel flames that turned bright-eyed boys into somber men.

More and more, Roberto fell back and rode alone. Like Jacob, he found no glory in killing, yet now there was blood on his hands that could never be washed away.

The tall boy gazed forward at his friends, not seeing how they could ever laugh again. His eyes lifted. From the front of the line, Jacob turned and looked straight at him. Something about the big man's grim assessment made him tremble.

Not far behind Roberto trailed Jacob's beautiful Apache bride. Often she retreated into her own mysterious world, yet when riled, her tongue could cut like a sword. Unarmed and small, she often showed the most courage of all.

By her side rode the tall writer known as Kane. Mea-a-ha would tell stories of the days of the Mimbres, and the young man would scribble in his book. Sometimes he wrote down what she said, but often he wrote about the Apache girl and the way she said it.

Jacob watched them smiling at each other as they talked. He knew their friendship was close, but under the circumstances maybe it was for the best. It eased Mea-a-ha's fears and gave her a reason to be happy.

Keeping this band of riders alive took all of Jacob's strength. There would be more killing on this journey to perdition. Besides, Kane could give Mea-a-ha much that he couldn't, and for that the big man was grateful, yet jealous. Everything comes at a cost. It was yet to be decided in what currency all debts would be paid. For now Jacob did his best to forget such things and focus instead on the battle that lay ahead.

Jacob glanced over his shoulder one last time then turned and faced the trail. Yes, a price had to be paid, and he alone knew what it had to be.

Last rode the Apache Warrior Nah-kah-yen and Jacob's best friend Jube. At any other time, these virulent men would have been mortal enemies, slashing at each other's throats. Neither man held any love for his foe, yet a deep respect had grown between the warrior and the buffalo soldier. They were equals suckled on the same poison, neither to be regarded lightly.

McCrae twisted in his saddle and scanned the horizon one last time. "Well, it looks like we eluded the Mexican army."

Brooding, Jacob did not share the young officer's enthusiasm. "An army is like a snake. It's safer when you can see it."

Mason was hoping for a little more assurance, and gave a half-hearted nod. "What's your plan?"

"Same as it's always been."

Shaking off his gloom, Jacob cleared his head with a deep breath. "We will reach the fat Mexican's ranch mid-day tomorrow. There, in one glorious swoop, we will vanquish the ruthless vaqueros, rescue the Mimbres, and race the Mexican army to the border on dead horses, draggin' four women and a baby."

The big man gave a sardonic sneer. "You can celebrate now if you like."

Kane turned to the girl. "It looks like we have some time. Would you like to work on your story about the puppy?"

Mea-a-ha took a breath of fresh air. "Kane, tell me about towns."

The writer was surprised. "Towns?"

"Yes. Jacob says there are towns so big, a man could walk for a day and never cross them." Her eyes filled with excitement. "He says there are houses filled with all the food you can eat." The Indian girl bounced in her saddle. "...and there are more houses filled with beautiful dresses."

Kane smiled. "You mean stores. Yes, that is true."

"Oh, tell me about it," Mea-a-ha pleaded.

Amused, the writer reflected as much to himself. "I guess civilization would seem quite wondrous to…" Kane paused, but Mea-a-ha blushed and finished his thought.

"A savage."

"You know I didn't mean that."

Mea-a-ha bowed her head. "I know, but maybe it is so."

Leaning toward her, Kane caught her eyes. "Maybe it was so, but it is for you to decide what you are to be," he teased. "I see you running through those stores filled with beautiful dresses, and trying them all on. People watching stop and say, 'Who is that amazing girl? Is she a savage?' Others say, 'No. Why, she is surely a princess from a foreign land.'"

Mea-a-ha giggled. She loved the dream. "Are there really places like that, where there is plenty of everything…and beautiful dresses?"

"Yes, Mea-a-ha. Where there is plenty of food, people are safe, and pretty young girls spend their days shopping for beautiful dresses."

The girl's laughter burst out of her and carried down the trail. "Oh, Kane, you must take me."

Kane looked at the grim man leading them. "Does Jacob mind you spending so much time with me?"

Lowering her eyes, the Indian girl shook her head. "No. He is near, but his mind is far."

Her answer helped ease a growing guilt. Kane was writing the girl's story, but sometimes he wondered how it looked with them being together so much. "You could ride with him."

Mea-a-ha shook her head again. "No. His heart is full of war." Apologetically, she added, "It is no place for a woman. The death in his eyes scares me, and I can only be in the way." Her voice trailed to a whisper. "Still I do not understand why he is so…" She tried to smile, but looked away.

Almost a year ago to the day, it had been the young writer's fortune to learn from a courier of Jacob's assault at Apache Springs. It inspired him, and he wrote of something he had no idea about, nor did a hungry nation. So he sold his story of a glorious battle and its unlikely hero.

This time Kane was learning first-hand of what he never knew. He'd seen courage and sacrifice, love and hate, and the grotesque faces of countless dead. The one thing he had not seen was glory.

"Mea-a-ha, in the story I wrote about your husband, I exaggerated and was fanciful. I glorified him as a dashing hero larger than life." Kane paused in his guilt. "…but he's not that way…and yet he is. On this fool's adventure, we have fought many battles, and I think we would have lost them all if not for Jacob." The writer stared forward once more. "He's not the hero I imagined, but he's more, if you know what I mean. He is so hard. I could never be like him."

The Indian girl nodded. "He is cold from battle, so the days are lonely, but at night when he holds me, I know he is still there." She forced a sad smile. "It is the days that are long. Thank you for your friendship, Kane. Sometimes it is hard to be alone."

Kane watched with sympathy as the little Apache hid behind a curtain of dark hair. "It is strange that we are friends. Your husband is a hero and I...." The writer paused. "Jacob said we are to die... Mea-a-ha, if you had never met him...do you think you could have loved a man like me?"

His question surprised her, but she understood it had more to do with him being a man than it did with their feelings for each other. Outwardly he appeared bold and dashing, but inside him there was a frightened little boy. Her heart ached for him. Mea-a-ha assured him with a smile. "A woman loves a man for many reasons. You are kind. Your heart would warm a woman."

She was going to let that be her answer, but somehow the words just came. "If I had not met Jacob, maybe..." Suddenly she felt embarrassed and ducked her head.

"Mea-a-ha." Kane reached for her again, but the Indian girl pulled away. "No. Please. I have given you my friendship. Now you must respect me and earn Jacob's respect, too. Go ride with the men."

In the same breath, she had shamed him and inspired him. Kane lifted in his saddle. "Thank you, Mea-a-ha. I will let Jacob know he can count on me."

With a snap of the reins, the young man spurred his horse to a gallop. As he made his way to the front, his heart quickened. On paper his words flowed with eloquence. Yet facing this man he admired and feared unnerved him. His mouth was dry.

"Jacob."

The big man lifted his head from his gloomy thoughts. "Morning, Kane."

"Sir, last night you led a raid. Your leaving Lieutenant McCrae in command was understandable. But I believe, Sir, that you left me behind because you felt I had little value."

Jacob slowed his horse and tilted back his hat. "I did, Kane. I took the men that could fight. Had I needed them, I would have taken the boys. You would have been my last choice."

The young man froze. This wasn't what he was expecting. The buffalo soldier's brutal affront was like a fist to his stomach. By a man he regarded a hero, he was deemed less than children. Kane clenched his jaw and took it.

Shaken, he held Jacob's pitiless stare. "Thank you for respecting me enough to give me the truth." His face burned, but Kane did not waver. "I'm not courageous like you, but if battle comes again, please allow me to do my part. If nothing else, I can take a bullet. I think I'm worth that."

Whipping his horse, Kane whirled around and galloped as fast as he could to the rear. His face was flushed with anger as he flew past the Indian girl without catching her eye.

Mason watched the wounded man disappear. "Kind of hard on him, weren't you?"

Jacob rode on. "Kindness can kill a man. He knew the truth. It's one less thing to hide from."

Jacob had said his piece, but inside he knew his cruelty was spawned by something more. His voice fell. "Guess we all got something to hide from."

****

The state of Chihuahua was a lot like the New Mexico territory, empty. Yet in the remote high mountain surrounding the Mexican desert lived the mysterious Terahumara Indians. There was little known about them. They had sought refuge from the Spaniards centuries ago and stayed hidden among the lofty peaks, forsaking all outsiders. The Americans would find no welcome, and traveling with Apaches made it worse. The two tribes were bitter enemies.

Jacob chose speed over stealth. He hoped they could slip past unaccosted. If the Terahumara were watching, they could make trouble he didn't need. For now his only hope was to ride forward and trust in luck.

Nightfall brought the exhausted riders to a series of deep arroyos. Spanish bayonets grew in abundance, lifting their naked branches skyward. Here the ground grew rocky, obscuring their track. Jacob led the Mimbre Riders a thousand yards off the trail to a secluded spot that offered shelter from prying eyes. He left Juan to watch the trail behind a rocky ledge at the mouth of an arroyo.

The horses were stripped and herded into a deep cleft. There was no spring. The animals would be rationed a little water from the canteens.

They would need nourishment for the days to come, so Jacob risked a small fire. Balancing the cook pot on the stones, Mea-a-ha welcomed something to do. When cooking, she became the center of attention. Tonight, she needed it. The men would hover around her, saying nice things. Mason would make polite compliments. Jube would tease her and the boys would say, "Hurry up. We're starving." This night only one voice was missing.

Kane sat alone in the rocks just beyond the firelight. Occasional smiles from the girl let him know his presence was missed. It helped.

Watching from his perch, he counted the number of times the Apache maiden glanced at him, and at her husband. His heart beat quickly. She was watching him more. Perhaps it was that his attentions were on her and Jacob was busy with thoughts of killing, but the writer gladdened just the same.

His trail had been lonely, too, and he was still hurting from Jacob's insult. For Kane, there was some vengeance in the girl's secret attention.

He never intended to care for another man's wife, but when he closed his eyes at night, visions of the beautiful Apache girl filled his dreams.

When the meal was ready, Mea-a-ha scooped up a plate of beans for her husband and gave it to him with a kiss. She then filled two more plates and made her way to Kane. The other men were left to fend for themselves.

The writer eagerly took the bowl from the girl, letting their fingers touch. It was a small thing, but it brought closeness.

Mea-a-ha leaned against the rock by Kane's side and sipped from the edge of her spoon. "Very quiet day." Her voice was soft, but carried a hint of rebuke. Kane chose to say nothing.

The girl stirred her meal, letting it cool. "You talked to Jacob. Then you rode away."

Tensing, Kane lowered his plate and stared into the fire. "Jacob told me if it came to a fight, he would choose the boys over me. It hurt."

Mea-a-ha's eyes darted uncomfortably. "How terrible. I am sorry."

They both took a few bites, letting the awkwardness pass. She touched a healing hand to his shoulder. "I think you are a brave man." The Indian girl hurried away.

Kane took another bite, savoring it for the first time. Another night would pass in blissful dreams.

As Mea-a-ha returned to the fire, Jacob reached out and pulled her into his arms. He pressed his lips to her ear. She pulled back, wanting to scold him. There was a hungry glint in her husband's eye. Tonight, they would sleep away from the others.

While Jube was knocking down the fire and the boys were spreading out their bedrolls, Jacob stepped through the smoke and made his way to the young writer. Startled, Kane rose to his feet. He was nearly as tall as the buffalo soldier, but easily fifty pounds lighter. The big man's size made him feel like a gangly youth. Jacob nodded to him.

"Daniel is going to relieve Juan's watch on the trail. We are doing two-hour shifts. You will relieve Roberto. When you're done, wake the camp. It should be about an hour before dawn."

Jacob started to walk away, then stopped and turned. "Kane, you've done what is expected of you. I don't need any more heroes."

The young man met his gaze. "Thank you, Sir, but if the opportunity should arise, I hope to disappoint you."

"Goodnight, Kane."

On a dark, sandy ledge farther up the arroyo, the Indian girl snuggled beneath her husband's arm. His flayed hand covered her soft stomach, pressing her to him. Mea-a-ha rested her head on his bicep, using it for a pillow. He had been quiet for a long time, but she knew he was not asleep.

Turning, she kissed his neck, then bit him. He jerked. "Ouch! What was that for?"

His Apache bride scolded. "You hold a naked girl, but your thoughts are elsewhere. I should bite you very hard."

The big man caressed her. "Sorry. I want more than anything to find a way to get this naked girl safely home. It consumes my thoughts."

His words earned her forgiveness and a healing kiss. "You will." She did not know how, but nights were for dreams. "Jacob. You know Kane killed the Indian, Nah-kah-yen castrated."

Uttering a long sigh of exasperation, he gave her a sharp pinch. The girl jumped in his hand, but he held her tight. "Loving stray dogs is a part of you, but when you lie in my arms, don't be thinkin' of other men. Is that clear, little Apache?"

The girl quietly nodded. "It's just that he's hurting, and you are a hero to him. A kind word from you would help."

Rolling over on his back, Jacob pulled Mea-a-ha onto his chest and tucked her head beneath his chin. "I already talked with him."

She nuzzled. "Good. Maybe my puppy will find the courage to join your pack of wolves. He will do good. You'll see."

Mea-a-ha pressed her hands against Jacob's chest and rose up, straddling him. The blanket slid from her shoulders. She lingered for a moment, welling with emotions that even the night could not hide. Her heart was in too many places.

A sudden breeze off the desert below swirled the long strands of her hair, scattering the hazy moonlight behind her. It glowed like silver-laced wings lifting from her delicate shoulders. Jacob took a deep breath. He held this angelic vision in his hands, but it was like holding a dream. There was a part of her that would never belong to him. The savage land laid its claim to this Indian girl. At times he felt she would dissolve before him. Like her people, she would vanish.

Jacob swore to himself. He would never let that happen. With his dying breath, he would find a way to save her.

Mea-a-ha suddenly jumped to her feet and stared defiantly down at the campfire. A faint red glow from the dying embers outlined the dark shapes of the men sipping their coffee. She knew Kane was watching. He could see her shapely silhouette etched in silver by the moon. She wanted him to. He must understand she was Jacob's woman.

The big man's hand reached behind his head and grasped her slender ankle. "Where is your heart, little one?"

She was stunned that he would ask. "Do you not know? It is here on this ledge."

He affectionately rubbed the back of her leg. "Lay with me. I don't think I want to share your beauty this night."

Turning, she knelt beside him and took his stubbled jaw in her small hands. Her hair fell about his face as she planted a slow tender kiss on his lips. "Let them look. My heart is only for you to command."

Jacob held her by the small of her waist and lifted her body above him at arm's length. "No one's heart is for another to command. A caged bird can never take wing. You are free to flutter where your heart leads you."

Lowering her to his chest, he wrapped her slender body in his firm embrace and kissed her softly. "I'm only saying that at this moment, I want your heart and every delicious thing attached to it."

Jacob rolled over, pressing her to the ground. "Tomorrow and the days that follow, stay with Kane. Be as close to him as you can. Killing must be done if I am to save this sorry lot... well...there is one thing I know; coward or not, he would die to protect you."

Jacob kissed her neck. "I'm not so blind as you think, but right now I need him guarding you and not following me into battle."

Mea-a-ha's eyes sparkled in the darkness. A guilty weight lifted from her heart. "You surprise me. I did not know my big ol' bear could speak so gently." She nuzzled her nose next to his ear and giggled. "...Let's find every good-tasting thing attached to my heart."

The muted crunch of dirt beneath the heel of a man's boots awoke Jacob. It was dark save for a billion stars. Kane knelt by the slumbering couple. "Jacob, wake up."

He caught the glint of a pistol as the big man released the hammer and set it aside.

"Is it time?"

A shiver ran down the young man's spine. Maybe it was seeing the gun, or just the cold night that made him tremble, but his eyes darted to the girl hidden beneath the blanket. He took a deep breath. "Not yet. I think I saw something, and I thought I'd better tell you."

Jacob lifted up on one elbow. "Let's have it."

Kneeling at the edge of the blanket, Kane spoke in a low whisper. "I'm not really sure. The arroyo is dark, but a herd of antelope went through a little while ago. I could hear their hooves on the rocks, and their white patches caught a little starlight."

Kane took another breath, calming his nerves. "After the herd moved through, it grew silent. I started to relax when I think something slipped through behind them. I wasn't sure. At first I thought maybe a large cat was hunting, but as it left the other end of the arroyo, there was a heavy thump on the ground. It sounded more like a horse's hoof than a cat. I thought I'd better tell you."

Jacob sat up and hurriedly slipped into his boots. "You did the right thing, Kane. Stay with her until I return."

The big man took his rifle and was gone.

Mea-a-ha grudgingly awoke. Tucking the blanket under her chin, she rubbed the sleep from her eyes. Kane looked at the stars, then back to the girl. A quiet moment passed as the two young people grew comfortable being left alone. In a rustle of blankets, Mea-a-ha sat up beside the writer and yawned. "Morning." A soft, sweet sleepiness lingered in her voice.

Kane found the girl's hand and squeezed it. "Good morning, I hope."

Closing her eyes, Mea-a-ha leaned her forehead against his shoulder. "Too early."

She shivered. Instinctively, he slipped his arm around her, offering warmth. Yearning for a few more seconds of sleep, the girl accepted his kindness.

Kane stared off into the darkness. There had been a few sounds below when Jacob left. Maybe he took Jube or the Indian with him. Jacob respected them...but he left him to protect Mea-a-ha. That was respect, too.

Looking down, he smiled. She had fallen asleep in his arms. The girl lying so innocently against him made his heart quicken. Kane pulled her close. Her sweet fragrance filled his nostrils. Only a loose blanket separated them. He could tell she was naked.

The young man struggled with his thoughts. He would not betray Jacob's trust. Still, she leaned against him, and he could not be faulted for a little joy in holding her. For this brief moment she belonged to him. He felt the weight of her body in his hands, and held a little more tightly. They breathed together in a long deep breath that for a stolen moment made them as one.

Slowly, a faint tinge of gray above the hills dimmed the morning stars. The girl stirred and blinked her eyes open. She leaned her head away in surprise, then giggled with embarrassment and fell back against him like a rag doll. "You can hold me while I wake up." She opened her lips in a soft sleepy yawn. "Morning." She giggled again. "I already said that."

Kane hugged her. "It is nice to hear, no matter how many times you say it."

Mea-a-ha placed a hand against his chest and pushed away. There was barely enough light to discern his gentle smile. "Find my dress. I think Jacob threw it over there." She pointed a bare arm.

Releasing her, Kane crawled to a low bush and started untangling the soft doeskin dress from its branches.

The girl lifted her head to the morning sky. It was still dark enough to protect her modesty. She stood and let the blanket fall away. A cool breeze kissed her bare skin, sending a shiver down her spine.

Mea-a-ha lifted her eyes to the heavens and remembered Kane's words about feeling insignificant. Wrapped only in starlight, she felt that way now, small and innocent. It was like being bathed clean of all sins.

Stamping her feet free of the blanket, she stepped onto the cool sand and waited quietly. Kane turned and spied the Mimbre girl's feminine shape tinged in pale blue light. He froze with an audible gasp. Mea-a-ha searched his face, then stepped closer and tugged at the dangling fringe of her doeskin dress. "Are you going to give it to me?"

When he did not move, she took the garment from the young man's hand. "Maybe you should turn around."

Taking a deep breath, Kane boldly touched a finger to her face and let it trail down her slender neck. "It's not seeing you. It's...well, it's..."

The Apache girl guessed his thoughts. "...It is standing next to a naked girl."

He stroked her cheek. "It's knowing the naked girl is you."

Enchanted by his luring words under the shimmering stars, her heart fluttered. The night was gone, but the day was yet to come. In this moment out of time, she found herself pulled closer. Her hand brushed his. They were touching. How nice it would be to fall naked into the dashing young writer's arms, wrapped in the love she was missing. Mea-a-ha's heart beat faster, but there could be no excuse for what she was feeling.

Seeing the struggle in her eyes, the writer cupped his hand to her cheek. "I guess the night makes a thin cloak."

Tilting her head, Mea-a-ha kissed the palm of his hand, then stepped away and quickly pulled the dress over her head. "Problem solved." She giggled. "No harm."

Kane groaned. "No, but I wish there were a billion more stars."

The girl reproached him with a bit of humor. "Men." She looked around. "Find me my moccasins. Where did he throw them?"

The young writer dropped to his knees and searched the ground. Mea-a-ha fell beside him and gently touched his arm. "Jacob trusts you to protect me. That's a good thing."

Kane leaned his face dangerously close to hers. His breath stirred her hair. "I think maybe he was testing me. I'm not so sure I passed."

Mea-a-ha pinched his cheek. "You passed."

When Jacob returned to camp, everyone was stirring. Mea-a-ha and Kane were descending the trial from the ledge, carrying the folded blankets. The sky held a red hue. Jube eyed the young couple, then turned to his friend. "Find anything?"

"A lone rider passed through the arroyo." In the early light Jacob's eyes narrowed, as he faced the Apache warrior. "I think it's Rutaio."

Without a word, Nah-kah-yen jumped on the back of his pony and rode off. The young lieutenant listened in amazement. "How can you tell so much from a hoof print?"

Jacob started to answer, but Daniel interrupted. "The hoof prints would be shoeless, meaning an Indian. Smaller too, an Indian pony. Indians hunt in parties, and never at night, making it most likely a scout. After my chase from Tres Castillos, I told you that Rutaio's pony had pulled up lame. The tracks my father saw were of a pony that favored one hoof."

The boy turned to the big man and grinned. "No?"

Jacob mussed the boy's hair and beamed. "Pretty good, my Son. What else can you tell me?"

Daniel grew serious. "Rutaio is coming this way."

Mason nearly jumped. "How do you know?"

A chuckle rose behind him. Tossing his saddle on his horse, Jube answered. "It is turnin' light. Rutaio won't see our tracks, so he'll backtrack, stayin' in the bottom of the arroyo ta' search for prints. Nah-kah-yen knows this n' will find a hiding spot on a ridge. Problem is Rutaio will know this, too." Jube winked. "Gets interesting."

Astonished, the young officer shook his head. "I feel like I'm blind."

The companions headed out in single file, taking their usual positions. Darkness still hung in the arroyo, and Jacob hurried the band forward, making the most of its cover. Soon the sun would rise and the night's reprieve would be lost. Already a red glow outlined the shadowed hills.

After a short distance, the trail climbed sharply, heading up a steep knoll. As Jacob made the saddle, he caught the morning light. Mason could see the big man holding his Winchester in his hand. The officer quietly slid his own weapon from the scabbard. He was learning.

Starting down the other side, the crack of a rifle echoed through the low hills. The report seemed to zigzag towards them, bouncing from one hilltop to the next. Jacob continued on without pause. Suddenly there was a flurry of distant pops breaking across the arroyos.

Jacob turned to Daniel. "Is Snow Raven fit for a run?"

The young Apache nodded. "His heart is strong."

"Then go." With a kick of his heels, the brave horse shot down the dusty ridge and around a bend. In a moment he was lost in the distant folds of the gray hills.

The rest of the Mimbre Riders hurried down the trail, Jacob leading them at a full gallop, but there was no catching the boy. Pulses quickened with the new pace. As they made their way through the winding arroyo, the volleys became more distinct.

It had only been minutes since they heard the first shot, but it seemed like they would never come in time. Every gun was held at ready, anxious for their friends.

As they reached a wide spot where sunbeams lit the trail, Jacob pulled to a quick stop. In front of them staggered a wounded pony with a bloody hole in its neck. The poor creature was suffering. Jacob fired a single round to its head.

In a side canyon gunfire rang out, much closer now. Turning in his saddle, Jacob quickly issued orders. "Kane, keep her here. Jube..." His friend whirled around. "I know; guard the rear."

Jacob slapped his reins. "The rest of you follow me." Mason and the Mexican boys spurred their mounts, tearing up a small sandy draw. They rode less than a thousand yards when straight ahead puffs of smoke burst from a low wall of rock on a far ridge.   Jacob raised his hand, and the riders slowed to a cautious walk.

Coming around a small bend, Juan pointed."Look!"

On the ridge above them to their left, Daniel knelt on one knee. He was taking careful aim at the distant rocks. His Winchester smoked, and the boy calmly levered another round.

A little farther ahead behind a sandy mound, Nah-kah-yen held his ground. He was laughing and taunting more than shooting, though bullets were politely exchanged. "Rutaio. Why do you not hunt the Apache now? Did not Victorio meet you in the open? You hide like a rabbit?"

Several rounds exploded in the dirt near Nah-kah-yen in reply. The Mimbre warrior laughed out loud. "Rutaio, bring me your scalp. Is it attached to yellow skin?"

"You killed my pony, poor shot that you are, and I will not walk to an Apache dog. Come and we will see whose hair falls the easiest."

Nah-kah-yen glanced behind him and saw the others. The warrior fired several rounds, then, kicking his pony, hurried back to his companions. It was one of the few times Mason remembered seeing the Indian smile. "Jacob, I know your thoughts. Let us go find Mary Lost Pony and leave this Terahumara scorpion alone with his shame."

The Apache waved his rifle, summoning Daniel from the ridge, and then galloped back to the mound. "Rutaio. If you survive the desert and the humiliation of telling the Mexican general how a single Apache chased you under a rock, then you come for me. I will be waiting."

Rutaio fired back. "I will come for you, Nah-kah-yen. I will piss on my bullets so as you die you will know they were mine."

The Mimbre Apache gave a victory yell and raced past his friends.

Lieutenant McCrae stared in disbelief. Completely flummoxed, he turned to the buffalo soldier. "Jacob, he has dreamed of killing this Indian since our first battle, and now he just rides away? I don't understand."

Jacob watched Daniel make his way down the ridge and then turned back to the lieutenant. "To an Apache, dishonor is greater than death. He knows Rutaio will follow. Until then he will suffer in shame as Nah-kah-yen has. This was a victory for all Apaches."

Mason looked back to the rocks. "Rutaio will track us. Why don't we finish him off?"

Jacob shook his head. "It could cost us lives to dig him out of there, and it would cost us time. We can't afford to lose, either."

When Daniel reached them, the buffalo soldier headed their party back the way they came. Lieutenant McCrae held back, watching the rocks. Two lessons learned this day, and the sun had yet to rise.

Chapter -16-
El Ranchero

The bleak hills finally gave way to the open plains. Here, livestock could feed on the tall grasses and bitterroot that flourished in the alkaline soil. Springs fed by the low mountains provided water for both man and beast.

In an eroding dry wash less than a dozen feet deep and not much wider, the companions quickly hid from sight. The jagged cut, strewn with rock, twisted and turned for a short distance before dissolving into the grassy plain. A small spring oozing from the crumbling walls flowed little more than a dozen yards to a shallow pool, where it gurgled beneath the thirsty rocks and disappeared.

Grazing right to the edge of the wash were the vast sheep herds of the fat Mexican rancher. A mile beyond, rose the adobe walls of his sprawling rancho. Except for knocking on his door, the first half of their journey was done.

For a long time Nah-kah-yen faced west, his hair blowing in the breeze. It was the same breeze that blew across the rancho. Closing his eyes, he took a deep breath, convincing himself that the fragrant wind carried the scent of his Mary and their son. At last they were within his reach. He had kept his promise to return. Honor was restored, but being near did not put his family in his arms. The warrior's heart ached.

Dropping from the ledge, the warrior faced the buffalo soldier. His savage heart burned. "Black Gringo, Apache cunning will not open the tall gates...I..." He cast his eyes to the ground. The Indian knew he needed the soldiers' help, and the only thing he had to barter was his life. He cursed in frustration. "Give me victory this day. Let me see my woman and child one last time. Afterwards, I will go willingly with the white officer, but save my family."

Jacob stood before his small band of misfits. Anxious faces, both tired and frightened, stared silently. The rescuers were done in, but one more battle had to be fought. They awaited his verdict, wondering how they would cross the last deadly mile. As tired as they were, he saw in their eyes a willingness to fight for a friend. It saddened him. He knew that none, save Jube, truly understood the violence to come. Now, as futile as it was, he must risk everything he loved on a fool's quest. All rationality failed as this small band followed their hearts.

There was nothing left but to see it done. Jacob set his jaw and drew himself up to his full height. "There ain't going to be no debate. We do this my way or I take my family and ride out." He looked squarely at the Indian. "Is that understood?"

Nah-kah-yen nodded, grateful beyond measure for the buffalo soldier's help.

The big man then turned to his wife and son. "You refused to listen to me, and so here we are at perdition's flame. From now on you will do exactly as you are told without any argument. Is that understood?"

Accepting his scolding, both Daniel and Mea-a-ha whispered their agreement.

Jacob turned to the others. His face was grim. "Here's how we play it. Roberto and me are going in alone to bring the women out. The rest of you will wait and be ready to ride with the devil on your tail."

A collective gasp betrayed the company's astonishment, but none more so than Roberto. "Me?" His voice was high.

Jacob held the boy with stern eyes. "Yes, you. There are others bolder and more foolish, but you have kept a level head. I've been watching you on the trail. Your friends have always been able to trust you, so I am counting on you now."

"But what can I do?"

Jacob reached out and put a firm hand on the boy's shoulder. "I've given this a lot of thought. You're Mexican. You speak the language, as do I, and you are tall enough to be taken for a man, a young one leastways. Here's the plan. The Rincon family is known even down here across the border, as are their fine horses. From now on, you are Vicente Rincon, come to buy breeding stock for your father."

Jacob looked to the Indian. "Greed will open the fat Mexican's gate where guns will not. Greed will win us an invitation to spend the night. Hopefully we will find the women and escape in the dark. That's it."

While the Indian stood in astonishment, Jube chuckled and clapped his hands. "Jacob, I always said, what you do best is thinkin'. I figured we'd be riding against the walls, guns a-blazin' 'til the last man was cut from his saddle. It's poetry, pure poetry."

The big man started dusting the grim from his clothes. "The Mexican army is still behind us. Poetry won't stop them."

Jacob squared with his lifelong pal. "If we don't return by sunrise, promise me you'll get my family back home."

Jube saluted his friend. "Ya' got my word. They'll see the Hollow or see me die."

Turning to his wife and son, Jacob pulled them into his arms. "I have done what you have asked of me. Now it is your turn to keep faith. You must promise you will follow Jube out of this country." He looked to the boy. "Daniel?"

The boy clenched his jaw to stop a trembling lip. "I promise, Father."

Jacob hugged him tightly. "Take care of your sister. Let her never go hungry."

Releasing the boy, Jacob took his wife's face in his hands. "Promise me, little Apache, that you will obey me this one time."

Mea-a-ha fell into his arms. "I promise." She lifted her teary eyes. "But you will return."

Jacob kissed her and stepped away without answering. "Kane. Give me what money you have left. We may need to flash some Yankee greenbacks."

As Kane extended a handful of bills, Jacob's voice dropped low. "If I don't return, you bought yourself a good woman."

He motioned to Roberto. "Mount up, young Vicente Rincon. We've got four hours of daylight. If you lie convincingly, maybe we will dine with our enemy. If not, four hours of daylight is all we've got."

****

Circling around, the two riders came in on the long road, from the west. Jacob knew it could be a short ride. He had lived his life as an honest man, and now their survival depended on how well he could lie. It wasn't a natural talent he possessed, but he consoled himself that he had been good at Five Card Monte, so he would rely on his poker face and trust in luck.

The big man grinned at the nervous Mexican boy. "Relax, Vicente. Remember, you are a wealthy American rancher. Gold knows no borders. This fat Mexican will be honored by your presence."

Throwing his shoulders back, Roberto tried to look important, but it lasted for only a second. Inside, he was sick with doubt. "Maybe gold knows no borders, but we don't even know his name and yet we come all this way to buy his horses? It doesn't make sense."

"I didn't say the plan was perfect." Jacob seemed to take it in stride. "A man makes his own luck. That's why I trust in it. Play your part, Vicente. Life is as simple as a game of cards. Today we open with a King."

The boy trembled. "I'm the King?"

Jacob laughed. "That you are."

"Well then, we're bluffing."

The big man would not despair. "It's what you do when you are holding a losing hand."

Roberto rubbed his sweaty palm on his trousers. "With twenty guns, the rancher has all the Aces."

"Son, you can't win if you are worrying about the odds. Many's the time two pair beat a full house. We ain't betting on our cards, we're playing our bluff."

In the distance, men moving on the wall told the unlikely pair they had been spotted. It wasn't long before the gates were thrown open and five vaqueros came riding out, waving rifles and screaming. Jacob risked one last word of advice. "Remember, you are a Rincon, and you command respect."

With their faces twisted in vicious snarls, the vaqueros came thundering at them. Roberto sat as tall as he could, trying to mimic the big man's cool demeanor. A bitter cloud of dust swirled from the horses, stinging Roberto's eyes. The boy was sure they were going to be killed right there in the middle of the road without a chance to speak.

The armed men pulled to a quick halt with two vaqueros taking up positions on either side. When the dust settled, an imposing Mexican with broad shoulders draped with double bandoliers held the center of the road, blocking their way. His eyes were hard and his voice scraped on his yellow teeth as he rasped an evil threat. "Amigos, you are on Don Sebastian's land without an invitation, a very dangerous thing. What is your business?"

Remembering Jacob's last words, Roberto ignored the man's question and asked one of his own. "Thank you. I know where I am. Who are you?"

Taken back, the vaquero puffed out his chest. "I am Miguel Antonio Quintana. I am Don Sebastian's foreman." He started to speak again, but Roberto cut him off and nodded to Jacob. "This is my foreman. I am Vicente Rincon. I have come to talk business with your master."

The Mexican stared at the young stranger--unsure, then at the black giant edging towards him. He pulled his pony back a few steps. "I have heard of the Rincons. He noticed the fine stallions the men were riding. "You breed horses."

Roberto patted some dust from his arm. "Take me to Don Sebastian so I may state my business."

Miguel Quintana eyed the strangers for a moment longer. His threat had lost its venom. Clearly this odd pair was not the usual trail bums, and the cut of the Black Gringo told him he was a man who could not be bullied. "I will escort you as far as the gate, and then I will see if Don Sebastian wishes to entertain you."

Without further word, the foreman whirled his pony around and headed back at a full gallop. Roberto glanced out the corner of his eye at the big man. He risked a quick smile. The boy knew he had done well.

When they reached the tall gate, the foreman disappeared inside. Jacob pressed his Buckskin against Roberto's pony. "Well, now we know the rancher's name." He winked at the boy.

Their presence seemed to create a stir. More men joined the wall while small barefoot boys scrambled to peek out of the cracks in the gate. Jacob realized that their interest was not so much in the arrival of strangers as it was in seeing a black man. Jacob tried to look ferocious so as not to disappoint them.

After several minutes Miguel Quintana returned on foot. Removing his sombrero from his head, he addressed Roberto. His demeanor had changed to being overly formal. "Don Sebastian sends his deep regrets, Senor Rincon. He is very busy. If you wish to come back tomorrow, he will be happy to see you."

With the army on their tail, tomorrow was out of the question, and the boy knew it. Jacob saw the confusion on Roberto's face and quickly prodded his horse forward. "Thank the gracious Don Sebastian, and give him our apologies for arriving unannounced. But our time is short, and there are other ranchos that might be willing to do business with the Rincon family. Good day."

The foreman sputtered as the black man turned his mount around. Roberto tipped his hat. "Good day, Senor." The boy tried to hide his dismay as he followed Jacob away from the gate.

When they were out of hearing range, Roberto whispered, "Did we fail? Did I do something wrong Senor Jacob?"

The hard face of the big man gave up nothing. He stared forward, intent on leaving. "You did fine. We didn't fail. Still playing cards. The king is on the table and the fat man is trying to run a bluff of his own."

The boy looked at the man and mustered a smile. "We just played a card face-up with a stack of chips on it, didn't we?"

Jacob grinned. "You got it, boy. The Rincon name carries respect. So Don Sebastian is trying to show us he's an important man, but we're calling his bluff. "

Roberto looked stunned. "Are you sure, Senor Jacob?"

The soldier rode on. "Nope."

Just then, hoofbeats could be heard barreling down behind them. Jacob grinned. "But I'm takin' bets."

Miguel Quintana galloped past them and pulled to an abrupt stop. He looked a whole lot less formal. "Senor Rincon, excuse me.

Don Sebastian has decided his other business can wait for such an esteemed family. He asks that you forgive the confusion and be his guest for the evening." The foreman's face was almost pleading.

Roberto nodded to his companion. "Jacob, what have you heard of Don Sebastian's stock?"

The big man shrugged, showing little interest. "They may be worth a look if the price is right."

The boy glanced at the evening sun before addressing Quintana. "Very well. It is late. We will accept Don Sebastian's kind offer. Lead the way."

Once inside the walls, they rode down a broad, dusty lane past gated courtyards with many small adobe buildings. Some had narrow walkways, and others just opened into the lane where rust-colored chickens pecking in the dirt cackled their protests as they dodged the horses' plodding hooves. Along the way, vaqueros with guns stopped and stared. Apparently strangers were not too common. And by the snarls on their faces, nor were they welcome.

At the end of the lane was an impressive two story hacienda surrounded by a wide porch with massive adobe columns stretching up to a narrow wooden balcony as yet unpainted. Some walls of the dwelling were stucco, while others were exposed adobe brick. It spoke of grandeur not yet realized.

As they dismounted, Jacob bumped into the boy. "No one hurries in poker. Play your cards slowly."

The boy understood what the big man was trying to tell him and took a breath to calm his nerves. He shook his fingers, which, moments before, were balled into fists.

A short, whiskered servant tugging on a stained coat too small for his belly greeted them on the porch. He nodded to the foreman, who stepped aside. His part was done.

With a low bow, the starchy gent led them through two large carved doors and into a wide hallway that opened into a cavernous room. Roberto took in his new surroundings.

While the hacienda was as large as the Rincon home, it lacked the elegance. There were no fine works of art or hand-embroidered tablecloths like Senora Elena Rincon kept neatly in place. The smell of stale food hung in the air. Still, the ranch was sprawling and the house told of a man of some wealth.

On the right side of the hall, a wide door was suddenly thrown open. "Welcome to my home." The fat Mexican Nah-kah-yen had described stepped before them and offered Roberto his eager hand. "So you are Vicente Rincon, no? Of course I have heard of your family. News comes often across the border. Your father has done well among the gringos. I am Don Jose Alverez Medina Sebastian."

The Mexican easily weighed more than three hundred pounds. He was imposing, and yet moved quite rapidly for a fat man. His thick jet-black hair was slicked back and greasy. It was the kind of hair one noticed because it didn't lay natural on his broad head. His entire countenance was distinctive, but it was his eyes that disturbed Roberto the most. They seemed at odds with the permanent smile painted on the fat man's face.

Before the boy could return his greeting, Don Sebastian abruptly bellowed down the hall to a servant woman stepping out of a room with linen folded over her arms. "Yessenia, you old woman. Bring wine for my guests and be quick."

Finding his wits, Roberto cleared his throat. "Most gracious, Don Sebastian. Wine would be refreshing after our dusty trip."

Smiling broader, Sebastian gloated. "It's imported all the way from Spain."

Roberto tried to act visibly impressed.

Their host escorted them into his office and offered a chair to the young Mexican, but left the black man standing. The young boy, unsure he could perpetrate their ruse alone, stood behind his chair, gripping it like a shield, and quickly introduced his companion. "This is Jacob, our highly respected foreman. I trust his opinion more than my own in the matter of horses."

The portly Mexican stared intently at the big man as if passing judgment. "Rumor had it that your father had a Negro." He puffed out his chest. "Times are changing. I, too, have recently acquired three servants of late—Apaches." He rubbed his hands. "And one of them is a gringo."

The ownership of a white woman seemed to give the fat Mexican great pleasure. His body shook with excitement and his voice rose in pitch and volume. "For Mexicans of true nobility like your father and I, the tide is turning. The arrogant gringos are thieves who will be driven from our lands. THIEVES!!"

Anger boiled in the Mexican like water thrown on molten steel. Roberto stepped back, expecting him to explode in a violent rage.

With great difficulty Sebastian quickly controlled the battle being waged behind his eyes. He took a breath and grew quiet, measuring his guest's response to his outburst.

Regaining his dignity, he calmed his voice. "Yes, thieves. That is what they are. Thieves." His words trailed away.

Turning without another word, their host crossed the room and settled his great bulk into a padded chair that groaned in protest. "Come, sit, sit."

As the two men seated themselves, Sebastian's eyes narrowed. The smile remained, but now it was as sharp as an assassin's blade. With only an imperceptible change, his countenance grew menacing.

"I know Luis Rincon has a son about your age, but we get many vagabonds making false claims." Sebastian took a cigar from a box and tapped it on the desk. "Wanting my gold, no doubt."

Striking a match, he leaned forward, blowing smoke in the boy's face. "How is it that you come so far across the desert without even a packhorse?"

Roberto froze. In all the commotion he hadn't thought of this. The fat man had been overly friendly, putting his guest at ease; now, his penetrating eyes screamed *liar*. The boy was sure Don Sebastian had seen right through them from the beginning. It left him speechless.

Jacob leaned forward. "I set it on fire."

Don Sebastian choked. "You what?"

Showing no emotion, Jacob continued. "Someone was following us two nights back."

He mocked the Mexican. "Wanting our gold, no doubt. When we got to the top of a narrow arroyo, I set the packhorse on fire and sent it racing back through them. Gunned them down by the firelight. It was real pretty."

The fat man coughed and spit out his cigar. "That's horrible."

Sebastian cleared his throat, then shoved the weed back into his mouth and took a hasty puff. "Horrible, but sheer genius." He laughed. "A flaming horse—I will have to try it sometime. Did you find out who they were?"

Jacob curled his lip in disgust. "Three filthy Apache buck. Heard they were all dead. That's why we traveled without escort."

Roberto came to his senses. "Enough of this. Don Sebastian, if you know of my father, then the horses we ride will tell you who we are. We want to buy good stock to increase our bloodline, which, no doubt, you have already guessed. We have come all this way because we are not satisfied with wild Mustangs and gringo breeds. Father wants some tall Spanish stock, and he is willing to pay top dollar to whoever has a good bloodline worth buying. So my question to you, Don Sebastian, is--Have we wasted our time?"

The big Mexican grinned from ear to ear. This is what he wanted to hear. He started to speak when the servant woman, Yessenia, returned, carrying glasses. She was followed by another woman lugging a heavy earthen jug. They quietly poured the fermented liquid and started to leave, when Jacob grabbed the second woman roughly by her cheeks. She was young, little more than a child. He guessed it was the one called Son-gee. "This one of them Apaches you was talkin' about?" He broke into a lecherous grin. "Maybe you got something other than your wine that could loosen our purse strings."

The Apache girl pulled away in fear. Don Sebastian laughed out loud. "I have heard Negroes have hot blood. It will be a pleasure dealing with a man after my own heart."

Jacob joined in the laughter and swatted the girl on the bottom as she scurried away.

Chapter -17-
Nightfall

Waiting is a hard thing. Waiting to learn of his family's fate was more than the warrior could bear. Nah-kah-yen continued pacing as he had done since Jacob left. The fate of Mary and their son rested in the hands of a soldier. Old hatreds die hard. The warrior beat his fist against the sandy cliff. Had he made the right choice?

It was not Nah-kah-yen's temperament to stand quietly by while others took action. Time and again, he looked to his pony with an overpowering urge to charge the walls. No! He had given his word. Spitting a heavy curse, he continued his pacing. Family before pride.

The rest of the companions tried to make the best of the unnerving silence while waiting in the growing shadows by the small pool. Jacob was gone and there was nothing for them to do but endure the slow passing of time.

Jube had made his promise to lead the Mimbre Riders home at dawn if Jacob did not return. Worried glances from Mea-a-ha let him know how hard a vow it would be to keep.

The Apache girl sat barefoot on a rock at the water's edge with her knees tucked under her chin, and silently stared into her own reflection. She had not moved since Jacob rode away. Her husband was in the lair of a jackal and she had sent him against his own will.

Mea-a-ha felt resentment growing towards Jube. Come dawn, he would force her to leave. An anguished sob squeaked from her throat. It wasn't his fault, but she'd make him pay. Her eyes burning with tears, she glared at him and returned to her reflection.

Lying in the tall dry grasses above their hiding place, Juan took first watch. Beyond the vanishing sheep herds, the sun lay like a giant ball, half-buried on the dusty horizon. Earlier, he had watched two tiny dots move on the distant road. It had to be their brave companions. Juan did not envy his tall friend now. Roberto must be terrified. For the first time, being small didn't seem so bad.

The boy broke off a dry blade of grass and chewed it, knowing he was in for a long wait. "Holy Shit!"

Juan slid quickly backwards, almost falling over the high ledge. "Senor Jube, Senor Jube. Holy shit, the Army is coming!"

Suddenly everyone was on their feet. Jube scrambled up the crack in the wall until his chest and arms were above the ground. Juan lay on his belly and crawled to him, pointing to their left. Jube cursed. Out of the foothills, a short distance away, rode a column of men. Somehow the Mexican army had caught up with them much sooner than expected. Their worst fears had been realized. Jacob was caught between the vaqueros and the Mexican army. His luck had finally run out. Jube's hand instinctively went to his gun, but he knew it was useless.

The grim soldiers made their way towards the adobe walls outlined on the horizon. For the moment, the rescuers hiding in the ravine had gone unnoticed.

A lone Indian scout rode farther afield, coming closer to their hiding place. He stared for a moment, then, turning, whipped his pony and followed the main host.

Jube watched them trail away, then dropped back to the bottom of the ravine, his large boots landing with a heavy thud. "Damn their hides. They's headed to the ranch."

A cry escaped the Apache girl's throat. Mea-a-ha dashed to her pony, but Jube caught her around the waist, lifting her off the ground. She screamed. "Let me go, let me go, we have to warn Ja..."

Jube cupped his hand over her mouth and tried to calm her. "Shh. You'd just get him killed. Jacob will see 'em comin' soon enough. It's his play."

Mea-a-ha sobbed helplessly, but she stopped squirming and accepted Jube's wisdom. He put her down. The girl angrily jerked away and wiped her eyes.

Not yet consoled, she clenched her fist and looked up into the soldier's face, demanding some kind of assurance that Jacob would be okay. Jube put a thumb to her cheek and dried a tear. "Trust in him, little Apache. It ain't good. Won't lie ta' ya' 'bout that, but he ain't never let us down. Ya' gots ta' trust. We waits until dawn like we promised." He lifted her chin. "Like-we-promised."

Mea-a-ha pulled her face from his hand, but grudgingly echoed his words. "Like we promised."

Daniel, who had expected Jube to charge forth, needed more. He shook with a young boy's rage. "We must attack. On horseback, we can cut them down before they reach Jacob." He looked at the men, knowing how absurd he sounded. It embarrassed him. "Well, we can... We can! Father can't face them alone. He..." A sob broke in his throat. It was run or cry.

Daniel tore past the small pool and disappeared in the winding ravine. Kane started to go after him, but Mea-a-ha pressed a hand on his chest and sobbed. "Let him alone. Even boys have tears."

Lieutenant McCrae climbed to the ledge with his field glasses, and watched until the army disappeared inside the adobe walls. He slowly came back down. "How'd they get here so fast?"

Jube could only shake his head. "We miscalculated."

"That we did. They must have given up after you stampeded their horses." Mason looked to the girl. "Well, we haven't heard any shooting. That's good news... isn't it?"

Mea-a-ha's eyes lifted hopefully, eager for anything to hold on to.

All of a sudden Daniel came running back. "Hide, get the horses back. A vaquero is coming up the ravine."

The boy caught his breath. "I think he's lookin' for strays."

In a frenzied rush, everyone scrambled, pulling the animals back as far as they could to the end of the draw, but it was no use. With all their horses, there simply wasn't enough room to hide. A sinking feeling turned Jube's eyes to the sky. It was still half an hour to dark. He licked his lips. "Our luck done run out twice, boys. It had ta' happen." He drew his pistol.

Mason grabbed his arm. "No! You shoot and they will hear it at the ranch. It's the bullet that's sure to kill Jacob."

Mea-a-ha gasped. Everyone frantically looked at each other, then cast a terrified glance down the ravine. Not a breath was drawn as their hearts beat away the fleeting seconds. All they could do was wait helplessly for the vaquero to appear. Someone would fire a shot. If not them, then the vaquero and it would all be over. Their long journey to rescue the Mimbre women had come to a bitter end as Jacob had foretold. Jube looked to Mason and Nah-kah-yen. "Damn it, boys."

Weaving her way through the tall men, Mea-a-ha led her Indian pony forward. Her voice, though meek, uttered a firm command. "Nah-kah-yen, draw your knife and follow."

Barefoot, she picked her way through the stony ravine until she reached the edge of the tiny pool. She positioned the spotted pony to partially block the view. Her sweet face coloring with sadness, the little Apache stepped into the water and let go of the reins.

Jube drew a breath, realizing what she was going to do. The vaquero would see her first. A pretty Indian girl would lure him in. If she could entice him to come close enough, distract his attention long enough, Nah-kah-yen might have a chance with his knife before they were discovered.

The vaquero must not see anyone but the girl. His attention must be drawn to her and her alone. Jacob's life hung in the balance. This Mea-a-ha knew all too well. The guns of the men were useless; only she could save her husband now.

Mea-a-ha's moist brown eyes darted pitifully to her friends. For the first time she finally realized how Jacob must feel. She had brought him to this, and now a price had to be paid.

Sickening with fear, her trembling fingers dropped to her side and slowly lifted the hem of her buckskin dress. She paused, then pulled it over her head and let it fall.

The courageous girl shuddered, and then taking a breath, she threw her shoulders back. For Jacob, she'd be a naked savage once more.

A patch of evening light danced on the water. Mea-a-ha stepped into it and stopped. Her Apache skin blazed a brilliant red in the dying sun. She was beautiful. As the evening shadows slowly cloaked her companions, the girl stood bare. She would be a candle in the night, blinding the vaquero's eyes to what was not yet hidden.

The enchanting Indian maiden dipped her hand and played as though she had not a care in the world. She was every young man's fantasy, a pretty girl caught bathing alone in a hidden pool.

As the rider appeared, she pretended not hear the tramping of the pony's hooves on the hard stone or see the young vaquero climb from the saddle, his eyes only for her. The girl splashed the cool water on her glistening skin then knelt in the quiet pool, drawing the man's vision down to the sparkling light. He was almost on her before she looked up and froze. A sweet, innocent child too terrified to move.

The vaquero was young and handsome, more a boy than a man, not much older than Daniel. His eyes were kind and his face shined as he gently reached out and caught her hand. He smiled softly, assuring the trembling maiden he would not harm her. His pulse beat rapidly. She was the first naked girl he had ever seen.

Over his shoulder, Mea-a-ha watched Nah-kah-yen rise from the shadows. Dying on the inside, she lured the boy with a trusting smile and timidly opened her arms, accepting his protection.

The gallant vaquero reached to lift the delicate angel from the water. A blade glinted in the evening light, raising high, then struck deep into his back. She was the angel of death. The boy's mouth open in a gasp he'd never breathe. Mea-a-ha's cruel betrayal burned in his eyes. "Why?"

Horrified by the evil deed she'd done, Mea-a-ha shrank away from his outstretched hands. In a heartbeat, Kane was at the shore. She rushed into his arms, then turned her head and looked back as the stricken boy fell to his hands and knees in the pool, fighting desperately for a life he would never live.

Nah-kah-yen's dark eyes reflected the steel blade as he plunged his knife downwards once more. The young vaquero stretched his hand to the girl and collapsed. His life's blood swirled in the water, lapping at her feet. Mea-a-ha buried her face against the writer's chest, wishing it was she who had suffered the mortal wound. Kane picked her up and carried her away.

Chapter -18-
The Uninvited Guest

The evening sun painted the white stucco walls in crimson. Even the air itself seemed to glow red. For Roberto, it was an evil omen foretelling how their charade would come to a grizzly end.

Splashing goblets of wine, they made their way past several small buildings while the fat man boasted of his Spanish blood on his father's side. He saw himself as an aristocrat. Mexican peons were of a different race. "…and you will see, young Rincon, that even my horses carry the same noble Spanish blood. Like the Sebastian men, it is superior, as a man's blood is superior to a woman's. While it is true that once long ago my Castilian ancestors took Indian squaws for wives, the male line has remained, where as the lowly peons have intermingled to the point that their bloodline has dwindled. They are little better than the dim-witted savages that run naked in the hills."

Don Sebastian tipped his cup letting the red wine roll down his double chin. He emitted an evil chuckle amid his final gulp. "If you stay for a while, we could hunt some Indians, no? It is good sport."

Roberto turned away and leaned on the railing. How could he pretend to be so evil? Still, there was so much at stake. He took a breath. "Si. It would be good sport. Maybe we could set another pony on fire."

A dozen horses of great conformation were paraded in a large corral. Vaqueros, snapping whips, kept them moving in front of the young boy. Don Sebastian made sure they understood the importance of his visit. He was a man of gluttony who salivated at the smell of money, blood, and women. Surrounded by high walls and twenty armed vaqueros, he had no need to hide his lust.

Roberto whistled and tipped back his sombrero, eager to change the subject. The horses were tall and spirited. "Andalusian!"

Don Sebastian slapped the boy on the back and gloated. "Do you think your father would be willing to loosen his purse for such horse flesh?"

Roberto smiled. "My father will not think my trip a waste. That makes me happy, and that loosens my purse strings."

Roberto stepped away from the railing. "Enough for tonight and this dwindling light. I am hungry and tired. Tomorrow after breakfast we will talk of money that I'm sure you will find to your liking." The boy did not forget the reason they came. "And tonight maybe we can satisfy my hot-blooded foreman's appetite. The trail has been lonely for him."

Sebastian laughed and rubbed his hands. "Fear not. He will find the delicate meat enough to fill his hunger."

Just then, a low rumble erupted from beyond the wall. It rose to the unmistakable sound of hoofbeats. Soon the creaking of leather and ringing of metal tack beckoned the vaqueros to the double gate. As it swung open, Roberto's hand went instinctively to his pistol. The feared Mexican army had come. Jacob was beside the boy and bumped his arm away.

A heavyset man in a broad sombrero, sporting a peppered mustache, rode through the arch, followed by a company of dour-faced men. Their clothes were dirty and torn, telling of the unpleasantness of the trail. Jacob leaned close to the boy. "Vicente, a new hand has been dealt. Play your cards well."

The man with the big mustache headed straight towards them and paid no attention to anyone else. His sunburned eyes squinted with anger. Roberto's stomach tightened as he watched the Mexican army pour through the gate. He felt like a penned rabbit facing a hungry wolf. It would only be a matter of seconds before they were placed against a wall and shot.

Don Sebastian stepped in front of the advancing soldiers, bringing them to a halt. "General Vasquez, how good it is to see you. What happened to the white stallion I gave you?"

The general snapped. "You gave me nothing. I paid you twice what it was worth." He looked at the rancher's guest and sneered. "It was stolen by gringos."

The fat Mexican laughed. "Did the gringo steal your army, too? You had twice this many men the last time you visited my ranch."

A vein twitched down General Vasquez's ruddy forehead. "The cowards stampeded the horses through our camp under the cover of night. A detachment of my men are returning on foot. We will need more horses, so do not be so quick to laugh, or maybe I will buy them elsewhere."

Don Sebastian seemed not to care. His humor remained unchanged. "How many gringos have invaded our poor country?"

The general fidgeted, not wanting to answer. From his side, an ill-tempered officer leaned in his saddle and spit on the ground. "There were twenty of them; perhaps more, but they attacked at night and fled on good horses, not like the ones you sold us."

Sebastian looked astounded and scoffed. "But you outnumbered them four to one, surely a few gringos seeking gold..."

The angry officer snapped. "These men were not miners. They had to be American soldiers, fighting the way they did."

The beady-eyed man kicked his mount past the fat Mexican and scowled down at Jacob. "There were filthy buffalo soldiers among them. Our Indian scouts could smell them and see their black hides beneath the moon." He pushed his horse closer and spit at Jacob's feet. "I am Captain Moralis. Tell me, Negro, by what trail did you come here?"

Jacob grinned, "Are you suggesting I attacked your army?" He laughed aloud in the officer's face.

The captain hissed. "You are American. No? Answer my question before I run you through." He grabbed the hilt of his sword.

The big man's eyes narrowed. "I am an American, and I used to be a soldier, a real one. If I'd attacked your little play army with twenty U.S. Cavalry, you wouldn't be here right now."

Rage flashing in the man's eyes, he grew livid beyond control. With a vile curse, he drew his sword. "You impudent nigger…"

With one hand, Jacob grabbed the man by his bandolier and pulled him from his saddle. Arms flaying, the little man slammed into the hard-packed earth, his lungs compressed with a raspy grunt.

For a moment, he lay stunned by the impact of the Negro's deed, then gaining his senses, the enraged captain tried to rise. Jacob pushed him back down with his boot and took his sword. "Stay where you are until your temper cools."

The big man's words had barely left his mouth when the clatter of rifles drew his eyes to a line of heavy muskets cocked, threatening death. There was no love for Americans, and they would not tolerate such an affront.

A message unspoken was clear: humble yourself or die. Showing his contempt, Jacob brought the Mexican's blade down over his knee and snapped it in two.

Don Sebastian hurriedly stepped forward with his arms spread wide. "General, you are on my ranch. These men are my guests, as are you. They came alone to buy horses. There is no army, so put away your foolish weapons and we will talk like civilized men."

Moralis cursed his way to his feet, ready to fight. The general waved his hand, silencing him, and then turned to the American. "Senor, forgive my foolish officer his anger. We have lost many men, though most of them were only Indian scouts. Still we do not like gringos in our country, no matter their color. You would be best to learn a little respect, or I will have my men teach it to you with the tongue of a whip."

Shaking off his shock, Roberto caught a fire in Jacob's eye and realized it wasn't in buffalo soldier to back down, no matter the cost. If pushed, it would end here in a shower of lead.

Rejoining the game, Roberto stepped forward. "General Vazquez, allow me to introduce myself. I am Vicente Rincon, son of Don Luis Antonio Rincon. Jacob here is our trusted foreman. Forgive his temper. The trail was long. We have come only to buy horses. It is said, 'Gold knows no borders.' Trade is good for both countries. No?"

Twisting in his saddle, the general studied the young man. "You do not look like a gringo soldier, and I have heard of your family, though I thought you were older." The general let his doubt hang in the air before continuing. "We will discuss your purpose here later. For now I suggest you teach your Negro some manners."

Vasquez turned to Don Sebastian. "As you say, I am your guest. With your leave, we will water our horses from your troughs and bed the men down outside your gate. Afterwards, Captain Morales and I will meet with you and the Americans to learn their reason for being in our country."

Don Sebastian smiled. "Please, you and your captain will be guests in my house. I will have beds prepared for you." He laughed. "Then you and Senor Rincon can bid for my horses."

The general had never cared for the fat Mexican, but he respected his wealth and position. "I accept your offer." He looked down at his officer. His voice grew cold. "Get in your saddle, captain." Vasquez turned his horse and rode away.

Moralis glared at the tall black man and then climbed on his mount. "You will pay for this insult," he said, then spurred his horse after the general.

Jacob smiled at Roberto. "Well, Vicente, I think that went rather well. Only a few days in Mexico and we are dining with a general."

Don Sebastian laughed. "I have never known a Negro before, but if they all fight like you, then it explains why the gringos bred you to slaughter the savages."

Jacob handed the broken hilt to his host and grinned. "Only the bucks. Squaws we got use for."

The Mexican walked towards the house, laughing and holding his belly. "We think alike. I am sorry the general will be here tonight. He is no fun." Sebastian raised a bushy eyebrow. "But beware of him. Vasquez is a ruthless pig, and Morales is his pet snake. Both have venom."

"Drink, my guest...Yessenia, more mutton and bread. Be quick, old hag." The fat Mexican's vulgarity was unappetizing at best. Bits of food seemed permanently stuck to the portly man's greasy chin. His arms flailed as he laughed at his own crude jokes, sending wine splashing from his goblet. Roberto turned his head in disgust. It would be a long night.

Despite their host's bad behavior, the meal was quite delicious, especially after a week of biscuits and beans seasoned with trail dust. There was plenty of food with jugs of strong wine to wash it down.

To keep the banquet coming, Don Sebastian had Yessenia enlist the help of the three Mimbre women. For the greedy Mexican, these poor girls would serve another purpose this night. He would have Vicente's gold, and he cared not what kind of flesh he sold, be it horse or Apache.

Giving the stout nectar time to dim the senses of the Mexican youth, General Vasquez folded his hands under his chin and faced the boy with a cold, calculating stare. "Senor Rincon. By what route did you enter our country?"

Turning his attention from the Indian girls, Jacob lowered his fork. It appeared they were still suspect. Roberto finished chewing a bite of mutton and took a slow deliberate sip of wine. The boy was learning. Fumbling his goblet onto the table, he focused his eyes on the general. "We entered south of Deming. Do you know the trail?"

Captain Moralis answered. "Yes, we have patrols watching that route. It is surprising they didn't see you."

Jacob finished his drink and belched. "We saw them. They just didn't see us."

The captain bristled, but hid his anger behind a disinterested sneer. "Tell me, boy, since you seem so eager to speak for your master, one of the colored soldiers we are chasing rides a tall Buckskin. Shot at him myself the night of the stampede. What color horse do you ride?"

Holding up his glass, Jacob motioned to the Indian girl carrying a jug. He made the captain wait while she poured. Though the corner of his eye he could see Morales's impatience growing. The Mexican's presence complicated the rescue of the Mimbres. Jacob needed to get rid of them for his plan to work. He smiled up at the girl and held her by the waist while letting his advisories fume.

The Apache finished filling his glass and tried to pull away, Jacob teased her a moment longer before turning to the captain. "I'm guessin' you checked the stables or you wouldn't have asked. Us darkies prefer Buckskins. Perhaps you didn't know that." Jacob grinned. "Like I thought all Mexicans only rode burros."

The captain's hand twitched, spilling his drink. One of the Apache servants quickly filled his glass while another wiped up the stain. Morales waved them away and glared at the big man. "You find this humorous, don't you?"

Jacob continued eating. "I find you laughable."

The big man's face grew serious and he leaned towards the captain, his disdain for the Mexican officer evident. "It takes more than your daddy buying you a commission to make you a soldier. That's how they do it down here, isn't it?"

Morales jumped up, knocking over his chair. "If I had my sword, I would teach you who is a soldier."

A smile, both wicked and amused, spread across Jacob's face. Taking a last bite of mutton, he slid back from the table. He had found a way to get rid of the captain at least. "Be careful, little man, do you forget that the U.S. Cavalry also uses sabers? Perhaps our good host could find two blades of equal steel, so we can settle this like men."

Born with a blood lust, Don Sebastian clapped his chubby hands. "A duel with swords, marvelous." He struggled from his chair. "We can do it in the main hall. Later I'll have a painting done. Simply marvelous." Sebastian detested the captain and loved a good fight, as long as he wasn't involved. He laughed, spilling wine on his silk shirt, then laughed some more.

General Vasquez rose from his chair and faced Roberto. A fight was not to his liking, but there was nothing he could do without losing face. "Senor Rincon, liquor will not excuse your Negro's bad manners. He has offended the Mexican army, and I will not stand in the way of Captain Morales to teach him a much-needed lesson. You will find the refinement of a well-bred Mexican officer is no match for your hulking beast. It will be like a matador slaughtering a dull-witted bull."

The general bowed to his host. "Bring your swords, Don Sebastian."

Morales measured the size of the big man, but his hatred of the American was enough to carry the fight on. Jacob's words touched a tender nerve. The captain's father had bought his commission. Still, while knowing little of military tactics, he fancied the sword. The ill-tempered captain had fought many duels to back his hasty tongue. With cold vengeance, he would reclaim his honor and leave the black gringo lying in a pool of his inferior blood.

Morales downed his wine and smashed his glass against the wall. "Before I run you through, Negro, I will cut your tongue from your head and see if it still wags so freely." He pushed past the men and stormed into the great hall.

As they trailed out, Roberto leaned close to Jacob. "Are we still bluffing?"

Jacob winked at the boy. "Better to have them mad, than to have them thinking."

Don Sebastian pulled two crossed Spanish blades from a frame on the wall. His hacienda was filled with tokens of war and manhood, though imagining a man of his girth using such weapons seemed most absurd.

Hurrying to the center of the hall, Sebastian held a sword high in both hands. Their chubby host enjoyed his part and made it quite a spectacle. To his right stood Captain Morales and the scowling general. To his left stood the black gringo with the Rincon youth as his nervous second. To Roberto, the thought of Jacob wielding a sword seemed so unlike him, and the swaggering captain was brimming with confidence. The boy's young mind swirled with serious doubt.

Don Sebastian looked at both men. "I would say keep it clean, but I think quite the opposite is true." He laughed and handed the men their swords with a ceremonious bow of his head. "Make it a quick thrust and keep the bleeding on my wood floors to a minimum." He laughed and quickly stepped out of the way.

Morales slashed the blade back and forth, feeling its balance. His eyes gleamed with a cold, deadly eagerness. Taking a step back, he assumed a pose worthy of a heroic painting and held it.

Jacob shrugged indifferently and handed Roberto his glass. He punctuated the tenuous moment with an impertinent belch and took a stance more akin to that of a sluggish bear.

Without warning, the captain emitted a shrill yell and made several short lunges, driving the big man back. Jacob knocked over a small table in his retreat. A lamp crashed to the floor and broke. Morales laughed at the Negro's oafishness.

Staying at sword's length, the combatants slowly circled each other several times. Captain Moralis commanded the floor with continuous short, quick jabs of his sword. Each step of the black soldier was in response to the captain's movement. The Mexican was taking his time, enjoying the feel of death in his hand. He licked his lips, relishing the victory to come.

The highborn captain measured the American and saw nothing to warrant respect. He gave another yell and with several advancing steps, drove his sword deep at the big man's belly. Jacob slid to the side with amazing speed for a man of his size. The captain's blade caught the fold of the big man's shirt but missed its mark. At the same time, Jacob flipped his sword in his hand and gripped it like a dagger. With tremendous force, he drove it downwards, impaling Captain Morales's outstretched foot to the floor.

The captain's eyes bulged as he screamed in agony and tried to pull back. It was hopeless. Panicking, the little man dropped his sword, and with both hands grabbed the hilt of the one sticking through his foot.

Jacob took advantage of the officer's plight and drove his immense fist square into the captain's face, knocking him out cold. The fight was over as quickly as it had begun.

Retrieving his wine from the astonished boy, Jacob turned to the speechless general. "Been a soldier most of twenty years. That ain't something you 'kin buy." He emptied his glass. "Senor Vicente told you we were here to do a little horse tradin'. And I told you if I was commanding twenty American soldiers, you'd be dead. Both are true. So let it be."

Pulling the sword free from the floor and the unconscious man's foot, Jacob handed it to Don Sebastian and smiled. "Kept the bleedin' in the boot. Ceptin' for a little nick, your floor's okay."

The fat man was speechless. In all his days, he had never seen such a fight, if that's what it could be called. Regaining his composure, he started chuckling. It rose in volume and pitch until he was laughing out loud. "Well, General, honor has been satisfied. I agree with the Negro. Let it end. They are simply horse buyers, and are clearly not an army, as you can see."

The general looked ready to burst. He glared down at his captain and shouted. "Guards!" The door quickly opened and two Mexican soldiers rushed in. General Vasquez pointed to the floor. "Carry him to the surgeon's tent."

Stepping past the prostrate man, the general, full of rage, faced the black man. "You are your own undoing, Negro. I am convinced now more than ever that you are one of the Americans we are hunting. I do not know where the rest of your Yankee rabble is hiding, but it would take a man like you to elude the Mexican army. It is no coincidence your being here or riding a Buckskin. Do not think me a fool. In your arrogance, you boast of being a soldier when playing a dumb servant would have served you better."

Turning to his host, the general bowed. "I will respect your home, Don Sebastian, but I will hold you responsible for these men. Tomorrow I will scout the surrounding trails. When I find the rest of his troops, I will expect you to turn these two gringos over to me for swift execution." The general bowed again and stormed out of the house followed by his guards.

Jacob stared after them. "Guess that means he ain't spendin' the night."

Don Sebastian's eyes narrowed. He looked to his guest, less sure. The general's doubt was convincing. It all did seem too coincidental. Sebastian's voice suddenly grew cold and deadly. "Tomorrow I want to see the color of your money, senor. Or…" He drew a finger across his throat and made a sickening sound. "The general will have your heads. Do not expect a pleasant death."

Instantly, Jacob's smile disappeared. His eyes darted nervously and his voice almost shook as if the threat of their host had left him unhinged. "Don Sebastian. Please, you leave us no choice. We will tell you the truth." Jacob held his breath for a moment as though he feared to speak, and then blurted out. "We have not come to buy one of your stallions." He paused, letting Sebastian think the worst. "We have come to buy all you have…and more, if possible."

Don Sebastian's eyes grew wide as Jacob continued. "We would rather not have told you this, as it will only strengthen your position, but now it is necessary for you to believe us. Senor Luis Rincon has received a contract from the U.S. Government to supply the finest horses in the land. They wish the best horse flesh for the high-ranking officers from the border forts to Santa Fe." Jacob bowed his head. "It is an order the boy's father cannot fill, and it would embarrass him greatly to fail. It is a matter of honor. That is why he sent us here on this desperate mission. We want all your horses and more, if you can get them."

Realizing what Jacob was doing, Roberto cut in. "Please, Don Sebastian, from one noble Mexican family to another, we need your help."

The fat man nearly danced. His insatiable greed pushed all doubt from his mind. "I knew it, I knew it. There was something you were hiding." He laughed out loud and patted Roberto on the back. "Come, let's finish our drink and celebrate now that we are rid of the boring general."

Escorting his guest back into the banquet room, he shouted as he went. "Yessenia, Yessenia, bring your savage bitches and more wine for my wealthy guests."

Pushing his chubby hands on the arms of his chair, the Mexican raised his great girth on wobbly knees. He laughed as he had done all night and motioned two of the Indians to his side. His lack of caring was such that he had never even bothered to learn their names. He regarded the Indians as mere animals, deserving no more thought than the meat left on his plate.

Shaking with terror, the women knew what awaited them. They had known all night. The fat man's constant groping and lecherous drooling had left no doubt, and now the moment had come.

Catching them under each of his fat sweaty arms, he hugged them to his blubber. Their horrified faces filled with revulsion. "My wife said if she caught me bedding one of these little beauties, she would lay a dagger to the family jewels." He roared with laughter. "I sent her and my three ugly daughters to Chihuahua only this morning. Let her spend my money and find three husbands who are blind.

"To seal our bargain, I offer you these delicious wild fowls of the desert. Though less valuable than horses, they are definitely more tasty."

Proving his point, Sebastian opened his salivating jowls and rudely licked the tender faces of the squirming girls he held in his left arm. "Sweeter than wine."

Laughing, he lifted his two captives onto their toes and captured a breast in each hand. He squeezed until they whimpered in pain, then roared with amusement.

Jacob emptied his goblet and pushed away from the table. "How do you communicate with these savages?"

Sebastian pressed his rubbery lips to those of the white Apache girl, nearly burying her petite face in his mouth. "With a whip. I will not degrade myself by mimicking the howls of wild animals. They will learn Spanish or I will peel the clothes from their backs."

Gulping his drink, he kissed her again, staining her delicate cheeks as he drooled his wine.

With a tremendous belch, Sebastian laughed and pushed the youngest girl into Roberto's lap. "The tiny one is for you, my young friend, so pretty, but she could not survive my weight." He laughed at himself and patted his great belly. His mood quickly changed as he turned and crushed the blond girl to him. "I hate gringos. They are so high and mighty. Tonight I will enjoy teaching this little white dove to sing prettily for her master."

The Mexican looked above the girl's head and snarled at the lone woman cringing in horror as she tried to hide in a shadowed corner. He pointed to Jacob.

Clutching her throat, the trembling Apache pried herself from the wall and hesitantly made her way to huge black man. To her he was all things evil—a dark, menacing serpent come to devour her, and now she must deliver herself into his gaping arms.

When she had edged close enough, Jacob grabbed her wrist and jerked her roughly into his lap. He laughed as she kicked and struggled. The girl pushed at his chest with both hands, but he bit her neck and kissed her hard, to the fat Mexican's laughter.

Coming to his feet, Jacob lifted the girl in the air and twirled her into a darkened corner of the large room. She screamed and prayed for death.

Don Sebastian shoved his hand down the White girl's dress, but paused in his lechery long enough to taunt Roberto. "What is the matter, Vicente, is she too thin?"

The boy smiled nervously.

"Come, young Rincon. Do not let your Negro best you. Fill your hands."

Roberto raised a sweaty palm and slowly cupped it to the girl's small breast. With a final glance at the Mexican, he pressed his lips to the whimpering Apache. Better to steal a kiss than trade words with the vulgar drunk.

Don Sebastian turned his attentions to the white girl. Grabbing the top of her blouse, he violently ripped it away. Screaming, she pulled free and tried to cover herself, but the cruel drunk caught her hair and yanked her back hard. Unable to stand, she crumbled to her knees, only to be jerked back up to her feet. Sebastian slapped the girl with his chubby hand to settle her down.

Sobbing helplessly, she submitted to his will. He would devour her like a piece of meat. Somehow the fat man managed to lift her into his arms. She cried silently as he tore at her remaining clothes. Roberto shut his eyes tightly and tried not to hear the poor girl's sobs. For now they must play the fat man's game.

In the corner of the room, Jacob continued kissing the Mimbre girl he was given. Their faces were hidden from the Mexican, who was now occupied with his own sins. Sliding his mouth across her cheek to her ear, Jacob whispered in Apache. "Mary Lost Pony?" He lifted his head. Disbelief mixed with the terror in her eyes. He kissed her roughly. "Nah-kah-yen is alive. He sent me to get you. Your husband is waiting."

Mary pulled back, searching the black man's face. She could not believe what he had said. Was she going mad? Tears flowed down her cheeks. Jacob risked a gentle smile and then bit at her ear. "Keep your fear. The Mexican must not know. There is danger this night." Jacob ripped the flimsy blouse from her shoulder. "Scream to the other girls. Tell them tonight we escape."

The Apache woman searched his face once more, wanting so desperately to believe. She had to believe, or else there was no hope.

In the giant's sad eyes, Mary Lost Pony found truth. For whatever reason, this man would protect her, and he had given her permission to scream. Until now even that had been denied her, as it had been for all Indians. Releasing a lifetime of injustice, Mary screamed for her people. She raged for the lost souls of Tres Castillos and the forgotten dead scattered on so many trails with no one to mourn them. Filling her lungs with the promise of freedom, she cried out to Lori White Feather and Son-gee. "My warrior has come. She told them to take heart. This would be their last shame."

Little Son-gee pushed a hand against Roberto's chest and gazed with a child-like hope into the young boy's face. He winked and hid her astonishment with a tender kiss.

The fat Mexican dropped Lori White Feather's shredded dress to the floor and staggered to the door with his delicate prize limp in his arms. "Follow me, my good friends. There are rooms at the top of the stairs. Enjoy the savage flesh tonight. Tomorrow we will conclude our business in gold."

Huffing and puffing, the Mexican managed to get to the top step. He had thrown the naked girl over his shoulder so he could pull himself up by the banister with his hands. Jacob carried Mary the same way, but Roberto cradled Son-gee gently in his arms. Sebastian turned and laughed. "Vicente, you are a young romantic. These animals will not appreciate your kindness. Consume them like succulent steak. Love is beyond them."

Still laughing, Don Sebastian pointed to two rooms and waited for his guests to enter, then stumbled to the end of the hall. His evil reverberated from the rafters as he disappeared into the bowels of the darkened chamber.

Jacob quickly pushed the door shut behind him and set Mary on the bed. She scrambled to the headboard, then dove back into his arms. "Please tell me it is true. Please." She was crying hysterically. "Please, please, please be true. My heart could not take one more cruelty." Jacob hushed her with a kiss. "It's true, Mary."

The Apache girl gasped for air, struggling to breathe. Her trembling hands reached out for the big man's face. She was full of doubt. "But how? Why would you do this for an Indian?"

Jacob smoothed her hair, trying to calm her. She was shaking uncontrollably. "I had no choice." He smiled. "Little Mea-a-ha is my squaw."

Mary froze. "It's you..." Her eyes suddenly filled with understanding. "We have heard of you. Mea-a-ha's black warrior. It is true."

The Apache fell into his arms, crying. "I thought we would never be rescued. I was sure Nah-kah-yen was dead."

She had endured so much grief. Mary's body went limp as she exhaled her agony in a wail that came from deep within her soul. Her torture was finally over.

Holding the girl, Jacob rocked her gently, letting her cry herself out. He felt her pain, but time was short. "Shhh... Mary. Listen, we are in great danger. We must wait until the house is silent; then, we can escape. After Sebastian is asleep we will get blankets and food if we can. Where is your baby?"

The girl took a deep breath, struggling to come to her senses. "He is in a room off the kitchen. Yessenia is a good woman. She will watch him until I return." Mary pressed her hands to her face and cried. "Poor Lori White Feather. Is there nothing you can do?"

Jacob shook his head. "With soldiers near, we must wait until the Mexican is asleep. We can't risk him shouting the alarm."

Her heart breaking for her friend, Mary clutched the big man's shirt, her eyes pleading. "What if it were Mea-a-ha?"

The big man's shoulders slumped. If it were Mea-a-ha, the hounds of hell could not keep him from breaking down the door. Lori deserved no less. Releasing Mary, Jacob pulled a long knife from his boot. "This may be the death of us."

Chapter -19-
Friendships and Darkness

The cold starlight sparkled in the little pool, adorning it with silver jewels. It should have been beautiful, worthy of a lover's poem, but Mea-a-ha lingered at its edge, knowing she had killed her first man. Inside she was dying. A part of her that was innocent was lost forever. The girl wept.

Standing in the shadows of the ragged cliff, Jube watched the poor child suffer until it knotted in his stomach. The soldier's voice broke in an anguished whisper. "Christ, Kane, ain't no one gunna' blame ya if ya kin' ease her pain. She's earned that much from us."

The tall writer slowly rose to his feet. In this Indian girl was the embodiment of love, and being part of a murder was more than her gentle heart could bear. He knew the price she had paid for the lives of her friends.

Quietly, Kane made his way through the dark to her side. Several hours had passed since the evil deed, and still she shook with grief. He put his arm around her. "Come sit with us. You shouldn't be alone."

Mea-a-ha could not tear her vision from the now-quiet water where the young vaquero had fallen. Her voice trembled weakly. "He was just a boy, and he had done no wrong."

The writer stroked her hair. "Sometimes it happens that way."

"Does it? Do we have a right to destroy what is good to survive?"

Kane shook his head. "It's a terrible thing."

Slowly, she lifted her teary eyes. "Is this what you fear, Kane? Killing?"

He stood silently, thinking. "I guess maybe it is. It's not dying I think of, it's killing. The Indian I killed yesterday, it haunts me."

Kane tried to make sense of it. "It doesn't seem right, but maybe sometimes it's necessary. Maybe we need to be more like Nah-kah-yen and Jacob."

Mea-a-ha threw herself against him and cried. "No. It hurts. I don't want to be like them."

Pulling the girl from the water's edge, Kane led her away. "I know. It leaves you sick."

She sobbed. "I can't go back yet. Take me for a walk."

"If it will make you feel better, little warrior."

"Please don't call me that. I'm a girl."

Leaving the pool, the couple silently made their way into the empty night, each praying that the darkness would hide their sins. Mea-a-ha closed her eyes even to the stars and let Kane guide her away. She emptied her tormented mind, desperately trying to lose the haunting image of the young vaquero's accusing eyes.

In the writer's embrace, she found comfort. Tonight she needed him. Mea-a-ha sobbed. "Kane." She spoke his name and nothing more.

They walked slowly, her steps stumbling as they went. He couldn't bear the Indian girl's sadness. Stopping, Kane just held her, listening to her breathe. Each quivering sob told of such sorrow. Her damp cheek was warm against his. "Yes, cry it out, my darling."

She crumbled against him. Tears fell like a needed rain. "It hurts."

"I know."

The girl surrendered her emotions into his care and cried. Kane kissed her forehead. "I know."

His heart opened to the innocent Apache and took her in. Her agony, her love, her soiled beauty was his. She folded softly against his chest and wept. The young writer stroked her hair.

Turning the girl in his arms, Kane lifted her tear-stained face and tenderly kissed her soft lips. Mea-a-ha dropped her head and leaned against his coat. "No, Kane."

They were two young people all alone, tangled in a grotesque nightmare. He could hide his feelings no longer. Lifting her face in his hands, he pressed his lips to hers in a long, slow kiss. She did not resist. When he released her, she fell away, trembling. "Please take me back."

Kane pulled her close, feeling her warm body, his hands not only holding, but touching her. The writer's embrace was intimate. "Please, Kane."

Even now when she needed him most, Mea-a-ha could not give herself to this handsome young man.

Relenting, Kane let his arms fall away. "As you wish, my darling." His anguished voice was barely a whisper, carrying injury of his own.

They walked slowly back the way they had come. Mea-a-ha slipped her hand into his. "I'm sorry."

Kane pressed her fingertips to his lips. "Mea-a-ha, perhaps I should be sorry...but I'm not. If I could make you surrender, I'd carry you from this pit and lay you beneath the stars."

She snuggled against his arm. "I need you, Kane. Please let me trust you."

The writer hung his head. "Very well. If that is your heart."

"I don't know my heart any more. But it is what must be."

Rising to his full stature, Kane tried to be strong. "I will be your friend and swallow my feelings. But if I grow cold, please understand it is because I could find no middle ground."

Mea-a-ha took a few steps and then fell to her knees. Kane quickly knelt by her side. He felt selfish and cruel. "I am sorry. I..." His voice trailed away.

The Apache girl leaned closer to the ground, burying her face in her hands. "Everyone says, 'Wise little Mea-a-ha,' but I don't even know my own heart. How wise is that?"

The young man pressed his head against the fallen girl. "It's not your fault. It's mine. I am sorry, not for kissing you, but for not being stronger."

Mea-a-ha slowly lifted herself and crawled back into his arms. She closed her eyes, accepting his comfort once more. "Jacob said I could have you for my friend. Where he must go, I cannot. He did not want me to be alone, but..."

The injured girl's delicate fingers clutched at the writer's coat as she pulled herself closer. "He doesn't know how dark it is. He doesn't understand... Just hold me."

Kane brushed her cheek with his lips and finished her thoughts. "...that when all is dark, and death overwhelms us, we sometimes need more from our friends than the cold light of day will allow."

Hugging her tight, he whispered. "It is dark now, my love. In this fragile moment we only have each other." Lowering his head, Kane nuzzled her. "I do not mean to betray Jacob...but tonight, so far away, maybe he would understand. It is not your beauty I desire, but the warmth of your heart."

The girl slipped her arms around the young writer's neck. Slowly, she took a breath. "Kane, hear my words. You may have one last kiss. After that, if we cannot survive without each other, then we must die with what honor is left to us. My heart belongs to Jacob."

Holding the Indian girl as tight as he could, Kane closed his eyes. "Forgive me, my beautiful savage. I will save my last kiss, and hope that someday I can earn it."

When they returned to the grotto, Mea-a-ha slipped her hand from Kane's and sought out her brother. She dared not spend the night in the young writer's embrace. Already she felt the others were beginning to question her friendship with the man called Kane.

Mea-a-ha's mind and soul were in turmoil. Her husband was in the jaws of the enemy, a young vaquero lay dead by her design, and Kane... how had everything gone so wrong?

The little Apache felt weak, like her heart might stop beating. Only now it was racing wildly, and she couldn't calm it.

Miserable beyond all measure, she dropped beside her brother and rested her head on his shoulder.

Mea-a-ha shoved her clenched fists between her knees and pouted like a small child seeking comfort from demons haunting the night.

Daniel could hear her breath quiver. He slipped his arm around her and pulled his sister's head to his chest. She snuggled closer, trying to make herself comfortable. Several short sniffs told the boy she was crying. He hugged her and whispered. "Crying is good. Tears wash away the pain."

The girl snuggled deeper. "It seems like it is all I do on this terrible journey. I wish we were back in the Hollow."

Daniel smoothed her hair. "Jacob wanted us to stay in the Hollow, but I disobeyed. I am sorry, my sister."

Mea-a-ha lifted her head and quickly wiped her eyes. "No, I didn't mean that…It's not you…" She started crying again. "Just hard to know what is right anymore."

For a long time the boy remained silent, searching for the words he knew he must say. He took a breath. "Some things are right, and it is not a matter of knowing. We just do."

He stopped. A heavy weight was on his heart. "We owe Jacob everything. I know you are hurting, my sister, but…well, we owe him everything. It is how we behave."

The girl's tears burst anew, drenching her cheeks and soaking her brother's shirt. She threw her arms around his neck and struggled to speak. "I know. I love him as much as you."

Daniel swallowed a tightening lump. "Do you love Kan…" Mea-a-ha pressed her fingertips to his lips. "Please, Daniel. Don't. It is hard to explain. Jacob understands…" She paused, "…most of it."

The boy needed to know. "But, do you love him?"

Mea-a-ha tried to nod and shake her head at the same time. "It is hard. There are different kinds of love. If not for Kane, I would have perished. Please understand."

Daniel stiffened. Mea-a-ha knew he did not accept her answer. She wanted to explain, but she didn't understand herself. Her lips parted, praying for the right words…none came. She crumbled against him, sobbing. There was no defense. Her heart was laid bare for his judgment.

Holding her close, Daniel softened. His sister was hurting. He did not understand, but he loved her. "You saved all our lives today. That was very brave."

The boy's words were meant to bring comfort. She was grateful. The tears slowed just a little. Daniel wiped them for her. "You're kind of pretty, too…for a sister."

A small chuckle bubbled in her throat. Her tiny hand slapped his chest. "Don't tease me."

He folded her fingers in his. "Juan won't ever be the same."

Mea-a-ha blushed. "Daniel! I won't be able to look at him if you don't stop."

The boy grinned. "Poor Juan, having to see my sister all nak..." Mea-a-ha clapped her hand over her brother's mouth. "I'm going to cry."

Daniel kissed her hand and pulled it away. "You win. I'm already soaked."

"I hope you drown." Mea-a-ha settled against him and closed her eyes. Her brother's teasing had eased her pain. Maybe she could sleep now.

The young boy wrapped his gangly arms around the wounded girl and stared at the stars in turbulent thought. He filled his lungs and released the soothing air in a long, slow exhale. 'Too much to think about.' Turning to his beautiful sister, he smiled and let his troubles go. There would be another day.

As peace returned, Daniel toyed with her hair and gently brushed it from her face. He felt better, too. "Mea-a-ha."

She nuzzled her head in acknowledgement. Daniel continued. "I don't understand everything, but as long as you love Jacob... well, if you would rather spend the night with someone your own age, it's okay with me."

Mea-a-ha kissed his cheek without opening her eyes. She felt very tired. "I'm staying right here with my baby brother. So if your arm falls asleep, too bad." Wiggling, she made herself comfortable. "Goodnight, Shidizheé."

The silent stars floating above twinkled serenely. A cool breeze dried the last tears from her cheek. It was over. Brother and sister were at peace.

"Mea-a-ha"

"Yes."

"Juan would hold you."

"I said goodnight."

The Mimbre Riders, as Kane had named them, picked their holes among the rocks and surrendered to fatigue. Only Jube remained awake. It was always possible that someone would come hunting the fallen vaquero. The burden that had been Jacob's was now his. He stared into the endless night. It would be a long vigil.

While Kane and Mea-a-ha were away, he had talked with the others. If dawn came without Jacob, Mason would help him get the Indian girl and her brother out of Mexico. Juan could not bear the thought of leaving Roberto behind, but a promise was made, and come the red glow of morning, he would obey Jube's order to ride.

Nah-kah-yen would not go with them. He had returned for his Mary. Come morning, with the sun to his back, he would charge the wall. At least she would know he tried.

Hearing footsteps, Jube lifted from his thoughts. It was Mason returning from his turn at watch. The officer settled down by the buffalo soldier. "All's quiet. Maybe they aren't searching for us." He rested the butt of his Winchester in the dirt between his boots and put his weight on it. "Four hours to dawn. It seems like a long time, and yet it doesn't."

The black man felt no need to respond. McCrae was just thinking out loud.

The young man peered into the shadows around him. He could hear nothing. Everyone was asleep. "Jube, it may seem wrong to say, but if it comes to it, I think it's best that Nah-kah-yen dies here."

Mason shook his head as he tried to make sense of it all. "Never knew an Indian while I lived back East with my mother. They were just an enemy out West to be killed. You know...dreams of glory." He stretched out his leg and then bent it back. "After fighting beside Nah-kah-yen, getting to know that wise little girl and her amazing brother, well, it's not in my heart to take the warrior back to be shot. I will because it's my duty, but it's not in my heart."

Mason scanned the dark once more, wondering where the girl was. "She's a pretty one, and boy, what she did today. But it takes a special man to forsake civilized people for a ... well, you know. Jacob's giving up a lot."

The black man broke his silence. "He's gotten a lot." Jube was surprised by his own answer. The Apache girl had given Jacob a reason to live.

A heavy blade of guilt suddenly stabbed deep in his chest. Jube avoided the girl as much as possible. Her being Apache made him uncomfortable. Still, he knew her worth. Jacob was a lucky man. "Guess I've been a mite unkind to her. Kept my distance. Maybe I coulda' made things a bit easier on the little Injun."

Mason shrugged his shoulders, then changed his thoughts. "So the hour's coming. Guess you've been thinking a lot about that, too?"

The sergeant frowned. "Some."

McCrae gave a soft chuckle. "Funny. You and me, two soldiers, committed to wiping out the Apache nation, and here we are in a foreign land risking our lives to save them. How'd that happen?"

Jube shook his head. "Danged if I know." He sat in thoughtful silence. "Maybe its 'cuz they is fighting desperately for a lost cause, n' they ain't gived' up hope. So maybe all mankind gots' hope. You n' me is just two men among millions. They are the last of the Mimbres. If that don't matter, then nothin' does."

Jube was quiet for a moment. "Yes, sir. Jacob's a lucky man."

Mea-a-ha stirred in her slumber. The Indian girl did not wake, but somehow she knew it was Jube. His big hand rested tenderly on her shoulder for a long moment. He tucked the blanket close to her cheek, and then was gone.

Chapter -20-
Candlelight and Starlight

With an unnerving creak, the door slowly opened a hairsbreath. Pressing his eye to the crack, Jacob searched the cavernous hall. A single candle flickered yellow on a narrow table set against the wall. Moving quietly forward, his shadow loomed menacingly against the black rafters, a harbinger of the evil deed he was about to do. On this night, Don Sebastian would die.

Jacob glanced at the door Roberto had carried the Mimbre girl through. He wanted to warn the boy, but he dared not linger or make the slightest sound. He would deal with the Mexican rancher first.

Feeling the weight of his knife, Jacob turned his mind to what he must do and made his way to the end of the hall. Cautiously he pressed his ear to the heavy black door of Don Sebastian's chamber. He expected to hear the bed creaking or the girl crying, but there was only silence. Jacob took one last look behind him and carefully lifted the wooden latch with the blade of his knife. Inching the door ajar, he peered at its edge until he could finally see. The big man lowered his weapon and pushed the door all the way open. There was no more need for stealth.

The pale-skinned Apache girl stood naked at the side of the bed. Don Sebastian's fat body lay equally exposed before her. A jeweled Spanish sword driven through his throat impaled the evil man to the mattress. Beneath his head, a bright red circle on the white sheet mocked a halo. He was dead.

Jacob stepped close to the girl and touched her arm. She didn't move. "Lori." He shook her. "Lori."

Slowly the dazed girl raised her eyes and then gazed back at Don Sebastian. Her angelic voice was soft and whimsical. "He was drunk. It was easy." She reached out a tapered finger and traced the jeweled hilt. "His eyes were closed. I called his name so he would see me kill him."

The girl tilted her head in a sad frown. "He didn't laugh. I expected him too, but he didn't laugh." Lori raised her faraway stare to the big man beside her. "Maybe he didn't find it funny." She collapsed in Jacob's arms.

An old clock in the great hall downstairs struck three times, filling the cavernous hacienda with a deep foreboding tone that seemed to say; "Hurry. Time dooms all men."

No longer listening at doors, Jacob slipped breathlessly into the darkened room. On a small table in the corner, an iron candelabrum burned low. Between the pillars of a canopied bed, he found the young couple locked in a passionate embrace. Roberto's shirt was unbuttoned and hanging off his shoulder. Son-gee looked up, then quickly slid off the bed and pulled her dress down to her knees. Jacob rolled his eyes and tossed the Mexican boy his coat. "We're here to rescue them."

Roberto hurriedly tucked his shirt in. "It weren't my fault. It was her doin'. I think she's grateful."

Ignoring the boy's defense, Jacob roughly shoved Roberto's hat on his head, covering his eyes. "Come on, Don Juan."

Fumbling with his button, the youth followed the big man across the hall, continuing his protest. "We don't speak the same language so we just kept kissing." He paused and grabbed the girl's hand, dragging her along. "Never rescued anyone before."

As they entered the room, Mary Lost pony was slipping a dress over Lori's head. The closet was full of fine Spanish dresses for the Sebastian girls. Mary chose the nicest one. Tying a pink satin ribbon, she finished dressing her charge. Clothed as Lori was, no one could tell she had been raised Apache since she was ten years old.

Roberto turned his eyes from Lori and looked to Jacob, questioning. The big man ushered the boy towards the door. "Sebastian threw in his chips, drew the wrong queen."

Mary wrapped Lori in a blanket then handed one to Son-gee, and draped another over her arm. The Mimbre women were ready to go.

Taking the lead, Jacob headed down the broad stairs. Son-gee hung on Roberto's arm. Lori clung to Mary, her glassy eyes unblinking.

When they reached the main hall, Mary tugged at Jacob's sleeve and whispered. "The general left a guard outside the front door, I took him food. We can go through the kitchen after we get my baby, but the guard will see us when we try to ride away."

Jacob frowned. That wouldn't do. Pulling Son-gee off Roberto's arm, he spoke to her in Apache. She was the youngest and most innocent. The guard would never suspect her of treachery. "Son-gee, you must act frightened. Draw the guard inside. He will follow you."

Trembling even more, the wide-eyed girl looked to the older woman standing by her side. Her terror was real. Mary Lost Pony took the blanket from her. "It will be over soon, my child."

Loosening several buttons, Mary slid Son-gee's blouse off her shoulders and then shoved her towards the door. The others quickly got behind it. Tears of fright rolled down the young girl's cheeks, making her plight even more believable.

Holding her crumpled garment to her breasts with one hand, she gripped the big iron handle with the other and jerked it open. As the surprised guard whirled around, Son-gee babbled frantically in Apache. He reached for her, but she backed into the room, imploring him to come inside. Without hesitation, he followed her through the door. It shut hard behind him. The startled man spun around. A large fist smashed his nose into his face, sending him flying across the room. He was out cold before he hit the floor.

Snatching up the soldier's rifle, Jacob raised it high in the air and slammed the heavy steel butt down hard on the man's leg, just above the boot. It made a sickening snap. The big man handed the musket to the stunned boy. "He gets to live, but I'll be damned if I will have him riding after us."

With a candle from a nearby table, the two men and three Mimbre women quietly made their way down a long dark hall. With Sebastian dead, the large hacienda seemed strangely empty, like walking through a graveyard at night. Sounds unnoticed earlier in the night now echoed with growing alarm. Son-gee gripped the Mexican boy's arm tighter, her eyes prying around every corner.

At the end of the hall were three low steps leading down beneath a stone archway. Mary squeezed ahead and pushed open the small door to the kitchen. A lamp burned on the table. Yessenia sat in a wooden chair, cradling the baby in her arms. She raised her head and stared. There were tears in her eyes for the Apache girls, but now their presence told a new story. "Is he dead?"

Jacob nodded. The Mexican woman kissed the sleeping baby. "Good."

She rose from the chair and handed the child to his mother. Stepping away, she looked up at the big man. "This evil place will die without Don Sebastian. You must take me with you." Jacob's eyes grew wide with surprise. The woman folded her hands to her breast, pleading. "They will kill me if you leave and I do not sound the alarm."

Roberto spoke up. "Senor Rincon will give her work."

Jacob headed for the back door. "There's an eternity between now and then. She'd do better taking her chances with the soldiers."

Releasing a sigh, Jacob turned to Yessenia. "You'll need a sack of food, and you must get a blanket." He patted her hand. "We will try."

The old woman quickly scurried about, robbing the pantry. Jacob looked to Roberto and shook his head. "It's a heck of a mess. Lori's in shock. Mary's got an infant at her breast. Son-gee is glued to your arm like dead weight, and now we're dragging an old woman. Don't know how we are going to fight our way out of here."

Jacob paced the room and came back to the boy. A plan was forming in his head. "We came here to buy horses. We'll take the best of 'em. The women are light and the horses swift. If by some miracle we get past the Mexican army, we should be able to outrun them for awhile. Women tire easy, but it's the only chance we have. A man has gotta' make his own luck, and tonight we need it by the buckets."

Yessenia returned with the supplies. The time had come. Taking a moment, Jacob looked at the trusting faces of the desperate women. They had lived on the dark side of hell. Their fearful eyes told him he was their only salvation. If he failed it would be their death. It would be everyone's death. He couldn't let them down. Tonight of all nights, he had to believe this insane rescue was possible. He must find a way.

Jacob touched his finger to the soft cheek of Mary's sleeping baby and gave her a reassuring smile. "Someday you can tell this little Apache warrior how he rode into battle by the side of a buffalo soldier."

"Let's ride."

Blowing out the candle, Jacob opened the door and stepped into the starlight. It was one night he wished were darker. For the briefest moment, he listened intently; then he moved from the sheltered archway. An alley led to a tiny courtyard surrounded by low adobe walls and sharp cactus, each little more than shadows. Expecting the worst, Jacob slipped his pistol from his holster and hurried forward.

With the women between them, Roberto brought up the rear. The air was cool and eerie still. The rescued and the rescuers glanced anxiously from side to side, eager to be gone from this dreadful place.

At a small gate, the women bunched behind Jacob and tried to quiet their breathing. The big man waited, but time was against them. From here on out, their only concealment would be the moonless night. Summoning their courage, they slipped into an empty lane that led past the bunkhouse, and then to the stables. Roberto could hear the soft swishing of the women's dresses and feared that other ears might be listening as well.

Less than a dozen feet from the bunkhouse, Jacob suddenly stopped with a harsh whisper, "Drop!" The women melted to the ground and froze. The buffalo soldier had heard something they hadn't. A rusty hinge creaked faintly. The discernable tramping of bare feet on the stone walkway outside the bunkhouse door sent a chill through their hearts. Had they been found? Was it over? Would their flight end in a hail of gunfire?

Straining his young eyes, Roberto could barely make out the shape of a short man leaning against an adobe column.

A match burst to life. In the brief moment, Roberto glimpsed the frightened faces of the women before him; the glint of Jacob's outstretched pistol; and the ruddy complexion of a sleepy Mexican with rumpled hair. The boy held his breath, waiting for Jacob to pull his trigger. It didn't happen.

Lighting his smoke, the man blew out the match. Luckily, the flame was so close to his face it blinded him to the crouching figures just yards away. Roberto struggled to quiet the pounding in his chest with no success.

Soon dawn would break. Every second was precious, but the sleepy vaquero could not know their hurry. Several times he raised the quirt to his mouth. Smoke curled around the red glow, then his hand would drop to his side, cinders swirling and fading in the air. The man was so close Roberto could smell the warm tobacco on the night air.

Rolling a husky cough the man cleared his throat, took another drag, coughed again, and spit.

Huddled in the lane, fearing the worst, time was counted in heartbeats dwindling away, heartbeats that might be their last. Every second became maddening. Roberto wondered how much longer it could go on. His own gun sweated in the palm of his young hand; his fingers cramped.

Then with a sudden awareness, Roberto realized that the Mimbre girl Son-gee was pressed against his arm, her tiny hands clutching at his sleeve. He could feel her tremble as she wiped a frightened tear on his shoulder. How fragile and innocent she seemed. Deep inside the boy, a growing warmth he'd never known charged every muscle in his body. His own fears faded as he swore a silent oath to protect this tender girl with his life. Ever so silently, he slipped his arm around her. In the dark shadows of a lonely lane, a boy took his place as a man. He faced forward with grim determination. No harm would befall her—not this night, not on his watch. Roberto's heart calmed.

The red glow lifted to the Mexican's face once more. He took a final drag, then tossed the quirt to the ground. It was over. The man would go back to bed and they'd make their escape.

As Roberto started to breathe, a new sound arose, water splashing on dirt. The vaquero was peeing off the steps. This, too, the boy could smell, adding to the agony of interminable delay.

At length the man's stream slowly trailed off, trickled, and ended. With a final cough, the door creaked open and shut. The vaquero was gone.

Without a word, Jacob rose and moved on. The women followed, terror quickening their feet. By the time they reached the stable, they were almost running. Once inside, the women released their panic in emotional squeals as they bunched together, seeking comfort in each other.

With no way to see what they were doing, Jacob struck a match. To Roberto, it seemed brighter than a haystack fire. It burst in brilliance for a second and then died, but it was enough time for them to spot the horses and gear.

Now in pitch black, working by memory, they quickly saddled their own horses. Then, grabbing four bridles from the wall, Jacob and Roberto picked mounts for the women. There were horses in the corral, but the men took the ones from the stables. These were the fat Mexican's very best. Four tall Andalusians carrying four small women— it might just work.

The men moved quickly, and soon all the horses were ready to ride. Their luck was holding by a prayer. They had gotten farther without a gunfight than Jacob had expected.

The night air felt cold as they let the spirited horses into the open lane. Without a word, the giant man lifted each woman, one after another, and set them on a saddle.

They were mounted and ready to ride. Jacob glanced to the eastern sky then grabbed the boy by his arm, pulling him back inside the stables. He hurried to the row of saddles on a long railing.

"Cut all the cinches." The buffalo soldier pulled his knife.

"Yes, sir." Roberto did the same.

It was a risk that took precious time, but Jacob knew what he was doing. Twenty belts were cut. Twenty vaqueros would not ride this night. When the cry at the gate was sounded, the vaqueros, caught up in the heat of the moment, would no doubt race to pursue as men do. Jacob figured that when they found their saddles slashed it would slow them down long enough for them to learn that Don Sebastian was dead, and hopefully they'd realize the escaping Indians no longer mattered. There would not be paid for the long chase by a dead man.

Hurrying from the stables, Jacob and Roberto tossed all the bridles into the watering trough and returned to the women.

Now only the army at the gate remained, and the gate itself. Jacob had already thought of that. When he threw the bridles in the trough, he drew a bucket of water, intent on making his own luck as he always had.

Mounting his saddle, he led his band of women quietly down the lane. The hooves of a half-dozen horses cannot be silenced. Jacob could only hope that the sleeping vaqueros were roused by the slow loping of the horses through the thick adobe walls they would not be alarmed. Perhaps they would stir reluctantly in their beds, but steal a few more winks. He was counting on human nature.

Several yards from the gate, Jacob dismounted and hurried ahead on foot. Quietly lifting the bucket, he poured the water over the iron hinges to silence their squeaks. He slid back the bolt, then returned to the boy and whispered his plan. "When I throw open the gate, lead the women at full charge. Make this your greatest ride. Let nothing stop you. I will catch up with you if I can."

That was it. There would surely be at least one guard, but there was nothing more Jacob could do. He gripped the bolt. The next ten seconds would determine their fate. If the guard was caught by surprise, if the women could ride fast enough, if the Mexicans were slow to respond, if, if, if. It was now or never.

Summoning his strength, Jacob threw the gate wide open. Slapping his reins, Roberto charged through. The women stayed at his heels, and the night exploded with thundering hooves. A startled soldier jumped into the middle of the road, shouting as he leveled his musket. The boy knew his duty. Without hesitation, flames leaped from Roberto's hand. The dark form crumpled to the ground, his screams trampled by the fleeing horses.

Curses of men kicking from their bedrolls, awoke the night. The big man climbed to his saddle and hammered back his gun. Win or lose, it would be a ride to remember.

Jube raised his head. The distant popping of rifles rumbled across the dark, grassy plains. "To your saddles, to your saddles, everyone!" His voice rang loud and clear. "Awake, we must ride."

Throwing back their blankets, everyone scrambled to their feet. Horses stomped and whinnied as the startled companions rushed at them in the dark amid cries of confusion. Trying to bring order, Jube shouted above the din. "Jacob done made his play. The shootin' means the Mexicans ain't got 'em yet."

The buffalo soldier grabbed the saddle horn and mounted up. "Ride, ya' sons-of-bitches. Follow me."

Whirling their horses, everyone obeyed the black soldier's command. Haste was needed. The time had come. This night, hope and fear rode together.

Moving faster than was safe, Jube led his band splashing through the pool and down the rocky ravine. Hearts beat and hooves pounded around turn after turn as they raced to the aid of their friends. Nah-kah-yen's rifle was already in his hand as he whipped his pony to catch up to the soldier.

The dry wash straightened out and the horses found greater speed. Soon the sandy walls dropped away and the would-be-rescuers were in the open, charging west across the broad plains.

Far to the south, distant flashes mapped out a running battle. Jacob was being pursued. The burst of gunfire clearly showed two groups, the hunters and the hunted.

Racing onward, Jube kept pace, but he did not close the distance. After years of fighting by Jacob's side, he knew his old friend well. At some point Jacob would turn north. Jube rode on.

The night was full of stars filtering through a misty haze. The steady drumming of hooves and the distant pop of guns blended with the horses' rasping breaths. Torn from their slumber and rushing into the night, it seemed like a terrible dream. Disbelieving minds fought to understand as their senses jolted with the crack of every gun.

On they went. Their speed was great, but the ponies were becoming winded. Jacob still hadn't turned north. Jube had expected it to happen long before now.

The chase continued farther into the plains. Onward they charged. Jube glanced to the east. Soon dawn would break. Jacob must turn into the hills before it was too late. There would be no eluding the Mexicans after light.

The fire from the soldier's guns died away. Then, out in front of them, flames leaped, and the chase renewed. Jube suddenly realized this pattern had happened several times before. Fool! Why hadn't he realized it sooner? The black man pulled to an abrupt halt. All around him, his companions jerked their reins and came barreling to his side. Mea-a-ha, frantic, cried from the dark, "Jube, we must help him."

In a desperate rage Nah-kah-yen roared. "To battle, to battle," but Jube's deep voice thundered above them all. "Follow me!"

He turned his horse around and they raced back the way they had come. It made no sense, but he was their leader, and they had promised to obey him. Their hearts sick with doubt, the Mimbre Riders turned and raced away, abandoning their friends.

Surrounded by a sea of darkness with the flashes of light disappearing in the distance, it all seemed wrong. With every stride in the opposite direction, Mea-a-ha's fears grew worse. What was Jube doing? She wanted to scream, beg him to go back. The distant shots, the droning of hooves jumbled her mind.

They had ridden for some time, almost back to the mouth of the ravine, when Jube slowed to a halt. The coughing of the horses died away, and all went silent. The fearful riders edged forward to the buffalo soldier's side.

Precious time was slipping by. Why had they stopped? Behind them the gunfire was all but lost in the distance. Their friends were far away. For a moment longer, the silence held, then Mason finally whispered. "Jube. Where's Jacob?"

The burly soldier was slow to answer as he strained his ears to the night. Finally he risked a few words. "That's him back there on the road, sho' enough."

Mea-a-ha pleaded. "Then why, Jube?"

"Shhh..." Jube listened a moment longer. "Ol' Jacob was firin'. Firin' when the dark could of hid 'em. He's leading the army away. Iffin' I'm right, Roberto is somewhere out here lookin' for us...Shhh."

Jube pushed his horse forward and stopped. "Listen."

Ever so faintly, a hoof scraped on stone. Then there was silence. Then another hoof scrape. "Wait here. It could be soldiers."

Jube headed on alone. Daniel started counting the seconds. He would wait for Jube if he must, but his heart wanted to race to his father's side. Surely Jube must have a plan to ride to Jacob's aid. He must.

Unable to think, the boy lost count and waited silently with the rest. Interminable seconds slowly passed. Then, above all hope, Jube's voice carried softly through the dark. "Nah-kah-yen...come get your son."

A trembling unmanly cry escaped the proud warrior's lips. He kicked his pony forward. A moment later the brave's voice gasped with emotion, and everyone knew he held his child in his arms.

Riders hurried forward, becoming aware of others joining them from the opposite direction. Women wept aloud. Soon they were all whispering at once. Horses bumped together, arms reached out, hugging invisible strangers. Everyone scrambled from their saddles, embracing whoever they could find. There would be time enough later to learn their names.

Nah-kah-yen's voice shook with emotion. "Mary!" A woman cried in response. At last the Apache held his family in his arms.

"My husband, I thought you were dead."

The warrior laughed, releasing his fears.

There was great elation for the companions old and new, but this fragile moment was for the Mimbre warrior and his small family. The incomparable journey with all its hardships had been for Nah-kah-yen. The family torn asunder was whole once more. Their joy was a victory shared by all.

Jube raised his head to the east. A faint light heralded the dawn. Slowly, dim faces took form in the dark. Mary Lost Pony released her husband and embraced a small figure beside her. "Mea-a-ha, thank you."

The old friends cried. Their worlds had changed since they last met. Mea-a-ha held out her arms. "Can I hold your baby?"

For a brief moment they pretended the Mimbre tribe still remained.

Daniel stepped forward. "What of my father?"

Jube placed his hand on the boy's shoulder. "Don't worry about yo' daddy, Son. Alone, the Mexican army ain't never gunna' catch him. He is only in danger when he's strapped with us."

The Indian boy teared with relief. "But…"

"He'll find us when he's ready."

Roberto appeared in the gray light and stood by his friend's side. "Don't fret, Apache. After what I've witnessed tonight, it's the soldiers who should tremble in fear."

Juan joined the other boys. "See. It is us who needs your gun, not your father."

For the first time, the boys hugged. This night, they had grown— Roberto, most of all.

Jube raised his voice. "Best mount up. We're in danger here." The urgency of escape suddenly returned. Reluctantly, the friends pulled apart and climbed in their saddles.

Lieutenant McCrae noticed a white woman who had never dismounted. She sat silently holding her reins, dressed as if she were attending a royal ball, and not escaping across the harsh desert of Mexico. Mason went to her. "Miss. Can I help you?"

The girl slowly lifted her eyes but did not answer. He reached out and touched her hand. "We have to go, ma'am."

Roberto rode past. "Lori, this is Mason. He's a friend."

The concerned look in the boy's eyes told the lieutenant that the girl would need special care.

Mason took the reins from her hand. "Here, Miss Lori, I will lead you."

Heading out, Mea-a-ha hurried her pony to Jube's side and spoke softly, not wanting to alarm her brother. "Jube, Jacob will come soon? Yes?"

The soldier's eyes saddened." It's the Mexican army that'll come soon. Anytime now there'll be enough light for 'em ta' see they is chasin' only one man. Then they'll leave some soldiers on Jacob's tail and turn the rest around ta' find us."

The girl's face fell. Jube reached out a big hand and rubbed her back. "I'm right sorry, little Apache. Ain't no kind way of sayin' it. We's gots' lots of hard ridin' 'for we is out of danger. It could be days or more 'afore ol' Jacob can shake free. He warned us. It's just plum amazin' we got this far. I'm mighty sorry, but it'll be some time."

Mea-a-ha sniffed. "Thank you, Jube. I'm glad you're here." She lowered her head and fell back in line.

With Jube in the lead, the party hurried for the nearest hills, and for a moment the threat of the soldiers seemed far behind them. The murmur of voices full of emotions greeted the new day.

Daniel and Juan rode behind Jube, leading the packhorses. The boys were the best of friends, and always happiest when together. They looked behind and grinned. Something had changed in the short night. The young Mimbre Son-gee pressed her mount close to Roberto, her hand tightly clutching his. Their tall friend glared at them, knowing he would be in for a lot of teasing. The Indian girl didn't seem to care. This brave youth had rescued her from a nightmare, and she would not leave his side.

Next in line, Mason looked to his own charge. He was holding the reins of the silent one, unsure if the girl even knew he was there. As amber light broke over the mountain, the lieutenant could see her skin was pale. Her hair was yellow and full of curls. She was the White Apache he had heard about. The girl was adorned in a beautiful layered dress tied with pink silk ribbons. Compared to the clothing of the Indian women, she looked more like a frilly laced doll, her porcelain lips pursed in silence. Captured by Apaches and enslaved by Mexicans, Mason wondered if she had always been this way.

Mea-a-ha and Kane rode side by side, their hands, too, almost touching. On this desperate journey, their hearts held them together when courage failed. A friendship had crossed its bounds, and neither knew how to find their way back. The stallion and the mare moved together until their legs brushed. Mea-a-ha lifted her eyes to the adoring stare of the handsome writer, then slowly turned away.

The brave Mexican woman Yessenia rode alone. She had not been a slave like the Mimbres, but still she had suffered terribly under Don Sebastian's cruel hand. Before the Apaches had been caught, she had been the only woman and had not escaped his coarse brutality.

The old woman was now among strangers. She did not know where she was going, nor did she care. The people surrounding her were kind. That alone was a vast improvement. Well past fifty, Yessenia would start her life anew if they survived the next day.

Lastly came Nah-kah-yen, the Mimbre Apache. Out of the annihilation of his people, he had saved his fledgling family. Despite the danger trailing them, he couldn't take his eyes off his beautiful squaw and child.

Mary Lost Pony gazed upon her husband with deep admiration. Somehow beyond all hope, her brave warrior had returned from the dead to rescue her from the darkest of evils. Just as amazing, he had accomplished it with the help of his strange friends of many colors. If life gave them only one day, it was all worth it. Her family was together again.

Chapter -21-
Saddles

East of the mountains from where they had come, the vast desert stretched to the Rio Grande. Mesquite, creosote, saltbrush, yucca, and Spanish bayonet grew where little else could. It had proven an unyielding barrier that took its toll on the rescuers and their horses, but here on the western slopes, the land was green from the spring rains. Wide, grassy valleys bordered by scattered trees spread for miles across a rolling terrain. Grama grass, juniper and oak mingled with the higher mountain's pines, offering a welcome change.

All around the fleeing riders, the land was beautiful and full of life. Jube had spotted peccary crossing the trail, and even a spotted jaguar at dawn. Small parrots squawked in the trees, while hungry eagles soared overhead.

Shaking off his wonder, the soldier had to remind himself that every moment in Mexico their lives were in great peril.

Jube squinted his weary eyes. In the far distance, hazy mesas broke the pale blue morning skyline. The high bluffs of his own country were still days away, but not so for the Mexican army. He hurried on.

It was a race to the border now, and he knew they could make time if they stayed on the plains. Still, they would be less visible sneaking through the foothills. It was tempting, but Jube figured the army was at least an hour behind and hopefully more, so while the horses had strength left in them, he held his charges to a fast pace over the endless meadows.

The morning air was cool, and a prolonged gallop seemed advisable. He rode alone, reflecting on what had happened and fearing what was to come.

Against all hope, they had rescued the Mimbre women. It was a feat worthy of the writer's pen, if they lived to tell the story. The Mimbre Riders; was what Kane had named them. Jacob called them fools.

By noon, Jube started pushing more towards the foothills. They had good horses, but they were suffering from the trail and the battle. Don Sebastian's Andalusians were fast, but they didn't have the stamina of horses bred for the desert. Maybe one more day and all the animals would be done in.

The women, unaccustomed to the jarring of horseback riding, were tiring too, and the baby was beginning to fuss. It would do no good to kill them all after that they had gone through to rescue them.

Sighing, Jube slowed the ponies. He had done what he could to extend their lead. Now they would settle in for the long chase.

The Mexican soldiers were leathery men, bred to the saddle. How the women would fare after another twenty hours on horseback, Jube didn't know. He would push them as far as he could.

With Jacob gone, Lieutenant McCrae felt his place was at the front by the buffalo soldier's side. Unfortunately, the white Apache girl made that all but impossible.

She still hadn't spoken a word. He thought; 'How strange and very sad she is.' Her vacant stare held a story that Mason wanted to know, so for now he would stay with his charge.

Tugging her reins, he turned forward and continued on. Had it not been for the girl's presence, his thoughts would have no doubt been on Nah-kah-yen. Seeing the warrior with his wife and child after what everyone had gone through to bring them together left him with a disquieting truth. It was his responsibility to once more tear this little family asunder. Mason looked at the silent girl, comforted by the distraction of his new duty.

A late lunch was eaten in the saddle. The young lieutenant passed the girl a biscuit along with some dried meat. She took it without comment, though her eyes lingered briefly before withdrawing back into her own world.

Undaunted, Mason offered his canteen. "Here, Miss Lori, a sip might do you good."

The girl's eyes look up from the saddle horn, where they had been locked all morning. To the young officer's surprise, she reached out and took the canteen from his hand. He watched as she took a long, slow drink. When the girl was done, she wiped her lips with the back of her hand, then hugged the canteen to her breast and lowered her head once more. After a long silence she whispered. "Thank you."

At least she spoke English. Mason smiled. "You're welcome, Miss Lori." He knew it was too soon to engage her in conversation, so for now he would just try to ease her fears. "Don't you worry; I won't let anything hurt you."

The unending trail with so few breaks made the day long. Jube had pushed them hard. He knew that in the days to come it would be more difficult, so he would demand as much from his small band as he could. The Mexican soldiers would have to wear blisters to make up the distance that ol' Jacob had bought them with his early morning charade. Jube felt confident that on this day at least, they would increase their lead. He wished that was their only problem.

Daniel left his friends and galloped Snow Raven to Jube's side. He tried to calm his breathing. "Jube."

The black soldier stared straight ahead. "I see 'em."

The boy looked surprise. "You've seen the Indians on the ridge?"

Jube nodded. "Yep. They're stayin' out of range, an' I've only seen two, so I guess they ain't gunna' try anything while it's light."

Daniel scanned the trees. "I think there are three. Should I tell Nah-kah-yen?"

"Guessin' he knows n' doesn't want ta' worry his squaw. Drop back and tell 'em I want ta' talk with 'em. Stay with his woman til' he returns." The boy started to fall back. Jube quickly added, "Try to let Mason know without alarmin' the girl."

As Daniel galloped to the back of the line, he made eye contact with the lieutenant and quickly glanced to the ridge. That was enough. The officer understood. Daniel hurried on.

A moment later the warrior came riding forward and settled in by Jube's side. "Terahumara. Maybe scouts. Maybe not."

Jube nodded. "Any ideas on what they will do?"

The Apache warrior tightened his grip on his rifle. "They will disappear. Then ambush us along the trail. Test us."

Nah-kah-yen was silent for a long moment. Finally he spoke with cold resolve. "It will be your battle."

The brave kicked his pony and raced back to the rear. Jube understood. They had depended on the Mimbre before, but this time someone else would have to lead the fight. Nah-kah-yen would protect his family first. After all he'd gone through to get them back, Jube couldn't blame him.

When Daniel came forward again, Jube summoned the other two boys as well. His jaw was set, and his eyes were pinned to the horizon. They knew something was up, and their young hearts began to race. "Boys, iffin' I call ya', we is gunna' do a little soldiering. Apache, you flank left. Roberto and Juan, flank right. Keep yo' wits. Don't get strung out, n' don't get ahead of me."

The commanding tone of Jube's orders reminded the boys that he too had once been a sergeant in the U.S Calvary. "Keep the pressure on 'em. Let them make the mistakes."

Juan saluted. "Yes, Sir, Sarge.'"

That was all. The boys fell back. Roberto deposited Son-gee with Yessenia, and had the old woman assure the young girl that he'd return for her. The lanky youth then galloped back to his friends and took center position as they rode three abreast. Son-gee thought how bold her tall Mexican hero looked as he rode to protect her. It brought her needed comfort.

Glancing at each other with dry mouths, the boys shared the realization that they were now the first line of defense. Jacob was gone, and at barely sixteen, the brunt of the battle would fall upon them. Like it or not, the burden of men is to go in harm's way, to surrender their lives in the protection of others. Death was an acceptable price. This night it was theirs to pay.

Watching the hills, Mason pretty much figured out that he was needed right where he was. Lori still held his canteen like a child cuddling a rag doll. If it came to a fight, she'd slow him down, but there was no other way.

Twisting in his saddle, the young officer stared at the writer until the man finally looked his way. Kane realized something was up. The lieutenant scanned the hills and loosened his gun in the holster, then turned and continued riding as though nothing was wrong.

Mea-a-ha was staring across the grassy planes, dreaming of when Jacob would return. Lost in thought, she suspected nothing. Kane was not sure of the danger, so he would not alarm her. His hand fell to the butt of his black Colt .44.

Fear once more tightened his chest, but this time it was not for himself. Jacob was gone and the Indian girl's protection was his alone. Kane grew angry at the thought of anyone trying to hurt her. He clenched his teeth. If it came to fight, this day he'd stand.

Up ahead, the trail narrowed as it wound between a line of large, gray rocks. The manzanita and madrona tangled with the wavy leaf oak, limiting their vision to just a few yards.

Without turning around, Jube spoke in a low voice. "Apache, what's your count?"

Daniel calmed his voice. "Five."

Juan looked at his friend with surprise. He had seen only two braves. The boy shrunk in his saddle. It would be the one he didn't see that would get him.

Pulling his reins, Jube brought them to a halt. He had not seen the Indians for some time, and if ever there was a perfect place for an ambush, it would be in the thicket ahead. He raised his voice. "Mason, Kane, let the womenfolk rest. Get 'em out of the saddles."

The two men quickly dismounted. Mason didn't waste time being polite. He plucked the startled girl from her horse. She tried to stand, but he sat her down beneath the oak brush. "Stay here, Miss." He went to help the others.

Kane did the same with Mea-a-ha. Her eyes grew large with fear. This was not the way men treated women unless there was danger. She grabbed Kane's hand as it slipped from her waist.

"Kane?"

"Get beneath the brush and be still."

Mea-a-ha trembled. Something was dreadfully wrong. She looked behind. Nah-kah-yen already had his family out of sight. He alone stayed with the horses, his Winchester held across his chest.

When the commotion settled, Jube pulled his rifle from his scabbard. The boys quickly did the same. If the Indians lay in wait, they knew now that the black gringo was aware of their plan.

Jube measured the setting sun. It was his only hope. In a minute, it would be behind them, blinding the attackers. He would have one chance to find the savages. Then twilight and shadows would give the advantage back to the Indians.

Mason tied the horses and hurried back to Lori's side. He drew his sidearm. In an instant, the women all knew that danger had found them. Son-gee cried and clung to Yessenia.

Kane slipped his .44 into his hand and stepped to the middle of the trail. Lean and tall, dressed in black, he looked deadly as a panther. Mea-a-ha was surprised how bold the timid writer had become. With a sudden gasp, she realized it was for her. He would stand his ground, kill, and die for her.

"Get ready." Jube searched the dense brush ahead, figuring out where he would be if he were an Indian. A thick scrub oak moved ever so slightly less than thirty yards straight ahead. Kicking his horse, Jube fired his Winchester with one hand and charged forward. "Wake up ya' mangy redskins. Its time to die."

Thunder and curses filled the air. An Indian jumped from the bush. Daniel's rifle cracked, and the man fell dead. Whipping his horse faster, Jube fired wildly and raced on. If he could make it through to the next outcropping of rocks, he would be behind the Indians, and they would have to fight in two directions. Overhead, leaves dropped as bullets cut their path.

Daniel fired into the dense underbrush twice more and then flanked a wide left, intending to come around from the side. Roberto took the high ground to the right. Galloping a short distance from the trail, he jumped clear of the saddle, firing as he landed on the ground.

Alone in the middle, Juan fired to both sides of the trail, laying down cover for Jube. The Indians instinctively ducked as the hail of lead tore a broad swath through the path, but only for an instant. Moving to new positions, their own reports joined the vicious melee.

It all happened in a brief second. A second was all Jube needed. Reaching the rocks, he whirled his horse around and levered three more rounds before diving to the ground.

Like someone blowing out a bright lantern, the sunrays flashed and were gone. Colors evaporated, leaving the glen a deadly shade of gray. The initial engagement was over and all fell silent.

Taking advantage of the momentary reprieve, each man reloaded his weapon and reassessed his position.

Juan, realizing he was in the open, kicked his pony forward and raced to a large thicket. As he leaped from the saddle, he caught movement in mid-air. The boy crashed to the ground and quickly flattened out. Flames burst through the dense brush as bullets zinged inches above him vibrating the air.

Unable to swing his rifle in the tangle, Juan drew his pistol and frantically returned fire while scooting on his back. He had made a bad decision. The boy quickly reloaded and fired again.

From a distance, the thicket looked like it was in flames. Juan was in trouble and there was nothing anyone could do without rushing forward to a fool's death.

Rolling onto his belly, the boy dove between some rocks barely a foot high. As soon as he hit the ground, bullets came from the opposite side. Juan twisted onto his back again and fired blindly in both directions, then laid his pistol on his chest, trying to be a small a target as possible. The Indians emptied their weapons on his position. His leap was another bad decision. He was pinned down and surrounded with nowhere to crawl.

Once more everything went quiet. Calming his breathing, Juan listened. There was movement from both directions. They were coming for him. The gray turned to black. His heart was pounding, and his mouth hung open and dry.

Juan's mind raced. If he raised and fired in one direction, the other Indian would put a bullet through his back. All he could do was wait for them to find him. The scraping sounds grew closer, and he wanted to scream. Suddenly it came to him. Juan screamed. "They're coming for me. I'm deep in the rocks. Fire at me. Fire. Fire. Fire!" He let his own gun blaze in the air so his friends would know where he was.

Swearing, Jube raised his rifle to his shoulder and squeezed the trigger. He levered and squeezed again. The boys followed the soldier's lead. From three directions, bullets flew towards their young friend, cutting down the thicket around him like the Grim Reaper's scythe. Amid the maelstrom, a voice cried out in agony. The deadly barrage had found a mark.

As each of the rifles spent their last round, silence returned, save for the distant wail of a woman who could not withstand the strain. From the darkness her shrill voice rose, then slowly died away. Friend and foe alike tensed to the haunting cry.

Jube finished loading his gun. He could only hope that Juan was still alive. Cupping his hand to his mouth, he hollered. "Juan, if you is there be still. Let 'em wonder." In response, a rifle cracked, and a bullet ricocheted off a rock near Jube's head, cutting his face. Blood trickled down his cheek. Spitting his anger, Jube fired back.

It was a standoff of the worse sort. He had failed to drive the Indians out or even find their positions. Now they were so close that no one dared move lest they be heard. It was impossible to attack and death to withdraw. Jube's only conciliation was that at least one, maybe two Indians lay dead.

Blinking dirt from his eyes, Juan laid motionless, fearing to remove the branches that had dropped on top of him. He was still alive. The Indian who had screamed lay dead, just feet away.

Several minutes passed while both sides waited for the other to lose their nerve. Faint sounds broke the silence, but never long enough to find a target. Jube thought of throwing a heavy rock in hopes of drawing them out, but he realized it would do no good. The boys were just as apt to shoot as the Indians.

Suddenly there was a rustle of brush high to the east. In quick answer, Daniel's rifle fired in rapid succession, five, six, seven, rounds. His barrage was met with an angry rebuke that tore through the dark, seeking to silence the arrogant youth. Someone of the boy's equal had challenged him, filling the night with a deadly roar. Standing his ground, Daniel answered bullet for bullet.

Then eerie silence once more. The exchange ended in a draw. Another tense moment passed. Higher up and farther back, an evil chuckle echoed hauntingly. It rattled on, increasing in pitch and volume before slowly trailing away. "Pretty good shoot."

The voice erupted into evil laughter. "Pretty good shoot, Apache boy. Tore my shirt."

It was Rutaio. "Where is Nah-kah-yen? Does he hide with the woman while children fight?" The Indian laughed again, then shouted in a voice that quickly turned to hatred. "Nah-kah-yen... Apache dog. Sleep while you can, for you walk in the land of the Terahumara. I will return with many braves and bring the soldiers, too. We will fill your women with the seeds of our young while you burn slowly at the stake." His voice seethed with vengeance. "I will cut you open and build a fire in your belly. Do you hear me, Nah-kah-yen? I burned Victorio, and I will burn you."

A cold, deadly voice rose from the dark trail. "Rutaio. Why do you hide? Did I not leave you in a hole trembling like a rabbit? Come, Rutaio, fight me now."

"First you must suffer. Watch for me. I will be behind you and in front of you. Look for me in your sleep. I'll be there, Apache."

His evil voice trailed away. The Terahumara warrior was gone.

Chapter -22-
Shadows and Shadowed

The light of the moon waxed and waned with the drifting clouds that hung low over the grassy plains. The Mimbre Riders' flight through the foothills had been revealed. Fearing another ambush, Jube hastened his companions across the shimmering sea of green. Shadow and light flowed like water with each gust of wind, creating an eerie wake that left a disquieting mood.

Still, they had been lucky. Save for a few scratches, no one had been injured in the attack. The boys had held their own against grown men. Jube had praised their bravery.

Yessenia translated for Son-gee while the shy girl hung by Roberto's side, sure it was he who had driven back the Terahumara single-handedly. It made the boy that much more a hero in the young girl's eyes. Roberto wrapped an arm around the slender beauty, silently fulfilling his role.

Daniel and Juan accepted that for the time being, the three amigos were now just the two hombres. However, their tall friend would have to suffer their teasing for having this pretty young Mimbre by his side. It was made worse because the girl saw no reason to end the kissing that Roberto had started when he rescued her. Apparently it was a gringo custom that the Apache willingly embraced. Roberto sneered at his friends, and then defiantly gave the Indian girl a quick peck.

Jube watched the young lovers and mused to himself. 'Kisses from the Mimbres and bullets from the Terahumara'. Injuns were hard to figure. He had never faced the Terahumara before, and they were definitely on his mind.

The Terahumara were mountain people, known for their endurance. They alone were equal to the Apache when it came to speed. Jube rubbed his weary eyes. After days without rest, the band of rescuers had been robbed of sleep once more by Rutaio's vengeful attack. They were dog-tired and Jube knew that tomorrow his small band would start falling apart.

Yessenia took the baby from Mary, giving her a much-needed respite. The infant slept quietly in the old woman's arms. It made her feel less alone. She thought of her own children, now scattered to the winds.

Riding past the boys, Mason moved out front with Jube. The haggard buffalo soldier welcomed the company of the officer, and McCrae hoped the change of scenery might do the silent girl some good. Maybe it would draw her out of her shell. There was some improvement. Though he still held her reins, he noticed that she occasionally kicked her pony forward to stay by his side.

"Jube, we were lucky again today." Mason spoke as much to himself. "Mexicans and now Indians, how long can it go on?"

The soldier shook his head. "Don't know. When you is up to yo' ass in wolves, it best to forget you is the rabbit, n' jes' fight like a grizzly bear. It's all we can do."

"Well the rabbits are getting mighty tired." Mason took a moment to smile at the girl. Reaching out, he patted her pony's neck. His kindness to the horse was intended for her. It was as close as he dared get. Mason let his hand linger until he caught her eye.

Like the others, she was exhausted, only it seemed to settle deeper in her. His heart went out to her. "If you ask me, Jube, we are in greater danger of collapsing from fatigue than being attacked again. At some point we are going to have to risk a little sleep or fall from our saddles."

The buffalo soldier sighed. "Guessin' there ain't no point in helpin' the Mexicans kill us by ridin' the women into the ground. Death if we do, death if we don't. Yes, sir, it's a hell of a game."

A short distance brought them to a shallow depression. There were no arroyos or even a dry wash, just a low spot that might give them a little shelter from distant eyes.

Jube frowned. "This will have ta' do. Can't go back into them foothills."

Mason agreed. "I'll help the boys hobble the horses."

Swinging his leg over his saddle, Jube realized how tired he was. "Tomorrow is going to be grueling iffin' it a good day, n' murder iffin' it ain't." He looked up at the starless sky. "Might see some rain come mornin'."

"Could use a bath." Climbing down from his mount, the young officer held his hands up to the pale girl, but he did not reach for her. "Miss Lori."

He wanted the next move to be hers. Mason waited patiently. Perhaps she would have preferred he just take her, like an adult would pick up a child without asking. Instead, he waited for her to respond.

Lori lifted her eyes, awakening to the man who had taken possession of her. Her face was troubled, but she slowly unfolded her arms and leaned towards him. Mason gently lowered her to the ground. The girl remained silent, but did not pull away. Taking her hand, Mason escorted her to the others. "Here you go, Miss Lori. I'll find you a bite to eat, and then you can rest."

The girl's eyes followed the officer as he walked away.

Sitting her pony, Son-gee watched Mason and Kane help their female companions from the saddle. She was as young and as agile as the boys, and quite capable of getting down herself, but she held out her hands to Roberto and waited. The boy glanced at his friends, then awkwardly reached up and lifted her down. Behind him, he heard snickering. Juan squeaked. "Oh! Daniel, please help me down!"

Coming up from behind, Jube cuffed Juan on the back of his head. "If ya' boys gots' that much energy, ya' can stay up while the rest of us gets some shut-eye. Daniel, ya' take first watch, n' Juan can relieve ya' in a few hours. Ain't no one else gunna' stand guard tonight. Ya' take turns relievin' each other."

Rubbing his head, Juan protested. "That ain't fair."

Jube cocked an eye. "From here on out, you boys is the main defense until Jacob returns, n' ain't nothin' fair about any of this, so get use to it."

"What about Roberto?"

Jube showed no sympathy. "Seem ta' recall the two of you catchin' shut-eye while Roberto was parlaying with the fat man. Guessin' he's been up longer n' you. Wonder he ain't dead. So when you is cryin' about what's fair, keep it straight." Jube broke into big grin. "'Till then, you two rascals is playin' cupid for yo' friend. Ya owe 'em that much for all the watching over ya' that he done."

Leaving his charge with the old woman, Mason mustered the strength to hobble and strip the horses. They needed a good brushing, but it was beyond him. He had stayed out of the last fight, but the trail was taking its toll on everyone, including him. There had been plenty of death and little sleep. Mason felt that he'd eventually reach a point where he got so tired, that when he closed his eyes, he feared he might never wake up.

As he pulled the bridle from Lori's mount, the officer turned with a start. Beneath the sliver of the sinking moon stood the Indian squaw, Mary Lost Pony. She was trembling more than the cool night warranted, and her large eyes were tearing with fright.

Clasping her hands under her chin, she timidly approached the officer, only to stop abruptly a short distance away. A struggle was going on inside the poor girl. She looked like a stricken deer ready to bolt.

Summoning courage, she willed her feet to move a little nearer. The Mimbre woman took several breaths to calm her breathing, and then found a trembling voice. "My husband says you are a soldier." Her body shook with the decree. "I have not spoke with a Pony soldier ever. Only have I run from them."

A strained smile on her fragile face pleaded for kindness. "It is hard to understand a soldier helping an Indian, and yet you have ridden across this evil land for me."

She edged a tiny step closer. "Of this great thing you have done, I want much to thank you."

For the Apache squaw there was a debt to be paid, even if it was to a feared enemy. She had expressed her gratitude to the others one by one, but facing the white officer was the hardest of all, so she had left this meeting for the very last.

Reaching a hand into her pocket, she drew out a thin leather cord and then lifted her eyes to the soldier. "If you please, I made this from my own necklace while we rode." She held it up. "There are three beads. It is for you, for saving my family, and to remind you of the father, mother, and child who are grateful."

Her eyes darted in embarrassment. It was not much, three simple stones for a man who had come so far. The woman blushed, fearing that her gift was too foolish. She held the necklace higher. "Please, I prayed over the beads for magic to keep you safe."

Coming to his senses, Mason drew a long breath and slowly reached out his hand, but his empty fingers closed short. "Thank you, Mary. It is a good gift, but I do not deserve it."

"Please. It is all I have to repay you." Her voice trailed to a desperate whisper.

Mason ached, knowing that to refuse would be a dishonor for the Mimbre woman, yet how could he accept such a precious gift when it was his duty to destroy her family? The evil of the deed burned in his chest, and there was nothing he could do to ease the pain.

Swallowing his guilt, the young officer feigned a smile. "I thank you, Mary."

As he took the necklace, he clutched her hand. "Mary...no matter what happens in the days to come, know I will treasure your gift always."

The Indian woman's eyes sparkled in gratitude, and then she hurried away.

As he watched her disappear, Mason sickened. Mary Lost Pony was as loving as an innocent child, but she would grow to hate him, and justly so.

His hands shaking, Mason placed the leather cord over his head. These three stones would be his shame to bear.

"Soldier." Mason turned. It was Nah-kah-yen. "I did not send Mary to do this thing. It is her heart."

Mason could not hold the warrior's eyes. His voice fell in a raspy whisper. "I know. You are a man of honor."

"Would you have it otherwise?"

The young man hung his head. "Perhaps it would be easier if you weren't. You could just sneak off in the night."

"You would follow."

"Yes." Mason sighed. "It is my duty."

"You are a man of honor, too."

Nah-kah-yen slowly turned to walk away. "I have my family. For this I thank you, so I will keep my promise."

"I am sorry, Nah-kah-yen."

The warrior grinned. "Be at peace, brave soldier. I think neither of us has to worry. The day we speak of will never come."

The weary companions tried to empty their minds, hoping to hide in untroubled sleep. They were caught in a terrible dream, and tired as they were; even rest had to be fought for.

Walking away from the others, Mea-a-ha waded through the knee-high grass, staring into the empty night.

A warm breeze, the kind that precedes a storm, lifted long, dark strands of hair away from her melancholy face. She folded her arms, fighting a cold growing deep inside. Mea-a-ha hurried on, unsure of where she was going. She was worn to her soul, and her head hurt. Nothing was clear any more. Her wisdom failed her. Life and death, right and wrong, swirled together, screaming guilt at her from a growing void.

One man had held this tiny band against the unrelenting storm, and he was gone. She had not been able to bridge the chasm that had opened between them.

Jacob had vowed to never kill again, but she had forced him to come. Now each new day brought more death and greater distance. He had grown so cold. How long had it been since her man had told her he loved her?

The Apache girl clenched her fists and beseeched the wind. "Jacob." She searched the dark, her heart desperately hoping for a reply she knew would not come.

"You shouldn't be out here alone."

Mea-a-ha gave a start. It was Kane. She frowned and turned back to the turbulent grass. "I am Apache." She said it as though the name held some magical spell that would protect her.

The writer came close. "Jaguars hunt on these planes. A little thing like you could be snatched away in an instant. The cat would not know that you are Apache."

Mea-a-ha's face locked in a huffy pout, angry that he would frighten her with such things.

Stepping past the girl, Kane stared into the vast expanse. "He's a lucky man to have your love." The writer sighed. "I envy him."

Kane moved further into the night. "I know I am not his equal. There is no choice between a hero and a coward. Still, I can't help caring for you."

Shamed, the young man hung his head, his voice pained. "How could I have known something so beautiful would capture my heart on this savage trail?"

Giving up some of her anger, Mea-a-ha came quietly to his side and rested a light hand on his arm. "You were very brave today."

"I did nothing."

"You kept me safe." She leaned close. "Seeing you standing over me, your gun drawn—you would have died for me, wouldn't you?"

Kane drew a deep breath. His voice was low. "Yes. For you."

"That is no small thing. I will remember it always."

Lifting the girl's gentle hand from his shoulder, Kane held it tenderly. "Is that your way of saying you care for me?"

Mea-a-ha lowered her head. "I care. You know that. Must you make me say it?"

He folded her hand and pressed it to his lips. "Mea-a-ha, tomorrow we could be dead. Maybe tonight is all we have. Yes, I want to hear you say it."

The writer let go and turned away. "I want to know that if I die, someone cares. I would like to think that a beautiful girl will shed a tear…that you would shed a tear."

Stepping behind him, Mea-a-ha leaned her head softly against his back. "I care. If you die and I live, I will weep. But you ask for more. You want me to love you, and I can't."

Kane stirred uncomfortably. "So you deny me love, my beautiful savage. Here at death's door, would you also refuse me the truth?"

The Indian girl reluctantly shook her head. "No."

Turning, Kane took her hands. "Then tell me you don't love me, if that is the truth."

Mea-a-ha tried to pull away. "Please, Kane."

"Tell me."

"Kane, please…I..."

"Tell me you don't love me."

The Mimbre girl struggled. She couldn't answer. It was the one question she feared to ask herself. Mea-a-ha started crying. Kane gathered her into his arms and held her gently, letting her sob. "That is what I wanted to know."

"You are cruel."

She took a breath, trying to control herself. Kane wiped her tears. His small victory allowed him this liberty. Mea-a-ha felt foolish and tried to turn away, but he lifted her chin and held her lips close to his. "You promised me one last kiss. If I asked, would you give it to me now? An honest kiss. One that speaks the truth when your words cannot."

Stunned by his boldness, Mea-a-ha closed her eyes and breathed a trembling whisper. "I...I promised."

The writer leaned close, letting his breath warm her lips. "A passionate kiss?"

Mea-a-ha's pulse raced, not knowing how she'd respond. Would she lie cold in his arms, or yield to an unspeakable truth from which there was no return?

Kane let their closeness linger until the girl thought she would faint, and then abruptly he released her. "No! I don't think you could...even though you want to every bit as much as I do."

He jerked away. "If you can't be honest with me, little Apache, at least be honest with yourself."

Kane turned and hurried into the night. Mea-a-ha dropped in the grass and beat her fist against the earth. She was furious at him. How dare he force her to reveal her heart and then coldly walk away, leaving her alone with her own emotions?

A long time and a lot of tears passed before Mea-a-ha felt in enough control to return to the camp. She hurried through the tall grass. The wind was picking up. It was late. Everyone would be bedded down.

As she got close, her heart sank. She had forgotten Daniel was on guard. Mea-a-ha hesitated as the distance between them faded. She had been gone a long time, and he knew she had been with Kane. Mea-a-ha paused quietly beside him, feeling the need to say something, but her mind could only hear the screaming of her guilt.

It was no use; the silence between brother and sister became too awkward. Mea-a-ha started to hurry away when Daniel reached out and took her hand. He didn't speak; he just looked up at her, waiting.

Mea-a-ha relented and brushed his hair. "I was hoping Jacob would come...foolishly looking for him, I guess. Kane followed me to make sure I was okay."

Exhaling in anxious frustration, Mea-a-ha dropped to her knees. "Nothing happened."

She pulled her hand free. "Daniel, we didn't do anything." Her voice sounded more defensive than she intended.

Mindful of his duty, the boy turned away, searching the grassy plane. Mea-a-ha held her breath, waiting for his verdict.

Daniel finally looked up into her eyes. "I just wanted you to say goodnight."

Covering her face, Mea-a-ha hid her shame. "Oh, Daniel." She kissed his cheek and hugged him. "What you must think."

The boy shrugged. "Now is not a good time to think. It is a time to survive. That's what you are doing. Isn't it?"

Mea-a-ha teared and kissed him again. "Goodnight, wise little brother." She hurried away.

Slipping quietly into camp, Mea-a-ha hid in her blanket and wiped her tears. Too distraught to sleep, she tried to make out the darkened forms in the churning grass around her. Rifle in hand, Jube sat propped against his saddle. His hat was pulled over his eyes, but she knew he would stay awake as long as he could. The weight that Jacob had carried for so long was now on this man's shoulders. She felt sorry for him. Like Jacob, he endured his charge without complaint, and like Jacob, he was changing. His laughter came less often.

Mea-a-ha's stomach knotted at the thought of this affable giant growing silent as men do when life wears them down. Right now she preferred the anguished wails of women. It was better to feel terror than to feel nothing at all. The Indian girl whispered a prayer. "Please Ussen, not Jube."

She turned her thoughts away and searched for the others. Close by, Roberto and Son-gee lay beneath the faint stars, their hands entwined outside the blankets. She smiled, glad for the young romance. Fewer eyes would be on her and Kane.

To the west, Lieutenant McCrae, ever gallant, had placed his saddle next to Lori White Feather's, blocking the chill wind. He was like that. The girl innocently leaned her head on his shoulder, accepting his kindness.

Mea-a-ha scanned the shadows one last time. The others were lost in the dark. She curled into a tiny ball and buried her hands beneath her moist cheek. She missed Jacob. Where was Kane? The wind howled in the distance. Tonight she would sleep alone.

Chapter -23-
The Storm

"Time to ride." Jube's husky voice jarred the weary souls from their fitful slumber. Without a word, the blurry-eyed companions struggled to their feet. Men moving more by habit than will started throwing saddles on the horses, giving the women a little more time to face the day.

It was darker than before. Low clouds blotted out the stars. The wind had grown colder and spoke with a low roar that seemed to crawl through the grass like a hungry lion on the prowl.

One by one, the women carrying their folded blankets stumbled from the dark and were helped into their saddles. No one helped Mea-a-ha. A lump tightened in her throat as she struggled to get her foot into the tall stirrup.

"Let's move out." Jube shouted to be heard above the wind. "It's now or never."

Mea-a-ha rose in her saddle, her worried eyes straining against the coming storm. She could only make out Yessenia behind her and McCrae with Lori in front of her. Where was Kane? She shivered.

"Bow your heads to the wind n' say yo' prayers. Then save your strength. You is gunna need it to survive this day. Keep 'em movin' boys." Jube's command drifted down the line of silent forms glued to their ponies.

For several hours they rode in silence. The mournful groan of the wind blowing through the pampas was too much to compete with. No one had the energy to talk anyway.

Dawn came without a sun. Only the graying of the sky spoke of morning. As her vision increased, Mea-a-ha craned her neck, identifying each of her companions as the night slowly surrendered to a bitter day. Kane was not among them. She counted again. No. He was gone. Panic rose in her breast. Had Jube not realized Kane was missing? Kicking her heels, she bent her head against the wind and galloped up the line. When she reached Jube's side, she was out of breath. "Jube, Kane is…"

Far in the distance, a lone rider led the way. Mea-a-ha was near tears and couldn't hide her distress. Jube pressed his horse against her pony and leaned down. "He asked to ride point."

The buffalo soldier held the girl's eyes, reading more than she wanted. Mea-a-ha turned away and stared at the distant figure. Poor Kane, she felt his loneliness. He was doing what he had to do to survive without her.

Mea-a-ha felt miserable. "Where's Jacob?"

Jube shook his head as the first raindrops began to fall. "Don't know, little one. This storm will make it harder for him to find us." The soldier's words trailed away as he spoke more to himself. "Could sure use 'em."

In the distance, lightning volleyed and thundered like canons doing battle in the gray clouds. Patches of light burst and faded. Had their moods been different, it would have been beautiful. Subtle hues of red and gold illuminated the low hills that marked their long path to safety.

Suddenly a tremendous bolt cracked overhead and rain burst upon them, icy cold.

Resigned to their fate, Jube shouted above the growing torrent. "Raindrops the size of hen's eggs. If it keeps comin' down like this, we can jes' float our way home."

Mea-a-ha pulled the drawstring on her hat and crawled inside her coat as much as she could.

Barely visible in the sheets of rain, Kane was now little more than a dot. It alarmed her that he was so far ahead. She glanced behind and saw that everyone was bunching together for shelter against the downpour. Their efforts were futile.

Another bolt of lightning tore across the sky with an explosive crack that set the horses bucking. Screams rose from the women and angry curses from the men as they willed the horses to obey.

Frantic, Mea-a-ha hollered to Jube. "Kane needs to come back." She squinted against the driving rain until she found him again. As she watched, a wall of fog rolling from the west cut between then like a heavy curtain being drawn closed. The solitary figure was gone. "Kane!"

In seconds, the menacing gray shroud swept over the riders dark and evil. Visibility dropped to only a few yards. Mea-a-ha pressed close to Jube, screaming, "We must go after him!"

Without waiting for an answer, the Indian girl whipped her pony forward. All of a sudden she felt a tingling, and then a blinding flash of light exploded before her. The sound was deafening. Sparks danced on the water and raced up the moist blades of grass. Her mare panicked, bucking and clawing the charged air.

Mea-a-ha jerked tight on the reins, but the pony reared higher, sending her tumbling backwards. She landed with a jolt in a pool of icy water that instantly soaked through her dress.

Clenching her fists, she shrieked in exasperation. Drenched beyond misery, Mea-a-ha struggled to her feet, shivering against the freezing wind that bit at her skin.

Before she got her bearings, Jube rode up, holding the reins of her pony. Reaching down a big hand, he caught her arm and hauled her back into her saddle. "If you ain't a soggy piece o' toast."

Lieutenant McCrae drove his mount forward, shouting. "Sergeant, we got to get to the shelter of the foothills before we drown or get smote by lightning."

Jube nodded. "Let's turn 'em, Lieutenant."

Shaking violently, Mea-a-ha struggled to raise her voice. "No! Kane."

Jube shouted. "It's him or us."

Cursing above the storm, the men started driving the frightened horses into a new direction while behind them a black rolling fog consumed all light.

With a roaring wind, the pounding of hooves, and booming thunder, the violent storm assailed them like a demonic foe, but Mea-a-ha was deaf to it all. Kane was gone.

She shut her eyes. Surely he would find them…but how? How could he know they turned away? He would come back and they'd be gone.

With the rain stabbing at their backs, the riders whipped their horses onwards through the gale. They had to find shelter quick. Nothing else mattered. Mea-a-ha alone, tugged against her reins, but her pony would not obey and instead followed the others.

The storm had struck across the open plane with a vengeance, and fleeing into the hills seemed little better as the rain turned to an icy sleet driven almost parallel to the ground. The freezing air sapped what precious little strength they had left. Their bodies and minds grew numb.

Mea-a-ha shivered uncontrollably. Her soaked buckskins stiffened with ice and stuck to her skin. The wretched girl closed her eyes. Slipping into a stupor, she fought for survival. All things faded from her mind save the image of a lone rider bending against the storm. At first the figure appeared tall and lean like Kane, and then grew large and stern like Jacob. Her faint heart beat. She dare not cry a name lest it betray her. The dream faded. Mea-a-ha's only companion was the howling wind. There were no warm arms to hold her, no heart to care for her tears. She was all alone.

At last a shallow arroyo opened before them. The beleaguered companions followed it for several miles, or at least it seemed. No one could tell for sure. They were in a whiteout, and time was measured by agony endured.

Twisting around a bend, the gully deepened enough to offer some shelter from the wind. The angry howl became an icy hiss that hunted them through every branch and stone.

As the wind surrendered some of its fury to the ragged terrain, frozen faces began to find their voices. Everyone was suddenly mumbling at once, releasing their fears. Mea-a-ha blinked her eyes and slowly returned to the world of the living.

Coming to her senses, she listened, but no one mentioned their lost companion. Warming with desperation, she cried. "We are safe, but what of Kane?"

Jube jutted out his frozen chin. "We ain't safe. Ridin' from one danger to the next, n' we gots' ta' keep goin'."

It was an answer the young girl couldn't accept. "Jacob would not leave someone behind."

The clamoring silenced. Without a word, Jube kicked his mount and headed on down the ravine. Mea-a-ha immediately regretted her outburst. But what of Kane?

No more was said, and the company quietly followed the buffalo soldier through the damp haze filling the arroyo.

Mason slowly raised his head and looked to his charge. Lori was shivering. Her lips were blue. Shaking off his numbness, his sense of duty returned. "Jube, we need to find shelter and risk a fire if we can find anything that will burn."

There was a murmur of agreement, and the party pulled to a stop. They had run as far as they could.

With the help of gunpowder emptied from shells, an unwilling fire was coaxed to life beneath the shelter of a tall, overhanging rock. They were in a small clearing bordered by a sparse stand of brittle gray trees.

Smoke from the damp wood swirled upwards, blending with the dismal fog while all around them the lingering storm moaned through the stiff oak brush, refusing to surrender.

Without being told, the boys stood guard, their backs to the pit, while the others huddled together, seeking warmth from the small yellow flames that threatened to die.

Tending the fire, Mason knelt on one knee and held Lori close, giving her what warmth he could. She accepted the young officer's kindness without question and leaned her head against his shoulder. He offered a sympathetic hug, and tucked her blanket to her cheek. "You will be warm soon, Miss Lori."

Dropping an armload of dry underbrush against the rocks, Jube poked a shaggy branch into the coals and held his breath until it smoked and caught fire. "Might as well rest while we can. Iffin' the Mexican army is still comin' in this storm, they'll be dead when they gets here."

Mea-a-ha lifted her moist eyes and reached for his sleeve. "I'm sorry, Jube."

With a forgiving smile, he pulled off his glove and felt beneath the Indian girl's blanket to see if she was drying. "No harm, little Apache. We is all worried."

The lieutenant slowly came to his feet. "Best have the boys rub the horses down, and maybe give them a bit of grain. If we are to survive, it will most likely be at a dead run."

Cold as they were, the three boys showed little sign of tiring. Such were the rewards of youth. Without complaint, they wiped their runny noses and shouldered the responsibility of grown men.

There was nothing more to be done. McCrae tossed another branch on the fire and then stumbled to a dry spot against the cliff and slumped to the ground. He was more tired than he realized. His heavy eyes closed, surrendering to exhaustion.

Searching the gaunt faces of her companions, Mea-a-ha shivered one last time and then drew a determined breath. A hot meal was sorely needed. Cooking was her responsibility. Kane's disappearance did not change that.

Rising on stiff legs, she shuffled to the packhorse and retrieved a sack of beans and a blackened pot. She sighed. At least she would be the closest to the warm flames. Mea-a-ha stirred water from the canteen into the beans. Little bits of ice flowed with it.

A soft hand on her shoulder turned her vision upwards to the wrinkled eyes of the old Mexican woman. She offered the Indian girl a caring smile and knelt beside her.

Untying the cord on a sack, Yessenia produced provisions of her own and quietly added an onion to the pot, along with a few dried peppers.

Too cold and sad for words, Mea-a-ha's mouth twitched in gratitude.

Roberto vigorously rubbed a mare's legs with a burlap sack. It was a good way to stay busy. While others thoughts were on survival, his were on the pretty Mimbre girl, Son-gee. He had gotten his first kiss. Roberto couldn't help but smile. That's not something a young boy forgets. Even now it warmed him. They had ridden into this violent land where death hounded them at every turn, and then in one bright, magical moment the terror was all swept by a simple kiss.

It seemed impossible. He'd come to help others. This was their story, and he now had one of his own...a girl, a strange and beautiful girl. She did not even speak his tongue, but he was closer to her than he had ever been to anyone before, and nothing else mattered, not even his friends' teasing.

A small hand reached past him and pressed the burlap to the horse's leg. Roberto turned his head. Son-gee's shining eyes looked up at him. The boy smiled and turned back to his task.

"Beans." Mea-a-ha cleared her throat. "Beans are ready." She and the Mexican woman filled the tin plates for the eager hands reaching over their shoulders. The boys stopped their work, happy to answer the call.

Roused by the commotion, Mason rubbed the sleep from his eyes and pushed back his hat. He gave a start. Lori White Feather knelt beside him with two plates in her hands.

Hiding his surprise, the young officer took her offering and nodded politely. The girl settled beside him. She took a few bites, and then stopped. "Thank you." Her voice was sad and sweet.

Mason smiled softly. "My pleasure, Lori."

She savored the warm food and let a moment pass. "I'm not crazy."

Mason's eyes showed sympathy. "Pity. Out here it might be a blessing."

The lieutenant watched the girl for a moment and then returned to his meal. "Yes, ma'am, a real blessing."

"Look!" Daniel pointed into the icy fog. A dark rider on a drenched horse came loping into view. Kane had returned. A cheer went up among the huddled companions. Overjoyed by their friend's return, everyone stood as the writer brought his horse to a stop.

More dead than alive, the tall man eased from his saddle and dropped to the ground.   Jube grinned. "Thought you'd written yo' last chapter."

Brushing crusted ice from his shoulder, Kane tried to shake the numbness from his mind. The storm had taken its toll. Slowly a glaze faded from his eyes. He wiped his face, blinked and turned to the black soldier. His lips twitched to form words. "Saw Indian ponies in the fog."

Everyone froze. Jube scanned the thick haze, half-fearing the Indians were upon them. "How many?"

"A dozen maybe." Kane shivered and blew into his hands. "Followed them until they headed back into the hills for shelter, several miles north of here."

Kane shook the numbness from his head. "They don't know where we are."

Jube breathed easier. "How did you find us?"

"Dumb luck."

The soldier stuck his hands in his pockets for warmth. "We is gunna' need all the dumb luck we can get."

A small figure pushed through the men and held up a steaming plate. Kane looked down into Mea-a-ha's worried face and then slowly took the warm meal from her hands. She lowered her eyes. "I thought you were dead."

Kane's voice croaked thick and raspy. "Some problems don't go away that easy." He stepped past her, drawn by the fire.

The Indian girl stared as he walked away. After fearing the worst, her heart needed more, but he made it plain; her feelings were no longer his concern.

The others all gathered around Kane, happy for his safe return. A clamor of voices rose with questions, some answered, some not. He was alive, and that was all that mattered.

Mea-a-ha filled a plate of her own and moved away from the others. She would let him be, but as the men talked, her eyes kept drifting back to him. He seemed different. How did he survive alone in that terrible storm, and how had he found the courage to follow the Indians? There was a strength in him she had not seen before, but it was cold, like... Mea-a-ha gave a start. He was trying to be like Jacob. It was why he rode point, to prove himself to her.

Kane lifted his eyes past the huddled companions all talking excitedly. The girl's heart was breaking. He took another mouthful of beans and turned back to the conversation. Some problems don't go away that easily.

The storm was subsiding. A pale yellow glow penetrated the clouds, casting faint shadows on the thawing ground. Soon there would be puddles and mud.

Daniel stepped away from the fire and scanned the distant hills. Behind him, his companions barely noticed. If anything, they were sure the valiant boy who had proven his worth with a gun was readying for danger should it come. This wild Apache kid with his fast hand gave them comfort when there was little else that could.

Daniel's eyes searched the fog with one thought on his mind: When would his father return? He had become a killer of men, but inside he was a little boy hungering for the safety of his father's arms.

"Hey, Apache." Daniel turned around to see Roberto standing behind him, holding Son-gee's hand. His tall friend cast a nervous glance at the Indian girl. "Can you help me?"

Daniel welcomed the relief from his own thoughts, and grinned. "You want me to teach you how to kiss?"

Roberto turned red. "I think I got that taken care of." He sneered at his friend, and then nodded to the girl. "Son-gee said something to me. 'Shils aash.' Can you tell me what it means?"

The Apache boy stifled a chuckle. It only meant 'My friend.'

Filled with mischief, Daniel did his best to look serious. "Sure I can. She called you her husband."

Roberto looked stricken. The color drained from his face. "Her husband!"

Daniel nodded and looked to the girl. "Shils aash."

Son-gee smiled and shook her head in agreement. "Shils aash."

She was sure Daniel was telling Roberto he was her good friend. Roberto swallowed. "But why?"

The Apache boy pretended to be astounded. "You slept with her in your arms last night, did you not?"

"Well, yes, but..."

Daniel scolded. "Apaches are a simple people. You are married by Indian custom. It is an honor to welcome you to our tribe, my brother."

Eyes bulging, Roberto tried to hide his fear from the girl. "But I'm only sixteen."

The Mexican boy's distress encouraged his cruel friend. "Apaches don't know age. She is fertile and will bear you many sons. That is all that matters."

"But..."

Daniel mugged deep alarm. "Roberto, you must keep her. It would be great shame to an Apache maiden if you slept with her and turned her away."

"But I didn't sleep with her. I... I mean I only slept with her. I didn't... You know."

"It is the same thing to Apaches. Remember, we are a simple people. Would you dishonor her, and break her heart after all she's been through?"

Roberto looked at the girl and shook his head. "No. But..."

Stepping past his bewildered friend, Daniel took Son-gee's hand and spoke in Apache. "My friend is a brave warrior."

The girl nodded in agreement. "He is very brave, and my good friend. 'Shils aash.'"

"Yes. Shils aash." Once again, Daniel did his best to look serious. "Roberto has saved your life. Do you agree?"

Son-gee shook her head. "Yes. He rescued me from the fat man. Very brave."

"Then it is done."

She looked confused. "What is done?"

"As is the custom of his people, Roberto claims you as his squaw for saving you."

Son-gee's eyes grew wide. Her mouth dropped open. "But I am only fifteen."

Daniel shook his head. "It doesn't matter. Mexicans do not know years. They are a simple people. You are his wife. If you refuse him, he must fall on his knife. It is a matter of great honor. Do you wish to kill him after what he has done for you?"

The Apache girl looked at the pleading eyes of her rescuer and misinterpreted his fear. Her heart melted. "No. I could not."

"Then it is done." Daniel placed the girl's trembling hand in Roberto's, who was shaking even more. "My friend, you must kiss your bride in front of a warrior of her tribe."

Roberto looked confused. Daniel rolled his eyes. "Me!"

The young couple stared at each other, accepting their fate. They could not believe they were married, but neither could bring themselves to shame the other.

Roberto leaned down. Son-gee raised on her toes. They kissed. Daniel put his hand over his heart. "As acting chief of the mighty Mimbres, I pronounce you husband and wife." He repeated his words in Apache. The young girl turned nervously to her husband with wide eyes.

As the newlyweds blushed, Daniel hurried away to tell Juan before he burst.

Chapter -24-
Battle of the Clouds

Captain Moralis tensed in his saddle. The cold bit at his injured foot. Releasing an impatient hiss, he looked across the windswept pampas. Soon the storm would lift and the chase would begin.

The black gringo had humiliated him and led them on a fool's chase. If he were to regain the respect of his general and the soldiers, he must find the Negro and even the score.

Many scouts had been killed, but the Terahumara Indian Rutaio had returned, seeking vengeance of his own. He had sent messengers telling the general to come quickly. Together they would pick up the trail of the Mexican boy and the Apache squaws. The black gringo would come to protect them. Moralis had little doubt that the half-dozen men the general had sent after the Negro would not return. Finding the women was the only way.

The captain winced as a stab of pain shot up his leg. He did not understand why the gringo soldier cared about the savages; it made no sense, but if he came this far into Mexico to find them, he would not abandon the women now.

In his bitterness, Moralis found reason to smile. He would kill the Negro. He would kill them all. His hatred of gringos of any color was only match by Rutaio's hatred of Apaches.

"You nurse more than an injured foot and a broken lip, my worthless captain."

Moralis sneered at the general who rode up to his side. "The fight is not over."

"For me it is."

"What!" the captain stared in disbelief. "We must hunt them down. We must!"

You hunt them down. There is no profit in killing this man Jacob, or whoever he is. We tried several times and failed. It's a fool's errand. Take thirty men if you like, and all the scouts. I do not care. As for me, Don Sebastian's ranch is a greater prize. It will be my new headquarters after I marry his widow."

The pitiless captain grinned. This was to his liking. He would be in charge and vengeance his alone. "My profit lies in another man's blood, my general. Save me one of Sebastian's daughters. I will return your army and the head of this buffalo soldier before the week is done."

General Vasquez laughed. "Do not discount this gringo. Luck rides with him."

An evil smile cracked open the captain's battered lip, bringing a new flow of blood. "So does his weakness. He cares."

****

Holding his collar to his face, Mason leaned into the wind. "The storm will blow itself out in another hour or two."

Jube stepped back from the bitter ridge and rubbed his eyes. "Well, we will ride now n' add to our lead."

He filled his lungs. "Mount up, ya' lazy bones. We is chasing the clouds."

For several hours Jube pushed his blanket-draped companions through a storm that was slow to die. Across the lowlands, the black veil was lifting. A chill wind bent the wet grass like waves on a green sea. In the foothills, the heavy clouds still hung gray only a few feet off the ground. A trail snaked through gloomy arroyos and over endless rolling hills.

Hoping to slip past the Indians unnoticed, Jube chose the shelter of the mountain. It was a dangerous gamble.

Not knowing where an attack might come from, he placed the three boys behind him and the three men at the rear.

With Jacob gone and Kane keeping his distance, Mea-a-ha joined the women in the middle of the procession. She alone had started this journey with the men. Though a woman, she had survived every battle and endured the grueling trail. The other women accepted her as one of the rescuers, equal to the men. It comforted them now that she had joined them.

Mea-a-ha lifted her eyes and watched the big man out front. In many ways he was nothing like Jacob. Laughter often flowed from Jube, even in the darkest hours. The hulking soldier found time for foolish jest. His thoughts were simple. But now Jube was their leader. He fell silent, turning to stone like Jacob. While others sought solace on the trail and healing from their wounds, Jube was constantly searching left and right, never resting. His mind was bent under a great weight. Each member of the troop feared for their own lives, but Jube feared for them all. He was changing, and it made her sad.

The young girl suddenly whipped her pony forward and hurried to the front of the line. She realized that she, too, had an important part to play as one of the rescuers.

Slowing to match the soldier's gate, Mea-a-ha gave him a naughty grin. "Jube, do you remember when we first met?"

Jube reddened, recalling a vision of the small naked savage he'd once captured. "I remember. Why do ya' bring it up?"

A smile broke across her lips. "It was the only thing I could think of that would wipe than frown off your brow."

"Well, some things is best not remembered."

"Why? Was I ugly?"

Jube eyes darted to the small girl by his side, knowing she was taunting him. He opened his mouth then closed it. Matching wits with the little Apache could be more dangerous than the dozen Terahumara Indians.

Mea-a-ha cocked her head. "Sometimes when you look at me, I think you remember." Her tone was accusing.

"Okay, I am no longer frowning. Can we drop it?" Jube shook his head. "Jeez, couldn't ya jes' asked me 'bout fried chicken iffin ya wanted ta' put a smile on my face?"

Mea-a-ha laughed. "That would just make you hungry."

Jube smiled comically for the girl's benefit and then turned his attention to the trail. Mea-a-ha had accomplished what she had intended. Letting the moment pass, they rode in peaceful silence. It was something they seldom did together. Being an Indian and a soldier had made it difficult.

Still, Jube couldn't help but admire the girl. She was as clever as she was beautiful, and she was right. Sometimes when he looked at her, he did remember.

As if reading his mind, she raised a reproachful eye. "That doesn't look like a fried chicken smile."

Jube grinned. "It ain't." He stared a little longer than necessary before returning his gaze to the horizon.

It was Mea-a-ha's turn to blush.

She felt safer riding by his side, and it saddened her that the color of their skin kept them apart. "Jube, do you still hate Apaches?"

"Dang, girl. If ya' don't come up with the most... Maybe it ain't hate, but ya' gotta' understand, a lot of my friends was killed by Injuns."

"All my friends were killed by soldiers." She looked injured. "...and I never killed your people, Jube."

The soldier shifted uncomfortably, knowing he could not say the same. "Jes' ride with me, little Apache. I ain't such bad company."

"Jube. Do you hate me?"

The soldier gave a big sigh and looked down at the girl. "No, little one. I don't hate ya'." He remained silent for a moment and then smiled softly. "Been thinkin' on that lately after what ya' done for us back there in that pool. Guess ya' wouldn't know 'cuz I ain't never told ya' but..." He reached out and cupped her delicate face in his big hand. "I've kinda' takin' ta' loving ya'...like a baby sister. You is part of my heart now. Guess that makes us family."

Flushing with emotion, Mea-a-ha sniffed back a tear. "Damn you, Jube. Don't you make me cry." Overcome, she leaned over and hugged him with both arms. Returning her embrace, Jube lifted the girl out of her saddle and just as quickly set her back down. He stiffened. "Join the women."

Mea-a-ha looked up at him, questioning, then followed his eyes. On a ridge across the arroyo, the legs of several Indian ponies protruded briefly beneath the fog, and then disappeared just as quickly.. "Jube!" Mea-a-ha gasped.

"Quick. Do as I say."

Mea-a-ha turned her pony around and hurried past her brother. Daniel's Winchester was shouldered and pointed at the clouds. His gentle, boyish face was hard as flint.

The Terahumara were on a ridge parallel to their own. With the Indians on higher ground, they were too close for Jube to turn his back on them and run. He would have to hold the trail.

Had the Indians spotted them? The buffalo soldier shook off his fatigue and readied for battle one more time. His dark eyes narrowed as he searched the gray mist while at the same time keeping a watch on the narrowing ridge. A cold fog swirled about them, opening and closing as an icy breeze buffeted the mountain.

For a tense moment there was no trace of the Indians. Jube held his breath. Perhaps they were gone. It was a foolish thought, and he knew it. A single hoof stepped from the clouds for an instant and disappeared. With each break in the shroud, Jube tried counting the number of ponies, but it was like counting sparrows in flight. Giving up, he cursed. There had to be at least a dozen. Maybe the same ones Kane had seen.

Ahead, the trail rose to another saddle that brought the two ridges closer together. The arroyo between them grew shallow, affording no protection against an attack. Jube nervously glanced ahead. The saddle was less than a hundred yards away now.

Back in line, Mea-a-ha's heart pounded wildly. She looked up to see Kane riding by her side, his shiny black pistol gripped in his hand. He said nothing as he placed himself between her and the Indians.

Hooves fell quietly in the damp grass. Everyone held their breath, fearing to make a sound. It was as though the empty silence were a magical wall. If the Indians could not hear them, then they were safe; an absurd hope, but for the moment it quelled the terror in their hearts.

Jube glanced ahead. They were almost to the saddle. If they made it, maybe they could hold the narrow pass, or maybe the two trails would separate and the Indians would take another direction deeper into the hills. Maybe...

A sudden gust of wind raced up the slope, tearing the clouds asunder. Luck failed. All was laid bare. A line of warriors, guns at ready, stood facing the rescuers. There was less than a hundred yards between them.

Cursing, Jube looked down at his thin line strung out across the lower trail. Kane alone stood with the Mimbre women. Jube's blood-curdling roar shattered the silence. "Kane! Get the women below the ridge!"

Jube raised his rifle and fired like a madman. The guns of the boys roared and smoked a second behind.

From the high ridge, the Indians returned fire and then quickly broke rank, retreating into the trees behind them. Some held their ground while most raced north around a knoll and into the next arroyo, disappearing from sight.

Fearing the Indians were trying to surround then, Jube charged over the saddle with the boys close on his heels. Here the clouds hung dark and heavy in a large bowl hidden in thick pine. Shots cracked and reverberated in the stagnant air, and the pale red glow of muzzle flashes in the heavy fog warned them that the warriors were already there.

Jube fired as he jumped from his horse. "Find cover n' stay low. If ya' can't see 'em, poke holes in the clouds 'til they scream." The boys dashed for the trees as bullets zinged through the clouds.

Over the ridge, Jube could hear the steady fire of the men. He cursed. His ranks were broken. A bullet ripped the bark off a tree by his head. Whooping and screaming, Indians on ponies came charging though the mist. The others would have to fend for themselves. Jube threw his rifle to his shoulder. "Here they come, boys. Make 'em bleed."

Mason and Nah-kah-yen held the low ground, spending their ammunition. Kane lay flat in the center of the ridge, firing his Winchester rapidly left and right in an attempt to suppress returned fire. His only thought was to not fail the women, not to fail Mea-a-ha. He fired like he had gone completely insane. Discharging his last round, Kane drew his Colt and, rising to his knees, fanned every round.

The unremitting crack of the savage's rifles and their echoing report came from everywhere. Huddling below the ridge, Mea-a-ha hung close to her pony's neck in a dense stand of damp pines. As bullets dropped branches overhead, the women drove their horses in closer. A ricochet cut too close. Son-gee screamed and closed her eyes.

Mea-a-ha looked up at the ridge. Kane had brought them down, and then returned to fight with the men. He could have stayed but he didn't.

As she returned her eyes to the frightened women, a thick gray cloud once more fell upon them, dark and cold. The wall had returned, only now it separated them from their protectors—at least those who were still alive.

In the crowded confines of the trees, there was nothing to do but wait. Every shot strained their nerves closer to the breaking point. Son-gee wept openly. Mea-a-ha reached a hand towards the child. Suddenly a blood-curdling scream erupted behind the young girl. Mea-a-ha stared in disbelief as Son-gee was ripped from her saddle.

Indians were upon them. Mary's horse reared against the attack, driving a warrior back. Before Mea-a-ha could react, an arm curled around her waist. Suddenly she was hanging in mid-air, locked in a mighty grasp. Kicking, she tried to free herself, but the brave held firm while whipping his pony forward. In an instant she was gone.

Fading behind her, Mea-a-ha caught a glimpse of Mary Lost Pony driving a knife into the neck of a warrior. Blood coated his bare chest as he crumpled. As they charged through the trees, a stiff branch slapped Mea-a-ha in the face, leaving her stunned. She shook her head, trying to clear the terror from her mind. Scream. She had to scream!

Digging her fingernails into the bare arm that held her, Mea-a-ha emptied her lungs. "Kane, KANE!" It was no use. The warrior jerked her violently and squeezed until she thought her ribs would crack. He shook her again before allowing her to breathe. Helpless, Mea-a-ha sobbed and stopped fighting.

Hanging her like a sack, her captor headed on down the steep hill. She had been stolen. The Mimbre Riders had come to an end. Through her tears she could see Son-gee thrown over the back of a mounted Indian just ahead. The young girl wailed and beat her fists to no avail. Yelling a victory cry, the brave ignored her pitiful assault and kicked his pony to greater speed.

Mea-a-ha balled her fists and struck the warrior's arm in futility. Stolen! She'd never see her beautiful home in the Hollow again. As a possession of this Terahumarian, she'd huddle in the dirt by campfires and forever be a savage. Her despair was even greater than her fear. She wept.

As the painted brave carrying Son-gee entered the next stand of trees, a dark blur broke from the thick shadows reached out and plucked the rifle from the Indian's hand. Before the startled warrior could react, the butt of his own gun caught him hard across the temple. The blow sent him crashing to the ground.

Mea-a-ha screamed. Charging out of the fog rode a giant of a man. Jacob had come. With no time to change his grip on the weapon, he wielded it like a club. The warrior holding her brought his sights to bear and pulled back the hammer. With not an instant to spare, Mea-a-ha twisted and sunk her teeth deep into the muscle of his shoulder. Roaring in pain, the Terahumara's bullet went high.

Before he could lever another round, Jacob was upon them. Mea-a-ha heard the skull of the Indian crush beneath the powerful blow. Blood spattered her face and clothing. She went flying through the air with the lifeless body tumbling after her. Hitting the ground, Mea-a-ha looked up into the face of the dead Indian. An eye was missing from a shattered socket. She frantically scrambled out of the way.

In a heartbeat Jacob was beside her. She lifted her head in disbelief, but a strong hand pushed her back down. "Lie still."

There was no time for sentiment. The big man looked at the rifle he held. The stock was broken. Jacob handed it to Mea-a-ha. "It should still shoot if you need it for protection."

He ripped a bandoleer of cartridges from the body of the dead warrior. "Hide in the trees until I return."

Mounting his Buckskin, Jacob charged up the ridge, and was gone.

Mea-a-ha scrambled to her feet and rushed to Son-gee, crying and hugging her. "Are you okay?"

The young girl pulled her tangled hair from her face and nodded. Mea-a-ha held her close. "Come, we must get back to the other women."

On the ridge, the shooting suddenly stopped. Crouching, Mason gripped his Winchester and ran through the fog, searching for Kane. The writer rose, soaked from the wet grass. He was shaking but he'd held his ground. "Where's Nah-kah-yen?"

Mason shook his head. "The crazy Indian charged into the clouds."

Dropping to his knee, Mason shifted his gun. "Maybe he's why they stopped shooting…don't know."

Beyond the saddle of the hill, sporadic shots continued. The faint voice of Jube barking orders at the boys let Mason know the buffalo soldier was still alive. A disbelieving chuckle escaped his lips. "Kane, you find the women. I'll help Jube. Somehow, I think we won."

Jube raised up from behind a broken log. Time and again, the warriors had charged, but with each attack, they had driven them back or left them dead. The courageous boys held their own.

With the last assault by the Indians, a mounted figure charged past him from behind, firing at full run. All Jube saw was a blurred shadow in the dense fog. Daniel, who had been by Jube's side seconds before, had jumped on Snow Raven and tore after the rider. Their charge broke the attack. The Indians retreated into the blanketed pines. Parting shots echoed their retreat as the Terahumara disappeared.

"Jube?" Mason edged over the ridge. "Jube?"

"I'm here. Be careful, don't know who else."

The lieutenant made his way to the black soldier's side and hollered to the boys. "Is everybody okay?"

"Si. We're okay, Senor Mason." Coming up out of a clump of trees, the two Mexican youths returned, leading their horses. "Where's Daniel?"

Jube gave a toothy grin and rubbed Juan's soppy hair. "I gots' an idea, but let's wait n' see."

Chapter -25-
Together

High in the sodden clouds, Rutaio made his way deeper into the lonely hills. He had tried to capture the Apache's squaw, so he used an attack as a diversion. It wasn't his desire to kill the warrior, not yet. He must suffer first.

While trailing the gringo, Rutaio had spied the Mimbre couple riding together. He knew her well. Raping Nah-kah-yen's woman would have been sweet vengeance, but the braves he sent never returned. Something had gone wrong.

The bitter Terahumara warrior climbed from his pony to relieve himself. The other Indians rode on by. There would be another day.

Rutaio turned to a bush, loosened his loincloth and proceeded with his business. He hated Apaches. There was no particular reason. He simply was the kind of man who needed someone to hate. The fierce Apaches had been decimated by the Long Knives, so Rutaio found it easy to kick them while they were down. Already he was reveling in his next assault. Yes, he would have Nah-kah-yen's woman. The Apache would hear her last painful screams until his knife silenced her forever.

As he soaked the ground with his urine, a cold steel blade pressed tightly to his throat. He gasped; every muscle froze. Only his bowels kept working as a voice hissed. "Rutaio, it is fitting that you die pissing. There will be no warrior's death for you."

With one swift cut, Nah-kah-yen's blade sliced deep into the Terahumara's throat. Rutaio collapsed in his own puddle. The Apache knelt on the dead man's back and with an angry fist gripped his hair. With another stroke of his knife, Nah-ken-yen pulled away the Indian's scalp and held it high. "Victorio. Sleep, great chief. Vengeance is done."

Jube and Mason made their way down the ridge with the boys dragging close behind. The battle in the clouds had worn them down. They were cold and tired. It didn't feel like a victory, more like an escape.

Sour-faced, Kane pushed his horse up the steep slope, returning with the women. Mea-a-ha jumped from her pony and ran to Jube. "Where's Jacob?" She was frantic.

Breaking into a tired grin, Jube hugged the girl to his chest. "I knowed' it was him. I jes' knowed' it. Your ol' bear's back, ain't he? Now maybe I'll get some sleep."

Just then two horses came galloping over the saddle of the mountain. The big man held his feathered Winchester in his hand. Mea-a-ha broke free of Jube's grasp and ran to her husband. Barely slowing, Jacob reached down and scooped the girl off the ground, hauling her up before him. She threw her arms around his neck and cried.

For the Apache girl, a lifetime had passed since they were together. She feared he'd never return.

After a long hug, Jacob opened his eyes and looked over the girl's head at his old friend. Jube was grinning ear to ear. "You was suppose to sneak in n' out of the ranch with Mimbre women, not bring the Mexican army n' these mountain savages with ya."

Jacob took a moment to give the Indian girl another kiss. "Told you it wasn't a good plan."

Tucking his arm under Mea-a-ha's knees, Jacob swung his leg over the saddle horn and dropped to the ground. He looked into the drained faces of his friends. "Sorry, I would've been here sooner, but I came up a few bullets short leading the army away and…well, I've been busy."

Setting Mea-a-ha on her feet, Jacob reached out a long arm and pulled his son to him. The big man's eyes closed as he hugged them both. Daniel buried his face against his father's shoulder. There were no words large enough, and men don't cry. A quiet moment spoke for what was in their hearts.

Juan pushed closer. "How'd you find us, Senor Keever?"

Jacob laughed. "The clouds were raining lead. Could have found you with my eyes shut."

From somewhere high on the shrouded peaks, rose an eerie blood curdling wail that sounded like a bird of prey soaring on the wind. Mary Lost Pony clutched her throat and gasped. "The evil one is dead."

Jacob hugged his family close. "Come, let's get off this accursed mountain.

Too tired to climb back into the saddle, he led the rescuers down the steep slope on foot. An emotional Son-gee tucked herself under the tall Mexican boy's arm. He had no idea what terror had befallen her. The story of the battle would wait. For now it was just good to be alive and together again. Roberto kissed the girl and walked on.

As the horses passed, Mason looked around, searching. Not far away, Lori White Feather stood, watching. She wondered if he would. Slowly she came to him and offered her hand. "I am here, gallant soldier."

The lieutenant smiled and drew her close, then slowly followed the procession off the hill. Hours ago he might not have held her hand, but now, after their harrowing escape from death, it seemed right. Mason lowered his head. "Like I told you, Miss Lori, it helps to be crazy."

The girl leaned against him. "Don't know what's not crazy anymore."

Hanging far back, Kane waited for the others to disappear before he followed. Mea-a-ha had been stolen by Indians right from under his nose. He was supposed to guard the women, and he failed. Once again, Jacob was the hero. It hurt him as much as seeing the Apache girl in the big man's arms again.

****

By late afternoon they were skirting the foothills, and the low sun was peeking beneath the clouds. Mea-a-ha closed her eyes and faced the hazy orange ball. Bathing in its warmth, she was finally dry, but she was still shaking.

The violent battle in the clouds played over and over in her mind. She couldn't stop thinking about it. She'd been stolen. Had it not been for Jacob, all that her new life had given would have been taken away.

Her people were gone, and she missed them dearly, but like the changing of the seasons, her future now lay ahead in the white man's world. Mea-a-ha suddenly wanted to be in her little cabin cooking a meal on her cast-iron stove. The days of fire pits and huts were over. She would never be a savage again.

The cloud in her eyes told Jacob his wife was in deep thought. Leaning over, he touched a finger to her nose. "Hey, little one, no frowns on such a pretty face."

Mea-a-ha lifted her chin high. "That's Mrs. Keever to you. You were late."

For several miles, Mea-a-ha rode with Jacob and Daniel, happy her family was finally together. They were safe for now, or at least as safe as they could be.

After a while, Jacob gave her a kiss. "I best give Jube a spell. He's earned it." With that he kicked his stirrup and headed to the front.

Mea-a-ha watched him for a long time. She was still learning about this man who was her husband. The depth of his strength was deeper than she'd known. He was a hero, not just by deed, but by the essence of his nature. It was simply who he was. Jacob was her husband, her protector, and lover. Having her life nearly ripped from her suddenly made things clear. She smiled.

Their short ride from the hills together was all she'd get, and she was grateful for it.

Sighing, Mea-a-ha looked over her shoulder. Her heart ached for the sad figure brooding far behind. He had much to learn about war and himself, but he had tried his best to be a hero, too. She could only guess how her friend Kane must feel. They needed to talk, and now was as good a time as any.

Pulling her pony aside, Mea-a-ha smiled at Daniel. "I'll be back, my brother."

The writer saw the girl stop. A part of him wanted her near, but it was useless to talk. All she could offer was pity. Kane wished he could ride away, but he knew every gun was needed, even his.

As the distant between them closed, he tried to pay her no attention. Sitting her pony, she watched him ride past her and then kicked her heels and settled in beside him. She gave a sideways glance. "Kane?"

Here it came. The writer acknowledged her with a tip of his hat and nothing more. "Kane!"

He remained silent. The Indian girl rode quietly for a moment and then tried again. "Kane, There has been too much said, and too much unsaid. The only thing I want to say is, you are my friend."

Kane stared straight ahead. "It may be the only thing you want to say, but I'm guessing it isn't the only thing you're going to say."

A bit exasperated, Mea-a-ha's expression turned to a scowl. "I also want to thank you for being near when I needed you."

The writer pulled his horse to a stop. "You don't need me now. So why don't you ride back up front and be with your husband where you belong." His voice was terse. "Just leave me alone."

Mea-a-ha lowered her head. "Be angry if you like, but we are friends, and you are being mean."

Kane turned towards her, his eyes smoldering. "Do you want me to show you my true feelings? Do you want me to open my heart, so you can turn it cold?"

"Kane!"

"No, Mea-a-ha, you allow me neither the truth nor the right to protect myself. What is it you want from me?"

"I want you to be noble. There is more in your heart than you know."

The Indian girl turned away, her lip suddenly quivering. "If you are so smart, then you should know my heart struggles, too." Her sweet face drooped in an injured pout. "What you want is not ours to have."

Mea-a-ha waited for him to say something, but Kane only looked away. She released a frustrated hiss. "You are a dumb friend." Wrinkling her nose, Mea-a-ha fumed. "Ask me to stay because I am your friend, or tell me to go away because you don't care."

Kane broke into a grin. "Ah, heck, little Apache, you know I care. Do I have to say it?"

Mea-a-ha lowered her eyes, knowing what he meant. "I'm sorry."

The writer chuckled. "In all the world, that's the rarest sound, a woman saying she's sorry. At least I can say I lived long enough to hear it." He leaned out and brushed a knuckle to her cheek. "I'm sorry, too, but don't think you won this argument. This is not a victory...my little friend, because you want to stay."

Mea-a-ha smiled and looked towards the hills. "It's a victory."

"Expected ya' here a mite sooner." Jube pulled his hat down over his eyes and kept riding. "Roberto said ya' didn't cozy up to this Moralis feller. Guess there is jes' somthin' 'bout you n' captains."

Jacob cocked an eye at his friend, not wholly appreciating his humor. "When he catches up with us, I'll introduce you, and we'll see if you still feel like being charming."

Tilting his hat with a knuckle to the brim, Jube looked over his shoulder with a heavy sigh. "Indians to the right of us. Soldiers up our ass, n' we is draggin' women, n' babies on dead horses. Best thing I can think of is, with the ammunition almost gone, our load is a mite lighter."

Jube gazed sorrowfully at the weary band of riders. They had nothing left to give. "Everything is closin' in fast. We ain't gunna' make it home, is we, Jacob?"

His question didn't need an answer. Women, children, n' babies, they weren't a fighting force. There would be one last massacre for the Mimbres.

"Jacob, it's been a pleasure ridin' with ya' all these years. Heck, never cottoned to old age, anyway."

Swearing, Jacob balled his fist. "Damn it, Jube. There has to be some good come of this." He turned in his saddle and hollered. "Lieutenant McCrae."

The young officer lifted his head to the urgent call. With a reassuring nod to Lori, he kicked his mount into a gallop. When he got to the front, Mason pulled to a quick stop and saluted the sergeant. Somehow it seemed appropriate. "Jacob."

The big man took a moment to measure the young officer he had led into Mexico. The Mimbre trail had turned him from a boy into a man. Now was the time to find out what kind of man. "Lieutenant, we got about another day and that's it."

Jacob paused and let the severity of their situation sink in.

Mason took off his hat. His eyes slowly turned back to their small ragtag band of Indians, Mexicans, coloreds, and gringos. A violent ride for the sake of a desperate dream had bound them together. They were now his friends, and the sergeant's words just proclaimed their deaths. It was a hard thing. "Yes, Sir, I understand."

Jacob crossed his gloved hands over the pummel of the saddle and stared into the distance. "It sure would nice if some good were to come of this."

Mason stiffened. "Yes, Sir. You want to know if you turn the Apache loose, will I trail him or stay with you and die."

"Mason, he's tough. If we hide his trail, Nah-kah-yen might be able to get his family through. There'd be some purpose in our deaths."

Holding his answer, the young officer once more gazed down the line at the proud warrior, his squaw riding faithfully by his side, holding their baby. This impossible journey had been for them.

The lieutenant lowered his eyes. It didn't matter. His duty was to see this Apache hung. All his training, everything he believed in and lived for demanded he complete his mission. Right or wrong, he was a soldier, and he had sworn an oath to a nation and his own father. He would return with his prisoner.

Mason returned his hat to his head and tugged down resolutely on the brim. "Jacob, your family is going to die with you. Do you think his is any more deserving?"

The big man's eyes showed deep sadness. "There is no greater love than I have for Mea-a-ha, and Daniel is my heart, but yes, I do. It's not something I can put into words."

The big man paused and swallowed a lump in his throat. "There's a terrible wrong that can be made right. That little baby back there growing up free will give some purpose to our deaths. And even if he didn't, it would still be right."

The lieutenant shook his head. A man is only as good as his word. It was all he had left. Mason came to his full height. No matter what Jacob wanted, he had to stand by his oath. His decision was made.

As he started to speak, Mason took one last look at the Indians he'd condemned to die. Riding by his side, Mary Lost Pony placed a motherly kiss on her baby and then looked upon her husband with love and admiration.

Mason's hand slowly lifted to his chest, capturing three small beads. Halting his breath, he stopped and stared into his glove. What was it she had said? 'So he'd remember the family he had saved.' The young man quietly smiled. Three small stones for him to bear...and protect.

'Orders are orders.' He'd heard that since he was a small boy, but there was something far greater. Above all things, a soldier must protect what is good. If he failed in that, he failed everything. No oath or allegiance to duty could justify the unnecessary death of an innocent child. 'For the love of a son.'

Mason lifted his eyes. "Sergeant, it would be my honor to die at your side."

Without another word, the young man slapped his reins and galloped back to his place in line by the yellow-haired girl. He would play out his part quietly. There would be no metals pinned on his chest, no hero's welcome—only the knowledge that in the darkest hour, he tried to do what was right.

Jube cleared his throat with a tired chuckle. "Now, there's an officer I might accuse of havin' a heart."

Jacob took a breath and turned to his loyal friend. "Jube, this ain't your fight either, and you ain't going to make no difference to the outcome. We can let the Apache go after dark, and at first light you could head out. Tell what happened here. You're the only one who could make it."

The sergeant shrugged. "Guessin' ya' had ta' make the offer, but ya' knowed' it was a waste of air. How long a man lives ain't so important as how well he lives. Them boys back there is as much my responsibility as them Mimbres is yo's."

Jube prodded his horse forward, speaking over his shoulder. "I knows' ya', Jacob. Ya' never give up. The Mexicans will win tomorrow, can't be but not; still, I suspect it will be like they won at the Alamo." He chuckled again. "Gots ta' see it. Maybe I can die as bravely as ol' Davy Crockett. Least ways, there will be a dozen empty Mexican saddles afore I drops ta' my knees, I guarantee ya' that."

By evening the grassy plains surrendered to broken ground. The desert had returned. Coming to the lip of a lonely arroyo, Jacob scanned the horizon behind him one last time and then led his band down the incline. Here they would have some shelter. "Boys, build a dry fire."

Sliding from the saddle, he lifted Mea-a-ha to the ground. "You got some beans?" He gave her a wink. "And maybe a little fist of your secret sugar. Make it special, little Apache."

Mea-a-ha tensed. Something felt wrong. Her sad ol' bear was smiling. It was the kind of wrong you feel when something seems too right. She reached for him, but he let his arm drop as he pulled away.

Beans! She needed to make beans. Mea-a-ha found herself trembling and didn't know why. She sought the old woman. Yessenia came to her side. "I will help you, my dear."

"We need a pot, and, and water, and…"

"Shhh." The old woman put her arm around the Mimbre girl and led her away. Mea-a-ha looked behind her. Maybe she was just being foolish.

Trailing in, Nah-kah-yen lead his family down the dusty rise. He looked up as he passed the white soldier McCrae. Oddly, the young man was grinning. "Good evening, Apache."

The warrior frowned. "Not so good." He rode on by.

While Mea-a-ha and the old woman cooked the meal, Jacob sat close by, watching her. If there was just one day left that was his, he'd spend it loving this angelic girl. He lifted his eyes to the light sound of boots. "Daniel, how is Snow Raven?"

The boy looked to his father, surprised by his peaceful demeanor. "He is almost healed and ready to chase the moon."

"Good."

Jacob reached out and mussed the boy's hair. "Give the horses extra grain tonight, Son. Give them all that's left."

As they sat down to eat, Mea-a-ha leaned on her husband's shoulder. He kissed her warmly, but turned away from her questioning gaze. "Kane! Come join us. It is not good to always sit alone."

Stunned, the young man stopped chewing and stared at buffalo soldier. Unsure what was going on, he stood and slowly walked towards the big man.

"Sit here with us." Jacob pointed to a boulder next to Mea-a-ha and took another spoonful of beans, savoring them slowly.

Kane risked a questioning glance to Mea-a-ha. She shrugged and shook her head. Swallowing his last bite, Jacob set his plate aside. "Thank you, Kane, for taking care of Mea-a-ha. She can drive a man crazy. I'm proof of that."

The big man rose to his feet and looked down at the couple. "Out here there is only fear and love. When death fouls every breath you take, it's easy to get them confused. What's right ain't always easy to see…an' what's needed ain't always right."

He held their eyes for a moment, studying them. "We are all trying to survive, and no one can ask any more from you than you do your best."

Turning away, Jacob stepped into the warm glow of the campfire. "Listen, everyone." He waited for all eyes to fall on him. "We came into this country for one reason. It was to bring a family together that should have never been torn apart. Well, we sure as hell did it. We also won a few battles that by all rights should have been have lost. I don't think the Mexicans will soon forget us."

The soldier's face darkened. "Tomorrow…tomorrow…" he paused and started over. "Well, about that family." His eyes shined.

"Nah-kah-yen, why don't you tell our writer friend here, and the others that don't know, about the Fortress of Juh."

The Indian came to his feet, surprised that the buffalo soldier knew the story. He was surprised even more that he would ask.

Stepping away from his family, Nah-kah-yen searched the face of the big man, trying to understand. "Of this we do not speak, black gringo, but I think it does not matter now."

The warrior turned to the others. "There is another band of Apache even more forgotten than the Mimbres."

His voice rising, Nah-kah-yen pointed to the west. "High on a great Mesa in this land you call Mexico is the secret Fortress of Juh. It is the home of the Nednhi, the lost Apaches."

He stopped and looked into the faces of his friends, knowing this secret would die with them. Nah-kah-yen filled his lungs with pride and regret. "Their chief is a great warrior named Juh. To climb his Mesa, there is only one trail up the steep cliffs. Even if it were discovered, no army would dare attack such a fortress for only one man can go up at a time. Because of this, the Nednhi live without fear."

Nah-kah-yen bowed his head. "It is where Victorio was leading our people when they were slaughtered at Tres Castillos. This fortress was our dream."

After a somber pause, the warrior cleared a tightness in his throat. "When the Apache are gone from the land, and even the trees forget our names, the Nednhi will survive. Search, and you will not find them, but they are there, watching, always watching like eagles in the clouds. That is what I can say about the Fortress of Juh."

The warrior stepped back, leaving everyone in awe. Kane wrote furiously in his book that remembers, looked up into Nah-kah-yen's concerned eyes.

The writer slowly returned his pencil to his pocket and thumbed through the few pages he had just written. It was an amazing story. "What the hell." Kane tore the page from his book and threw it into the fire. After watching it burn, he smiled at the Indian. "Where would be the magic if all secrets were told?"

Jacob placed his hand on Nah-kah-yen's shoulder. His voice softened. "Brave warrior and good friend, hear me. We release you from your promise. Take your family and go to Fortress of Juh."

Nah-kah-yen was astonished. He looked to the white officer. "You would do this?"

Mason grinned. "The U.S. Army can't be wasting good rope hanging every unpleasant Apache that comes along. I think our country will survive without stretching your neck."

Jacob nodded. "It is dark. If you leave now, two ponies might make it out unseen. We will cover your tracks."

The warrior knew what tomorrow would bring for his friends. His gun was needed. Nah-kah-yen shook his head to protest, but Jacob stopped him. "Your duty is to your family and the memory of Victorio. You must complete his journey."

His eyes darkening, Jacob glanced at Mea-a-ha, then back to the Indian. His voice dropped low. "Your staying will change nothing. Take your family and go."

Nah-kah-yen gripped Jacob's hand. "Soldier, against my oath, I call you friend." He looked to the young officer. "You too, Long Knife."

Urgently he turned to his wife. "Woman, go to little Mea-a-ha and get your crying done. The journey of the Mimbres continues. We go to the Fortress of Juh."

Mary Lost Pony came to her feet. She didn't understand what was happening, but for the first time there was hope in her husband's eyes.

The camp suddenly came alive with excited voices. None of them knew what tomorrow would bring. Their friends were departing and somehow it seemed like good news. If the small family was escaping, then surely they were escaping, too. Jacob must have plans.

Daniel rushed to his side. The boy was shaking. His father had found a way to make it all right. "Father."

Jacob turned from the group of men and took his son in his arms. "What can't be undone, is undone. Will you forgive your Pa now?"

Daniel threw his arms around the big man. "I'm sorry, Father."

Hugging the boy, Jacob pressed his head to his chest. "You've got your miracle, my Son. Had you not disobeyed me, Nah-kah-yen would not have his wife and child."

He lifted the boy's chin. "You did right, but not all things can be undone. There is a price to pay."

Daniel looked up sheepishly. "I know, Father, I'm still going to be punished when we get home, but we saved a Mimbre family. It is worth a thousand whippings."

Jacob closed his eyes. He had traded his own son for another man's child.

A gentle hand touched his arm. "Have my boys made peace?"

Jacob reached out and pulled his wife close. "All's forgiven, little Apache. All's forgiven."

Mea-a-ha searched her husband's face once more and started to ask what changed his mind, but he stopped her. "Have you said your goodbyes to Mary?"

The girl nodded. "Yes. Thank you, my husband, for letting them go. I love you." Out of the corner of her eye, Mea-a-ha caught Kane smiling from the shadows. "Thank you for so much."

Jube slapped the young lieutenant on the back. "Best get this treason done, if we is gunna' save these Injuns."

Mason untied the reins of the Indian ponies and walked them to Nah-kah-yen. The warrior grinned. "Your scalp would have looked good on my lance, but I think I will value your friendship more, young soldier."

The Apache jumped onto the back of his pony and greeted the loving faces of his friends. His eyes came to rest on Jacob. "I will tell my son what happened here. The story will be told as long as campfires burn."

Nak-kah-yen finally turned to Mea-a-ha. His eyes saddened. "And you, little Apache. Had you not shooed the hungry wolves from a freezing fool, you'd all be safe in your homes. For this I am sorry."

Mea-a-ha reached up and touched the tiny hand of his baby. "Do not grieve us, brave warrior, we are not dea..." She stopped cold. Her eyes darted to her husband and then back to the warrior. Their faces told the whole story. Mea-a-ha struggled to control her breathing. "We...We followed our hearts. That's worth something. I think. It is no small thing..."

Lowering her head, Mea-a-ha whispered, "Teach your son what happened here." She could say no more.

Jacob stepped forward and put his arm around her. "Nah-kah-yen, this arroyo is hard rock. Follow it until first light, and ride out of history, my friend."

The big man tenderly kissed his tearing wife and then looked over her head at Nak-kah-yen and his family as they vanished into the night, and whispered. "You are our victory. Ride, Apache--Ride for us all."

Chapter -26-
Return to the Abyss

The moon did not rise. Mea-a-ha lay in her husband's arms. "Is there no hope?"

"There never was."

Mea-a-ha sobbed. "You told me, but I would not listen."

"Nah-kah-yen's family is safe from harm. That is what you wanted."

"And now eleven must die. I..." It was too much for her to bear. "...we must flee."

"Soon. The horses need rest. Sleep while you can, my love."

"The air is cold." Lori White Feather looked up at the starless sky. Mason reached from his blanket and found her hand. "It is cold, but it is ours to breathe."

The girl rolled closer to the young soldier. "You say it as though it is fleeting. Is it?"

Mason squeezed her hand. "Best you get some sleep, Lori."

"Are you still protecting me?"

"...It's a soldier's duty."

"I did not ask the soldier. I asked the man."

"...The man is protecting you, too, but for another reason."

Lori pulled her hand from his and let her fingertips rest on his face. "Mason? If tonight is all we have, are you ever going to kiss me?" The girl slid from her blanket and into the young officer's embrace. "I do not fear death, my soldier. It has already visited me."

She lifted her soft lips to his. "Its dying unloved that I fear."

"I wish I understood your tongue, little princess." Roberto drew the back of his hand down Son-gee's bare spine and kissed her shoulder. They had bedded down away from the rest. The boy smiled at a lone star breaking through the clouds. "We have sealed our marriage, and yet I never got to ask you proper. I want it said. 'Son-gee, will you be my wife?' "

Rolling onto her back, a soft arm uncurled and then encircled his neck. "Ro-bear-tow, Son-gee." She pressed her lips to his long and hard. The Indian girl did not understand his words, but she knew his heart. Cradling his hand to her cheek, she murmured. "Squaw." It was a word he would know. She belonged to him.

The young girl giggled, and kissing the tips of his fingers, slid them down to her belly. It was their first night, but somehow she knew. She would bear him a fine son.

****

"Father." Daniel rested his hand on his father's arm. Opening his eyes, Jacob lifted his head from his saddle. "Soldiers?"

"Indians."

The big man was out of his blanket, kneeling by his son. "How many?"

"I have not seen any. I only sense them. The insects no longer speak."

Jacob understood. "Wake the others. We ride."

The companions had learned to rise quickly and quietly. Soon, the horses were mounted. Jacob rode to the back of the line. "Jube, keep 'em straight. Push 'em hard. The horses are tired, but if we can hold the Indians back, they will fade with the sun. Let's ride to daylight."

With that, the buffalo soldier turned his Buckskin around and silently moved past the others until he reached Kane. "Writer, take care of our little Apache. Don't ever leave her side. See you in hell."

When he reached the front, Jacob leaned in his saddle, whispering instructions. "Juan, ride with Yessenia. We will have a guard for every woman. She should not ride alone."

"But..."

"Don't worry, boy. There will be plenty of fighting for everyone when this day is done."

After the Mexican youth rode away, Jacob spoke quietly to Daniel. "I will not lie to you, boy. Your gun is fast, and though you grieve those you've left dead on the trail, kill twice as many and it will not be enough." He handed the boy an extra box of cartridges. "This day we ride as father and son. They may never know our names, but let them learn to fear our family just the same." Jacob drew the famed Winchester from his scabbard. "Move 'em out."

The attacks were coming more frequently now, and Jacob knew they would never let up. The Terahumara would either wear them down or exhaust their ammunition. Either way, they would never see another setting sun.

Coming out of the arroyo, a fresh breeze filled Jacob's nostrils. He patted his horse. "Come on, Mister, let's do our best."

For a thousand yards, they rode without resistance. Jacob maneuvered the band away from the foothills and towards the open plane. The Terahumara would have to give up cover to follow. The night would be won by inches.

Dawn was near. It was the best time to attack. If an assault was successful, the victors could hunt the survivors down by light of day. Jacob didn't intend to let that happen. The morning sun would lay bare his enemies, and the heavy Springfield would keep them at bay.

Because of the Terahumara reluctance to attack outright, Jacob guessed that they number less than two score. A number far greater than his own, but the Indians would not give up half their number just to claim victory. That was the white man's way. If they couldn't take the gringos in a surprise attack, they would follow and pick them off one by one.

To his right, Jacob heard the faint click of Daniel's deadly revolver. A second later it thundered and was quickly answered by a mortal scream. "Ride!"

The small party bolted into a run, praying the horses would find their footing on the broken ground.

Amid savage howls, shots rang from the dark, and bullets filled the air. From far behind and to his right, a defiant barrage sought to blunt the Indian's attack. Jacob knew that his son and Jube had turned to face the enemy. Their bold courage would buy them time. "Hee'yah!" He pushed the horses harder, snapping the reins. "Hee'yah!" By meanness and bullets, he would hold them till dawn.

A round whizzed past him from directly ahead. Their escape had been cut off. Jacob raised his rifle and fired three spaced shots in the exact opposite direction. There was another deadly cry directly in front of him. Suddenly, without warning, he collided violently with two warriors. The horses reared and screamed. Men struggled to control their mounts, but the Indian ponies were no match for the giant Buckskin. One pony fell over on its back, crushing its rider beneath him. Jacob shoved the muzzle of his rifle into the exposed neck of the startled brave and pulled the trigger, nearly blowing his head completely off. The lifeless body dropped into the shadows as the soldier rushed on by. Whipping his horse forward, Jacob pushed on. "Hee'yah!"

Galloping from behind, a mighty stallion quickly overtook him. The father's heart beat. It could only be Snow Raven. Daniel had returned. With a yell of his own, the boy charged ahead. His young eyes were keener than his father's. If there were any more Indians before them, the devil would have his pay.

Shots became random and then died away. The Terahumara had broken off their attack. It was over as quickly as it started.

For several more minutes, Jacob urged the horses onwards into the new day. If they could run forever then maybe there would be a chance, but he knew it could not be. The horses were already spent. Grudgingly, Jacob slowed to a walk. In the early light, he could see Daniel far ahead. The boy had stopped and was turning around.

When he closed the distance, Daniel's eyes glinted in the morning sun. "I think they fear us, Father."

The big man pulled to a stop. "It will make them think twice before they try it again.

Turning in his saddle, Jacob waited for the rest to close up the line. Roberto and Son-gee came first, followed by Juan and the old woman.

Searching further, Jacob cursed. Mea-a-ha's pony came galloping up without her. He whipped the Buckskin around, but then caught sight of Kane, with Mea-a-ha held safely before him.

As the pair drew up alongside Jacob, the girl reached out and Jacob drew her into his saddle. She was shaking. "Warriors charged out of the dark, shooting and screaming. My pony stumbled, but Kane pulled me from the ground."

Brushing the hair from her face, Jacob kissed her. Then with a nod to the young man, he handed her back. "Round up her pony and keep her with you. I've got to check on the rest." Jacob rode away.

Mea-a-ha turned in Kane's embrace. Overflowing with emotion, she threw her arms around his neck and pressed a long, hard kiss to his lips. Leaning back, she searched his startled face and then slipped from his saddle. She caught her pony, and with a backwards glance hurried to Yessenia.

Heading to the back of the line, Jacob rode past Mason without stopping. The officer was reloading his Colt. Lori White Feather seemed more alive than he'd ever seen her. Further on down the trail, he could see Jube cussing and holding a hand to his horse's head. "Damn them Injuns, nearly shot ol' Buck's ear plum off. Leastwise put a hole in it."

"Had a bad go of it?" Jacob knew that when things got rough, Jube would fuss about everything else.

"Ya think they'd have somethin' better ta' do n' skulkin' in the dark fo' a bunch o' Mexicans who most likely ain't gunna' pay 'em anyway. Jes' cussed mean. Theys' worse n' Apaches."

Jube wiped his bloody hand on his shirt. "No offense, Jacob. Mea-a-ha not included."

The grizzled sergeant looked around and swore. "Damn, Jacob. That son of yours. You n' me been doin' this a long time, but that boy... He rides between bullets n' lays 'em cold. Might not have fought 'em off had he not come when he did."

Jacob stared back up the trail. "Don't want to see him that way, but I guess it doesn't much matter now."

Jube tore off his neckerchief and wrapped it around Buck's ear. "Our horses is done in, n' we didn't gain much ground. Damn Injuns."

"Keep watching for the soldiers, Jube. Something tells me they are closer than we think, or the Indians wouldn't have attacked out here in the open. They want the women before the Mexicans get to them, and they took a foolish chance."

"They will jes' keep comin. Sorry sons o' bitches."

"Yes, Jube, they'll just keep poking until they find our underbelly."

Mea-a-ha stared at the front of the line. Jacob was pushing hard. The men looked spent and the women were sobbing. It was too much. Jube had let them rest when he was in charge, but Jacob was relentless. Morning and noon had passed without food. They were so tired. If the soldiers didn't kill them, Jacob would.

"Mea-a-ha."

Leaving her thoughts, Mea-a-ha looked up at Kane. He was exhausted too, but there was a fire raging in him that burned away the pain of the trail. The girl knew she was his tinder.

"Little Apache. Will you explain your kiss?"

"You rescued me. I am grateful."

"No, Little Apache. A peck on the cheek would have been just payment. You kissed me."

The Mimbre girl returned her gaze to the big man out front. She belonged to her husband, and right now she longed to be by his side.

Kane reached down and took her hand. She tugged her arm, but he held firm. "Please let me go."

"You kissed me. Once you said I had one last kiss. Was that it?"

Mea-a-ha wept. There was no time left for hiding. If the truth was to be spoken, it would have to be now. "Maybe, and if it is, Kane, then I want you to know I care."

"You care?"

"...Much." Her voice broke.

"You love me."

She bowed her head. Kane released her hand. "...but you love him more."

"Yes, but he will not let me be with him. Even now here at the..."

For a moment the young man was silent, then he broke into a grin. "It's okay. I just needed to know...here at the end."

Mea-a-ha raised her eyes. "You know?"

The young writer stared at the distant figure out front. "It is why Jacob is pushing so hard. It is why you have finally told me you love me."

"Those were not my words."

"But it is your heart."

She whispered. "It is my heart." Mea-a-ha looked away. "There shall be no tomorrow, the problem is solved."

"The problem is solved, my darling, but Jacob has given you to me this day. So until the end, you are mine."

"To protect. Not to claim."

"I claim your heart. At least a part of it, and that is enough. It is worth dying for."

"Then claim me if it is your desire, but when the end comes, you will take me to my husband."

The writer nodded. "With my dying breath."

Mea-a-ha searched the young man's face. "You are not frightened of death."

"I am terrified." He swallowed a nervous chuckle. "…but love conquers all. You are mine to love and protect. If killing buys me one more moment with you, then at last I have a reason to fight."

"Then you have found what you came for."

"That and so much more."

With Jacob and Daniel taking the lead, the other men followed in line, each escorting one of the women. Jube as always brought up the rear.

Until now they had been damn lucky. The enemy had not expected an experienced adversary of Jacob's worth, and he had used the element of surprise to his advantage.

He'd kicked sand in the face of a slumbering giant, and while the giant was blinking, he stole the Mimbre women and ran, but now the Mexican army was on to him. His horses were done in and ammunition was running low. There would be no more surprises, and the American border was a faraway dream.

Jacob slapped his reins, urging the big Buckskin on, but it had nothing more to give. He reached out and patted the horse's neck. "Come on, ol' boy, better to drop dead trying, than give up. Let's crawl for another mile."

One mile brought another, and a few steps more. All day he pushed them without stopping for a meal, or even breaks for rest. Sensing their doom, horse and rider spent everything they had. Eventually the sun sank low on the western horizon.

Jacob rubbed a hand across his eyes. Not far ahead lifted the fateful towers of Tres Castillos. They had come full circle.

In this solitary place, Victorio and his Mimbres had met their tragic end. It was also here where the rescuers had their first encounter with the Mexican army. Only a few days had passed, but it seemed a lifetime ago. For good or ill, the fate of so many lives had been changed by this lonely mountain. If there was a hell on earth, Tres Castillos was it.

Yet as the day had slowly waned, each of the companions began to secretly hope that maybe their leader's grim prophecy was wrong. Jacob could see it in their eyes and knew better. Something didn't add up, and the back of his neck began to prickle.

"Look!" Juan shouted, pointing to the foothills to the east. A band of warriors trailed from an arroyo less than a thousand yards away. Seeming to be in no hurry, they kept their distance, forming a parallel line to their own.

Mason, riding behind Jacob, switched sides with Lori. "Jacob, what are they doing? Will they attack?"

There were a dozen or more against seven men. Jacob shook his head. "No. I don't think that's their plan."

Suddenly Jube let out a whoop from the rear. Riding out of the sun, the Mexican army appeared, galloping over a shallow rise. They were further away and farther behind, but they too took up a parallel line.

Jacob cursed himself. He had been a fool. While he had kept close to the foothills, seeking concealment in the arroyos, the Mexican army had not followed as he had expected. Instead, they'd moved out into the plains, where they could make better time. It was their country, and they knew the land. They also figured that the gringos had to return by the route they'd come. Tres Castillos offered the only water.

The Indians had played their part by slowing them down. It had all been planned from the beginning. In his blind rush, the buffalo soldier had made a fatal mistake, and in doing so he had condemned his friends.

Mason counted as best he could. "Appears to be a score n' ten. Plus the Indians." It was half what they expected. He glanced to the stones rising in the distance ahead. "Maybe there are more hiding in the rocks, and we're surrounded."

"Maybe. Maybe not." The big man kept moving forward. "...But what they got is more than enough to get the job done."

With soldiers to the left and Indians to the right, they were running a gauntlet. Jacob judged the distance to the tenuous shelter of the stones at the base of Tres Castillos. It was still too far to make a run. The enemy could easily collapse on them before they could make it, and even if they did make it, the end would be the same.

The situation was hopeless. 'Hopeless.' That was a word Jacob didn't like. He tugged his hat and set his jaw. "Never give up." He knew he must try.

Easing into a gallop, Jacob sought to close the distance to the rocks without causing alarm. If he broke and ran, the enemy would be upon them, but if he held his line it might slow them down and buy the needed time.

Jacob thumbed back his hammer and rode on, his eyes darting left and right as lumbering hooves drummed against the cold, hard ground. Like a condemned man climbing to the gallows, he was counting feet and grasping seconds of life.

For a moment it looked like they might actually make it, but then the doom of a trumpet sounded from the ranks behind them. Suddenly the Indians started closing the gap and pulling ahead to block their escape. It would end here in the open.

With a deadly cheer, the Mexican army increased their gait, and the distance began to collapse.

Jacob's lip curled, ready to give the order for a valiant charge against the Indians. Maybe a few of his small band would break through. Maybe a lone rider would be overlooked and this day yet remembered. He turned to the brave youth riding by his side.

"I love you, Son."

The young Apache cocked his head. His face shined with admiration for his father, but his eyes glinted with mischief so cold that it stole the big man's breath. Without losing another heartbeat, Daniel spurred his horse, leaping far ahead. Offering one last smile to his father, he ripped off his hat and threw it to the wind.

As Snow Raven bolted, the boy stood high in his stirrups and screamed like a wild savage. His roar filled the air, drawing every eye on the field to him.

Daniel leaned to his pony. "Fly, my friend, fly."

The mighty stallion charged forward, unimpressed by the enemy line. Thundering towards his foe, the raging youth tore off his shirt and let it wave on the wind like a banner before letting it fly away. The setting sun lit his skin red. He was Apache, and he wanted them to know it. For Mexicans and Indians alike, it was a name that struck fear. A Mimbre warrior had returned to fields of Tres Castillos.

Taunting his enemies with cries of scorn, Daniel raised his rifle high and claimed the middle ground between his friends and the Indians.

The Terahumara did not know his words, but they recognized the Apache tongue. The young warrior was challenging them, daring them to face his deadly gun. There is a saying along the border: "If you see an Apache, you have two choices; run or die." It was words he wanted them to remember now.

From their first encounter with the bold Mimbre in this same mountain valley not so many nights ago, and in all the battles since, they'd learned to fear this wild youth. They told stories while licking their wounds by campfires about the warrior whose rifle thunders death. Some whispered that he was the spirit of Victorio raised from the dead that no bullet could kill.

The small mountain ponies of the Indians were no match for the Painted stallion's blazing speed. The braves snarled like angry dogs, but slowed their advance. It was not their battle, and the promise of blankets and beads bought only so much blood. Let the Mexicans strike first if they wished to die.

"Now, you fools." Jacob screamed and raced for the trees. With whip and threats, the tired horses were commanded to run. Behind them the trumpet sounded again. Mexican curses muddied the air. The rout began.

Guarding the rear, Jube jerked his reins, whirling old Buck around. A wall of thundering horses and raging men raised a cloud of dust before the lone man. Throwing his Winchester to his shoulder, he emptied it on the closing ranks, then drew his revolver and emptied that, too. "Welcome ta' hell, ya' sons-a-bitches." Kicking his horse, Jube turned and chased after his companions while reloading at full run.

Out front, Daniel claimed a barren mound. Snow Raven clawed the air. Mocking the warriors, the boy turned his stallion and charged back down the valley. This time his gun awoke, sending its deadly promise. The lead Indian tumbled from his saddle; then another slumped over his horse and dropped out of line. The braves returned sporadic fire, but veered away.

Passing his son in flight, Jacob pulled up hard. "Mason, get them to the rocks. Kill the horses if you must, but get them to the rocks." Firing with one hand, the big man's gun spoke to the left and right as he turned and charged back down the line.

Advancing from the rear, Jube came to his old friend's side and spun around. "Sho's' a pretty sunset. Couldn't pick a better day to die." His rifle belched. "Here comes, yo' boy." Jube emptied his gun and grabbed a fistful of shells. "They'll pay for ol' Buck's ear."

Snow Raven reared to a halt, and the Apache youth joined the men. Now three Winchesters flamed in the evening sky. Half a hundred rounds were set free. The Mexican army flanked wide, avoiding the deadly barrage. It slowed the attack, but still they came.

Bullets rained all around the courageous three. With a sharp crack, a splinter of wood burst from the stock of Jube's gun. "Damn!"

A heavy slug tore Jacob's canteen from his pummel. He fired in answer and then looked over his shoulder. "Bless him, Mason has made the hill. Let's get the heck out of here."

Lieutenant Mason McCrae of the U.S. Calvary came to a stop beneath a tall stone where a lone raven perched. He turned his exhausted horse and shouted to the boys. "Dismount and form a line. Kane, keep the women moving. Make for the high ground."

The writer jerked his reins. "I'll stand with the men."

"I have no time to debate your worth. The women need you more."

Mea-a-ha screamed. "Kane, we must go."

His face darkened. She reached for his arm. "You promised to protect me."

"Damn you, girl, I'm trying." Kane slapped his reins and headed up the hill. Mea-a-ha waited for the other women to pass and then hurried to Kane's side. "Let's make for the towers."

With the Mexicans in close pursuit, the three riders broke through the trees. Mason barked. "Fire!" Roberto and Juan obeyed the lieutenant's command. Their guns bellowed with insolence at the advancing army.

For this moment, the fragile line was the boys' to hold. Juan felt as though his hands were made of clay. He couldn't fire fast enough. Bullets cracked the rocks in front of him, and a screaming round tore the sombrero from his head. His ears rang with the deadly roar, or was it the terror welling within?

Suddenly Jacob was kneeling beside him. "You're doing good." The big man fired with ease. Where seconds before the boy had seen angry soldiers swarming towards him, now only empty saddles remained, but there were plenty more to take their place.

"Mount up!" In a hail of bullets, men and boys scrambled to their saddles.

"Ride while ya' breathe." Jube barked and headed up the hill.

Juan whipped his pony, eager to obey when suddenly a loud gasp by his side turned his head. Roberto stared at him unmoving, his eyes glazed in disbelief. Slowly the tall boy leaned forward in the saddle, blood flowing from a hole in his chest.

"NO!" Juan stretched out a hand as his friend started to fall. "No!" Save for the ring in his ears, all went silent. "Roberto!"

Pushing the Buckskin forward, Jacob caught the boy as he tumbled from the saddle. The big man lifted the brave youth with ease. "Ride, damn it, ride."

Juan mechanically grabbed the reins of Roberto's horse and followed the big man.

The carnage unfolded in a slow-moving nightmare. All around them, smoke curled, and flames from muskets seemed to hold in the air. In horror, Juan looked behind. Jube had stopped. With Mason by his side, the buffalo soldier stood his ground, firing volley after volley. The Mexicans poured through the opening in the rocks. Unable to pull his gaze away, Juan watched in disbelief as his pony drew him further up the mountain. He heard a muffled scream. The bold lieutenant's gun burst from his hand and flew through the air. Blood spurted from a hole in his wrist. Soldiers filled every space. Jube swung his empty rifle like a club, taking off a Mexican's ear.

Juan's horse charged up the hill, and suddenly they were lost in the trees. The young boy turned and closed his eyes. It was as Jacob had foretold.

Ducking beneath the branches and twisting around rocks, they climbed higher. Their ponies slowed, and Juan anxiously pulled alongside Jacob to see his friend.

Roberto lifted his head. He was still alive. Behind them the shots of the soldiers faded. The young boy cried. "What of Jube and Mason?" He feared the howling Mexicans were already charging up the hill.

Juan tried not to think about it and looked to his friend. Jacob held Roberto to his chest, his bloody hand pressed tightly over the wound. They rode on.

Ahead, Jacob could see Kane urging the women through a narrow cut between the towers. It was a good choice. The cliffs spread out, offering protection. Here they could slow the army, giving the women more time to escape.

Son-gee turned in her saddle and saw Roberto hanging limply in the arms of the big man. Screaming, she turned her pony. Kane grabbed her reins.

Shouting for them to keep moving, Jacob pushed the tall Buckskin up the steep incline. The girl sobbed hysterically as they rode on by.

Bravely, Roberto lifted his eyes, assuring her with a weak smile. He breathed to Jacob. "Please, sir. Put me in my saddle. Son-gee will hold me and bind my wound." The boy was courageous.

Knowing he was desperately needed, Jacob lifted Roberto on to the back of his horse. "Kane, stay with him. Try to stop the bleeding and then get them home. They're yours now."

Just as Jacob turned, Jube and Mason, battered and bloody, whipped their sweaty mounts through the cut. The big sergeant's sleeve had been torn completely away. A deep gash cut across his leg. He winced. "Think I met that charmin' captain you was telling me about. Does he favor a sword?"

"Did ya kill him?"

"No, but his horse gots' three eyes."

Juan's voice trembled. "I thought you were dead."

Jube gritted against the pain and shook his bloody head. "Would have been, 'cept for that young Apache."

Just then Daniel charged though the cut. Snow Raven glistened in the last rays of the sun. The boy spit his anger. "Let them search the dark for their wounded and dead."

Mea-a-ha pushed her pony to her husband's side. Jacob pulled her into his saddle and held her in his arms. She cried. "Oh, Jacob, I'm sorr…"

"Shush, little Apache. No more apologies." He silenced her in kisses and put her back on her pony. "Be brave and trust me."

Reaching out a blood-stained hand, he cupped her cheek. "God, you're beautiful. I love you."

The Indian girl sobbed. Jacob turned his head. "Jube, push 'em hard. The night will hide you. I'll hold them as long as I can."

The two men locked eyes in the fading light. Without reply, Jube prodded Buck forward. Reaching into his saddlebag, he took out a box of cartridges. "It's all I got left. Make 'em count."

Mea-a-ha reached for her husband's arm. "Jacob."

He gave her a loving smile. "You remember your promise, little Apache, and obey Jube. Now get going."

"You're coming too. Yes?"

Jacob looked around. "Don't worry. This mountain has claimed enough lives. You'll be okay."

He could see she was full of doubt. There was no time to argue, so he set the truth aside and told her what she wanted to hear. "I was wrong, my love, we can make it, but you must go now."

Daniel waved his gun. "I'll hold them back with you, Father. Then we'll catch up together."

"No! There is only need for one rifle to hold this pass, and the trail ahead is uncertain. You remember your promise too, my son. With the wounded, Jube is going to need you more than me. You've been a good warrior; now be a good soldier. No more arguing." Mussing Daniel's hair, Jacob pulled away.

"Kane." He implored the young man. "I'm counting on you, Kane. Don't let me down."

Unable to look Jacob in the eye, the writer grabbed Mea-a-ha's reins and whipped his pony, trying to run from his shame.

Jube turned his horse. Already bullets were finding their way through the gap. "Let's go. Any more goodbyes and they will be ta' the Mexicans. We ride." He nodded one last time to his friend, and barked an order. "Daniel, take over as rear guard, little soldier. Do as yo' pappy says."

With a wave of his hand, he led the women and the wounded down the dark side of the mountain. "Don't be thinkin' we is out of trouble. Ol' Jacob will buy us minutes, but not hours, n' we still is days from the border, so none of ya' be makin' plans for tomorrow's social."

The buffalo soldier's familiar drone pulled them away from the horror of the mountain. He knew what he was doing. Everyone hurried their ponies. Danger was howling at their heels, and with Roberto gravely wounded, there was no time to breathe, and less time to think. The cold night settled in.

Chapter -27-
Darkness

For a time it was silent, save for the anguished sobs of little Son-gee. The crescent moon gave them both light and shadow. The companions came down off the mountain and into a long valley. It seemed peaceful. It seemed wrong. In the distance a rifle cracked, then another. Mea-a-ha's stomach tightened with each shot. She feared for her husband and wondered if the moon was on his side.

"Jube, how long will he stay?"

"Keep riding, little Apache. Jacob is doing what he hast ta' do." Jube reached a caring hand to her shoulder. "Check on the boy for me. Don't want to kill 'em by pushin' too hard."

Another shot echoed in the distance. Mea-a-ha clenched her teeth and slowed her pony, letting Roberto come alongside her. Son-gee held his reins. The young Mimbre girl turned a hopeful face upwards. "Please. Tell him I love him." She spoke in Apache.

Mea-a-ha brushed the boy's hair. Roberto lifted his head from his horse's neck. "Tell her not to cry…and she is beautiful. Please."

"Are you okay to keep riding?"

Roberto licked his parched lips and nodded. "If it means her safety, I will ride 'till I'm bones."

Mea-a-ha motioned the girl to her. "Come sit behind your brave young hero. The Rincon horses are strong, and I think you will calm the boy's heart. It is a good thing."

Son-gee gave a frightened smile and climbed behind her new husband. "You tell him sleep. I will not let him fall."

Lori White Feather gently pressed the tips of her fingers to Mason's bandaged hand. "It still bleeds. Do not let it hang by your side."

Gritting against the pain, Mason lifted his hand to his shoulder. "Lori… Back there when I got shot…the Mexicans pouring through the rocks, just me n' Jube, I was sure I was going to die." He paused to take a breath and calm his nerves. "In a moment like that, what's important gets real clear."

The pain seemed to leave the young officer's face. Straightening in the saddle, he looked at Lori and braved a smile. "All I was thinking was I'd never see you again. It grieved me more than death."

Mason glanced over his shoulder. "What Jacob is doing…well, we might make it. Chances are slim, but if we do…well, I got some money...what I'm saying is, it worked for Jacob and Mea-a-ha. Do you think there's a chance for us?"

Lori shuddered and gulped a breath. Her tearing eyes searched Mason's face. She was a white woman stolen by the Apaches. A brave had claimed her, and the fat Mexican had ravaged her. Surely he knew this. No decent man would want her. She feared to hope. "Mason, what are you saying? Your father is an important man; you can't..."

"My father isn't the one asking you to marry him."

Lori covered her face and burst into tears. "Mason, I can't let you..."

The gallant lieutenant grew stern. "Then I'm not asking, I'm telling. I'm going to marry you, Lori, and the world be damned. So best get used to it, Mrs. McCrae."

It was frightening how far the sound of a rifle could carry in the clear night air. Now the shots were little more than faint pops, but there were so many. Mea-a-ha feared Jacob was having a hard time; otherwise, he would have followed them by now. The shots died away, but they would start again as they had many times before.

Mea-a-ha had fallen back behind Roberto and Son-gee, trying to be closer to her husband. All she could do was cry. She felt useless. Wiping her face, she looked up. Kane was by her side. His head hung like a beaten man. He reached for her, but let his hand fall away. "Mea-a-ha." A tired whisper was all he could manage. "No matter how hard I try, I could never be like him or take his place."

The writer turned his eyes to the rising moon. "I wrote a book about him. Made him larger than life. Embellished every sentence with flowery proclaim. Oh, I was so proud of my skills."

Dropping his head, Kane returned to a whisper. "...and not one word I wrote comes close to describing the real hero of Apache Springs."

"Kane, you are a good..."

"No! Don't say it. Forgive a foolish coward for daring to think you could ever love him. I have pretended to be more than I am."

Suddenly Kane leaned in his saddle and pulled Mea-a-ha to him. "I'll take my last kiss." He pressed his lips to hers, telling of all his love. The girl tensed but remembered her promise. Molding to the writer, she wrapped her arms around his neck and kissed him long and tenderly. It was one kiss, but she left no doubt how she felt about her tall gringo.

The truth finally spoken, their lips parted. Mea-a-ha swallowed and took a breath of air. Her fingertips gently held his face. "It was no fool who protected my heart. Thank you, Kane."

Lifting her small brown hand from his cheek, he kissed it tenderly.

There was nothing left to say. Kane jerked his reins, and whirling around, raced to the back of the trail. He had taken what was not his. Courage matters little without honor. The writer vowed to make it right.

When he reached Daniel, Kane pulled to a quick stop. With a soft chuckle, he stuck out his hand and mussed the boy's hair. "Go be with your sister. She needs you."

Kane saw the young Apache's concern. "No soldiers will get past your brave father, and even I can guard the cold night air. Go now." He slapped Snow Raven's flank, sending the boy on his way.

Daniel caught up with his sister. She quickly wiped her tears. "Oh, Daniel." Steadying her breathing, she sniffed. "Did we do wrong? Was wanting to save our people worth what it cost?"

Mea-a-ha lifted her eyes to her brother. "So many have died. Much sadness."

The boy consoled her. "Father knew what it cost, and he came anyway when it was in his power to make us turn back. He saw it all when none of us could, but he did what he believed was the right thing, and that was to protect our hearts."

"Mine was not worth protecting. I failed him." Mea-a-ha sobbed.

The boy reached to her. "Kane?" He let the name linger, then smiled at his sister. "Do not think Father a fool. He put you two together, knowing he could not be there. I heard him tell Kane to protect you, to keep you always by his side. He told me the same thing, that I should never let you go hungry…"

Suddenly Daniel stopped. His mouth hung open. "Jube!" the boy shouted as he raced his pony forward. He had been so blind. Passing the other horses, he jerked to a stop. "Jube, Jube, we must go back."

Jube kept his eyes on the trail. "We keeps movin'."

Mea-a-ha galloped to their side. "What is it?"

The boy's eyes filled with tears. "Jube, you knew, and you let him. You're his friend."

His sister pleaded. "What?"

"Father isn't coming back. He said he'd find a way. I'm going to him."

"No! We is going on, like ya' both promised. It's what he wanted."

Daniel cried. "But he tricked us. He will die."

"He will die anyway. Your going back won't change that. We keeps' movin'."

Mea-a-ha hadn't let herself believe Jacob wouldn't follow. Hit by the truth, she wailed. "Jube, no."

The buffalo soldier held firm. "We keeps' movin'."

"NO!" Whirling around, Daniel kicked Snow Raven. He would save his father or die. As the stallion flew past, Jube reached out a huge arm and pulled the boy from the saddle. Daniel screamed. "Let me go!"

"I made your father a promise, too. You is staying."

"Let me go." The frantic boy kicked while dangling in the air. He beat at the big man's arm. "Damn you, Jube. Damn you, let me go or I'll kill you." He reached for his pistol.

"Sorry, kid." Jube brought his huge fist up under the boy's chin. Daniel's head snapped back and then the youth went limp.

Mea-a-ha screamed. "Jube!"

"No, little Apache. This boy is Jacob's heart. If ya' let 'em go back, then Jacob loses everything. It was his last wish. I need ya' ta' be strong. So does Jacob. Don't fail him again."

The black soldier's dark eyes spoke the terrible truth. 'Don't fail him again.'

Collapsing against her pony's neck, Mea-a-ha shook silently. Every breath was torture, a promise of a life she no longer wanted to live.

Faint whispers escaped between her sobs. "Jacob, Jacob, oh Ja.." Mea-a-ha lifted her head and pulled her hair from her face. Her eyes were vacant. Taking several breaths, she calmed herself. "I will not fail you again, my husband. We go on. Like we promised."

****

A lone raven abandoned his lofty perch and winged a silent path across the face of the waning moon. Jacob's keen sight caught the movement as he searched the night. Far below, the silver light shimmering in the tranquil lake calmed his heart. Even in death there was beauty.

Jacob wiped blood from a gash on his cheek and hollered. "Captain Moralis! How about you letting your soldiers go home? You and I can settle this on our own. That's what it's about, isn't it? You got your nose rubbed in the dirt. How about it? If your men kill me, ain't going to do your honor no good."

A cold voice reviled the night. "Vengeance. I want vengeance. If my men kill you instead of me, then I will cut off your head and use it to bludgeon the women to death that you try so hard to protect." He laughed. "Is one of those filthy savages yours?"

Jacob raised his rifle to his shoulder but then slowly lowered it. No. He would not let the captain know he had spoken so close to the truth. "I came to kill Sebastian, settle an old grudge. Took the women because they were there. Hope you don't mind. I figured you were more partial to sheep."

A pistol erupted below. Jacob laughed and fired at the flashes from the gun, and then he listened intently. A high, whining curse let him know he'd missed. The big man settled back into the dark.

Tilting a tattered box, he poured the last of the bullets into his hand. It wasn't much. He reached into his vest and found three more. It still wasn't enough. Jacob looked behind him. Moralis would eventually send soldiers around the spires if he hadn't already. When they found the passages not guarded by the other men, they would be on him like flies.

Jacob loaded the Winchester and then reached down and pulled his trusty Springfield closer to him. It had one last round.

Surprisingly, he had held the soldiers for more than an hour. An hour's lead takes a long time to make up. If Jube kept moving through the night, they might just make it.

A rock dislodged by a clumsy boot tumbled not far below. Jacob emptied a canteen and threw it aside. He would buy them a little more time. Judging the sound, he raised his rifle and fired three shots in a close pattern. A man screamed, then in answer, a hail of gunfire tore through the air. The heavy lead slugs hammered into the rocks above Jacob's head as they had done many times before. He chuckled. "Must think I'm ten feet tall. Not even close." He felt blood trickle down his neck from a cut in his ear. "Damn." He'd been hit by another ricochet. "If they don't shoot me outright, they'll whittle me to death."

Angering, Jacob fired again, then ducked as the deadly report shattered rock once more. He rose, giving a death-like scream. A man jumped up in the moonlight. "We got him. We got him." Taking careful aim, Jacob cut the fool down. "Moralis, go home while you still have some soldiers left."

"I think, black gringo, that I have more men than you have bullets. You have been shooting sparingly. Did you think I would not notice? Perhaps if you surrender, I will torture you for just a little while before I kill you. You like my plan. No?"

Jacob cupped a hand to his mouth and hollered at the Mexican soldiers. "Your captain is a coward. Why do you follow him?"

Moralis scoffed. "Nice try, but it will do you no good. They are paid to follow me, not to like me."

It was worth a try. Jacob longed to see his beloved Hollow one last time. He looked to his horse, saddled and ready to ride. For a moment, he was tempted to run, but no. Here he could buy a few more precious minutes for his wife and son. He'd never see his home again.

Coming to his feet, Jacob quickly stripped the saddle and bridle from the Buckskin. "Okay, Mister. This time it's the horse that lives to see another day. On your way, boy." He slapped his faithful companion hard on the flank. The horse moved a few feet and then stopped. Jacob cursed. "What's-a-matter? I'm giving you your freedom. Go home. Did you hear me? Go Home!" He slapped the horse again "Yee-ha!"

The Buckskin obeyed his master's command and bolted into the night. Watching him disappear, Jacob whispered. "Go, boy. Let this be our last battle."

He turned back to the cleft and drew a sad breath. "The killing stops this night, too." With death inevitable, knowing he'd never kill again gave the weary soldier solace.

A smile suddenly broke across Jacob's face. He'd gotten them all through, even his horse. "Guess there's a small victory in that."

His thoughts drifted as the night grew silent. Maybe the Mexicans had enough. No, Jacob knew Moralis would never give up. It was a foolish wish.

Crouching in the dark, waiting for the next assault, Jacob tried to make sense of it all, but couldn't.

He bemused, and then he remembered the old saying: 'At the brink of death, your life flashes before you.' Jacob remembered his old colonel's parting words. 'Some believe you should hang for the killings you've done.' He sighed. Perhaps the colonel was right.

A sudden trampling whirled Jacob around. The moment had come. They were behind him. Flames leapt out of the void. Jacob hit the ground hard, levering his rounds. There was a scream, and a dark figure fell not twenty feet away. Others scrambled back into the shadows. He could hear cartridges being slammed into breeches.

Rolling over, Jacob fired rapidly at the mouth of the cut. A Mexican pitched backwards.

With a silent curse, the buffalo soldier set the empty Winchester aside and picked up his old carbine. One shot, and five in his colt.

Turning, the big man raged. "Come on, Moralis, you son-of-a-bitch. Show your ugly face. I'm tired of this. Counting the Indians if they stayed, there's not but a score of you left. Hardly a good breakfast. So let's get 'er done."

He had talked too long. Once more there was movement behind him. Jacob waited until he saw the flash of the rifle. A bullet burned his neck, ripping the collar from his shirt. He fired and cursed himself. Had he let the man get closer, he could have stolen his gun. Jacob tossed the Springfield aside and drew his revolver. It was his last defense. He looked around. Which way would they come next?

Suddenly, from above, rocks came raining down. He dodged against the cliff, but the moonlight caught the barrel of his gun. Shots cracked from both directions. Jacob fanned his pistol left and right to silence them. For a brief second the quiet held, then a boulder hurling out of the darkness stuck his leg, knocking him down. He clenched his teeth against the pain. The dark shapes of angry men rushed at him. Jacob cursed and hammered his last round. Struggling to his knees, he grabbed the barrel of his carbine. If he could stand, he'd take one more with him. Soldiers poured through the cut, screaming for vengeance. They knew the gringo's deadly gun was finally empty.

Jacob swung the rifle, knocking the legs out from under a burly soldier. He swung again, aiming to crush the Mexican's skull. Before he could, a heavy blow from a rifle butt caught him across the side of his head. Blood gushed from his torn scalp as he slumped to his hands and knees. Growling, he struggled up, but another rifle stabbed into his ribs. His lungs emptied in a heavy gasp.

A reckless soldier grabbed for him. Jacob's big fist sent the senseless Mexican flying back. Three more took his place, clubbing him into the dirt. The big man was down. Howling like wolves, they stomped and beat him at will.

"Don't kill him. He is mine." The men landed their final kicks and grudgingly stepped away.

Struggling to breathe, Jacob focused his bloody eyes. In the moonlight he could see the glint on Morralis's sword. "I think I stick you many times before I cut off your head."

The ugly captain strutted forward. Jacob tried once more to rise. Moralis laughed and jabbed his saber through Jacob's hand. "That is for my foot, black gringo."

The big man snarled and lunged forward, wielding his buck knife in his good hand. A flat of a gun stock caught him hard in the face. Jacob collapsed at the captain's feet.

"Poor black gringo." The gloating captain slashed his blade deftly across Jacob's lip. "You talk too much and you don't listen so good, so first I'll cut off your ears." Moralis's eyes filled with a hatred welling up from a withered soul. His knuckles whitened against the hilt of his sword. This was the kind of fight the little man was suited for.

Gritting his yellow teeth, he threw his arm back and held it high, savoring his victory, but before his blade could fall, flames burst in the dark. Two soldiers beside him gripped their chests and fell dead.

Fearing for his life, Moralis screamed and slunk back into the shadows. The narrow passage erupted in streaks of flames and confusion.

Startled soldiers fired wildly as they scrambled out of the cleft, unsure who they were facing. The assassin's Colt .44 thundered again in rapid succession, driving them back.

From behind the flames, a lone man rushed to black soldier. Jacob struggled to see. Not Daniel, it mustn't be Daniel. The thin figure continued firing, dropping another man.

"Jacob!" It was Kane. His trembling hand reached out for the big man's shoulder. "Jacob, I…" As he turned to look down at his fallen hero, the despicable captain saw his chance. Moralis lunged out of the shadows, sinking his sword deep into the young man's chest.

Kane convulsed and gasped. He lifted his head to the captain's vulgar curse. Moralis pushed the sword deeper. The wounded writer gripped the blade with a bloody hand. So this was how it felt to face death.

Kane's eyes narrowed and he laughed. "I'll see you in hell." Raising his pistol, he thrust the muzzle to the Mexican's head and pulled the trigger. The two men collapsed together.

Roaring like a wounded bear, Jacob struggled to his knees, but the soldiers once more rushed at him, clubbing and kicking. The pale moon faded from his vision. Everything was going black. Only distorted sounds remained. He heard his ribs crack and felt the heavy thud of boots against his head as they stomped him again and again.

From the pack of wolves there were screams of murder that suddenly turned to screams of death. The Mexicans were dying. Hisses! There were hisses in the wind. Lying face-down in the dirt, Jacob parted his torn lips. "Arrows."

Chapter -28-
Return of the Mimbres

The sun was shining when Jacob tried to open his eyes. They didn't work. He was lying on his back beneath an animal hide. A gentle hand washed his face. He gasped. "Mea-a-ha?"

There was soft laughter. "No, black gringo. It is Mary."

The Mimbre squaw called to her husband. "Nah-kah-yen. He lives."

Jacob blinked his swollen lids to the sound of footsteps. A blurry figure bathed in light knelt beside him. "Easy, my friend. You have little blood of your own."

Rolling his head to the side, Jacob waited for his vision to clear. The next time he opened his eyes he saw several Indians stripping the dead soldiers. Nah-kah-yen knew his question. "They are the Nednhi. The Mountain Apaches of Juh. Do you remember? They watch the soldiers. That is how they found me. Runners told us of the battle."

The warrior looked at the naked dead. "It is befitting that here at Tres Castillos, the Mimbre are avenged."

Jacob struggled to lift his head. He felt like it had been replaced by a heavy stone. Gently, Mary helped him sit. "Be careful. Death may still call your name."

Wiping a bandaged hand across his vision, Jacob looked around. One eye still worked. Not far away stood Mister, chewing grass. Jacob muttered, "Stupid horse."

Blinking, the bloodied soldier looked past him. Beneath the shaded cliff lay the brave young writer, his face now ashen gray. Jacob turned to the woman. Is he..." Mary whispered. "He waits for you, but his time is short."

Jacob struggled. "Please, help me to him."

The two Indians supported their friend as he dragged himself to the young man. Releasing him, they stepped aside. Jacob raised himself on his good arm and tried to clear his head. He rasped. "Kane...Kane."

Summoning the last of his failing strength, the prostrate figure slowly opened his eyes. "J-Jacob. Will you tell her I died bravely?"

"I will tell her how you saved my life." Jacob took the young man's hand in his.

The writer rolled his eyes to the black soldier. "I...am... sorry Jacob for betraying you."

"You didn't betray me, Kane."

"I love Mea-a-ha. I tried to take her from you."

260

Jacob swallowed. "I wanted you to."

Kane's breath rattled in his chest. "Wh...You what?"

Lowering his head, the big man hid his eyes. "I didn't figure on making it out of this alive. A price had to be paid. It was the only way to save her." Jacob clenched his teeth and tried to breathe as his throat tightened against the truth. "I needed somebody to take care of her, to love her as I did. You're a better man than me, Kane. You could teach her so much that I never could. Treat her like a lady, and... your heart is not withered by death. There is a cloud about me. It makes her cry. You were her chance for happiness." Jacob squeezed the writer's hand, and offered a forgiving grin. "But you had to be a hero."

A thin smile parted Kane's ghostly lips. "Ironic... We wanted to be like each other." He coughed weakly, and then grew calm. "I guess... she's stuck with you. Love her for both of us."

"I will, and I will try to be kind and gentle like the courageous man who gave her back to me when he could have kept her for his own."

Kane closed his eyes, exhaling his final breath. "Mea-a-ha." He was gone.

Death gives no preference for the good in a man's heart. It devours all without caring what noble deeds they've done. Jacob lifted his eyes and looked around him at the butchery of nameless men whose bodies would be burned and forgotten. He angered at the injustice. Here beside him lay a man of worth. In his last hours the young writer had lived and died like the heroes in his books. 'The Hero of Tres Castillos.' He deserved better.

His mind reeling, Jacob tried to rise on one knee, but it was too much. Blood rushed from his head, and he collapsed beside the man called Kane.

Nah-kah-yen hugged his wife. "Maybe it is better that he too should die here, free from his torment."

****

Small green shoots, a promise of life, were already breaking through the cold, hard ground. In the eternal struggle, winter yielded to spring.

Mea-a-ha sat quietly on the step of the old hermit's dwelling in a patch of warm light. Her eyes searched the lonesome trail that wound its way down the mesa to the long valley from where they came a dozen days ago. She shuddered. As the Mimbre Trail had been for her people, so it was for this little Apache, a journey of death.

Wrapping her blanket around her, Mea-a-ha slowly stood and walked to the edge of the cliff. The two men she loved were gone, yet she remained. A cold wind blew up the crevasse. Maybe the day would see rain. It seemed fitting.

Daniel had not spoken a word to anyone since that terrible night, not even to Juan, who stayed faithfully by his side. Mea-a-ha ached for him, but she would be the last person he'd want to speak to. There were no arms left to hold her.

Stepping closer to the edge, her heart quickened. Beneath the rocks there was peace. No! It was the coward's way out. Her promise to Jacob was that she'd go on living. It was a punishment she'd bear.

The door opened and closed behind her. She took an anxious breath. It was Daniel. They made eye contact but then the boy hurriedly looked away, digging the toe of his boot into the cold earth.

He had come outside for a reason. There was a debt to pay. Stuffing his hands in his pockets, he slowly came to Mea-a-ha's side and joined her vigil, staring into the quiet abyss.

Mea-a-ha's heart ached for her brother. He had cut a wide swath of death. Jacob had warned that a bullet kills twice. Poor Daniel. She could hear his breathing rise and fall as he struggled for peace. Braving the distance, she gently rested her head on his shoulder. For a moment Daniel leaned towards her, then pulled away. "Who is it you wait for?"

She withdrew. Tears rolled down her cheeks. The boy lowered his head. "I'm sorry. That wasn't fair. I just miss him, and there is no one else to blame."

His sister looked so small and injured. Daniel put his arm around her. It was time he became a man, the kind of man his father had taught him to be.

Accepting his comfort, Mea-a-ha snuggled close to her brother's chest. "To blame is to not go on, but I do not know how to forgive myself. I am lost."

Leaning down, Daniel kissed her. "It is hard, but we have to start somewhere. It might as well be today... or now." He glanced back at the door. "I guess I need to tell Jube I'm sorry."

Mea-a-ha turned and curled her arms inside the boy's embrace, "My brother, Jacob gave us this chance. We must keep our promise."

Daniel hugged her tight and rested his chin on the top of her head, staring into the distance. He wanted to run away, but when he closed his eyes he could see his father sitting on his tall horse, telling him to go on and never give up. He would live for Jacob and make sure his sister never went hungry. "I love you, sis. You will always be taken care of."

The boy opened his eyes. His body shook. Mea-a-ha felt his heart pounding against her cheek. A cry choked from his lips. He struggled to speak. "Fa...Father!"

Releasing his sister, Daniel suddenly ran down the trail as fast as he could. Mea-a-ha whirled around. "Jacob!" She threw her hand to her mouth, struggling to breathe.

A dark shape of a giant man on a tall horse loped around the bend in the narrow trail that cut into the cliff. There was no mistaking him. Mea-a-ha started to follow her brother but stopped. Her knees turned to clay. The Indian girl's heart was breaking. She wanted desperately to go to him, to be wrapped in his arms and buried in kisses, but fear overwhelmed her. Mea-a-ha crumbled to the ground and cried with joy and shame.

Daniel was now a dark figure running wildly. She watched as the big man climbed from his horse and engulfed the boy in a huge bear hug. They stood without moving for what seemed like forever.

A fragile smile slowly broke through the Indian girl's tears. Jacob had returned. Nothing else mattered.

The father and son, still holding each other, turned and led the horse down the trail. As they came closer, she heard the fall of their heavy boots on the broken stones. Words were beyond them. How much alike they'd become.

The tear-stained boy looked at his sister, knowing it was her time. Taking the reins from his father, he gave a final hug, and led the Buckskin away.

Jacob's arm was bandaged and a dirty rag was tied around his leg. His clothes were filthy and torn. There were new scars on his face, and he shuffled like a man in pain. Mea-a-ha struggled to her feet. He had never looked more handsome.

Giving her a big grin, Jacob took off his hat and hugged the girl with his good arm. "Hey, little Apache. You sure look pretty."

Mea-a-ha threw her arms tightly around him. "You do too." Climbing onto the top of his boots, she stretched up and kissed him. "Oh, Jacob. I thought you were dead."

He held her tight. "My sweet little Apache, I've been dead for a very, very long time." He tucked her under his chin. "...but I think I'm ready to live."

****

Days passed in the baker's shack. Stories were told and retold. There was laughter and tears, joyous commotion, and reverent silence.

"Ya' come back for my biscuits. Yes, sir. Brought some new friends, and left some behind, I see. All wantin' my biscuits." The hermit laughed. "I'll make a tidy sum this year."

Lori whispered to Mason. "Does he have a name?" The old man heard her. "Hein, or Heinric, as best I kin' recall, but I can't remember anyone ever callin' me that, so maybe I'm someone else." He grinned at the girl. "My mother called me Dearie', n' my wife called me...well, never mind."

Yessenia took some dough from the baker's hand and started kneading it. "Maybe you should choose a new name."

The old man winked at the woman. "Don't have no need for a name, lessin' someone is fixin' on stayin' to use it, or take it for her own."

Little Son-gee would occasionally peek from the bedroom door and press her cheek against the rough wood frame. She didn't know their words but she would listen to their hearts. Then the young girl would return to Roberto's side. If his eyes were open, she would tell her own story as best she could.

Sitting on the edge of his bed, Son-gee would say, "Lori-Mason," then press her hand to her heart and give a romantic sigh, or she might say "Jube," and bray like a burro. Roberto understood. Sometimes the girl would whisper Mea-a-ha, then mimic tears. This made her sad.

Mostly Son-gee tried to bring Roberto good news, or use the words she was learning. "Hot-biscuit, drink-this, sleep-now, love-you."

Jube, for his part seemed unchanged. Life and death were the same to him. "Can't have one without the other." He would tell this to the boys as they tried to make sense of what happened. "How do ya' know what's warm, iffin' ya' ain't felt cold?" His logic was simple, and they usually understood.

The pale sun rose and set, and days passed with little change. It was as though time had stopped. No one seemed to know how to move beyond the terrible thing that had happened.

"Ya' looks like a man chewin' on gristle. Shores' tough to swallow." Jube stuffed his thick hands into his pockets and joined his friend at the edge of the cliff as he stared off into the warm sunset. "Ya' done pulled it off, Jacob. It's 'n amazing thing... 'n a sorry thing. Lot a killin'."

Lost in thoughts of his own, Jacob took time to dislodge a small rock with the toe of his boot, sending it over the ledge. It crashed far below and bounced several times before coming to a stop. "Lot a killin', Jube. Lot a dyin'."

"Yea...lot a dyin'. Tough ta' figure a man like Kane. Coward or hero, hard ta' tell."

Taking a long deep breath, Jacob exhaled it. "Maybe both. Guess that's the way it is for all of us. A man is known by how he lives. Perhaps Kane should be remembered for how he died."

Jacob turned to his friend, his eyes struggling for answers that would never come. "Lot a dyin' and a lot of livin', too. Kane probably lived more...and..." The big man faltered and then cleared his throat. "...and loved more...on the Mimbre Trail, than he did his whole life."

"Jacob, it changed him. That's for sure, done changed us all. Daniel n' the boys, Mason...n' little Mea-a-ha..." Jube stopped abruptly, wishing he hadn't mentioned the girl. "Yessir' Jacob, a sorry thing."

The two friends continued walking with their heads down. "Jacob, did we do wrong? Killin'? The likes I ain't seen since the war. Guess it was our own private war, ain't nobody gunna' ever know. Still. Did we do wrong?"

It was an answer Jacob didn't have. He walked another dozen steps in slow silence. At length he shook his head. "Did what we had to. Maybe we were on the wrong side of the law being down there, but maybe the law was on the wrong side of what's good and decent. We saved a family. Got to believe that's worth a little forgiveness."

Jube turned and stared down the trail that had brought them out of Mexico. "Guess ya' can't look at the price once ya' decide somethin's' right."

Shrugging his shoulders, Jacob's hard exterior dissolved into a soft grin. "Daniel said the same thing. We did what we had to do...nothing more."

Placing a big hand on his friend's shoulder, Jacob turned towards the shack. "Let's get some coffee."

Later that night as they sat in front of the fire, some reflected while others dozed. Lori curled in Mason's arms; Jacob stirred and smiled down at the slumbering girl he was holding. Remembering something, he looked across the room and then cleared his voice. "Daniel, drag my saddlebag over here, will you, Son?"

The tired youth rubbed the sleep from his eyes and did as his father asked. A moment later, he was curled back in his blanket on the floor, a little boy once more.

Jacob fished around underneath the leather flap with his good hand. Mea-a-ha lifted her head and watched him. He glanced back at her and then slowly withdrew a black leather-bound notebook. It was Kane's journal. "I think he would want you to have this."

Mea-a-ha was suddenly filled with emotion. Her eyes, moist with rising fear, searched her husband's gentle face. She struggled to speak. "Hav...Have you...you read it?"

Jacob shook his head. "No. Someday when you can read well enough... I think he would want you to read it first."

Trembling, Mea-a-ha took the book from Jacob's hand and hugged it to her breast. "Thank you."

She curled back into her husband's arms and tightly closed her eyes. Nothing more was said.

Late in the night, Mea-a-ha crawled from their blankets on the floor. Clad only in Jacob's big shirt, she wrapped it about her, and slipped silently beneath the stars.

An icy haze scattered the light of the placid moon lingering overhead. Mea-a-ha hurried down the trail, wishing it would go away. The cold stones beneath her bare feet mattered not. There was no place to go, but she needed to get far away from the hermit's shack. She started running. Tears streaming from her eyes, she ran until her lungs hurt. Where could she go?

Mea-a-ha slowed her pace and finally came to a stop. It was useless. She could not run from what she had done. The Apache girl started shivering. She was dying from a cold within.

Her emotions were tied in knots, and no matter how hard she tried to unravel them, they just got more jumbled. How had everything gone so wrong? All that once was, was undone. Even the magic of the Hollow would not repair the damage she had caused.

Against all odds, Jacob had returned. They had saved a family as she had wanted, and the threat of death was now a distant memory. She should be happy. Everyone was joyous, and yet all she wanted to do was cry.

Her anguished breath steamed in the frigid air. She was no longer wise or beautiful. In her mind, she was ugly and cruel. Unable to hold her grief, a painful wail escaped from deep in her throat.

"Are you thinking of him?"

Mea-a-ha whirled around. Jacob reached for her, but she pulled free and hid her face. He stepped closer. Again she backed away. "Don't!" Mea-a-ha struggled to breathe. "My husband, I've betrayed you."

"Because you loved him?"

Her tortured eyes lifted to Jacob. "Yes...because I loved him."

"He loved you, too. Very much."

Mea-a-ha cried with shame.

Jacob quickly reached out and pulled her into his arms. She tried to escape, but he wouldn't let her go. "You miss him desperately and you can't tell me, or let anyone know how much you hurt."

Mea-a-ha held herself rigid but could not stop her tears. "You shouldn't comfort me. Nothing can make how I feel be right. I should have been better. I should been strong."

Tucking a knuckle beneath her chin, Jacob forced her to look at him. "You would have died."

"Then I should have died, instead of him."

"You're missing something important, little Apache."

Mea-a-ha lifted her grief-stricken eyes to her husband, not understanding. He kissed her forehead. "War is hell, and it is the providence of men. Love is your strength, as the gun is mine, and without love you would have died. You and Kane needed each other desperately. I knew that when I pushed the two of you together."

"You knew?" The young girl searched her husband's face.

"It was the only way I could save you." Jacob let his arms fall away. He hung his head. "The shame is not yours alone. My love, you have known my darkness. I can't love and kill at the same time. It is I who failed you. I couldn't give you what you needed to survive. For that I am sorry. Forgive a tired soldier his weakness. I used Kane, and yet I hated him for being what I could not be."

"Oh, Jacob." Mea-a-ha rushed to him. "I knew, but I didn't understand."

He lifted her from the ground and held her tight. "Kane saved both our lives. It doesn't matter how."

Jacob cradled the girl to him. "Cherish the love he gave you, as will I. He was a hero and we will grieve him together."

Laying her head on his chest, Mea-a-ha wrapped her arms around Jacob's neck and closed her eyes. "Take me back; I think I can sleep now. For a very, very long time."

Bluewater Publications is a multi-faceted publishing company capable of meeting all of your reading and publishing needs. Our two-fold aim is to:
1) Provide the market with educationally enlightening and inspiring research and reading materials.
2) Make the opportunity of being published available to any author and or researcher who desires to be published.

We are passionate about preserving history; whether through the re-publishing of an out-of-print classic, or by publishing the research of historians and genealogists. Bluewater Publications is the *Peoples' Choice Publisher*.

For company information or information about how you can be published through Bluewater Publications, please visit:

www.BluewaterPublications.com

Also check Amazon.com to purchase any of the books that we publish.

Confidently Preserving Our Past,
Bluewater Publications.com
Formerly known as Heart of Dixie Publishing